Only a

Breeze

A Novel

Barbara Wesley Hill
Oct 2017

Barbara Wesley Hill

confffo

For **G**ene.

For constant encouragement
and extraordinary patience.
For caring—about everything.

conffo

And my **F**amily.
For cheering me on,
and believing in my goals.

Publication Data.
Title ID: 7199459   ISBN-13: 978-
1546930242
ISBN-10: 1546930248

BISAC Code: Fiction/Christian/Historical/
Romance

Only a Breeze: a novel / Barbara Wesley Hill
Oabgm8@gmail.com

ও৵ও৵ও৵

Acknowledgements.

As in everything, I thank God.

My gratitude to the authors and editors who have crossed my path in this past year, most of whom I have yet to meet. I have never experienced a more generous group.

Alison, thank you for all you did to put me on the right path.

Cover design by Rachel Bostwick.

~ 1 ~

Aleksander Nordin
Russia, 1934

Streams of sun came through the window, dancing... laughing, or so it seemed to Aleksander, again able to view them through his own bedroom window.

From the kitchen came the welcome sounds of clattering dishes and the low static of a radio, amid bits and pieces of conversation between his parents.

He touched the soft hand-made quilt, smiling at the things Mama had placed within easy reach of his bed—her way of reminding him of good times.

There was his school picture from the sixth grade, and a picture of Mama holding a baby girl, the sister he'd never known.

Beside it was his favorite children's story book, *The Wonder Clock*. How Mama had loved telling him of his sister, Blancha, who had gone to America before his birth.

Blancha had sent the book upon receiving news of his arrival, her only sibling.

"November, 1917
Dearest Mama,
I send this book for my baby brother in hopes of bringing thoughts of me as he grows.

I've been told this book, The Wonder Clock, or Four and Twenty Marvelous Tales, *is a favorite of the American children, as well as their parents.*

Of course, it is in English, but the illustrations are so beautiful, I hoped he would enjoy it.

How I do hope to meet him some day, as well as seeing you and Papa again.

Love, Blancha"

"It became a game for us," Mama said excitedly. "Your sister walked to the library every week to copy a story from the book into Russian for me. This helped me begin to learn English words. Blancha confessed she felt closer to us by sharing the language of her new country.

"It was good for you, too, Aleksander, having knowledge of the language of a far-away country. Before you were two, I had all the stories of the English children's book hand-written in Russian," wistfully adding, "in my dear daughter's *own* hand."

The happy memories flooded back. He smiled, appreciating home and all it meant to him.

As his injuries healed, he grew stronger each day. But his mind often drifted back to what had brought him to this point in his life.

❊ ❊

Growing up, working with numbers had been Aleksander's talent.

He dreamed of being an engineer.

By the time he'd completed sixth grade, it became apparent his dream was not to be. Not only would he not be able to go to the university, he would likely not even complete high school.

Completing the eighth grade in 1931, he knew he had no choice but to quit school. He realized he'd been afforded the opportunity for more education than many of his friends, but his father's health had deteriorated and he was no longer able to work. It was up to Aleksander to provide enough income for his family to survive.

Within weeks of quitting school, Aleksander was working forty to sixty hours a week.

"You are tall and muscular, Aleksander, with the energy of youth," Mama said proudly, "and *dependable*—that's why you get so many hours every week."

Da, and because I am on call for a half dozen merchants and farmers, with no guarantee of how much they will pay. I cannot question or they will not ask for me.

After his sixteenth birthday, he stunned his parents with a decision.

"I have joined the *Krasnaya Armiya* (*Red Army*). I will report next week to begin training."

"Aleksander, no!" Mama gasped, "I expected to have you at least two more years before the draft. I cannot bear it."

There was no outward reaction from Papa.

Nervously, he continued, "They did not question my age, Mama. They were pleased I had received eight years of formal education.

"The doctor looked me over and announced, *Da, he will be a strong soldier for Stalin.*

"And I was formally enlisted at that moment!"

He observed his parents, attempting to explain and comfort. "It's exciting, Mama... Papa... and perhaps I will be returning *home* in two years, though one cannot know. I will have a steady salary, *fifty* rubles a month at the beginning. The army will provide my food and shelter, so I can send the greater part home to you. I expect to make more by the end of a year."

Aleksander served a year and a half in the Red Army.

"I am well and happy," he wrote in his letters home, though far from the truth. But it did please him to be able to include forty rubles a month, keeping only ten for his own needs.

Early in the second year, a superior took notice of his work ethic and, after extensive questioning, began to use him as a courier. His salary was raised to seventy-five rubles, of which he sent sixty-five home.

Sent into dangerous areas and situations, Aleksander began to fear some of the larger packages contained smuggled items. The smaller packages concerned him even more.

Am I delivering threats? The rumors of labor camps are more rampant.

Perhaps I am delivering lists of names of those to be arrested.

I have no choice but to obey orders.

I'll likely never know whether I may have played any part in bringing dire circumstances to fellow Russian citizens. Perhaps I don't wish to know.

He began having nightmares that deliveries were equivalent to a death sentence. He continued to hope, even pray, for his own safety, and that his fears were only his imagination.

But I'm not sure God even knows my name.

Tap, tap, tap.

The sound, coming after midnight, was so slight, Aleksander thought it might be part of a bad dream. But he'd learned to be a light sleeper and slept in his clothes. He rose quickly, grabbing the gun by his bed. At the door, he listened.

He opened the door cautiously, only enough to see who was there. The cold air burst through the small opening.

A soldier—he didn't recognize him. As well as being pitch dark, the soldier's heavy jacket hood was pulled around his face.

"Nordin?"

"*Da.*"

"Sign for the envelope and leave quickly," he said gruffly, handing over a thick, bulky envelope. "Delivery must be accomplished before daybreak."

Aleksander complied, accepting possession and responsibility.

He closed the door and slid the bolt. *Clunk*!
The sound was loud in the quiet of night.

The envelope was heavy, more of a package.

It bore the familiar seals of the Red Army. He knew if any package should appear to have been altered, the courier would inexplicably 'disappear.'

He hastily pulled on his heavy coat and boots, concealing the large package inside the coat. Within minutes, he was on his way in the old army vehicle. The early morning was bitter cold—he had no idea how far below zero.

There were few lights along the way, silent except for the howling wind, which masked the sound of the old motor, and the added rattling when he hit the frequent holes in the crudely built road.

In just under two hours, he reached his destination, a large old building away from any town or signs of life. To a passerby, it would appear deserted. Turning off the motor, he sat motionless, scanning the area. Listening. Satisfied, he exited the truck, looking around once more before taking the first step to crunch through the ice and snow toward the darkened building.

He tapped lightly on the door.
Whap!!!

All was darkness. He knew nothing more of what happened.

Aleksander woke to realize he was in an unfamiliar room... alone.

Where am I? How? It's bright outside, daylight.

The pain in his leg was almost unbearable.

He suddenly remembered the stories.

My leg?

The stories... not of treatment... but of amputations.

"My leg!" he screamed.

"You still have two legs." The deep voice came from the next room, followed by a large, burly soldier. "But the left one is badly damaged. You are being sent home to have it amputated. I have your discharge papers and will take you to the first train. My orders are to inform you that you are no longer useful to the Red Army, but have met your service requirement. You will ask no questions and never discuss your missions."

Though it appeared they were alone, the soldier scanned the area. In a lower voice, he added. "You are lucky, Nordin. You will lose a leg but are returning home alive—not always the case."

Aleksander had pulled himself to a sitting position on the narrow bed. Most of his left pant leg had been torn off, his leg heavily wrapped in blood-soaked rags. The entire leg and foot appeared to be in one piece, but the piercing pain let him know he might not be seeing it much longer.

※ ※

Aleksander's trip home after the nightmarish evening, his last in the Red Army, was a disjointed memory. He knew he moved, or was moved, from and to several different modes of transportation.

He remembered seeing his mother's face, not sure it was real.

He'd been vaguely aware of Dr. Loban's presence. He'd removed the layers of bloody bandages from his leg, cursing the lack of treatment and resultant infection.

He slept through the next weeks. But the morning arrived when he was fully aware. He cried out, then slowly pulled himself up and threw back the quilt to mourn his missing leg.

There are two! Can it be?

He examined the left leg, then the right, thinking he may have been wrong about which had been injured. He pulled at the heavy gown he was wearing. The left knee was swollen. Touching it brought stabbing pain.

I felt it—it's still there.

Hearing his agonizing scream, his parents rushed to his room. Seeing him awake, examining his leg, they paused in the doorway. He became aware of their presence, watching him, smiling. His mother came to kiss his forehead. "My son, we are so happy to have you home. You will get stronger each day now. I'm sure of it." Papa put his hand on his shoulder, nodding agreement.

Oleg Nordin observed her handsome son lying in the bed, his thick blond hair mussed, his quick wit subdued, his sinewy body tired and used. She detected his attempt to smile, to ease her worry.

He is but a child, not yet eighteen. But he has become a man... too quickly, through the cruelties of war.

Dr. Loban came later in the day.

"Aleksander, you are a lucky young man.

"Your knee was badly crushed. By something comparable to a large pipe."

Dr. Loban paused, raising his eyebrows in question. Aleksander did not reply.

"By the time you arrived home, you had developed an infection; I've never seen worse. But we had little to lose, so I delayed amputation.

"I continued to treat it day after day. You may not be one hundred percent—your knee will give you some trouble. But after a few more weeks, you should be ambulatory, though probably with a limp."

"Dr. Loban, how can I thank you enough? I was told I was being discharged to return home for amputation. The Army washed its hands of me."

Perhaps God knows my name after all.

As time passed, Aleksander realized more and more how fortunate he was to be out of the Army. The rumors were growing about imprisonments, exiles and executions.

His knee healed and the pain grew less. Only a slight limp remained. He began to look for work, but had not considered the changes that had taken place while he was gone. Appearing embarrassed, his former employers all said the same, "We regret, but there is just no work."

He was viewed as a damaged man, and became disheartened.

"Aleksander?" His mother knocked lightly on his door.

He had not left his room today, and knew she would make another attempt to rouse and encourage. He couldn't shake the feeling of failure.

"*Da*, Mama, I don't feel well. I will rest today."

Through the door, she said, "*Gospodin* (Mr.) Sonchev has sent a message asking you to come to his shop to talk with him. He gave no reason."

He didn't answer.

"You remember the cabinetmaker, don't you?" she asked patiently.

"*Da*... *p*erhaps I will feel better tomorrow."

❈ ❈

In time, Aleksander became an apprentice to the best woodworker in his village, as well as the surrounding areas. Mr. Sonchev was best known for fine cabinetmaking.

He learned quickly, working by the side of the man who became his employer, teacher, and dear friend.

Oleg Nordin could see her son returning to his previous good nature, even the limp improving.

He rose cheerfully each morning, eating a hearty breakfast, and speaking enthusiastically about his day. "I never know what new skill I may learn from Mr. Sonchev. Woodworking is more complex than I ever imagined."

Within months, Aleksander had found a new passion. Each step of building top quality cabinets fascinated him.

From selecting and preparing the wood, and choosing the best design, to staining and finishing—he relished every phase.

"You are quick to learn," beamed Mr. Sonchev. "You will someday surpass me."

Aleksander delighted in the high praise. His mentor was a perfectionist. "I am learning from the *best*. I hope one day to be even *close* to your expertise, *Gospodin* Sonchev."

Four years passed... rapidly, Aleksander becoming more knowledgeable and adept in his craft each day.

✵ ✵

Going in to work one morning, he was surprised to be greeted by *Mrs.* Sonchev.

"Aleksander... there is no easy way to deliver my news... my dear husband died during the night." She broke down in tears as he embraced her. Through sobs, she said, "I wanted to tell you myself, but... I thought to have gained better control. He loved you so."

Shocked... unbelieving, he stammered, "But... he was strong... the stamina..."

"Yes, but it appears he had a heart attack... without warning."

She took his hand, saying, "I know he would wish you to continue his work."

Aleksander was twenty-one.

His mentor had given him a few fine tools, and Mrs. Sonchev agreed to a plan for his purchase of the larger saws and tools, so he kept the business open.

His aptitude with mathematics served him well in measuring and figuring the amount of wood needed, as well as pricing.

He'd begun doing the bookkeeping for Mr. Sonchev a year before his death, resulting in his knowledge of every detail of expense and profit of the business. The building being only a rental, he remained at the location, maintaining the business and its reputation.

Another year passed… then two. Woodworking was his life, engineering long forgotten. He made a fair living for himself and his elderly parents until their deaths, barely six months apart.

At times, usually at just the moment a large consignment of cabinetry or specialty piece came together beautifully, he would stand back to admire the work of his hands, and his thoughts would drift to the days of his boyhood.

Ah, the dreams I had. All changed and evolved in ways I could never have imagined. But I am content—this I know to be rare.

Life, however, is about change. At age twenty-four, Aleksander Nordin was about to happily begin a new chapter, realizing his life was not complete after all.

~ 2 ~

Vera Grekov

The café was noisy with the clatter of dishes, loud music, waiters calling out orders, and the chatter and laughter of the crowd. Aleksander and his friends met here at least once a week, enjoying the casual, friendly atmosphere, as well as the food.

The noise was part of what they enjoyed.

"The sounds of life happening!" shouted Yury.

The food had been consumed early on, but the friendly banter, and occasional wine or ale, could continue for hours.

Laughing at the latest joke, Aleksander glanced around the room, his focus suddenly halting on a woman across the café. It was Vera Grekov, a girl he'd known, or known of, most of his life.

As she stood to beckon the waiter as the group at her table dispersed, he was certain she had seen him, too, their eyes meeting for a split second.

Unexpectedly, he saw her with the eyes of a man who, until that moment, had not known he desired a woman in his life. Not any woman— Vera. In the same moment, his mind, or heart, quickly made the leap from imagining a woman in his life, to the thought of a wife— before he'd even spoken with her.

She has truly blossomed, his mother would have said.

Aleksander remembered her vaguely as a pretty girl. Today, stunning… a woman. She was about five-seven, with long, wavy, light brown hair.

Wearing no jewelry, she was dressed in a heavy off-white, cable-knit sweater and long dark wool skirt.

She is beautiful… but she seems to have a style, a way of her own. She appears relaxed… content. This is not common—most women seem one thing or step away from being content.

"I bid you fellows good night. I see an old friend."

His friends scanned the café and began to laugh. "Da, and better-looking!"

Aleksander rose and walked toward Vera's table. Closer, the hectic noise seemed to fade away, and he became more aware of her smooth, light skin.

Vera had been having a light evening meal with friends. The tight-knit group of six worked at the local school in varying positions and went out together about once a month.

Besides Vera, there were two additional unescorted women. One was a single cousin who worked in the school office, and was Vera's only living relative. The other woman worked with the cleaning crew—a lifetime friend, whose husband worked at night. There was one married couple, both instructors.

Rounding out the group was Zahkhar, also an instructor. She had known him a few years and counted him a good friend.

She was aware he would like to be more. She'd thought it not impossible, perhaps... in time. They had been out a few times and her feelings simply had not grown beyond friendship. Generally, their time together was with this group of friends.

Tonight, for one reason or another, they broke up earlier than usual.

"Good night, all," she said. "I will stay for another coffee before going home."

Zahkhar glanced around as if about to change his mind.

"Please don't change your plans. Earlier, you mentioned having paperwork waiting at home. I will stay only a short while. You know I am accustomed to walking alone in the area."

She smiled. He was a kind and thoughtful man. He wanted time alone with her, if only to accompany her on the walk to her flat.

He looked at her longingly. "Are you sure, Vera? I do not have to be in such a hurry. We could sit for a while and have a leisurely walk home. It is snowing again, but we are always prepared for that, eh?"

"Thank you, Zahkhar. You are very kind." Teasingly, she added, "Go. Get your work done. Perhaps we will see each other at lunch tomorrow."

He left reluctantly, causing her to contemplate her feelings for him again, more honestly.

I will probably never have romantic feelings for him. Perhaps I need to clarify matters; it's the only fair thing to do.

Vera was an only child. Her father had died when she was a teenager. After her mother's death a year ago, she had remained in their small flat. She knew her friends thought she would have made more changes in her life, but she did not feel the need. Though she hoped someday to advance, she liked her job assisting the instructors at school, and relished her volunteer work at the hospital. Her strong faith in God sustained her, she felt productive, and was blessed with good friends.

I can envision myself as a wife and mother someday. But... unlike my friends, I won't feel a failure if it doesn't happen. I will not settle for just anyone only to say I am married.

As Zahkhar left and she'd motioned the waiter to her table, she and Aleksander saw each other at almost the same moment. Their eyes met and she acknowledged him, but turned back to the waiter.

After ordering coffee, she turned slightly to see Aleksander out of the corner of her eye. He seemed to be concluding a conversation with his companions.

He'd be surprised to know how much I know and remember about him. Not only his name, family, and where he attended school, but about his giving up his dream of being an engineer. He quit school to care for his parents. He joined the army and returned with a serious injury.

Hmmm, I observed no signs of an injury. Presently, he is a fine woodcrafter. The village grapevine is rather thorough.

I recall a conversation. I was twelve and overheard Mother speaking with a neighbor. They commented about seeing "the Nordin boy, the one born during the October Revolution." They'd sighed, remembering the first they had heard of Lenin. Mother commented, "And who could forget Oleg's surprise at having a child so late in life?" They laughed, and her friend replied, "But a blessing since their only other child traveled to America years ago."

Aleksander Nordin, born in October, 1917, makes him two years older. I liked what I saw even during our school years.

❀ ❀

Vera felt a surge of happiness when she saw him taking long strides across the room, looking directly at her.

He was well over six feet tall with a muscular build. His hair was blonde, and his eyes appeared blue-green.

She turned further to give him a welcoming smile. She put a great deal of faith in a smile. She was not disappointed when he arrived at her table—his smile was one of pure pleasure.

He has fine straight teeth as well. For goodness sakes, he's not a horse to be measured by the look of his teeth! Still, it is something I notice.

She liked everything she saw.

"Vera Grekov?" he inquired. She nodded.

"I'm Aleksander Nordin. I believe we were in school together, but I haven't seen you in a long while. May I sit with you?"

He took her hand, strong yet feminine. As she began talking, looking into his eyes, she moved her hands expressively. He sensed she was taking his measurement at the same time— with those bright blue eyes, as well as her mind.

"Yes. Of course, Aleksander. I remember you."

His smile instantly warmed her, the touch of his hand affecting her in an entirely different way.

His heart soared. *Her voice is so gentle, kind... and sweet.*

She had sorted her memories of him. She was pleased.

He makes even work clothes look good—the plain brown corduroy pants and blue work shirt... just right. His hair is to his collar, curling slightly. His muscles... apparent even through the shirt.

"Vera, you are lovelier than ever. I'd enjoy catching up on what has happened in your life in the years since school."

"Thank you, Aleksander. I would enjoy that."

When the waiter returned with Vera's coffee, he ordered one for himself and two pastries.

They talked for hours, about their late parents, their work, and what they enjoyed.

The waiter finally reminded them of closing time. Neither had realized how much time had passed.

"May I walk you home?" he asked. "Or do you have transportation?"

Most in their village walked everywhere, though some had small motor bikes, and there were cars for hire.

"Thank you," she answered. "I live only a few blocks away. I'd appreciate your walking with me. I am not usually out so late."

"My fault," he replied, "but I regret not a minute."

Her smile assured him she felt the same.

Snow continued to fall steadily, but the air was very still. Since morning, everything around them had been covered in thick blankets of snow. At this time of night, everything in their world appeared peaceful and pure, the only sound being their boots crunching across the snow.

About half-way to her flat, he took her gloved hand as they stepped into a street. He never let it go, and she made no motion to pull away.

At her door, Aleksander desperately wanted to kiss her good night. This was not appropriate, but it was difficult to restrain himself. Releasing her hand, he raised his to her cheek, touching her gently. She was so close, smiling softly.

A hint of her perfume wafted through the cold night air, her lips tempting, her eyes intense.

As difficult as it was, Aleksander lowered his hand as they continued looking raptly into each other's eyes, without speaking.

I feel her vision goes much deeper… into my core feelings, my very soul. I have a sense of finding a part of myself.

"Good Night, sweet Vera. It is after midnight. May I see you again later today? I must work until six but could pick you up by seven." He felt rather desperate for her to agree. He only hoped his eagerness didn't cause her to back away.

Vera did not hesitate.

The nearness of him… he is causing me to tremble within… but at the same time, I feel comforted.

"Yes, Aleksander. I would like to see you again today. I will be ready at seven."

~ 3 ~

After the chance meeting at the café, Aleksander and Vera happily spent every possible moment together.

To no one's surprise, they married three months later.

He had lived in two sizable rooms at the rear of the cabinet shop since the death of his parents.

He'd been eager to show Vera his shop, but apprehensive about the living area.

"It is perfect!"

"Vera, even I wouldn't say that. It's been fine for me, but…"

"Darling, yes," she said tactfully. "It can use a few improvements—the first being *me*, I'll be here with you. I'll hang curtains, a few pictures, after we paint it, of course." She smiled up at him as she put her arms around his neck. He willingly leaned in as he embraced her in a warm embrace, kissing her passionately. Everything *was* perfect.

"Aleksander, it's practical to continue living here. It's big enough, and we'll save a considerable amount."

She transformed the two large rooms into a real home. They wanted nothing more.

Their love was deep, honest, and full of joy. Work continued for both.

They were building their future. But they lived for their time together.

She was the love of his life, beautiful, yet unaware of her true beauty.

Moreover, he thought her the most kind-hearted, loving woman he'd ever known. She was smart, with an amazing wisdom, yet maintained a practical view of life. He'd been right in his first impression—she was content.

She believed in looking to the future, but took things in stride, accepting the good with the bad. She never complained and did not understand anyone who did.

They were occasionally able to take holiday for a day or two but never tired of talking and laughing together—or of making love with equal amounts of fire and tenderness. It took only a touch to remind them of the surety and solidarity of their love.

Just after they'd celebrated their first anniversary, Vera returned home early from work.

Concerned she might be ill, he stopped work to go to her, but quickly recognized her mischievous smile as the one reserved for teasing him. She stood just inside the door, unmoving, gazing at him with the smile that was his alone.

"Vera," he began, giving her a perceptive grin, "you are home from work early, yes? I know it is not a school holiday. Did you leave only because we are wealthy and money does not matter?"

She began to sway her body seductively, smiling and gazing into his eyes.

She replied sweetly, "Ah, as most husbands, you are very clever… but you are not clever enough to know my secret today."

Taking a few long strides to her, he enveloped her in his arms, stopping her movement, and leaned down, covering her mouth with his.

She responded to his touch and melted into their kiss. After a few minutes, he raised his head and looked into her eyes as he continued to hold her.

Tenderly he asked, "Is your secret one I will know today, or will you take a while to tease me?"

Truthfully, she could barely contain herself.

In a low, almost shy, voice, she looked up at him. "Aleksander… darling… we are to have a baby."

She paused to watch his expression before adding, "I have been to Doctor Loban. We will have a little one before September."

Nothing could have pleased him more. Tears of joy filled his eyes as he lovingly pulled her closer. "Oh, Vera, how I love you."

His mouth again covered hers, her response eager, needing him. All other thoughts faded as their bodies came close, warming with love.

She had an easy pregnancy, though becoming self-conscious of her rapidly growing body during the last two months.

Loving her so deeply, Aleksander assured her she had never been more beautiful.

"All women have these feelings, Aleksander," his Aunt Raisa soothed.

"Continue to remind her of your love, and that she is more beautiful to you than any woman."

She patted his hand. "You are a good man and a good husband, Aleksander. Your parents would be proud of you. And Vera is proud to be your wife. Not to worry, she will again be your confident Vera as soon as the babe is here."

Vera continued to work at the school only a few weeks.

Aleksander, having all the orders he could fill, worked contentedly from early morning until dark, looking forward to their evenings of sharing a meal and dreams of the future with their child.

"Aleksander, you know of my curiosity about America, and my study of English books to learn a bit of the language—it was one of the first things we discovered we had in common, having some knowledge of English."

"Yes, but mine came because of my *sister,* who lives there. I still do not understand your curiosity, Vera. Americans are not liked in our country. Even Mama, who was so pleased to learn a bit of English through Blancha's being there, was guarded about speaking kindly of anything American."

"Well, your American story book, *The Wonder Clock,* is wonderful, and we will share it with our son… or daughter," she smiled with delight.

"Imagine someone who could conceive of twenty-four stories, one for each hour on the clock… each an adventure. To read them in a *foreign language* makes it more so."

"Yes, darling, we will share it with our child," he said, willing this conversation to end as he pulled her closer.

He looked forward to meeting this child created through their love.

But can I possibly love anyone as much as I love Vera?

❋ ❋

*W*aaaaaaah, waaah, waaaah!

"A beautiful, healthy boy," Dr. Loban pronounced exuberantly. "Exactly eight pounds, strong lungs, and a head full of blond hair. Mother and son are doing well—both crying at the moment."

It was the twenty-eighth of August, 1941. Impatient and anxious, Aleksander was allowed to see them an hour later. Vera's tears of happiness had dried, the babe asleep in her arms.

"He is perfect, Vera…. as are you, my gorgeous wife, Mother of our son."

"Look at that hair, Aleksander, and take his little hand… oh, his eyes are opening… to see his papa for the first time. Such bright little eyes, they seem to take everything in. Dr. Loban says this is not the case for a newborn, but I'm not so sure," she laughed.

"Aleksander, isn't he wonderful?"

Her tears began anew, as did those of the new father. They had never been happier.

~ 4 ~

Aleksander and Vera celebrated their love and the delight of having a child.

Nonetheless, something was creeping in to destroy their ideal life and the beautiful wife and mother, whose tiny son would not even know of her existence.

Mikhail was four weeks old when Vera held his soft warm body to her, contentedly giving the milk from her body to nurture his.

The noise of saws and hammering coming from the shop were actually soothing to her as she gazed at her son, this tiny miracle, in her arms, thinking of the happiness she and Mikhail gave each other at this moment.

Without warning, her body became limp, the smile leaving her face as her eyes closed, and one arm fell beside her. Mikhail's soft little mouth continued to pull at his mother for milk.

Her heart had simply stopped beating.

As the boy began to whimper, Aleksander became aware of a change in the atmosphere. The baby was crying softly, but he heard no soothing voice from Vera. He stopped his work and walked to their living quarters to check on his little family.

The baby remained on Vera's lap, though her left arm was limp and her eyes closed.

"Vera! Nooooooooooooooo, *please*, oh… God… noooooo!"

The loud, excruciating cry was a heart-breaking sound—to all who heard, and some so far away they never learned what sadness caused it.

He fell to the floor, sobbing, with an arm around his motherless son.

Even a babe, the one closest of all, would have been thought to have an imprint of such a distressing sound and moment on his memory. But there was none.

He only began to cry more urgently as he searched for his mother's milk.

Dr. Loban attempted to comfort Aleksander, shaking his head sadly. "Nothing could have prevented this. I discovered nothing unusual during her checkups. There must have been a defect in her heart, probably from birth, but undetectable."

Inconsolable, Aleksander screamed, "Undetectable? A defect? You should have *known*... given her something!"

Pausing between racking sobs, his voice barely audible, he groaned, "*I* should have seen... done *some*thing..."

Devastated, he grieved deeply for the love of his life, barely speaking during the funeral or in the weeks ahead

Well-meaning relatives and friends attempted to console him and help with the care of tiny Mikhail, but he was not to be comforted.

He made small attempts at allowing Aunt Raisa to care for the babe.

But he wanted him to himself. Mikhail was his connection to his beloved Vera.

I cannot bear their talk of her being an angel. In truth, their speaking of her at all, in the past tense. I have Mikhail, born of our love.

I will give everything for him to have a good life. But I will grieve my darling Vera's death until the day of my own.

❋ ❋

Life continues. Days pass, almost without notice at times—rapidly becoming years.

Aleksander remained firm regarding his wishes concerning his wife's memory. Therefore, they never spoke of her, and even as Mikhail grew, no one knew why he never inquired.

He was a delight—a healthy, happy five-year-old. He loved everyone, and bubbled over with laughter and energy.

"He talks constantly and is as inquisitive as any child I've ever known," a neighbor remarked to Raisa. "His never inquiring about his mother is unbelievable."

"Some things are not to be understood," Raisa answered, dismissively.

Life in Russia, however, was growing more difficult.

"Aunt Raisa," Aleksander asked one day, "Have you read or heard rumors of famine in parts of the country?"

"Yes, and many are complaining of our government not addressing the needs of the people.

"Yesterday, a traveler said food supplies are becoming scarce here in our own homeland, yet our government is still exporting grain in large amounts."

Aleksander added, "And I've heard Stalin seems also unwilling to keep an agreement to withdraw from Iran, causing more unrest here and in other parts of the world."

"Sadly, I believe it to be true, Aleksander."

Changes were happening fast, and he knew of nothing he could do about them.

❋ ❋

Aleksander's only sibling, the sister in America, was Blancha Nordin Aldredge. It was strange to have knowledge of a sister seen only in a few photographs.

Blancha had married and left Russia before his birth, never having been able to return. His parents had recounted her romance with an American soldier, with whom she had fallen deeply in love.

They had spoken to them of their dream to marry, but when military orders for his return to America came earlier than expected, they arranged their marriage quickly. Though they could not travel together, amazingly, she was able to leave a few months after his departure.

She corresponded regularly with her parents before their deaths, and they spoke proudly of her, more often within the family.

After Aleksander's father's death, his mother spoke wistfully of Blancha.

"Aleksander, I have written your sister the sad news of her father's death. Not being able to see him again will burden her heart. But, what of the time of *my* death? I want assurance you will correspond with her then."

"Yes Mama. Many years from now, I hope, but you have my promise."

"You are a good son. It is my hope a relationship might grow between you—though across the world, we are still family. Since her husband's death, we are the only family she has. She needs to feel our love. You will feel that need when I am gone."

"I regret I have never met her. She sounds very dear."

Aleksander hugged his mother and kissed her cheek, dreading the day he would have to keep his promise.

The unhappy day came sooner than expected. Aleksander wrote to the sister he did not know, to bring the devastating news of no longer having a living parent.

Her reply seemed to have been written the very day his letter had arrived.

"Aleksander, my beloved brother,

I thank you for your letter, though it brought the sad news of our mother's death. From her letters of late, I knew of her failing health.

Though we have never met, we are of the same blood, from the same cherished parents .I am so sorry you had the burden of burying them.

Also, the knowledge of not being there to help you with our dear mother and father in their years of deteriorating health has brought me great pain. I know you were a blessing to them from the moment of your birth.

Though I cannot regret marrying David and traveling with him to his home country, I feel a deep loss in never having seen you or being there to embrace you in love.

David was the greatest blessing in my life, in spite of the few years we had together. He was a good man, Aleksander. How I wish you could have known him.

Nonetheless, it has been impossible to return. Please know the depth of my love for you. I pray for you daily, asking God to someday allow me to embrace you. I hope you will continue to correspond with me about the occasions of your life.

With love from your sister, Blancha (Aldredge)"

Following the initial correspondence, their long-distance relationship continued.

They wrote at least several times a year, with the exception of the year following Vera's death, Aleksander being unable to write such words on paper.

When he finally wrote, it was a letter of sadness, but culminated with the news and joy brought to him by his new son, Mikhail.

❋ ❋

Aleksander had faced facts about the trouble in his country.

The idea grew within that America would be a better place for his son. With the news of a cousin's plan to travel there, the possibility became clearer.

He wrestled with it. He attempted to face the reality of the consequences if it grew to fruition. He made inquiries about America, travel requirements, and cost.

Aleksander stayed awake at night thinking of every conceivable consequence.

Finally, he wrote a letter to his sister to ask whether she would take Mikhail into her home —if he could arrange to send him to America.

She replied quickly.

"Dear Aleksander,

My happy answer is yes. I was overjoyed to receive your letter about the possibility of sending your precious son to me for safe keeping. Of course it has long been my prayer to meet you. Perhaps this is my answer.

As you know, David and I were not blessed with a child in our marriage, and I have little experience with children. Our marriage was much too short, a fact which I will not take time to discuss. I spent many years in dress-making, but have not worked in some years. I tell you this to let you know my health is not good, and I have little energy to give to a growing child.

The school here is good, though, and is close, so he could easily walk. His basic knowledge of the English language will be an advantage.

How gratifying it is to know this was made possible at your own birth, Aleksander.

Perhaps God himself guided my choice of the book, The Wonder Clock, *for you.*

I believe America to be a better, safer place to rear a child and it will afford him more opportunities. For you too, when you arrive.

My thoughts were to be honest about my abilities, but have no doubt about my eagerness to have him with me.

I will cherish Mikhail and care for him, the most precious thing in your life. I still have love to give and will love him as my own.

I will await your reply.

Love from your sister, Blancha"

❀ ❀

Blancha posted the letter and sat in her easy chair looking around her small home.

I can make room for Aleksander's boy if travel can actually be arranged. I am eager for it to work out. I pray God will give me the wisdom and strength to be good for my nephew.

Being widowed young, she knew little more than the work she had done in the dress-making shop, her love of reading, and attending church.

She had embraced the God of her husband and America, and was baptized while her husband remained alive. She attended worship services faithfully until her strength failed. Though not a great distance, mornings were more difficult.

She seldom even went to the grocery or the library she loved, and would read the books she owned again and again.

She was thankful for friends who visited. She kept fresh pastries to serve with the coffee, for which Americans seemed so fond.

"If Mikhail does make the trip," she confided in the one person she had consulted about her decision, "there is the question of Aleksander's arranging his own travel to America. The limitations of the United States are strict, and the cost prohibitive. Worse, the Russian government has a hard stance on allowing a young man to leave the homeland. He has, however, fulfilled his military duty.

"He even incurred serious injury—surely his military time would be taken into consideration. From his letters, I have no doubt of his doing whatever necessary to get here to his boy, or die trying."

She prayed for Aleksander and Mikhail, loving them from afar.

"God, please guide the future of Aleksander and Mikhail, and of mine. I believe it is your will that I take this child, and that I have made the right decision."

God will find a way for this father and son. I'm sure of it... most of the time.

❄ ❄

Reading his sister's letter, Aleksander was relieved and touched, though he had a knot growing in his stomach.

He hoped this was the right decision and that he would be able to carry it through.

Many things would have to work together for it to happen. Relatives who knew his cousin, Arta Nordin, assured him she was known for her good, honest character.

She had gone into a job at a local factory after a year of high school, where she apparently had a good work ethic. She had no immediate family left, and decided to pursue a better life in America.

Satisfied, Aleksander began researching the possibility of Mikhail's travel papers being added to hers.

Contacting Arta had presented obstacles, but after two conversations, she reluctantly agreed to take him with her.

"Only," she had stipulated, "with your assurance of my being able to quickly deposit him with your sister after arriving in America."

He began mentioning America to Mikhail more often, and being more diligent in their reading of *The Wonder Clock*, as well as speaking English.

"You think we might really go to another country someday, Papa? And meet your real sister? Would we take Aunt Raisa with us? I don't know if I'd want to live somewhere else…"

"Mikhail," Aleksander laughed, "you never let me answer your questions. You are too busy thinking of the next one."

That boys' conversation only pauses when I read to him. Such a talker. But how will I live without hearing his busy, happy, small voice, if I send him to America?

35

But I must do what I believe is best for him... even if my heart breaks again.

He had not had the heart to mention to Mikhail that he might not be going *with* him.

That information was not shared until plans were set.

Adding Mikhail to Arta's passage proved complicated, involving much paperwork and bending a few facts.

But after a few months, all arrangements had been made for Mikhail to leave with her.

❈ ❈

Waving from the ship was a very unhappy child. He was with a cousin he barely knew, and traveling out of his village for the first time—to another country and an aunt he'd never met.

From the dock, a most miserable father returned his wave. Though he forced a smile as long as his son might be able to see him, his tears flowed abundantly.

When Aleksander could no longer see even an imagined small shape on the ship, he collapsed onto the dock and sobbed.

.

~ 5 ~

Mikhail Nordin
America – Spring of 1946

Mikhail had in fact been brought to the small Southeastern town of *Mt. Seasons,* Tennessee.

The population was barely five thousand, varying with the seasons. It was located on the plateau almost at the top of a mountain. Most families who lived there did so because it was their place of birth, as well as the birthplace of their parents and grandparents.

Downtown consisted primarily of brick buildings original to the town's establishment. None had been noticeably updated over the years, but were kept spotlessly clean. Occasionally a new coat of paint on a door might be observed, or the addition of an awning.

Within a few blocks was the town's only drugstore, a small dress shop, a sandwich shop, a general merchandise store, a few assorted shops, and the only picture show, the *Ritz.*

Scattered in other directions was the school, three churches, a library staffed by volunteers, one grocery, two restaurants, a shoe repair shop, a small medical clinic and a service station.

Mikhail was frightened. "Everything is too *big* here."

Though the buildings in this town were not as tall as in other cities they'd traveled through, there seemed to be cars everywhere—and noise.

Mikhail was not accustomed to such… *busy-ness.* "It's pretty, though, and warm. I do like that."

"Yes," Arta replied. "Try to smile. We will soon be to your aunt's house."

Seeing Blancha for the first time, Mikhail was somewhat afraid.

He held Arta's hand as they approached the steps to her house. Apparently watching for them, Blancha came out onto the porch. She was short, and very thin.

Her hair is fuzzy… gray, like Aunt Raisa—I hope she's as nice. Her dress, shoes… everything… is black. I think her eyes are blue, like mine—but different, tired.

He looked at Arta, hoping she would stay with him.

I'm not sure Arta likes me much, but I'm used to her—she's stayed with me every minute since we left home… like she promised Papa.

Thinking of Papa, he felt the warmth of tears returning to fill his eyes…

Arta hasn't talked much to me and she said she would be glad when Aunt Blancha took over. But… maybe she's changed her mind.

Arta took her hand from him. She said to Blancha, *"Vy Blancha, da?"* ("You are Blancha, yes?")

"Da, Mikhail's tetya." ("Yes, Mikhail's aunt.")

"He is now yours. I keep promise. Do not expect to see me again. Goodbye, Mikhail." She turned and quickly walked away, without even accompanying him up the steps.

Blancha hadn't uttered a word to him, but held her arms out.

He climbed the steps, slowly, and briefly hesitated before going into her arms. She hugged him close and spoke to him quietly in the language of their birth. "Mikhail, I am your Aunt Blancha, your Papa's sister. I am glad to have you, his boy, here. You look like his pictures."

There were tears in her eyes. "I will do for you the best I can, Mikhail. Come. I show you your room." He took her hand.

What Blancha saw standing at the bottom of her porch steps that day was a small, very frightened boy, whose blond hair seemed to go in every direction. He had a few freckles scattered about on his nose, not noticeable unless you were looking for them.

His nose is a little bigger than his other features, but will sort itself out as he grows. He's a handsome boy, like his father. He looks directly at me with those large, decidedly-blue eyes—I like that—and the girls will envy those long eyelashes. But, his eyes also hold fear—a look I hope to soon remove.

He'd be surprised to know how fearful I am… of not being able to give him what he needs, or failing both son and father.

She so wanted to gather him in her arms and hold him a while.

She hoped to give him her love, and earn his in return. She knew it could not happen overnight. Perhaps, one day. She regretted having so little experience with children, and was past having the energy and wonder she believed a child needed.

With God's help, though, I will do my best.

She watched as he took clothing from his сумка для путешествий (travel bag). From a smaller one, he removed books, drawing paper and pencils. He turned slightly to look at her as he placed one of the books carefully by his bed. Her breath caught—it was the American story book, *The Wonder Clock,* sent to her brother, Aleksander, as a gift so long ago!

Recovering quickly, she smiled. Mikhail turned back to the book, but she'd caught his fleeting expression of pleasure.

❄ ❄

Two days after his arrival, Blancha took him to the Mt. Seasons Elementary School, where the principal, Mr. Matthews, met with them. He spoke alone with Mikhail, asking a series of questions to determine his readiness for school.

Though the principal smiled and was kind, Mikhail was nervous in this new environment, a stranger judging him.

Mr. Matthews brought Mikhail out of his office into the reception area. "He's done well with everything I've presented, Mrs. Aldredge.

"His need for a better knowledge of English words will be quickly resolved, I believe.

"He's very bright, and actually has a better grasp of English than I expected. I'd like to put him into a first-grade class to see how he adjusts."

Mr. Matthews spoke to Mikhail, slowly, kindly, "Our school will soon be out for the summer, but I'd like for you to spend the remaining time in a first grade classroom to get acquainted with our customs, Mikhail.

"When school resumes in the fall, you will most likely be in the same class room, but with a new group of children. You will be six then, correct?"

Mikhail thought he understood—he was listening carefully.

It was difficult to remember to answer in English, but he answered quietly, "Yes, sir."

Blancha was pleased as they walked down the long hall to the first-grade classroom, hearing sounds of teachers and children coming from the classrooms. At a side door, a line of children walked behind a teacher as they filed out to the playground. Mikhail observed them—they were not talking, but appeared happy. Several looked his way, curious.

Arriving to the classroom, they were introduced to Mrs. Wilson. She had him stand in front of the class as she introduced him to his new classmates.

"Hellloooo, Mikhail," the class responded on cue.

"When you return tomorrow morning, the children will introduce themselves to you," she explained.

Mikhail studied the array of new faces.

I wonder if they will like me... there are so many.

❅ ❅

The first full day of school, Mikhail felt Mrs. Wilson was staring at him as he struggled with the words on the spelling list.

I don't think they like me, the new kid from Russia. I don't look different from them, though. My hair is blond, like some of the others. Most have brown hair, but one girl's hair is red.

Papa said I was good with English because of our American story book we read every night. When Papa began talking more about America, we practiced speaking English. And on our long trip here, Arta made me speak English so we'd "be ready for the new country," even though she didn't talk much.

Everyone was wrong—the teacher doesn't sound like the other American travelers.

"Are you listening, Mike?"

"Yes, ma'am. I am called Mikhail—*Meek-ha-eel*."

"Yes, I know. Many of the children have what we call nicknames, though—usually something shorter than their regular name. Couldn't your American nickname be Mike?"

He looked around the room. The other children were smiling, so he answered, "Yes, ma'am."

Thus, his name became Mike to everyone other than Blancha and Aleksander.

"Miss Wilson, I'm not good at understanding the words when you say them."

"Mike, simply listen closely… and it's *Mrs.* Wilson, not Miss."

There were many words he did not understand when she pronounced them, though he recognized some when written on the chalk board.

❄ ❄

Happily, Mike soon made a friend. She helped him with the spelling problems and other things as well.

Her name was Anna, but he didn't meet her in school.

As he walked home from school on the second day, Anna stopped him on the sidewalk near his house to introduce herself. He knew right away she liked him.

A young woman with a ready smile, she had lived in Mt. Seasons all her life, and still lived with her parents.

"I don't live far from here, but was out taking a walk. I'm enrolled in college classes in a town down the mountain," she explained. "I hope someday to teach school, maybe children the age you are now."

Kindly, she said, "Honey, what you need is help understanding English with the *Southern accent.*

"You might just as well learn Southern cause that's where you've been planted. Anything else will just give you problems."

Confused, he asked, "Isn't this America?"

Anna laughed. "Yes, honey, you *are* in America. It's just that the American *South* is a distinctive difference."

She worked part time at Turner's Drugstore, the town's *only* drug store. Mike had noticed it earlier, and the large *RX* sign out front.

"What kind of store is an RX?" he asked shyly. She didn't laugh, but smiled and explained it was a way of saying medicines.

"We sell many other items, though—birthday cards, notebook paper, candy, Cokes, and, my favorite, fresh-dipped ice cream cones and milkshakes. You'll like it, Mikhail."

A few days later, Blancha gave him a few pennies and allowed him to walk to the RX. It was exactly as Anna said.

He'd never seen so much candy, and stood in awe of the glass display case. The assortment of penny candies was amazing. The chocolate bars were individually wrapped, several varieties—some a nickel, one a dime.

He watched as a customer selected penny candies. Anna took his selections out of the case one at a time, using tiny tongs, and dropped them into a small paper bag.

He decided on the yellow gum drops. They were *two* for a penny. If ever he had a nickel to spend, he hoped to have a Coke.

He'd seen milkshakes being made, but they were twenty cents. Anna gave him a hug as he left with his treasure.

I have so many! Maybe Aunt Blancha would like one. I can't wait to get home to show her.

On subsequent visits, Anna would sometimes sit with him at one of the tiny round tables.

She didn't mind answering his questions.

And she would occasionally pat his arm or hand as they said goodbye. A few words he asked about, she explained should not be used at all.

"They are not acceptable at school or in good Christian society, Mikhail," Anna explained. "Some Christians may use that language, but God is not pleased."

Anna seemed to enjoy using his born name, though sometimes she did call him Mike.

He didn't yet understand the word Christian, but Aunt Blancha was one, and it was about belief in God. Papa believed in God.

"What does *play* mean when it's not about going outside at recess?"

"It's a performance," Anna answered. "Sometimes there is singing and other times the students act out a story. Many of our words have more than one meaning."

Over time, he had a variety of questions. Her answers satisfied, though some still left him somewhat mystified.

"What do the boys mean when they say they went *skinny dippin' in the crick*?" (Swimming naked in the creek, or stream.)

"Why is it bad to curse but good to write in cursive?" (To curse means using bad, ugly words—*writing* in cursive means joining letters together by curving the letters to form a word.)

"What's so bad about being a Yankee?" (Yankees aren't bad—Southerners only think living in the south is ever so much better.)

And… "Mrs. Wilson keeps her ruler on her desk all the time.

"Sometimes she uses it to swat somebody's hand… so why is the *Golden Ruler* a good thing?"

"What we call the *Golden Rule* is in the Bible, God's Word, Mike. What Jesus meant was that one of your rules in life should be that you treat everyone else as well as you hope they treat you."

His eyes grew large as he processed these thoughts. Anna delighted in the workings of this child's mind.

❄ ❄

The school teacher insisted her name, or title, be pronounced correctly—*Misris (Mrs.)* Wilson. Not *Miz,* and most definitely not *Miss.*

If pronounced wrong, you'd likely get your hand smacked with a ruler in front of the entire class.

Why is she so cranky about her name, but had no problem changing mine to a nickname?

I don't know whether there is another first-grade teacher, but maybe I'll get a different teacher next year. Younger, like Anna.

Mrs. Wilson isn't as old as Aunt Blancha, but she's pretty old, over thirty, and kinda fat.

She wears lipstick and ear-bobs every day— I never knew a lady that did that. Aunt Raisa only did on a special day, like a funeral. Mrs. Wilson even wears stockings… hose every day.

At recess, Thomas confided, "When I see Mrs. Wilson's legs in her H-O-S-E (he spelled it out), I think of the word "hoss" (the pronunciation for horse in Southern)…

"Well, I imagine two hosses' legs and can barely keep from laughing out loud!"

The other boys laughed so hard, some had to sit on the ground, tears rolling down their cheeks, Mike joining in.

It's probably not nice to say something like that, 'specially about a teacher. I don't think I'll mention this to Anna.

~ 6 ~

Mikhail thought it clear he had no mother.

Mentioning this matter-of-factly at supper, Blancha grew visibly distressed. "Mikhail Nordin, you *cannot* be *born* without a mother! It's inside her you grow, don't you know?"

"You *knew* my mother?"

Her voice lowering, she answered, "No, Mikhail… I never knew your mother. I didn't know about *you* until you were already a small boy. But these questions are for your papa when it is the right time."

I'm not so sure about a person not being born without a mother… I don't think she knows either. I'm sure I would have remembered if I'd had a mother. I got a father, though… and I need him.

As Mikhail settled in at Blancha's, she explained, "I'm sorry I cannot play games and run with you, I'm just about worn out, honey."

So… if you could be a mother by getting a baby to grow in you, Aunt Blancha would surely have gotten one to grow in her before she wore out. I wish she had; then I wouldn't be as lonely.

His first night, he'd cried himself to sleep, but after a while he did think of this as home.

And how different it would be when Papa arrived.

He liked his small room and the large oak trees surrounding the house.

"Your room was a porch before it was closed in," Blancha explained.

"That's why there are windows all around and no heat. When winter comes, the door to your room will be left open all the time so the heat can get to it. I'll be making new pajamas for you, too, with feet sewn right in to help keep you warm."

❄ ❄

The school building was the largest building Mikhail had ever been inside—he couldn't wait for Papa to see it. The first-grade classroom was also large, having its own bathroom at one end. There was another separate room without a door called a *cloak room*, for hanging coats, jackets and hats, or to leave snow boots in the winter. The only time it was necessary to leave the room was for recess or lunch.

The lunch room was separated from the school by a short covered sidewalk. Lunch could be purchased or brought from home, but most days Aunt Blancha made a sandwich for him and sent money for milk. He was glad when his sandwich was made with sliced bread from the store; more often it was made from cold biscuits.

If he could buy lunch, his favorite was spaghetti day, with the dessert being a big greasy peanut butter cookie with a crisscross on top.

The walk from school was about two blocks through the alleys.

With nothing tempting him to hurry, he let his imagination take hold as he explored his new world.

At times, something would come to his attention peeping from a garbage can or corner. He'd found a perfectly good used billfold—Blancha called hers a bill-*folder,* an only slightly-soiled *Superman* comic book, a cap barely worn, and a nearly-full package of chewing gum.

When Blancha asked about the cap, he answered honestly, "Someone I didn't know didn't want it anymore."

The day before the school year ended, a heavy rain began just before the last bell rang. Mike put on his hat to go straight home.

The front door creaked as he opened it. As he removed his shoes and hat so as not to drip water into the house, he sensed something different. He smelled coffee. Aunt Blancha had declared she "could not abide" coffee in the afternoon.

Hey, we must have company—somebody important, 'cause Aunt Blancha generally doesn't do things she cannot abide. Papa! He loves afternoon coffee and would be very important.

Hurrying into the sitting area, his aunt sat across from a man who sat in their best chair with his back to him. It wasn't Papa—this man was tall, but skinny, with a gruff voice.

"Mr. Snider," Blancha announced proudly, "this is Mikhail, my nephew from Russia."

"Hello, sir."

Looking the boy over thoroughly, the man gave only a grunt. He then rose, nodded to Blancha, and left.

"Who was that, Aunt Blancha?"

"An unhappy man who has no heart," she answered, with an unusually short tone,

She left the room without asking about his school day or instructing him to wash his hands.

No heart? I thought you had to have one. Maybe they operationed it when he had a heartache or was heartsick. A hard heart means you don't love your children and a pure heart meant something about God. This is definitely a question for Anna. Aunt Blancha answers lots of my questions, but she doesn't talk a lot because she's worn out.

I still don't understand that—she said it meant real tired... but how can you be worn out if you still got more wear in you? Like shoes—nearly worn out means wear them a little longer, but worn out means no good, get another pair.

Maybe I won't have to ask Anna about being wore out... but I sure need to ask about not having a heart.

❋ ❋

Summer was wonderful—warm, sun almost always shining, no school, no homework, and more time outside. Besides Anna, Mike had made another friend. James was in the second-grade class.

Buzzzzzzzz! Buzzzzzzzz! Buzzzzzzzz!

The school fire alarm had sounded loudly and long for a fire drill. Students rushed from classes into the hallway to file outside.

Instructions were for moving along in silence, but the pushing, shoving, and giggling continued in spite of all warnings.

James had fallen from his line almost right in front of him as everyone rushed out, happy to be missing class. No one slowed down for James, but Mikhail stopped and quickly helped him up, whispering "hurry," as they smiled at each other.

James was taller than Mike, with bright red hair and a bounty of freckles. He lived at the edge of town, a mile or so from Blancha's, but was allowed to ride his bike to visit.

He talked about his parents often, as well as an older brother and younger sister—obviously having fun together as a family.

They hoped to go to the picture show before summer's end. James had been once and told Mike how grand it was. They read about movie stars in the old *Movie Life* magazine Mike had found.

"If only I had a bike," Mike bemoaned. "Even though James lets me ride on the back of his, it's kinda uncomfortable and won't go fast with the two of us riding." Aunt Blancha was not encouraging.

James confessed his bike came from the town dump. "Daddy found it and fixed it up. He had to put new patches on the tires, and got a pump for new leaks."

Mike wanted to visit James, and timed his request during supper.

"Aunt Blancha, James always comes *here* to play. He wants me to visit *him*. I could ride on the back of his bike some, and we'll walk part way… boy, these beans are good tonight."

Blancha only nodded about the beans. He helped clean the kitchen before quietly going to take his bath.

When it was time for bed, he asked casually, "So, is it okay if I ride with James on his bike over to his house tomorrow? I'd be back before suppertime." She looked up from her mending, paused for a moment, causing him not a little worry, but smiled as she rose from her chair.

"Mikhail, you are a good boy. You may go with James. I know you will mind your good manners."

Mike was elated.

But there were surprises coming his way. Things are not always as they seem.

❄ ❄

Mike greeted the milkman cheerily that morning, "Morning, Mr. Partin."

"Good morning, Mike. Up early today, must have a good day planned."

"Yes, sir, I'm waiting for my friend."

He'd come out to the front porch quickly at the sound of the milk jars clanking. He took the quart of milk and hurriedly put it into the ice box. It was only seven-thirty. James generally arrived around nine as he had to help his older brother, Robbie, with a paper route.

In case he was earlier today, he was ready.

At eight-thirty, he saw James riding toward him, but with a puzzling expression. Mike began happily waving and grinning to let James know he could go. James slowed and came to a stop at the steps, maintaining the unusual expression.

"I can go! Is it still okay? Did your mama say I could visit?"

"Yes, it's all right. But... I guess I didn't think you would ever be allowed to visit. I don't know whether you'll like where I live. It's different from your house... a *lot* different."

"Well, I know. You got a big family, probably noisy and everything—I'd like it."

"No. That's not it. It's... well, we don't live in a house. I never really *said* we lived in a house," James replied defensively.

Mike didn't understand. *Doesn't he want me to go with him?*

"Is it an apartment? They're called flats in Russia."

James took a deep breath.

"*No*, we live in a *tent*! I thought somebody woulda told you by now."

Taken aback, Mike didn't know what to say. He'd never heard of anyone *living* in a tent, only camping. He stood, unmoving, stunned into silence.

James stood for only a second before getting on his bike. Without another word, he pedaled quickly away.

Recovering, Mike shouted, "But... but I don't *care*, James, I was just surprised!"

James had disappeared around the curve.

Mike walked slowly up his porch steps and inside the house.

Blancha looked up from her coffee.

He mumbled, "James came by. He has to help out at home today, so I won't be going."

I still don't understand repentanance, but I know good Christians don't lie. I got a real sick feeling in my stomach, though... maybe that's it.

Every day he hoped to see James riding down the street as if nothing had happened. His living in a tent made no difference to him. Honestly, he was quite curious. Even if Aunt Blancha had a phone, he guessed you wouldn't have one in a tent. He considered talking to Anna but was ashamed of his behavior.

The next week he had three pennies and was allowed to walk to the RX. While he pondered his decision, he saw James. The druggist was handing him a small bag.

Mike suddenly felt sweaty and scared. He wanted to talk to him, to be friends again, but he didn't know how to go about it.

As James turned from the counter, their eyes met. Mike took a few steps and said in a low voice, "Hey, James, I got some pennies. I can't get us a Coke 'cause they're a nickel. But you could help me pick out some penny candies... if you want to."

"Okay," James replied.

By the time they left the RX, they were friends once more.

The next day, after they'd ridden a while and walked part way across town, a wooded area came into view.

"We live there, just a little behind the biggest tree at the right." James announced. "You know, this is the only time we've lived in a tent. We always had a house before—Daddy says it's just while he says up some money."

The tent was similar to pictures Mike had seen of circus tents, though not as large. James put the bike against the tree. The kick stand had been broken long before.

"No door, so we open the flap, and if we don't see Mama, we yell out so she knows who's home." As they entered, Mrs. Gosden rushed up to give James a quick hug and kiss.

"Mama, this is the friend I told you about, Mikhail—but he's called Mike now."

"Nice to meet you, Mrs. Gosden."

She leaned down to give him a hug. "I'm so happy to meet you. If it's okay for me to call you *Mike*, then you call me *Mama G*. We've been hearing all about James' friend from Russia and the fun you have. I got some good chocolate pudding ready for ya'll."

Mama G's hug was warm and comfortable—she was what his aunt in Russia had called *ample*.

He was amazed at the feeling of home—a kitchen area with wooden boxes stacked to make a table, and clotheslines stretched across the tent with blankets hanging from them, creating rooms of a sort. Mattresses and quilts were on the canvas *floor* to be used as beds.

Mike noticed a white metal pail with a wire handle beside one of the mattresses. There was a slim line of red paint around the top, with a matching lid.

Mike pointed. "What's that?"

"It's for... well... bathroom stuff... during the night."

"Oh." He wanted no more information on that subject.

The same type wooden boxes in the kitchen area were being used to store folded clothes. Others had cushions on top for seating.

"Dynamite came in these boxes at the road construction company where Daddy works." Mike then recognized the words *Dynamite– Danger* stenciled in red on each on each one.

James continued authoritatively, "They use dynamite to blast boulders out of the way. Boulders are really big rocks, bigger than a house sometimes. The boxes are usually thrown away or burned. So Daddy brings them home."

James was feeling more confident. "We take showers and use the bathrooms in the big bath house at the trailer park. Daddy pays them, kinda like rent.

"I get on the bus for school at the stop by the trailer park, so I guess lots of kids think I live in one of the trailers."

Mama G had used an extra-large dish pan to mix and cook the chocolate pudding. He'd always had it cold. This was freshly cooked, and still warm.

Mike remarked, "This is the best pudding I ever had."

"Why, thank you, Mike," answered Mama G.

Going into the woods to explore, they climbed trees and talked about all they wanted to do before school resumed. Later, they sat on a large low-hanging branch of an old oak tree to eat sandwiches.

"Boy, James, your mama is a good cook. I never had butterbean sandwiches before, but they're *good*. And…you know, I think the tent is great."

James grinned. "Yeah, I guess."

Before they realized it, the afternoon was gone.

Mike waved to James as he ran up the steps and into his house.

I'll just tell Aunt Blancha about James' mother, the chocolate pudding, and the woods. I won't use the word, house.

~ 7 ~

Blancha was about to sit to read after supper. "Mikhail, take the garbage to the can out back. Take a look around while you're out there to see if anything else needs to be done."

"Yes, ma'am." Not knowing exactly what she meant, he'd look around in case there was trash scattered or something out of place. He took the bag out, walking through his room to the back door. He put the bag into the old oil barrel serving as their garbage can, and began to make a quick scan of their small yard.

Not yet dark, he thought he saw something in the shadows at the edge of the yard.

Going to investigate, his daydreams seemed to get in his way—it resembled a bike tire.

Of course it isn't. It can't be.

Going around the corner of the house, he looked more closely behind the privet hedge where the item was partially hidden. He nearly lost his breath as he got hold of it and pulled on, yes, handlebars—it *was* a bicycle!

"Look, look, Aunt Blancha, look!" he began to yell. As he turned, he realized she was standing in the doorway watching. Her expression was one of total satisfaction, even the rare whisper of a smile.

"Aunt Blancha, where did it come from… can I ride it? It's not new, but the paint looks good… and tires without patches.

"It has a basket… a kick stand and everything… why is it in our yard?"

Mike took a deep breath and walked the bike over to Blancha, who had slowly made her way down the steps.

"It is for you, Mikhail. It can be an early birthday present so you have more time to ride in summer before you are in school again. Maybe we have more meals with just beans and bread, and not many treats at the RX, though. Would that be all right?"

Mike hugged his aunt tight. "Yes, Aunt Blancha, oh yes, this is the best present ever, and you are the best aunt in the whole world!"

"And I have a nickel for you. You can go to the new *Roy Rogers* picture show with your friend."

Mike could barely comprehend all this happening in one day, but was sure he would not ask her for anything else, *ever.*

As he got into bed that night, Blancha came into his room to tuck him in, as had become their custom.

"We didn't read together tonight. But we must remember not to miss many days. Mrs. Wilson assured me you would do well in the fall if you practice reading and writing English."

She bent slightly to pat the cover as usual, then his shoulder, which he'd come to think of as a small, soft hug.

As she leaned down, he reached up to her and put his small arms around her neck.

Surprised, she looked into his face.

"Aunt Blancha?"

"Yes, Mikhail?"

"I love you, Aunt Blancha… not just because you gave me a bike… just… I *love* you."

"Oh, sweetheart, I love you, too, so *much*."

She moved to sit on the side of his bed, and leaned further in to hug him tightly, kissing his cheek before slowly rising to stand beside the bed again.

"Sweet dreams. I will enjoy seeing you riding your bike tomorrow. Don't forget to thank God for this good day. All good things come from him… like *you*. Good night."

She left, partially closing the squeaky door. Entering her own room, her eyes filled with tears.

He's doing so well, even with his reading of the word lists. Our speaking English at home has helped.

"Thank you, Lord, for this boy," she prayed. "You have helped me remove the fear from his eyes, replacing it with joyfulness. Thank you for your love for us and the love between Mikhail and me. Please continue to protect him, and make it possible for Aleksander to be with us… before the year ends… please."

❋ ❋

Though they missed the Roy Rogers show, Mike and James were first in line for the first showing of the new *Lone Ranger*, agreeing it the best adventure of all.

A few weeks remained before school resumed.

Mike seemed to have gotten acquainted with everyone in town, and Blancha was no longer concerned about his riding out of sight.

His favorite place to ride alone was a separate section of town called *All Seasons*. A large ornate archway with double gates graced the entrance, though the gates were never closed. Most of the houses were immense, with beautiful flower beds and pots of flowers all around. There were hills just right for riding a bike up, and coasting down. It was always quiet, with only a few houses occupied. The *winter people* had not yet arrived.

"Most people who own homes there generally live in them only during winter months; some rent them out for the summer," Anna explained.

"So we refer to them as *winter people*. They have other homes in the northern part of the United States. You remember our conversation about the word, Yankee. It's much colder there, with heavy snows and ice, so they come here during those months because our winters are milder."

"It was a lot colder in Russia than here, but I don't look different… what do winter people look like?"

Anna laughed. "They are like everyone else. Their speech is different, though. English, but a different sound—an *accen*t. Sometimes we have trouble understanding them.

"I suppose they have trouble understanding us as well.

"In the South, we seem to talk more slowly, as if we have plenty of time. Northern folks seem to *me* to be in a hurry to finish."

The last week before school resumed, Blancha announced, "You're going to Vacation Bible School this week, Mikhail. It's at the church."

They attended the community church, a few blocks away, when Blancha felt up to walking.

"Whoever heard of a vacation school? Vacation means *no* school," he challenged.

"Many of your school friends will be there, Mikhail, including James."

He was not at all pleased with this new prospect, but on Monday morning, the last week of August and freedom from school, he rode his bike to the church.

Returning home, he happily admitted, "I *liked* it, Aunt Blancha. We sang and played games... we had *good* snacks... and heard stories about God.

"And I'm making a surprise... I can't tell you what it is yet... but you're gonna like it. We talked a lot about the Golden Rule and prayer. You were right... James was there... I can't wait till tomorrow!"

On Friday, the last day, crafts were taken home. He ran into the house, forgetting to be quiet as he slammed the front door.

"Aunt Blancha, you get to see my surprise today!"

Excited, he handed it to her.

"It's my hand print," he explained... "I got to put my hand in paint... then we made the frame for it from popsicle sticks... do you like it?"

"It is *very* nice, Mikhail. Thank you. This will go on my kitchen shelf."

Wistfully, she added, "You know, someday your hand will grow—you will be a man. But this will always be a sweet memory."

Mike was pleased—only special things were placed on her shelf.

~ 8 ~

Thousands of miles away, Aleksander waited anxiously every day for word of his Mikhail. But when a letter arrived, he was torn with a roller-coaster of emotions.

Shakily he opened Blancha's latest letter. He smiled—Blancha's opening line was always that Mikhail was doing well. Continuing to read, tears flowed again, missing him anew.

He replied as often as possible, but there was little to write. He was working every minute he could to earn the money necessary for travel when his papers were approved.

Dare I say 'when' my papers are approved? I must believe, or I could not go on.

He wrote,

"Dear Blancha,

I write only to feel closer to you and Mikhail, as I have no further news, and I do not want you to worry. I am fortunate to be working steadily, and am nearing my goal of earning the money for my passage. There is no word on approval as yet, though.

As always, Raisia sends her love, and many in the village inquire often of you both. I am pleased to hear that you are well, and that the burden of caring for a child has not been too great.

Indeed, I am pleased to hear that he has brought joy to your life as he has to mine.

And I am glad to hear of his new friends and discoveries.

Love from your brother, Alekxander"

And to Mikhail...

"Dear Mikhail,

I cannot tell you how much I miss you, but I smile to receive your letters and the pictures you've drawn. I am glad you and Blancha have found happy times together. I work hard each day for my journey to America to be with you both, but cannot know when that will be. Try to be patient, and continue to be a good boy for Blancha.

I love you, Papa"

Blancha explained that Aleksander was working as much as possible to raise money for his papers and travel to America. He would sell the large carpentry equipment last.

"Paper and postage cost money, too, you know. We must be patient."

Blancha wrote to Aleksander almost every week to let him know of Mikhail's well-being. She knew she had more time, and it had recently become a delightful task. Mikhail had progressed well and was content. She never failed to add, however, how much he was missed, and how much they both looked forward to his being with them.

School began in September, the day after the Labor Day holiday. Mike had high expectations.

Though he was in the same first-grade class room, Mrs. Wilson had moved away. The new teacher was Miss Parker. He had accepted his American nickname and introduced himself as Mike.

But Aunt Blancha and Papa will always call me Mikhail.

Winter seemed to appear overnight. It reminded Mike of Russia, causing a new wave of homesickness. But the cold wasn't as bitter, and the sun shone brightly more often.

At times, Blancha gave him a dollar and a grocery order to fill after school. He had only to give the list to the grocer and he would gather the items for him, which he could take home in his bicycle basket.

"This will save a bit of money as I will not have a delivery-boy to tip—*you* are my good delivery boy."

She continued her larger monthly order, though most families had groceries delivered weekly.

❄ ❄

School break for Christmas holidays began with a light snow.

With the radio playing Christmas music a few days later, Blancha was enjoying a second cup of coffee, and Mikhail was finishing his oatmeal.

Knock-knock, knock-knock.

"Aunt Blancha, somebody's at the door. Are we having company?"

"As a matter of fact, I am expecting a delivery. Go to the door and let him in."

Enthusiastically, he rushed to the door, shouting, "I see Brother Marshall out the window. Is *he* bringing your delivery?"

"Yes, open the door before he freezes."

Earl Marshall was the minister at the church they attended when Blancha was able, and Mikhail had gotten better acquainted with him when he attended the *vacation* school.

He quickly turned the lock and opened the door. Brother Marshall was holding a small cedar tree, thick with green branches and a distinct aroma.

"Good Morning, Mike. How about some help getting your Christmas tree into the house?"

"A Christmas tree… *ours*?" He stepped back to take hold of a branch in an attempt to help.

"You bet it is. I asked Blancha last week if I could bring it by."

Blancha beamed as she motioned the minister to a cleared space by the front window.

"Thank you, Brother Marshall. It is just right. It will be *perfect* after Mikhail decorates it."

Elated, he asked, "*I* get to decorate it?"

"Yes. There is a box in the corner of my bedroom with decorations. You are completely in charge of deciding where to put them on the tree. Go get it while Brother Marshall and I have a cup of coffee."

After the minister left, Blancha sat on the davenport watching Mikhail examine each item carefully before placing it on the tree.

What a lovely picture of joy. I wish Aleksander were here to see it.

"We hang the stockings on Christmas Eve," she explained. "On Christmas morning you will look inside to find a few surprises, and a gift may have been placed under the tree."

She gently added, "There will be only small gifts, Mikhail. I don't want you to be disappointed."

His eyes were as large as saucers. "I won't be disappointed, Aunt Blancha. I love Christmas. Everything is fun, even the way the house smells since we got the tree."

Choosing her words carefully, she added, "There *may* be a special surprise. I cannot tell you because I'm not sure… but we'll see."

Lord, please… make it possible.

Beginning to understand prayer, Mike remembered to thank God each night for his blessings. Afterwards, he'd tell him if he was sorry about any wrong-doing. *Repentanance* remained a bit unclear, but it was part of being sorry.

Requests were last… for *any*thing you wanted. If God's answer was yes, it would be given to you, but not always right away. If the answer was no, you wouldn't get it. And sometimes, God has to think it over—Anna said it *could* be a long time,

"God, thank you for the Christmas tree and for Aunt Blancha letting me decorate it.

"Thank you for the snow that makes everything so pretty. And, God, I'm glad you don't send as much here as you do in Russia, 'cause we can still walk outside, and my nose doesn't freeze.

"Please, *please* send Papa here. I hope you remember that 'cause I want *him* more than anything. I miss him so much. I'm trying to be good and keep my promise not to ask Aunt Blancha for anything else since she gave me the bike. You probably remember that."

I guess God is still thinking it over about Papa.

Still, he reminded him every night… if he didn't fall asleep too quickly.

❋❋

Finally, Christmas Eve.

The snow was no longer falling, and only five inches remained on the ground.

At breakfast, Blancha made an announcement, appearing unusually satisfied.

"We'll go to the special evening service at church tonight, Mikhail. I've always looked forward to the Christmas Eve service, but I've had to miss it the last few years. But tonight, you can hold my hand as we walk through the snow. You'll enjoy it, Mikhail. They'll be serving hot chocolate in the large parlor before the service, so we'll go early. I *think* a friend is meeting us there. We'll see."

With holiday decorations all over town, everything seemed to be adorned in red bows, greenery, and flowers.

Bells rang, cheerful holiday music played, and laughter abounded on every corner. Mike loved it all.

Miss Parker had taught the class about the red flowering plants seen most often during this time of the year. "They are *poinsettias*," she told the class, adamantly, "*not* 'po-in-sett-ers. *Even* if living in the South, you can certainly pronounce poinsettia correctly."

Though a big word, it was included on the spelling test.

Mike had liked her from the first day of school when she introduced herself. "My name is *Miss* Parker, not Mrs., because I'm not married. Some people call an unmarried woman a *bloom not yet picked*—and I know all about it." She had laughed. He hadn't understood, but sensed he should ask no more.

It was twilight as Blancha and Mike began their slow walk to the church building.

Crunching through the snow, Mike held Blancha's hand tightly, lest she lose her balance. Entering the building, they walked down the long hall toward the parlor.

Though Mike was anxious to hurry in case the supply of hot chocolate ran low, the walk from their house had tired Blancha. She was moving slower than usual. Then she stopped completely.

"Aren't we going for hot chocolate?"

"Mikhail, could we sit for a minute?"

As he sat beside her on the small bench in the hallway, he felt sad for her.

She was so tired. Nonetheless, he couldn't help wondering about the hot chocolate.

"Mikhail, someone is coming down the hall—you may want to share hot chocolate with him."

He'd wondered which friend of Blancha's was to meet them there. It was a minute before he turned.

Taking long strides down the hall toward them was Aleksander, his eyes and broad smile for Mike alone.

"Papa!" Mike jumped up to run to him, hardly believing. Aleksander grabbed him up into his arms as Mike wrapped his arms around him tightly. To Mike's embarrassment, he began to cry.

"Oh, Papa, you're finally *here*… it took so long… I'm so happy… we're going to have hot chocolate and hear the story of baby Jesus… Aunt Blancha didn't tell me you were coming… you must be my surprise… the *best* Christmas surprise in the world, even in the whole South… oh, Papa..."

He buried his face, wet with tears, in Aleksander's shoulder, squeezing him more tightly.

Aleksander couldn't be happier as he held his precious son once again.

Mike raised his head. *Papa is crying too.*

"I am so happy to see *you*, Mikhail. Ah, you have grown bigger, and more handsome."

With a grin, he winked, "Like your Papa, maybe?" His eyes hungrily took in the beautiful sight—his boy.

"I will never leave you again."

After a few minutes, Blancha stood. Aleksander drew her into his embrace, and the three of them stood with arms around each other, sharing tears and thankfulness.

"My prayers are answered," she whispered. "My dear brother, how thankful I am to have my arms around you at last."

Mike's squeal had caught the attention of several church members, who gathered to view the happy reunion.

Though Mike's priorities had changed, the hot chocolate was still plentiful as they walked into the parlor.

Blancha proudly introduced her brother to the minister and other friends, before they entered the sanctuary hand-in-hand.

As they walked home, Aleksander in the middle, hands clasped, the snow began to fall more heavily. This little family, however, was almost unaware of the cold.

Arriving home, coats were hung to dry, and they sat together on the davenport. Blancha couldn't take her eyes from Aleksander.

My dear little brother… strange to think of him in that way as he towers over me, strong and virile. So handsome—his blue eyes seem to be shining as his mirrored image sits in his lap. It is a beautiful Christmas Eve portrait.

"All is well, Lord. All is well. Thank you."

After getting Mikhail into bed, Aleksander came to sit with her.

They were both weary, from travel and life. He put his arm around her. "Blancha, my dear sister, I cannot begin to thank you for what you have done for us. Finally, we are together."

More tears of happiness were shed before retiring for the night. Aleksander made his bed on the davenport. He had traveled with little— everything fit into the corner of Mikhail's room.

Unlike most of the neighborhood, they slept later than usual the next morning, though the adults were gladly wakened by the small boy's joyous cries of, "Merry Christmas Morning!"

Blancha filled the percolator with water and was measuring coffee grounds. "Mikhail, you do not have to wait to see what might be in your stocking."

He was excited to discover fresh fruit, nuts, and a bag of candies inside.

Blancha brought coffee and hot chocolate into the living room, along with pastries she had planned ahead for their breakfast.

Aleksander had carved a finely-detailed wooden horse for Mikhail.

For Blancha, he had a small wooden heart, carved with an intricate design, for a necklace. He also delivered letters to her from several relatives and friends.

Under the tree were Blancha's wrapped gifts to them.

She had knitted a scarf for Aleksander, and purchased a shiny bicycle horn for Mikhail.

Mikhail had drawn a Christmas tree on heavy construction paper for Blancha. He'd carefully created it using bright red and green crayons and stickers, adding, "I Love You," under the tree.

Paper rustling, Blancha removed it from the wrappings.

"Beautiful, Mikhail, *this* will go on the kitchen shelf!"

To Mikhail's relief, she added, "Aleksander and I will share this since, of course, we know you love us both."

Relaxing before lunch, they were thoroughly content, basking in the love and togetherness they had so desired.

A thought came to Blancha. *When Mr. Partin delivered the milk yesterday, he spoke of a new movie,* It's a Wonderful Life. *He saw it in Nashville and said it was the perfect Christmas movie.*

I think nothing could be more wonderful… more perfect…than this Christmas, this family, and this day.

Late in the afternoon, they enjoyed a fine meal, for which Blancha had planned for a month. She'd prayed Aleksander would be there to share it with them, as he'd hoped.

She'd succeeded in surprising Mikhail with the entire menu of roasted hen, stuffing, corn, and sweet potatoes.

No beans.

And fruit cake for dessert.

~ 9 ~

After the holidays, Aleksander's priority was to find work. Up early, he made coffee and saw Mikhail a few minutes before school, then was out all day.

Within days, he had been to almost every business in Mt. Seasons, even outside of it as far as he could walk or ride Mikhail's bicycle.

He didn't take the bicycle often. He was well aware of the spectacle he must make, his knees in front of him even with the seat as high as it would go.

I must look like one of those circus bears, trying to fit my big, six-three body on something meant for a small boy.

Without a doubt, people knew he was "not from around here," before he spoke, though his English was fair. Most of the townspeople knew Blancha, and Mikhail, too, which seemed to smooth his way.

But he'd had no luck, not even possibilities. He'd had a small sum of money when he arrived, but was concerned the burden on his sister was too much. If he didn't find a job soon, he might need to go to another town to find work. If necessary, he would leave Mikhail with Blancha a little longer.

But I promised Mikhail I would not leave him again.

He did a few repairs around the house, trying to keep busy, as well as being helpful.

"Aleksander, the kitchen cabinet appears almost new," Blancha exclaimed.

She was pleased with the cabinet. More importantly, she was proud of her brother's talent.

Aleksander had almost rebuilt the cabinet. He'd made a new door from scrap wood found discarded at a home construction site. Even without proper tools, the cabinet *was* quite an improvement. He'd only brought a few smaller tools with him, the barest of necessities to a woodworker. But it was good to work with wood again.

Approaching the near-finished home, he'd hoped for available work, but the company had come from out of state. The scrap wood was good, though, the crew boss telling him, "Hey, whatever you haul off, we don't have to burn."

He began to mention not finding anything in Mt. Seasons, primarily for Mikhail's benefit, hoping to soften the blow if relocating were necessary.

"Papa, there's something I learned when I first got here. You can learn it, too," Mike announced at supper.

Aleksander raised his eyes from his bowl of soup. "Ah?"

"You gotta learn to speak *Southern* English, so you can talk better to the people you want to work for."

Fearing he might appear disrespectful, Mikhail added, "Your English *is* good… just… you *see* I talk different than when we learned English at home.

"It's *Southern* English, a little funny sometimes, but I know you can learn it."

He was excited now—there was something he could do to help.

Blancha glanced at Aleksander with a hint of a smile, and a slight nod. "It wouldn't hurt, Aleksander, it wouldn't hurt at all."

Aleksander was amused by them *both*—Mikhail, because he wanted to teach his own Papa how to speak, and Blancha, as he'd observed her speech being little different from his. But perhaps it was a different time.

The job search continued, along with "lessons" a few evenings a week.

Mike was doing well in school. He'd made new friends, and still liked Miss Parker very much.

Recess was shared with the second graders, including Thomas, whom he had gotten to know his few months of school in the spring.

One day, Thomas whispered loudly to the other boys, "My mother said Miss Parker is probably going to be an old maid since she's already twenty-eight and set in her ways."

Mike didn't know what an old maid was, but from Thomas's tone, he was sure it wasn't a good thing.

He'd learned a lot since coming to America, though. One thing more important than anything—everyone *did* have a mother. Aunt Blancha had been right.

Who was she? What was her name, and what did she look like? Do I look like her?

The question he was most afraid to ask was, *where is she?*

❊ ❊

Anna had caught a glimpse of Aleksander Nordin when he came into the drugstore to ask Mr. Turner about available work. She was arranging a new supply of *Screenplay* magazines.

Mike finally has his Papa, but for how long? He's tall... and very good looking. Mike favors him. He is anxious, I'm sure. Yet even with the strong voice, he appears humble in his inquiry. I hope he stays in town... for Mike.

But Anna wasn't sure it was her only reason.

She mentioned the situation to her parents and began making occasional inquiries of customers who came into the store.

When James came in with a doctor's prescription for his younger sister, he spoke to Anna while waiting for Mr. Turner, the pharmacist.

"Hi, James. Do you and Mike still spend a lot of time together?"

"We're still best friends, Miss Anna, but his class is at the other end of the school building. I'm in *third* grade now. I can't wait 'til summer, though."

"Does your father still work for the company building the new road?"

He answered proudly, "Yes, ma'am, and he got a promotion. Now he's the one getting the orders from the boss first, and telling the others what to do that day."

Lowering his voice, he added, "And we might get us a house soon."

Anna smiled. "Wonderful news, James. Did you know Mike's dad is trying to find a job?

"Maybe you could tell your father in case something comes up."

"Sure," he replied. He took his package from Mr. Turner and hurried out the door.

A week later, James remembered.

His father, Bobby Joe Gosden, "Bob J" to his friends, was happier with his job now. He'd resumed humming, and was talking about the possibility of getting a small house soon. "Just to rent, you know, because when this road is finished, we'll be moving again."

"Daddy, my friend Mike's Dad, the one who surprised him on Christmas Eve—he's trying to find a job. Do you know of any at your company?"

"No, don't know of anything… but I'll be thinking on it. I met Mr. Nordin, Alex he said, a couple of weeks ago and I thought him right nice. I was surprised he spoke such good English, better than mine I '*spect,*'" he laughed.

As James laughed with him, he added, "Mike's trying to teach him to speak *Southern.*" That brought more laughter from the family.

"It ain't so easy," added James's older brother, Robbie.

"For goodness sake, Robbie," replied Mrs. Gosden, "you know *ain't* is not correct in *any* kind of English. We're all glad *you* aren't trying to teach anyone."

✳ ✳

February came with snow and ice, and everything generally messy.

Aleksander had been plagued with a cough and cold for several days, which could no longer be ignored.

Blancha walked to the neighbor's house to call Dr. Moore, who stopped by later in the day. The doctor verified a low-grade fever.

"If you don't stay in a few days and take the medications, you are likely headed for pneumonia."

Mike was sent to the drugstore with prescriptions.

Blancha cared for her brother tirelessly, keeping up with the dosage schedule, making soup, and piling quilts and pillows around him.

At night, she added smelly rags around his throat and on his chest.

"Blancha, you will surely kill me with this smell," he complained.

She laughed aloud at his protests. "This cure I learned from our own mother."

Hearing her laugh was better than any medicine.

"When you are well and strong again, you will find work. And soon we have need of serious talk."

He was about to ask what about, and why not have it now, but Mikhail came running in from school, happily wanting to share news of his day.

A few days later, with cautions from Blancha, Aleksander continued his job search.

The only thing to do was return to each business in hopes something had changed.

He let his experience be known while hoping to make it clear he was not only available, but anxious and ready for *any* work.

❋ ❋

Mike finished his bath, putting on pajamas Blancha had sewn for him. She'd made two pair, one blue, and the other pale yellow. He liked the softness of the flannel, and didn't have to wear socks since they had *footies* sewn in.

He came into the living room and climbed onto Aleksander's lap, where he felt the world was good, right, and safe.

Tonight though, he was nervous.

Tonight, he would present his questions.

"Papa... I love you."

"Mikhail, you are the most important thing in the world to me—Blancha, too."

"You know I'm six now... I know things I didn't know last year."

Aleksander smiled, replying, "Of course. You are very smart."

"I need to know something else, though— something all the kids in my school know, except me."

Aleksander was puzzled and somewhat worried about the subject, especially since there was much about America he did not yet understand. By Mikhail's expression and seriousness of his tone, he could see it was important.

82

"What is this you need to know? If I can help, you know I will."

"Papa." A brief silence... he wasn't sure how to proceed.

Papa."

"What *is* it?"

He blurted out, "I know I have a Mama like everybody else. I want to know.... I *need* to know who she is... and *where*!"

He could feel Papa trembling. He'd never seen such an expression, pale, and quiet.

"Is it a bad question?"

Aleksander sat motionless.

Mikhail laid his head on his father's shoulder, tears beginning to fall. He didn't understand what was wrong, why this question was causing the expression on Papa's face. He felt a tear drop onto his face from Papa's eyes, and raised his head.

Blancha came into the room, intending to ask Aleksander if he wanted another cup of coffee before she retired for the night.

The scene before her was startling—when Aleksander looked up, she knew.

"Aleksander, shall I take Mikhail to bed and talk with him?"

"No, I will talk to him... about his mother," he said quietly.

Blancha left to go to her room, softly closing the door.

Aleksander had to gain control of his emotions, at least enough to speak.

His son owned his heart... but his mind wanted to drift back—he let it drift, to picture her again in his mind, feeling the loss again.

He could almost feel her touch, hear her voice… Vera was here with them as he began.

"Of course you have a mother, the sweetest any child could have. But she no longer lives in this world… our world. She is in heaven."

He paused. He'd thought to first make it clear to Mikhail he would never be able to meet her face to face.

"Before you were born, I fell in love with the loveliest, kindest, woman I'd ever known. Her name was Vera. She loved me, too, and agreed to marry me. She was to be your mother.

"Understand, she had to leave this world before she, or anyone, wanted."

He could see amazement in his boy's eyes.

"She was beautiful, her hair light brown, nearly blond, long and wavy. Her eyes were blue, like yours, and they sparkled with her smile. She was a cheerful person, laughter a part of her. She brought joy to my life as if I had never known what joy meant." Aleksander smiled, remembering.

"Like the song, *Joy to the World*?"

"Yes, when you are so happy… all over and deep inside."

Mikhail smiled.

"We were very happy together, and even more so when we found we were to have a child—you.

"The day of your birth was wonderful. We loved you more than anything on earth.

"We thought we must be the happiest people in all of Russia. You added to our joy."

He hugged Mikhail close.

"When you were just a few weeks old, though, something happened inside her heart, taking her to heaven. These things we cannot understand."

"Papa..."

"Mikhail, I'm sorry I have not talked to you about her. I loved her so much, as much as I love you. All these years I thought if I spoke aloud of her, my heart would shatter, and I would no longer be able to go on. And I wanted to go on. For *you.*

"I think about her often, and I should have shared her memory with you. I have only a few pictures of her, but I will get them out tomorrow.

"She died happy, son. I *know* because she was holding you safely in her arms, feeding and loving you."

They sat for over an hour, father holding son, their tears intermingling as they talked.

"It has been an important day for you, and we are both tired. You go to bed now and have sweet dreams, perhaps about the mama you now know something about. You will think of many questions, tomorrow or later, and I want you to ask... anything. I will try never again to keep anything hidden from you. Perhaps I love you enough for both a papa *and* mama."

Life does indeed continue, the earth revolving as if nothing has been altered.

Nothing *had* actually changed in Mike's world, but he felt different.

Mike missed the mother he hadn't known, but somehow felt better, more complete.

He'd felt loved all his life. Now he knew of another who had loved him.

Each day, he felt more comfortable asking questions. He had a small picture of Vera in a frame by his bed, bringing her to his mind more clearly.

He asked again and again to hear the story of Aleksander seeing her in the café that evening. He wanted to hear about the proposal, when they married, of their discussions of him before he was born, and the day of his birth.

Blancha was included in many conversations. She delighted in hearing their love story, and of their lives in Russia.

Unexpectedly, Aleksander felt almost restored since talking about Vera and their love —the love that brought their son into the world. His memories could again bring joy to him as they did for Mikhail. At last he was ready to make her a part of his past—his love not diminished, but he would grieve no longer.

❆ ❆

Finally, Alex, as he'd become known, had a job. Temporary at the road construction company, but work... a salary. Bob J had mentioned him to a supervisor when he heard they needed an extra man to build and paint signs.

He would pick up small supplies down the mountain as well, and have use of an old construction truck.

The road was more than half completed, but he was thankful to be employed, even temporarily.

Mike was introduced to his first *Valentine's Day* in school, and he declared it, "almost as much fun as Christmas."

They made cards the day before, each decorating a small box for the Valentines they would collect. His box was red, white, and blue.

"It's like the American flag, Miss Parker."

He carefully printed "Mikhail" on one side, and "Mike" on the other.

Culminating the day, cupcakes and punch were served by the *homeroom* mothers.

To Mike, life was just about perfect.

February, however, was yet to bring unspeakable alterations in their lives, as well as touching many others.

Though no one knew the far-reaching effects, the sequence had begun.

~ 10 ~

As soon as Mike opened the door, he sensed something wrong. It was the last Wednesday afternoon in February. He'd seen the construction truck, so knew Alex was home. The house was quiet and dark No smells of supper wafted from the kitchen. He closed the door quietly… it seemed appropriate.

Papa was sitting on the davenport. Waiting for him.

"Mikhail."

"Yes sir?"

A pause.

"Come sit beside me."

As Mikhail climbed onto the davenport, Aleksander put his arm around his son to pull him close.

"Today is a sad day, Mikhail. Your Aunt Blancha died this morning. She has gone to be with the angels."

"Noooo!"

"She is gone from us, son. She didn't come in for coffee before I was to leave for work, so I went to check on her. I believe she died during a peaceful sleep."

Mikhail began to cry in earnest. "She was finally *all* wore out, Papa."

Blancha had been only fifty-three, yet she'd seemed older. When he found her, he didn't know what he should do.

He hurried to a neighbor's house to phone Dr. Moore, who came immediately.

"I will make the arrangements, Alex, and sign the death certificate. She's at peace now, and in no more pain."

"Dr. Moore, I knew she had little stamina, but she never mentioned pain. Do you *know* what caused her death?"

"She had cancer. She'd known for some time. We know so little, but there are things she could have tried. She chose not to pursue them, so I prescribed pain medicine. Truthfully, I doubt treatments would have helped.

"She asked me to respect her privacy, but… Alex, you should know that she talked with me when she received your request to send Mike to her. The type of cancer she had was slow-growing. She was using pain medicine only occasionally, so I was in agreement that she could accept and be able to care for him."

The doctor placed a hand on Alex's shoulder, appearing regretful. "We… *I*… honestly thought she had more time. Perhaps, however, she felt she could go in peace now. *You* were *here*, Alex, the dream of seeing her brother had come true. Mike was a welcome bonus, but now he would be all right. I am truly sorry. She was a good woman."

Alex nodded sadly. "Thank you, doctor. She never indicated *any*thing," He broke down, sobbing for the loss of the sister he'd had such a short time.

Blancha had been heard to say that good things came in large doses. It now seemed as if bad things were to come in larger doses.

The minister, Brother Marshall, generously took care of most of the arrangements for the memorial service at the church on Saturday morning.

Blancha's friends and neighbors prepared lunch, and served it at the church building after the service. In addition, they brought liberal amounts of food to the house.

They had all been so kind and Alex was grateful. By afternoon, though, he was thankful for time to sit quietly with his son.

Knock, Knock—Knock, Knock!

The sound seemed amplified in the quiet aftermath of bidding a last good-bye to Blancha. The caller was making his impatience clear, obviously with no thought of being an unwelcome intrusion.

Wearily, Alex rose from the davenport, leaving Mike, and opened the door to a stern-looking man, who wore a dark suit and an unsympathetic expression.

"Good afternoon, I am Mr. Abe Snider."

Hearing that voice, Mike's head whirled around. *The man without a heart!* He rushed to stand beside Alex, looking Mr. Snider over. Still, he saw nothing different—he'd forgotten to ask Anna about it.

"Mr. Nordin, I have received information that Blancha Aldredge has died. Is my information correct?"

"Yes, sir. Please come in. My sister's memorial service was only this morning."

Alex had a bad feeling in the pit of his stomach.

90

This was not a friendly visit—perhaps he was a lawyer. Maybe it was to be good news, something about Blancha's business she hadn't revealed.

Mike recognized the nod from Alex to leave the room.

"Were you aware Mrs. Aldredge only rented this house?"

With a sigh of relief, Alex realized the man was only concerned about the rent payment. "Yes, my intention is to remain here with my son. Do you need a signature for a new agreement?" he asked, hoping the amount was not to be raised.

"No." Mr. Snider raised his voice slightly, answering bluntly, "I believe in talking plain, so as to be understood. Since you come from Russia, I'll put it *real* plain."

This morning, Alex had thought this to be one of the worst days of his life. His love of Blancha and their relationship had grown into a deep understanding and closeness. Since her giving Mikhail a home and his own arrival in America, he'd developed a heartfelt appreciation for her sweet, kind spirit. Her death had hurt deeply.

Evidently, Mr. Snider was to make it worse.

"Mr. Nordin, Mrs. Aldredge lived here with her husband, then continued to do so after his death. The house was owned by my late grandfather. He felt sorry for her and signed an agreement allowing her to live here for her lifetime, paying only a pittance for the privilege."

Mr. Snider seemed to be growing irate. "Though there were ways to break this agreement, my father honored it, as have I, out of respect for my father and grandfather.

"*However*, her life has ended and *so* has any agreement. By law, I must give you three days to clear out. This being Saturday, I'll give you until Wednesday noon, *most* generous anyone would agree. I have nothing more to discuss."

The man turned quickly, walking out of the house and closing the door behind him. He'd made it *plain* all right—no discussion.

The small house surely wasn't worth a great deal, but Mr. Snider was angry. The agreement, which obviously *had* been binding, was something about which he could do nothing. Until now.

Blancha's death clearly closed a chapter for him. But what was *he* to do—in only *days*?

Outside, as Abe Snider got into his car, he began to smile.

Finally. A long-awaited step to my next goal, completed, with none the wiser.

❋ ❋

And we know that in all things God works
for the good of those who love him…
Romans 8:28

Anna, along with her family and others with whom they worshipped, believed the scripture with all their hearts.

There would come a time, however, when they would admit to astonishment at the ragged path life sometimes takes leading to this.

❋ ❋

Though Alex recognized the depth of Mike's grief to be as great as his own, there was no choice but to tell him the purpose of Mr. Snider's visit.

He called him from his room, and they sat together as he told him as much as he felt he could understand.

"Where will we live?"

"I'm not sure. I wanted to let you know so you could begin to get your clothes and other things together. Don't worry. It will be all right."

Mike looked at him solemnly, tears beginning afresh.

"It *won't* be all right! Not without Aunt Blancha. When I had her, I just wanted you to be here. I asked God every night. Now you're here… but *she's* gone."

He cried out, "Aunt Blancha took good care of me, and everything she told me was right. I *prayed* it wrong!"

"Mike, no… oh, no," Alex pulled him onto his lap. "God doesn't do things that way. You knew Blancha was older and not well. She was much sicker than we realized, and was getting weaker all the time.

"She loved you so much—I believe she asked God to let her stay on this earth long enough to take care of you until I arrived.

"We'll both miss her forever, and we'll remember the way she cared for and loved us. Mikhail… she knew we loved *her*, too."

Mike was apparently sorting things out in his own way.

"Papa, do you remember I told you about the bicycle surprise?"

"Yes, that was special."

"I knew she didn't have much money and she said we wouldn't have many different foods to eat for a while. But, you know what?"

"What?"

"Aunt Blancha didn't smile a lot. When she told me the bike was mine, she smiled big... and her *eyes* were laughing. Do you think she was happier not to live alone before she went to heaven?"

This boy—he has Vera's great capacity for love and understanding.

"Yes, I do. You made Blancha very happy. She *told* me she had prayed to see us before she died—Dr. Moore reminded me of that.

"Her prayer was answered, Mikhail, and she would want you to always remember your good times with her."

Mike's tears stopped temporarily, as they prepared for bed.

"Papa?"

"Yes?"

"That man came here one time before you got here."

Alex was curious. "Do you know why?"

"No, and I didn't remember his name. He was here when I got home from school that day. I got excited for a minute thinking it was you...

But it was *him,* that man... he was in the chair, but he got up to leave when I came in. He wasn't friendly—he didn't even say hi when Aunt Blancha *introducted* us."

"Did Blancha tell you anything about why he'd visited?"

"No… she just said he was a man with no heart—I never did find out how you can*not* have a heart."

"Not having a heart is an expression, Mike. I think it means you are not a very kind or caring person."

My sister was right about Mr. Snider… which reminds me… she mentioned something about our needing 'serious talk.' About the house? Her health?

In any case, I'll never know. I doubt it would have made a difference anyway.

❈ ❈

In his morning prayer, Alex thanked God for his job and ample food in the house. The people of this town, most from the church Blancha loved, had supplied them with more than enough food for the remaining days in the house. He thanked God most of all for Mike, and asked blessings for this boy who had endured too many changes in his short life.

He had only a few days until… moving from this house. Past that, he didn't know. He asked for help from above.

He glanced around the kitchen. *Where do I begin?*

Mike came in with his sweet, mussed, still-sleepy appearance. "What's for breakfast?"

"Cereal today, buddy. After we eat, we need to begin sorting, and get ready to pack."

"But it's Sunday, we need to go to church. Can't we go?"

They had been in the habit of attending church if Blancha was up to it. But he was simply not in the mood today. There was so much to do.

"*Please,* Papa. It's nearly too late for Sunday school, but we have time to get to church. I know God wants us there."

God wants *us there… today?*

A realization washed over him. *I have just asked God to bless us. And he has. I've asked for help, and I'm struggling. Yet, a six-year-old had to remind me it's a day of worship.*

Humbled, he answered, "All right. Let's eat and get dressed. We do have a lot to get done this afternoon, though."

Joy returned to his boy's face.

Monday morning as Alex drove to work, he pondered the amount he might earn before the road construction was completed. He couldn't afford to miss any work. He would pack at night if necessary.

Alex greeted the men as he walked into the area where most gathered before beginning their individual jobs. "'Morning, Bob J, 'morning, Mr. Blackstone."

Mr. Blackstone, the construction superintendent, generally gave Bob J the biggest portion of assignments for everyone, including what might be needed from Alex.

Not a big man, but stocky, the superintendent had thick black hair and ruddy skin. He had an authoritative way about him, without being overbearing.

He wore work boots and khaki pants and shirt like many of the construction workers, but his were starched and generally spotless. Alex knew, however, that he had no problem getting onto a piece of equipment or down into the red clay with the men, if needed—the reason he had the respect of everyone who worked for him.

Today he motioned to Alex that he wanted a word with him.

"Alex, I was sorry to hear of the death of your sister. I understand you have a young son. Is there anything we could help with?"

We need a place to live!

"No sir. The flowers were appreciated—nice for the gravesite."

"We're nearing completion of the job here, actually ahead of schedule. Only a few areas need finish-work before the final inspection. I expect to be moving out of here in a couple of weeks, three tops."

Three weeks until there would be no work, possibly sooner.

"Yes sir. I've been grateful for the work, but I'll be trying to find work elsewhere."

"When I heard of your sister's death, I heard other things… like your needing a place to live. Is that right?"

"Yes, sir. The lease on the house is up and the owner wants us out… soon."

He looked at the ground, embarrassed Mr. Blackstone knew he couldn't even provide a home for his child.

"Times are hard, Alex. And I can't help a great deal. But I need a night watchman to keep an eye out while this heavy equipment is still here. Johnny Reese was doing it. He drove one of the smaller tractors, but since he has no family, he was just as happy to stay in that little work trailer at night and keep watch.

"I've sent Johnny on up to a job in Illinois to help my brother with another project. If you want the night watchman job for the remaining weeks, it's yours. You could continue to use the truck."

A warm place to sleep… no… there's Mike… couldn't work… a few more hours pay though…

Mr. Blackstone paused, observing him.

"I'm not suggesting this as a real solution to your problems. Just that I do need someone and if you could manage it, I thought it might work temporarily. For you and the boy. It's very small, one room, a fold-out bed, little cooktop and a small sink, but it's heated. No bathroom, you'd have to use the portable thing over by the equipment.

"But you'd be paid for the watchman's job, plus whatever we need you for during the day."

A place to go, a temporary solution.

"Mr. Blackstone, I'd be happy to do it. And it *is* a solution for now. My boy Mikha… Mike, won't give any trouble. He can ride his bicycle from here to school every day. Thank you."

The superintendent nodded. "Good. Start tomorrow night?"

"Yes, sir. Thank you."

A couple of weeks, maybe three… a paycheck and a warm bed. I must find another job, and a place to live by then.

Back at the house, it saddened him to realize how little Blancha had accumulated in a lifetime. In the living room, the only thing truthfully good enough to keep was an easy chair—maybe he could get it into the watchman's trailer. The sofa—Blancha had called it the davenport, which he'd learned was the manufacturer's name. It was uncomfortable as seating, worse for sleeping.

Her room consisted of an older bed, dresser, chair and a chest of drawers. The kitchen table and chairs was decent.

There was also Mike's small bed. But there was no choice. He had to leave it all.

That left Blancha's clothes, dishes, bathroom towels, and bits of things she'd kept.

"Knock, knock."

Walking to the door, Alex could hear humming. He knew it was the minister, Earl Marshall. He was known for his good nature and humming.

Opening the door, which no longer creaked, a gust of March wind pushed its way through. "Come in out of the wind... uh... Mr. Marshall."

Alex had not grown accustomed to the fact that the minister was not referred to by a title. He'd heard someone call him Reverend Marshall, and he'd quickly, but cheerfully, corrected them.

"None but God is reverenced here. I'm Earl Marshall, plain and simple, trying to teach about him."

This minister didn't fit the images he had of clergy. Nothing about his attire set him apart, though he was always dressed impeccably in a suit, starched white shirt, and tie.

Today, however, he was dressed more casually.

Earl Marshall was probably close to his age, maybe a couple of years older, not as tall, medium build towards the stout side, with light hair, which showed signs of thinning.

Alex knew little about him other than his being single, well-liked, and that he taught lessons of love from his pulpit.

He had a look… something difficult to define, though. There was a spark, perhaps simple sincerity, but he seemed to genuinely like everyone.

Entering the living room smiling, he said, "If you *must* title me, Alex, Brother Marshall will do, but I'd really prefer Earl."

"Earl, then. You've probably heard we have to vacate the house. I have a temporary place for a few weeks—and am in the process of deciding what to keep, though it can't be much."

"I was sorry to hear it, and dropped in to see how I could help—packing, cleaning, or disposing of things. Honestly, the *most* helpful thing might be that I have space in my garage you could use for storage, even furniture. My car barely takes half the garage so there's plenty of extra space."

He continued eagerly, "One of our church members has a large truck I could borrow."

Taken aback at this sincere, specific offer of help, Alex glanced around.

This isn't like the empty offers I've heard, in Russia, as well as here.

People say, "If there's anything I can do, let me know," as they walk quickly by or end a conversation.

I heard the idle offers when my parents died, after Vera's death, when I was in need of work in Russia and, more recently, when Blancha died—no, many did help in this instance.

But Earl's was no idle offer. He was explicit and seems in no hurry to leave. He's not just dressed casually, he's in work clothes.

Alex felt an unexpected wash of emotion.

"Thank you," Alex replied, hesitantly. "It *would* be a big help to have storage space."

"Good. I'll bring the truck tomorrow. Where can I begin now?"

"Well, I have no idea what to do with Blancha's clothes. I imagine they've seen a lot of wear, but certainly useful to someone."

"Great. I can load them in my car and take them to the church building. The ladies will be glad to sort and distribute them. Do you want to go through them first?"

"No. That will be of great help... Earl. Thank you."

"Fine. I'll get busy."

In an hour, Earl had cleared the bedroom closet and drawers. He had the clothing folded in stacks and began carrying them out to his car.

"I found a few smaller items you might want to look through. I put them in a blue box in which she had a few other things—it's not very big... rather ornate."

"Thank you again."

Earl was quiet for a moment, considering his thoughts.

Finally, he replied simply, "You're welcome. I'll go now with the load of clothing—it's probably time for Mike's return, and you need your time with him. I'll stop back by tomorrow."

"I appreciate your help. If nothing changes I may be here earlier tomorrow afternoon. There's less work at the site every day."

"There was something I'd meant to ask, Alex. I visited Blancha a few years back and seem to recall her mentioning her husband having a relative in town. She didn't say who it was, and never mentioned it again. There was no one at the memorial service whose family backgrounds I didn't know. Do you know who it might be?"

Genuinely surprised, Alex answered, "No. I'm sure you knew she'd married and left for America before I was born. She corresponded regularly and our parents mentioned her fairly often, but I remember nothing about a relative here. She never mentioned anyone after I arrived."

"Maybe whoever it was died or moved away long ago. It had just occurred to me. Well... I'll see you tomorrow."

Earl left, carrying a load of clothing to his car.

The unexpected presence of another person had somehow eased the situation.

But Mike would be home at any moment. The sight of his boy always filled his heart with love, though today he had a sense of dread. He wasn't the father Mike deserved, and was ashamed he could provide almost nothing for him.

As Mike bicycled home, he began to peddle faster, the wind so strong it seemed to help push him along.

What will Papa say about where we'll live?

He wanted everything to have been solved miraculously. Yet, at six, he'd already learned life didn't usually turn out like the fairy tales.

Though no one paid any attention to the small boy on an old bike, he was embarrassed as tears began to roll down his face once again.

As the cold air hit his face, cooling his tears, he scolded himself aloud, "Don't be a baby. Only *babies* cry!"

He'd tried to catch a glimpse of James during lunch or recess to talk with him about his aunt, and the question of where they would live. But he never saw him—hadn't seen him since the memorial service. He'd made other friends, but none he felt as close to as James.

When he rode into the yard, though wanting to hurry, he carefully parked his bike and put the kick stand down. The company truck was parked by the curb—Papa was home. He ran up the steps envisioning Papa standing at the door with arms outstretched and a big smile— assuring him there was good news.

He opened the door quickly. The house was quiet. As he came inside, Alex walked from the kitchen. No smile. No outstretched arms.

He walked slowly to the sofa, sat, and looked up at him with what Mike thought of as a sad smile, finally holding his arms out to him.

Mike hurried to the security of his papa's lap before noticing boxes in the kitchen, and the empty feel of the house.

"Mikhail…"

No miracle... and Papa has been calling me Mike—he changes back to my Russian name when he's real serious or upset.

Alex explained the situation with the construction trailer as best he could.

He wanted to be honest, but desperately tried to find words of comfort. No such words came.

"I love you—that will never change. Now... you need to finish getting everything together tonight. This will be our last night in the house. Tomorrow you will go to school and I will go to work for a few hours. You need to ride straight home tomorrow, as you did today."

Mike hugged Alex tightly.

"I love you more than anything, Papa."

As Mike walked to his room, he suddenly turned around. "Know what?"

"What?"

"James would be excited about living in a trailer. I like their tent, but James thought they were going to get a house... his daddy decided since they would have to move too soon... they wouldn't change where they lived. Anyway, he thinks the kids living in the trailer park are lucky—just wait till I tell him!"

Vera's boy. Remarkable.

As expected, Alex was only needed at the construction site for three hours. He did need the time at the house, but was thankful the night watchman's pay would begin tonight, for as long as it lasted.

Driving the company truck back to the house, his thoughts were on the best way to finish packing and moving out of the house.

They wouldn't be sleeping in the house tonight, but he'd have the rest of the day and until noon tomorrow to finish. He would clean after everything was out.

The seemingly cruel circumstance under which he was moving made no difference in doing what he thought was right.

He'd been inside about an hour when he heard the knock at the door. Earl. The name came more easily to mind.

Feeling comfortable as he opened the door to his new-found friend, he observed the large, borrowed truck he'd driven, the back loaded with empty boxes. They could most likely get everything in one load.

"'Morning, Alex. It's a beautiful day."

Alex returned the welcome smile, motioning him into the house.

Beautiful day? Not really—I'm still essentially homeless. But suddenly my load feels lighter.

~ 12 ~

"**W**e eat first, then work, Alex. We're going to the *Seasons Moon Café* for lunch, home-fried chicken, my treat," Earl announced. "I'm sure you've about finished the casseroles."

Lowering his voice and grinning, he commented, "At the very least, you've tired of them. We'll have plenty of time to pack up when we return."

The café was close by, as most everything.

It wasn't quite noon, ahead of the lunch rush. The red-checkered tablecloths, music playing from the jukebox, and everyone speaking, created a pleasant atmosphere. The waitress was at their table almost before they'd settled into the chairs.

"Hi Teresa, I'd like you to meet Alex Nordin. Alex, this is Teresa Jackson. She knows everyone in town and what most of us like to eat."

"Nice to meet you, Alex. Your usual today, Earl?"

"Yes." Turning to Alex, he commented, "Everything is good here, but today's special is fried chicken, mashed potatoes, fresh green beans, and homemade biscuits—my favorite, but order what sounds good to you."

"How could I go wrong? I've realized fried foods are popular here."

"All over the South, honey," replied Teresa.

"You might find fried chicken up North, but not like here. I guarantee it.

"Okay, fried chicken with all the *fixins* coming right up. And keep today's dessert special in mind, apple cobbler."

Shortly, Teresa brought the amply-filled plates of chicken and vegetables to the table, with a basket of hot biscuits, and two glasses of sweet tea.

Sweet tea was another thing everyone here not only liked, but seemed to expect. After the memorial service, several gallons of sweet tea had been brought to the house in nice pitchers along with the food.

Another thing to take care of—returning the pitchers and dishes to the church kitchen.

"If you can't manage it all, Alex, they'll put the leftovers in a doggie bag for you."

"Doggie bag?"

Laughing, Earl answered, "I guess it started when people actually did take bones and scraps home for their dogs. More likely nowadays, the dog never sees it."

Plenty for Mike's supper.

Conversation stopped for a few minutes as they began enjoying the meal. The café was almost full now, the noise level having risen significantly with conversations, laughter, the clanking of silverware and dishes, and the volume on the juke box turned up.

"Everything is *so* good."

"I *concur*. And, don't bother cutting the chicken. Just pick it up and go at it.

"I was told that in 'proper society,' which we aren't, but it's always acceptable to pick up anything having a bone," laughed Earl.

After a while Teresa stopped to fill their tea glasses and inquired, "What about the apple cobbler—ya'll gonna have some?"

"Yes, for both. I'd like coffee as well. Alex?"

Shyly, Alex answered, "Could I have milk with dessert?"

"Sweet milk coming right up."

Alex looked puzzled. "No... just regular milk, I think."

Teresa burst out with a loud laugh. "Honey, we got sweet milk or buttermilk. Don't know about another kind."

Earl interjected, "Teresa, I'm sure he wants sweet milk. And you can bring a couple of those containers, so we can take supper home, too."

Earl observed one of Alex's rare smiles. And he hadn't protested about adding dessert either. *Thank God, he's beginning to relax.*

"Don't be embarrassed by Teresa's laughter; it's her way. I guess the term sweet milk is another Southern thing."

"Well," Alex confessed, "I thought sweet milk was like tea—they would add sugar."

Earl couldn't resist laughing, but was pleased to see Alex taking it good-naturedly.

"Let's not explain *that* to Teresa."

Alex agreed.

"You probably know my mind is full of all I need to accomplish. But you have no idea what a help you've been."

Earl responded, more seriously, "It's good to feel needed, Alex. And you, my friend, filled a need of mine."

As if to quickly change the mood, he added with a laugh, "Hmmm, that sounded deep, didn't it?"

As they were leaving, someone called out, "Earl, hi! Where you off to?"

They turned to see Anna. Though Alex hadn't been introduced, Mike had pointed her out to him from a distance, and he'd seen her across the sanctuary at church. Mike had spoken of how beautiful she was.

He thought Anna pretty, but he wouldn't have described her as a beauty. He'd also assumed she was nineteen or twenty since she was a college student. On closer observation, he'd guess her to be at least twenty-four or five.

She was slender and petite, maybe five-six. She wore a pink turtleneck sweater with a slim-fitting black skirt. Her hair was thick and dark. Though pulled back in a ponytail held by a bright pink barrette, soft wisps escaped around her face. Her brown eyes seemed lit from within, hard to describe, but full of joy.

Earl gave her a hug. "Hi, sweetheart. We've just finished a plate of fried chicken, topped off with cobbler. Have you met Alex Nordin?"

Earl called her sweetheart. Seems another mark of the South, all the affectionate names. Even the waitress called me honey. I haven't adjusted to that.

Holding out her hand, she replied. "Not officially. But I'm happy to finally meet you, Alex. I know a lot more about you than you'd guess. Mike and I are good friends. I was so glad to see you with him Christmas Eve. I thought I'd seen him happy, but it was nothing compared to his look of *elation* that night."

Anna was one of the few people he'd known who looked at you directly. He was acutely aware of her brown eyes at that moment, as she gave him her full attention. Her smile seemed to fill her with a delight she expected to be reciprocated. *Now...* he could see the beauty Mike had described.

"Very nice to finally meet you," replied Alex. "Mike thinks so much of you. I've wanted to thank you for giving him your time and friendship when he needed it most."

She replied genuinely, "My complete pleasure. You two seemed in a hurry, though, and I need to get back to my group. I'll see you later."

Unexpectedly she gave him a brief hug, then turned back to Earl and hugged him tightly and kissed him on the cheek. Alex was simply not accustomed to this open showing of affection... but e*ven with your minister?*

Earl and Alex arrived back at the house, having discussed where they'd begin packing. Earl reassured Alex there was half a garage sitting empty at his house.

He could store anything he might like to keep. It was more of a relief to Alex than he had realized.

By the time Mike came in from school, the house was nearly cleared, and he was ready to go to the trailer with a small load in the company truck.

"I've stored a lot in *Brother* Marshall's garage, so we will have it for later." He had consented to call the minister by his first name, but it was not appropriate for a young boy.

"Good," Mike said, agreeably. "I didn't want to say, but I did have things in my bag I was kinda thinking I might not get to keep. Thanks, Brother Marshall.

"And, Papa, I got to see James during recess today and told him about our adventure of living in the *constructor's* trailer. He thinks it's great—I knew he would."

Frowning, Mike added, "Know what's funny?"

"What?" Earl and Alex asked almost in unison.

"Brother Marshall and Anna have the same last name."

"Nothing funny, Mike," answered Earl. "She's my sister."

Mike began to laugh happily. "I *love* Anna."

Alex was too taken aback to say a word. He sat down on the davenport and simply looked at them.

"You didn't know she was my sister, Alex?" Realizing the fact was obvious, he said, "I apologize. I assumed you both knew."

At least the long, tight hug, term of endearment, and kiss made a bit more sense.

❋ ❋

Mike showed no hesitation or surprise upon entering the one-room trailer, his home. He could stand inside the door and see it in its entirety.

"This *construction* company trailer is to be our home now, or for a few weeks."

"During the day the small mattress will be standing on one end there by the table. At night we'll let the built-in bed down from the wall, put the mattress in the floor space and one of us will sleep on each, however works best.

"Now let's see where we can figure to put our clothes. I didn't bring many. Your other things are stored in Earl's garage. We'll eat and read a while before trying out our sleeping arrangement. Oh, I have fried chicken for you—you're in for a treat."

They adjusted quickly. There wasn't much for Alex to do during the night. The bright street light near the trailer provided a measure of security. He set an alarm to wake him periodically, and used a spotlight to look more closely over the equipment stored nightly nearby. He was thankful Mike slept soundly.

Though Mr. Blackstone had mentioned his use of the truck to transport Mike being fine, Mike wanted to ride his bike. He would leave earlier in order to get to school on time.

The distance was well over a mile, but he was accustomed to riding as far around town. He knew people along the way and the area was safe.

"Mike, you know the way to the school and I trust you to go straight there and straight back in the afternoon.

I can easily take you and pick you up in the afternoon, so let me know if you are uncomfortable doing this." Mike shook his head.

"If the weather is bad, I'll take you or pick you up. Understand?"

"Yes, sir, but I like riding far," he grinned. "If I ask in the morning to go by the RX, or take extra time for something, can I?"

"Yes."

"Can I go to the RX *tomorrow*, to see Anna? I gotta tell her about knowing she's Brother Marshall's sister, and I haven't talked to her in a long time... please?"

"Yes, not long, though."

For Mike, all was well again.

There was less work at the site every day, so Alex spent his time searching for another job. With Blancha gone, there was nothing to keep them here. No doubt there would be more work available in a larger town. Still, he felt comfortable in Mt. Seasons.

And he knew Mike was content at school, and the area. But he couldn't delay long.

Mr. Blackstone had made it clear that when the inspectors accepted the completed road, papers would be finalized the next day.

Everyone and all equipment would be gone by the end of the day—could happen in less than two weeks.

On Friday of their first week in the trailer, a steady drizzle began just after lunch and looked as if it would remain for the day.

Alex waited at the school building that afternoon, parking near the bike rack so Mike was sure to see him.

Earl pulled up next to him and waved. He rolled the truck window down, asking, "Is student transportation *another* duty of yours?"

"I was actually looking for *you* and thought you might be here due to the rain. Wanted to see whether you two would join me for hamburgers at my house tonight. There will be a few others there, but you'll know most of them. Anna is coming, and promised a chocolate cake."

"I haven't had any better offers all week—didn't know you cooked."

"This is my one menu. Come whenever you can. Most will be there by six."

Suddenly feeling inadequate, always being on the receiving end of this friendship, Alex added, "Only if you'll let me pick something up to contribute to the feast."

"Here's the truth, Alex. I'd like to show you a cabinet on one end of my kitchen that's in bad shape.

"I'm hoping you'll look at it—to let me know whether you could repair it. I remember one you termed a repair in Blancha's kitchen and it looked like a new custom-cabinet.

"Anyway, if you could do it, I'd certainly be coming out on the good end—and if you say, no, you still have one of my great hamburgers."

"You're sure?" asked Alex, doubtfully.

"Wait till you see it. I can buy the wood, but wouldn't know where to begin doing the work."

All right, we'll be there before six. Mike will be especially excited to see Anna."

He didn't add that he might be looking forward to it himself.

The sky cleared within a few hours, and they arrived at Earl's house well before six.

Pulling up to Earl's, he admired the lovely old white frame home with its extensive porch, complete with a comfortable swing.

Earl opened the door to usher them inside. "Welcome."

"What a beautiful house," Alex replied, appreciatively.

"Thanks. Does need work—you'll see when I show you the cabinet."

Earl had not exaggerated. Though the inside of the cabinet wasn't bad, the door was badly damaged from age and use. It was actually a pantry door, narrow, and about five feet high.

Earl gave Mike a hug. "The other children are in the back yard on the swings."

Mike was out the door almost before he finished his sentence.

"Well, Mike is taken care of for a while. They're good kids. Their parents are Stan and Alice Abrams, from next door."

"I think I met them at church," Alex answered, turning back to the cabinet door.

"I can't see repairing the door, Earl—wouldn't be worth it. I can make a new door, much like the one I did at Blancha's, and use stain to blend with the rest of the kitchen, or even paint it. It being at the end makes it easier.

With limited tools, I can't do the finish work I'd like, but it will be a huge improvement."

"I knew you could do it. Let me know when you can go with me to get the wood, then work on it when you have time."

"Do you own the house, or does it belong to the church? That might determine the amount to put into wood."

"It's actually owned by my other sister, Mary. It's an old, but solid house, and Oak Grove Street is a good neighborhood. I think she bought it more or less as an investment, though she did mention she might someday return here to live. The owners died and their children offered it at a great price.

"Mary hasn't lived in it; she works in Chicago. She was considering doing some work to rent it when I accepted the position at the church here. The arrangement worked out well for us both.

"She won't accept much rent, so I try to make a few improvements here and there. I recently painted the outside."

Laughingly, he added, "That was the long answer—short answer, I'll pay for the best option."

"I'm still trying to process the fact of your having another sister. Seems I don't know much about you at all."

"We'll have to work on that."

Theirs had quickly become an easy, relaxed relationship. Alex was thankful to have this man, a friend, in his life, filling a long-time void.

People began coming in, including Anna with the promised cake.

Alex had never seen so much hugging and laughter, all seeming to talk at the same time. Alex felt the shyness and feeling of inadequacy creeping in again. These people had known each other all their lives. He was more than an outsider—he was a foreigner. Though he'd never been around people more friendly and helpful, he still felt inferior.

As Earl walked out the back door, promising hamburgers soon to come, Anna crossed the room, and gave him a quick hug.

As before, her smile could almost be *felt*. Tonight her dark hair hung below her shoulders. She wore a bright pink dress, almost the same pink as the barrette in her hair the day they met.

"Hello, Anna. Mike is out back. He was excited you'd be here."

"I'll be happy to see him, too. But truthfully, I was hoping for more time with his father."

The evening was the best Alex could remember in a long time. He began to relax, as everyone included him and Mike as if they had been there for years. Anna stayed by his side all evening. Glancing toward her several times, he felt he'd caught her observing *him*.

She'd talked with Mike for a while, but surprisingly, Mike had turned his attention to the other children.

He and Anna talked briefly about Mike.

"I know your circumstances, Alex. I want to know more about what *you* enjoy, the work you like, and what you *want*."

The hamburgers, and all the extras, were good, topped off with Anna's chocolate cake. She took little credit. "It's Mother's recipe. I've only recently begun to do it justice."

Alex thought about the evening as he drove back to the trailer. It was so good to laugh again. He felt he had talked too much about himself. But, every time he'd tried to turn the conversation around, Anna had asked another question. He smiled, imagining Anna sitting close to him, her beauty unveiled in her smile and eyes. Next time, he determined to find out more about *her*.

Next time? Why would I think there would be a next time? I am a foreigner, a man with a child, no home, and a part-time job which is about to end. And I have no prospects.

Those thoughts quickly erased his smile. He glanced over at Mike, who had fallen asleep almost immediately.

But, a nice evening. Nothing will change the pleasant memory.

~ 13 ~

Mike rode his bike to school Monday morning. Alex checked in with Bob J to see whether there was any work for him. Nothing needed today.

He decided to go by Earl's to see whether he had time to purchase wood for the cabinet. It wasn't yet eight o'clock so he thought to catch him before he left for the church office, or to make visits.

He'd learned Earl made numerous visits to the hospital in the nearby town. Though Mt. Seasons had a clinic with two doctors on staff, and a couple of beds used for overnight, the town wasn't large enough to support a hospital.

Earl also visited home-bound members. Without a phone, it might be difficult to catch up with him.

As soon as he'd knocked on the door, he heard movement inside.

"Good morning, Alex, up and out early, aren't you?" asked Earl as he opened the door. He was still in his pajama pants, bare feet, and a coffee cup in hand.

Feeling welcome and comfortable as he stepped inside, Alex laughed

"Well, you know my schedule isn't very full these days. In fact, after Mike leaves for school, I have nothing to do until he returns home. I've been making rounds again trying to find permanent work, but no luck.

"Of course at dusk I have the difficult job of… *watching*."

Though Earl laughed easily too, he replied, "Don't take the job of night watchman lightly, Alex. It shows a great deal of trust in you."

Alex nodded and sat down as Earl poured coffee for him and refilled his own large mug.

"If you have time this morning, we could buy the wood needed for your cabinet and I can begin working on it right away."

Earl finished his coffee, put the mug in the sink, and moved toward the door.

"Perfect timing, I'll dress and be with you in ten minutes. I need to be at the hospital around eleven as Billy Turney is having surgery, but that should be more than enough time. I think he's going to do well, but they don't have much family and I like to be there for them."

Alex followed Earl's car to the lumber yard. It didn't take long to get the wood. After it had been loaded into the back of the truck, he and Earl left in different directions.

Working on the cabinet until it was about time for school to be out, Alex left a note saying he'd be back the next morning unless there was work at the job site. In any case, there would be no need for Earl to wait, as he'd been shown where an extra key was kept.

Earl had laughed when he mentioned a key. "Most of the time I don't lock the door. Few people around here do."

Alex was astonished to think of leaving a house unlocked.

"We know one other in this town. We keep an eye out."

"Never had a problem. Anyway, most days you can just come on in, but if it happens to be locked, you'll know where to find the key."

He was pleased with the start he'd made today—he missed this kind of work. He could finish it tomorrow. As he left, he locked the door, probably to Earl's consternation.

The afternoon was beautiful, and it was tempting to go by the school for Mike, and go for ice cream. He knew Mike actually liked riding from school on such a day as this, so he decided to save the idea for another day. Truth was, he couldn't afford ice cream cones in light of the fact they would soon be homeless.

Alex continued to make visits inquiring about work, but it was time to face facts.

I can probably count on another week as night watchman and having use of the truck. I might have enough money to live on a couple of weeks, but no more... a couple of weeks.

As he sat on the trailer steps waiting for Mike, he again asked God for wisdom.

He thought of his mother. She would probably say, "God's wisdom should tell you to quit stalling and go elsewhere."

Okay, decision made, albeit not much of one. I'll complete Earl's cabinet tomorrow.

Since I'll soon be without transportation, I'll drive down the mountain to Jessups and begin inquiring there. The town is larger, and has a major hardware store and lumber yard. I have to have a job.

Mike had returned home, happy and bubbling over with school news.

Alex had begun noticing the addition of a girl's name in his conversations. Her name was Lindy.

"Today, I helped Lindy with her poster for history… she says I'm a lot better at drawing than she is… and Miss Parker said it was okay to help each other."

He began to laugh. "Lindy's cows looked like dogs, so I showed her how to draw them better.

"She helped me make my title line. She's real good at writing."

Continuing without taking a breath, "I saw Anna today… I guess she was working at the RX, because she brought things to the school nurse, and I saw her when we were outside for recess… she was leaving, but she stopped to hug me… you know, like she does…"

Oh… my son is beginning to blush.

"She wanted me to tell you hello, and to come by to see her sometime."

Alex felt a bit of warmth in his own face as he thought of Anna. It was with regret, but he did not intend to complicate that sweet woman's life.

After Mike took a breath, in his own very-direct approach, he asked, "What do you think we'll do when your night-looker-man job is over?"

There it is—what am I going to do?

At the same time, he couldn't stifle his amusement at the title he'd been given.

"I'm called a night *watch*man, but you're right about it being about looking all around.

123

"I hope to have something figured out soon, okay?"

"Okay. I'm supposed to read a chapter to you aloud. Can we do it now so we can tell stories or play cards later?"

Mike was satisfied. He trusts me. But I'm not living up to what he deserves.

He gave Mike a grin and answered, "Sure, get your book. We'll read right here before the sun goes down and I have to begin *looking*!" They laughed together.

The cabinet for Earl completed, Alex continued his job search, concentrating now in Jessups. He had to get something settled while he had transportation.

Saturdays were for Mike—a picnic by a nearby creek, tromping through the woods, or visiting the downtown area, which was frequently active with exhibits, barbershop quartets, food vendors, and always someone they knew.

On Sundays they attended Sunday school and worship, and would usually stop on the way home for a hamburger. Occasionally they also had ice cream, a special treat.

On the way out of church one Sunday, Earl stopped him and asked if he would come by his house Tuesday morning.

"Of course. My calendar is clear," he joked. "Something else to repair?"

"Something I want to talk about. Can you come by after Mike goes to school?"

"Sure. I'll be there by eight unless I'm needed for work, which I don't expect."

Alex made more job inquiries in Jessups Monday morning and had a few hours' work at the site in the afternoon.

Tuesday morning, he drove to Earl's just before eight. The day threatened storms again so he had dropped Mike off at school and was planning the afternoon in his mind. He'd have to be back before school was out.

Before he reached the door, Earl opened it, ushering him into the kitchen. Alex sensed something about him, but couldn't pin it down. He obviously had something on his mind. They sat down with coffee and fresh banana bread Anna had brought by. Earl seemed in no hurry.

"The cabinet looks great, Alex. I knew it would. I have something else in mind now, though, a bigger project. I hope you'll hear me out."

Alex could feel himself tremble—he knew it was time. *Time to stop the hand-outs, though genuinely given. Time to stand on my own feet, say goodbye to this town, and move on to a place with work and a future.*

"Earl, you have been more than good to us, but I have taken a close look at myself and faced facts. It just doesn't appear that Mt. Seasons can provide what we need, meaning working to build a future."

As he spoke, his voice rose. He began to sound almost angry, though at himself.

He continued, "I'll never forget your generosity, but it's time for me to quit *taking* and become responsible for myself and my boy again."

For several minutes, neither of them spoke. Earl concentrated on his coffee and Alex sat in the uncomfortable silence they'd never felt before.

"I asked you to hear me out, Alex. What I have in mind could fulfill your hopes for your future—if you can be objective for a while and think what you could *do* with this idea—not my part in it."

"I'll listen, Earl; I just cannot continue letting others take care of us."

"First thing—taking care of each other is what we're all about. It's the way God planned it. Helping each *other*, Alex. Later on, it will be you helping someone else who is having a rough time.

"Look, I know how hard you're trying, but you have no idea of where you'll go when the night-watchman job is over.

"Before I tell you about an idea I've had, I want you to make a promise to me. I want your *word* that when the job has ended, you and Mike will come here to stay with me for at least a week or two... until you can make a more definite plan. Will you do this for me as a favor—so I won't worry about you two?"

Alex was shaking his head.

"Temporarily, Alex, *please*... this will take a load off your mind... *and* mine.

"I have a phone you can use to make inquiries and will gladly help you with transportation. Please."

"I explained—I can*not* continue allowing you to take care of us."

More calmly he added, "But I do accept your offer of a place to stay for a week or two, for Mike's sake. And I'm grateful. Nonetheless, I have to find a job... soon."

"I agree. As a matter of fact, it ties in with my idea, a possibility—long shot so to speak—but an idea.

"As I tell you about the idea I've been pondering, keep in mind it is not to be a hand-out. Think of it as a hand-*up*. In fact, my friend, what I'm proposing might be the most work you ever did."

The mood between them relaxed. Earl laid out his idea. Alex listened.

Earl insisted his proposition was a business deal, an investment he would admit held risks.

"I have good instincts about people, Alex. I like you. I also trust you and know something of your business and experience in Russia— Blancha didn't talk a great deal, but told me enough that I knew of your character and morals before I met you.

"I've seen the pictures you brought showing a sampling of your projects there. I've observed *repairs* you've done here, and I've observed your attention to detail in every single thing you do. Let me emphasize, this idea is not a hand out.

"Alex, if this works out, I'll expect a good return on my investment."

Nearly an hour later, they rose from the table and walked out together.

Earl was pleased. "My day won't end until late, so I'll expect you back here in the morning, whenever you can make it. Then I hope we'll soon be taking a drive and making some decisions. Think everything over, okay?"

In spite of their lengthy conversation—more accurately, Earl speaking and Alex barely responding—he still had time to drive down the mountain to inquire at the homebuilders' association and one other. He was considering Earl's proposition, as he had agreed, but there were too many variables.

As before, no encouragement from either business. He stopped on the way back to put gas in the truck. The company furnishing gas for his personal business was not part of the deal.

"Fill it up," he instructed the filling-station attendant. While the young man cleaned the windshield, Alex cringed as he noticed gas had gone up to fifteen cents a gallon.

He arrived back at the school just as Mike was coming out.

Mike rattled on about the school day until they arrived at what he shuddered to call home. Yet… yes, he was thankful for it.

Later, as he lay across the mattress with Mike, he listened to news about school.

He heard more about Miss Parker, Mike's friend Lindy, and his getting an extra cookie at lunch.

Alex worked in a few questions, which he hoped were casual enough for Mike not to give it any thought.

What do you think about living in Mt. Seasons?

In an attempt to understand more of Mike's feelings, he asked specifically, "What would you tell relatives in Russia about living here?"

As Alex attempted to sleep, there was one thing about which he had no doubt—Mike would be crushed to leave Mt. Seasons.

He's done well with so many adjustments. Without me, he adjusted to his aunt, a new country and language, school, and new ways. He adjusted to a town full of strangers—and now he has friends of all ages all over town.

He smiled as he remembered Mike's attempt at helping him with Southern English.

But, after all, he is but a boy. Children can adapt a multitude of times when confident in a parent's love.

His mind assured him of one thing. His heart felt something altogether different.

The cold morning was sunny and calm. Mike again insisted he loved riding his bike to school, so Alex relented, which turned out to be a good decision.

As Mike rode out of sight, Alex heard a vehicle coming in close to the equipment.

He recognized Mr. Blackstone's bright red pickup truck.

There should be another name for that vehicle. A truck is a work vehicle, but I'm sure this one has never hauled anything.

A 1946 Chevrolet with a six cylinder engine, Bob J said, and in Mr. Blackstone's specifically-chosen color, swift red.

Mr. Blackstone *"wanted the men to see him coming."*

It doesn't even sound like a truck.

Alex had little doubt why he was here. He walked toward the truck—no need for Mr. Blackstone to get out.

But the superintendent got out of the truck, seeming in no rush. He wore his usual starched khakis with a light jacket, but today also wore a brown *Stetson* hat. Alex knew the brand, as he'd heard one of the men enviously mention their superintendent having several of them. It *was* a fine-looking hat.

"Good Morning, Alex. I'm sure you know why I'm here. Thought you might have a cup of coffee to spare."

"Of course, come in. I'll clear *the* chair for you." They both smiled, knowing it was no exaggeration.

Alex moved a stack of books as Mr. Blackstone removed his hat and sat down, seemingly quite comfortable in the shabby work trailer. He took the mug of coffee and leaned back.

Alex admired the man. He had no air of superiority nor did he seem at all out of place, in spite of being his superior in every status imaginable.

"You've made the small space work for you," he observed.

"Yes, sir, it's been fine. Mike called it an adventure."

"Well, you know why I'm here. Everything about the job has been approved, signed on the dotted line, so to speak. So we're finished.

"The men will start moving the heavy equipment out Thursday, and most likely get it out by the next day. Only this work trailer will remain, which I've asked Jerry Smith to haul out Sunday morning. His son will come with him to drive the truck."

"Yes, sir. I'll have our things out and be here when they come by to give them the keys. I've appreciated the time here and extra work."

"I have your last paycheck, including the hours for the rest of this week, and had the bookkeeper add a bonus. You've served the company well."

He stood to hand the check to Alex, who took it and shook his outstretched hand. "Thank you, sir."

The man was making no moves toward the door, but stood as if in thought.

"Alex, do you have an immediate plan, for a roof over your head, I mean?"

"Thank you your concern. I can't say I have a plan, but I have a place to stay for a while. We'll be all right."

"I thought of offering you a job, asking you to follow us to the next site. But I don't really think it would be the best thing for you and your boy. The pay wouldn't be any better, and you are capable of more.

"You're a good worker, Alex

"If you need a reference, call me or give the company address and my name to any prospective employer.

"I'll be happy to vouch for your honesty and hard work. I believe you can handle most anything coming your way, and I wish you the best of luck."

Mr. Blackstone had apparently had his say, and was opening the door to leave. The kindness and concern of this man was unbelievable.

Finding his voice, Alex replied, "Safe travels to you, sir. I can't thank you enough."

There was a brief nod and wave as Mr. Blackstone got into his truck. He started the motor and drove away.

Walking back into the trailer, mentally thinking what he needed to do first, he opened the envelope. A nice bonus would be twenty-five dollars, generous indeed. There was an additional *hundred* added to his regular pay!

He rose quickly from the chair to open the door, but the red truck was out of sight. He felt a gentle breeze, refreshing, cleansing.

He knew how much the extra money would help, and thought about the man who had given it.

He wanted to help, and never made me feel he was looking down on me. Most likely I'll never see him again.

Alex looked upward and whispered, "Thank you, God."

Good people. I seem to have been surrounded by them almost exclusively since arriving.

132

Life was smoothing out in slow and simple ways in this little Southern town so far from Russia.

But in a city less than two hundred miles away, someone else was making plans—which, if put into action, could turn a small breeze into an out-of-control hurricane in many lives.

~ 14 ~

Arta Nordin

The young woman moved quickly along the busy street in Nashville, Tennessee. Her eyes nervously darted everywhere as she plodded along. She hated this large city. She was beginning to panic, sweat forming on her forehead. Things had gone well for so long. Now she was unsure of everything. Well, almost everything. She knew she was not going to take the blame. She deserved better for all the years of having nothing, and all she'd gone through to get this far.

Arta Nordin had come across the world less than a year ago with Aleksander Nordin's son in tow. He'd been a good kid… still, an added responsibility.

She'd planned to leave Russia for America and was waiting for her papers to be finalized when, as though from a fairy tale, she'd met the handsome American man. He was the reason she had agreed to bring Mikhail Nordin—he insisted it was the kind thing to do.

Only later did she realize he had other ideas. She was hesitant about agreeing to his plan, but she did—she'd done a lot for him, for love. Nonetheless, she'd had the foresight to take care to provide a back-up plan, a little insurance… just in case.

It had been costly insurance, but might prove to be worth it. And it seemed the time was drawing near.

It was the kid's father, I'll say. I was an innocent, trying to help him out. He said he wanted a better life for the kid, begged me, claimed he had nothing but what he'd scraped together to pay the kid's expenses. So I did it out of the goodness of my heart. Barely related at all, but I wanted to help them out. I'm guilty of nothing more.

Yes, this would work... if necessary. She hadn't told her boyfriend before taking the action she thought might protect them. Actually, he was her fiancé, though she had not received the ring.

But he was angry about her acting on her own. If plans went wrong, he'd *congratulate* her for thinking ahead.

❈ ❈

Arta had lived all her life in a Russian village about twenty miles from Aleksander's, never expecting to travel much further. She was five-six, with straight dark blond hair, dull blue eyes, and an unusual figure—slim, but completely void of curves. She had no memorable features and was painfully aware of it all. To make up for it, she attempted to be agreeable and accepting of people and situations, doing so by remaining quiet on many occasions. Therefore, she was liked well enough, thought of as being attentive, and posed no competition or threat to anyone.

In 1945, she was thirty-two years old.

She had finished a year of high school and gone straight into an assembly-line factory job near home. She was a bright enough young woman, but like so many others, had no resources for further education. She'd had little ambition anyway.

Arta had rather expected to be married long before the age of thirty. Her dream was of being a homemaker, and raising her children with a dependable husband who treated her decently.

When she finally admitted to herself she'd had the interest of very few young men and *no* prospects for marriage, she became restless.

Arta began to recall life in Russia… and what had brought her to this place and time.

I remember the day I overheard the conversation between several people about an acquaintance who had gone to the United States. I couldn't get it out of my mind. A few months later, I filed papers and began saving money to finalize papers and travel. I had no qualms about leaving my home country. My parents were gone, and only a few aunts, uncles, and unknown cousins remained—no one I would miss, and no one who would miss me.

I stopped with the other girls that day after work… just to purchase a coffee or ale. Two young American men were there. They were watching us… interested.

I knew the other girls were curious about them, but certain of their parents' disapproval. I had no such problem.

The men came over and we introduced ourselves and talked briefly. I very much enjoyed it. They were nice... and handsome.

A few days later, stopping by the same pub, one of the men was there again. He smiled as I came in, and greeted me immediately.

"Arta," he began, beaming, "I'm so glad to see you. I must confess I have been here every day hoping to see you once more."

He was interested enough to make a trip there every evening... hoping only to see me again!

He asked me to sit with him—I was flattered.

His name was Tank Johnson. "Arta," he began intently, "I am drawn to you, in a way I can't explain. Your maturity as a working woman is so appealing, and your attitude so refreshingly different from American women I've known."

I could see no harm in an hour spent in public talking with the fascinating American. "After all," I told a co-worker, "he knows I haven't money or status. He has nothing to gain... except me."

We met there several times before he asked me to dinner. He was so wonderful, and obviously very attracted to me.

I remember his exact words that evening. "You're beautiful, in a classic, natural way.

"I love that you give your whole attention to our conversation."

He was in love with me!

"I cannot bear to leave you when I return to America, Arta," he whispered sweetly.

I thought I'd told him about my filing paperwork for permission to travel to America, but he appeared surprised and thrilled when I mentioned it.

I'd made that vow all those years before to remain a virgin until marriage, and made my standards clear to Tank early in the relationship. I knew he truly loved me when he vowed, "The respect I have for you is part of your appeal."

I nearly melted when he held my hand, groaning, "Baby, you're worth the wait."

I was older—a difference of six years, but he assured me it didn't matter. Nor did it matter that I didn't have money enough for my travel—he wanted to give me whatever amount I needed.

Remembering, Arta could see more clearly.

It was later, gradually, that he began to hint at something we might do to "assure our prosperous future in America."

He would wait until I was able to depart before he resigned his construction job and arranged his own travel. He'd be able to meet me soon. As my travel date grew close, he took me to that nice restaurant.

"Will you marry me, Arta?"

My dreams were coming true! "Oh, yes, Tank, of course I'll marry you."

"I have a ring in the States, a family heirloom. We'll marry there."

I pulled closer, and whispered that I was ready to give myself to him... that very night. I loved him so much and, after all, we were soon to marry.

Remembering, I thought he actually seemed repulsed as he pulled away so quickly. But, just as suddenly, his look softened. "Oh darling Arta, no, we will wait for marriage, as we agreed. It will be a sacrifice, but I will not let you break your vow of purity."

I bitterly regretted having taken that stance—I wanted to give myself to him... to show him how much I loved him... I was anxious for him to make love to me.

But I couldn't sully his pure image of me—I couldn't insist on his taking my virginity no matter how much I wanted it to happen! His respect reinforced my faith in his love for me. Yes, I could wait for our wedding night in America. Then... Miss Arta Nordin would be Mrs. Tank Johnson.... I thought.

And so it was... the first thing he took was my self-respect—I willingly offered myself to him, knowing it was wrong before the marriage bed.

It was almost as if someone spoke to her...

Oh? He took it from you? You offered yourself—he turned you down, Arta.

She began to cry in earnest, realizing Tank had *taken* nothing—she'd fallen for his line... and thrown her integrity away.

~ 15 ~

Panic enveloped Alex. No job, income, or... home.

He was thankful he'd accepted Earl's offer of a place to stay for a time. Another temporary fix, but it calmed his immediate worries concerning Mike.

Looking at the clock, he realized he needed to get to Earl's.

Obviously waiting for him, Earl opened the door as Alex approached the porch. He motioned him to the kitchen, poured coffee and sat. Alex continued to stand, neither speaking. Earl was simply waiting for an answer.

"Earl, your proposition of investing in, *buying* a business for me to run... you must know I'm not comfortable with your putting your savings into an investment for me. Neither of us can know whether it will pay off, and I'd have a hard time handling it if you lost everything because of me."

He'd thought Earl might interrupt. He didn't. He sat, giving his full attention.

Alex continued. "Last night I slept very little. One minute I'd be excited about the prospect of having a business again, doing what I really like—carpentry. Next minute I'd be honest, knowing it wasn't coming from my efforts, but from your money, your goodness and faith in me. I'm not sure I deserve it."

He finally sat. Earl remained silent for several minutes, finishing his coffee.

"What I hear is—you'd like to at least consider this, and *see* what I'm talking about. But, you're scared. Right?"

"Yes… that's most of it."

"Okay. I will say one thing. If the deal went through, and didn't work out financially—I would *not* lose *every*thing, only money."

Earl laughed, continuing, "So I'll make arrangements. I'm busy tomorrow until about two. Come over after school is out. Mike can go with us to check it out.

Back at the trailer, Alex's mind was reeling. He was filled with fear, but hope continued to raise its head. After eating a sandwich, he began to gather their belongings and prepare to tell Mike what was happening… as much as he could possibly explain.

Telling Mike about the short time schedule they had once more wasn't difficult. He knew the question in Mike's mind was only where would we go now.

"Our next stop will be Brother Earl's house. We've been invited to stay with him for a while. And we *may* have a plan, son. After school tomorrow, you and I will go to his house, and ride with him to check out some business ideas he and I have discussed. If it doesn't work out, we'll stay with him until I get some kind of job. I just got my paycheck this morning, so we're okay for now."

As Mike's eyes and grin grew wider, Alex realized he needed to reign in premature expectations.

"Now, Mike, these are just *possibilities* we're going to look at with Brother Earl. Do you understand?"

"It means maybe, doesn't it?"

"Not even a strong maybe, okay?"

"Okay." But the grin remained.

Most of their belongings in the back of the truck, Alex added Mike's bike on top and they were on their way to Earl's by three o'clock. The trailer and truck would no longer be his after Saturday. Whatever they decided, Earl still had space in his garage for the remainder of their things. All they'd have to grab Sunday morning would fit into a small bag.

While at Earl's, Mike would ride the school bus, and would still have his bike. Alex, though, would be going everywhere on foot. He had checked the county transportation schedule to nearby towns, if needed for his job search, but the trips were sparse and, he was told, undependable.

Earl was ready and waiting, anxious to see the property and Alex's reaction to it. He prayed it would be an answer to everything... well, *most* everything.

"I know I'm an optimist," he'd laughed, "but *realistically* optimistic."

"Mike, you can make some hot chocolate. There are marshmallows in the cabinet."

Mike headed to the kitchen and Earl handed Alex a hot mug. "We've got a few minutes. I poured fresh coffee when I heard you drive up.

"Thought you'd want to take a closer look at the bedroom you and Mike will have while you're here. It's not big, but I think you'll be comfortable."

"After a one-room trailer? Wonderful."

Earl showed him the closet space and pointed out the empty book case. "Though I had the extra bedroom set up, it hasn't been used since I've been here. You can use every corner."

"It's perfect," Alex observed heartily. "And, we'll see what happens with your idea, but in any case, I won't impose more than a few weeks."

Earl dismissed the thought and asked hopefully, "Are you eager to see the property?"

"Yes. Still apprehensive, but anxious to see it."

Earl called out to Mike, "Hey, Mike, you gonna stay in there all day? I bet I don't have a single marshmallow left, but get on out here. We're going for a ride."

Chair scraping across the floor, Mike shouted, "Yes, sir!" and came in quickly. "I didn't use all the marshmallows, Brother Marshall. You got some left... I was looking at the book on the table with all the pictures of people at church... I know almost all of them."

"The new church directory, yes. No one else has seen it except the ladies in the office, and volunteers who helped get it organized."

"Why isn't my picture in there... and Papa's?"

Earl grinned as he looked directly at Alex. "*Well-sir*, guess you have to ask your Papa. I'm hoping ya'll will be in the next one, though."

The three of them left the house to get into Earl's car.

"Where we going?" asked Mike.

Alex realized he had *no* idea where this place was—he hadn't asked. It couldn't be far, but he couldn't think of anything he'd seen fitting the loose description Earl had given.

Earl answered. "You'll see. I want your papa to see a building—walk through it and tell me what he thinks about it. It was a cabinet shop years ago."

Mike brightened, "Like our shop in Russia?"

He'd said "our" shop, Alex noticed. He felt out of control. "We'll have to see, Mike. We are just looking at it, that's all."

They drove to Main Street, crossed, and continued a few blocks further. Earl then veered to the right onto an older road.

Passing *Carter's Shoe Repair,* one of the busiest places in town. Alex remembered hearing of the place, but had not been in this area. Folks could have new leather soles or heels put on their shoes for a sight less than replacing them.

The shop itself looked as if it had been there as long as the town. The front was in need of repairs, including the banged-up door and shutters, and begged for a new coat of paint. He noticed, however, spotless windows and the recently swept sidewalk.

Mr. Carter is likely barely making a living, just getting by, like most people. Townsfolk care more about his ability to make their shoes last another year than the appearance of his shop.

I'm seeing the building through the eyes of a carpenter! I haven't thought that way in a while.

Just past Carter's, Earl rolled the window down and put his arm out to signal a left turn.

They drove another mile, passing several old houses, almost all in need of repair, but again, immaculate yards and porches. The people of Mt. Seasons took pride in caring for what they had. Admirable. This area was heavily wooded and houses set further from the road than in town. It had the feel of the countryside, quieter, slower paced, probably older residents.

Earl slowed the car and turned onto what seemed to be an old road, once paved, now full of potholes and broken pavement. Then he quickly turned again into a dirt drive, coming to an abrupt stop.

"This is it, Alex. Let's get out."

Mike jumped out, running to explore the property.

"Hey, these are great climbing trees… look, there are squirrels everywhere… and there's a dog house… I wonder where the dog is… I'll look for him."

Nearly blending into the overgrown woods was an old building, not large but a fair size. It appeared well built and still solid. Alex began considering the building's dimensions.

His eyes were quickly diverted to the left. A good-sized sign made of light oak, stood several feet in front of the porch. It had been beautifully carved with great detail.

Carpenter's Carpentry
Cabinetry Your Way
—Most Anything in Wood

Alex walked to the sign, running his hands slowly over the delicate carving, in awe of the work. He was overcome with emotion, surprising and embarrassing himself. He wasn't even inside the place, but there was a faint smell of woodwork in the air, a smell he'd grown to cherish.

"This is a work of love, Earl. This place meant a lot to the man who worked here."

Earl gave him a few minutes before walking up two steps onto the porch to unlock the door. He motioned for Alex to enter ahead of him.

Alex was astonished at the amount of equipment. The place was dirty from time, not disarray. Everything seemed to be in its place, each small tool apparently having a separate niche. The electric saws and other larger tools had seen years of use, and probably had their own formulas to keep them running. He was at home with this equipment.

He knew how to repair and work on all of it, but could never have hoped for so much.

Earl remained silent. He rambled around but, for the most part, observed Alex examining each piece. He touched them almost in awe, running his hands over the larger pieces and picking up the smaller ones as a child might in a toy store, where he'd been warned against causing damage.

From the small front porch, they had entered directly into the shop. At the far back right corner was a large, double-basin sink. It showed a lot of use but was solid.

Earl observed, "This old sink is porcelain over cast iron. It may be the only thing in the room I know anything about, but it will never wear out."

Alex walked to its left through a larger door leading into a sizeable room, perhaps used for storage, or an office of sorts. An old, heavy desk sat in one corner, the room otherwise barren. The door leading to the back yard was at the back of the room, a window on each side. Looking out, the area was wooded as far as the eye could see.

Through the other window he observed Mike, in his own world, exploring. There was a small outhouse at the edge of the woods. He'd be interested in what Mike would say about *that*—obviously a one-seater.

Going to the other window, he could see a lean-to which provided shelter for an old truck—very old, in worse condition than the construction truck he'd been driving.

He doubted this one had been moved or driven in years. Probably junk.

His excitement was obvious. It was like being in part of a dream, getting a glimpse of someone's life work.

"*Well*, Alex? I want to know whether you think the equipment is workable, usable, and enough of it. I want to know what else you'd need to buy to get started in business. First thing would be a phone, couldn't operate a business without one, a small item; but I want to know what big purchases we'd need."

Speaking more enthusiastically every minute, Earl continued, "We need to take a look at the old truck, see whether it might be usable—you'd certainly need it. Mrs. Carpenter said her husband had used it right up till he died, but didn't claim it was without challenges.

"The deal would be for the land, building, everything in it, and the truck. Mr. Carpenter had built up a good business. Mrs. Carpenter will *consider* giving the account books to the buyer, which would include a list of past customers and provide a good starting point. Tell me what you're thinking. I know nothing about this equipment."

"The equipment is more than I had before. It's old, but workable, I'd say. Doubt I'd need anything else. It appears we'd need only to buy materials, good quality wood, which *is* costly—we'd have to invest a lot in wood and stains before we'd ever make a penny."

Earl began to smile and nod his head. He raised his eyebrows in question. Still nodding, he put his hand out.

"Whoa!" Alex was unsure he could comprehend all this. "You really want to do it? You can afford it?"

"I *hope* so. We'll have to talk to Mrs. Carpenter more about specifics.

"There's no price listed on the property. But I've been given what I think is an educated guess on the value and probable asking price. So... I think I can. Partners?"

Alex put his hand out. They shook hands, embraced, and began laughing.

Only then did Mike come inside. He ran through the door, stopped, and looked around. "Wow, whose is this?"

Alex leaned down to pick him up. "What would you think if I said it might, just *might* be ours soon—ours with Brother Earl?"

"Hey, I'd *like* that... I think there's a dog around here too, Papa... would it be ours?"

Earl and Alex both laughed, and Alex answered, "Well, *if* there's a dog, Mike, I don't really know. I'd say probably not."

"Well, we already got a dog house out there. If there's not a dog, we should get one since we already got the house."

~ 16 ~

Returning from the carpenter shop, the thought, even *possibility* of running a carpentry business again… overwhelmed Alex.

"Home again," Earl announced. "A successful day, I'd say."

"Yes… I can't even comprehend it."

He turned to Mike, "Get in the truck, Mike. We've got to get back to the trailer. Earl, we'll see you Sunday."

"Sure. In the meantime, I'll make phone calls and hopefully set up a meeting with Mrs. Carpenter for Monday."

Alex planned to finish in the trailer the next day and spend Saturday with Mike. Mr. Blackstone had told him to leave the truck and trailer keys in the truck bed Sunday morning, but Alex wanted to be present when everything was picked up to assure there were no questions.

Earl had a plan. "I'll be there at eight-thirty. If the trailer and truck are gone, I'll pick you both up. If not, I'll take your things and Mike with me. I can take him to Sunday school, and you'll have the bike to ride into town, either to church or to my house."

"Have it your way, preacher," Alex replied. He was about to drive away, but leaned out the window. "Earl, I know the deal is far from being done. We'll see Mrs. Carpenter Monday, but I'd like to go over a few matters with you Sunday afternoon."

"Sure, as of now, my afternoon is free," Earl replied jovially.

❋ ❋

Sunday morning, Jerry Smith knocked on the trailer door at seven.

"Good Morning... Mr. Smith? I have hot coffee if you'd like some before I finish up. Here are the truck keys. Can you give us a few minutes?"

"Sure. Mr. Blackstone said I wasn't to rush you." The man seemed to hesitate, but continued, "Just... sooner I get going, sooner my day is finished. We ain't gettin' overtime for this—really thought you'd be gone already."

Alex noticed the younger man standing back at a distance. He was sure the man and his son were being well paid, but replied, "Of course. Here's your coffee. There's not room in here to offer you a seat, so you might want to wait in the truck."

He handed him the trailer and truck keys. "We won't be long."

By seven-thirty Alex and Mike were standing by Mike's bike, a paper sack full of things in the basket, and smaller items at their feet. All they could see of the trailer and truck was a cloud of smoke from the exhaust of the old truck.

"It's a bit cool this morning, Mike. I know you're bundled up, but why don't you head on over to the church on your bike? I'm sure someone will be there to let you in early. I'll just sit down by the tree and wait for Earl."

Mike was about to start out when they saw Earl's car coming down the road—an hour early.

He pulled up and opened the door. "Put the bike in the trunk and hop in. I know I'm early, but let me tell you—sometimes I think there's no need for phones in this town. All you need is Sister Hamby. Ah, don't even ask questions, most times even *I* can't figure how she knows so much so quickly. But she's the reason I knew to be here early."

They all laughed, Mike not sure he understood, but Alex was grateful for Sister Hamby. He didn't have to ask whether they were headed to the house or the church building. At least he'd had time to comb his hair and get a cup of coffee.

Alex had become more relaxed at church. People had accepted them. They were good people, and he hoped to attend more regularly when their lives settled down.

After church, Alex and Mike left with Earl. Following them were Earl's parents and Anna, all on their way to Seasons Moon for lunch.

On the way, Alex asked, "Earl, you haven't mentioned anything about what we've talked about to anyone, have you?"

"No. I didn't think it was time."

"Good. Mike, how about not saying anything about the shop we looked at—because we don't actually know anything yet. Okay?"

"Not about getting a dog either?"

"Not the dog either, they're part of the same thing."

"And, Earl, I'm buying lunch for the three of us. You best enjoy it—might be the chance of a lifetime."

He enjoyed feeling a part of this loving family. Pam and Bill Marshall were easy-going like Earl, and of course Anna was comfortable with everyone. Mike made no secret of assuring a seat beside her, pretty much oblivious to everyone else.

Sunday's special was chicken and dumplings, and pineapple upside-down cake, both new to Alex.

The meal was wonderful—but to Alex, the laughter and sharing of the week's news among the family was even better. He was proud of Mike for not mentioning the possibility of the shop, but he was engrossed with Anna, which may simply have overshadowed everything else. No one asked about his job or possibilities, which Alex appreciated. While they waited for dessert, Earl brought it up.

"My family is being thoughtful today, Alex, but they care about you, so I'll say this—Alex and Mike will be staying with me for a while. I had to insist, of course. But I have confidence that Alex's plans will soon improve, and I'm sure he appreciates you not questioning him. And for your prayers, which I know you've been sending up."

Alex nodded in agreement—he couldn't seem to speak.

As Pam and Bill Marshall looked at him, their kindness and caring was almost tangible. He felt enfolded in their warmth.

Pam spoke. "Alex, Mike… we feel you've become part of our family. You are good folks and we wish you good things."

Bill nodded. The moment was becoming too somber to suit him. "Absolutely. And Earl might be a *minister*, but I tell you he needs a little watching after—maybe the two of you can keep him out of trouble."

Everyone laughed as the chatter resumed, and dessert had been served.

Leaving the restaurant, Anna came around to put her hand on Alex's arm, capturing his full attention. Her sweet smile and loving nature was difficult to resist. She was especially lovely today in a simple black suit, accented by a soft pink sweater.

"I'm glad you'll be with Earl for a while. I just know things are headed in the right direction for you."

He could feel the warmth of her hand on his arm. He'd almost forgotten the softness of a woman's touch.

"Thank you."

She made no move away from him. They stood for a minute before moving apart.

"I hope to see you soon."

She's giving me another chance, encouraging me. I still have no real prospects… but she won't be patient forever.

"Yes, I hope so, too." He'd felt so unsure before, inadequate. Little had changed. But this time he looked into her eyes and put his hand lightly on her shoulder.

She returned his direct look. "Bye for now."

At Earl's, they unloaded Mike's bike, carrying it to the end of the porch, and brought their clothes and boxes into the extra bedroom.

Mike was eager to go out to find the neighborhood children. Alex sat in one of the comfortable chairs. Earl removed his tie and jacket before coming in to sit across from him, kicking off his shoes to put his feet on the large footstool.

"Okay, Alex, what's on your mind? I hope you're not having second thoughts."

"No. I'm sure there will be many questions when we talk with Mrs. Carpenter. This is something different."

"Let's hear it."

"This is about my making a home for Mike."

Earl stretched and leaned back.

"I can never say thank you enough for giving us a place to stay when I had no idea of what to do or where to go.

"I think it will work out fine. After all, you have a tendency toward being messy, and I'm good with cleaning house. Especially since I'm now living *in* one, instead of a room on wheels."

Earl grinned.

"First step comes tomorrow—if we can't come to an agreement with Mrs. Carpenter, the next step won't matter. But if it *does* work out, I have in mind to make the back room and part of the back area of the shop into a living area.

"We have enough stored in your garage for a good start... beds, chairs, kitchen table, enough dishes, and so forth.

"I'll admit we've gotten used to an indoor bathroom, but we'll adjust to the outhouse—lots of others do.

"Over time, I can improve the place. It's important to me for Mike to have the feel of being in our *own* home—more permanence."

"May I speak?" Earl asked quietly.

"Sure. I'm not thinking of leaving your house right away. You'd still be stuck with us at least a few weeks, maybe more. *If* this deal should work out, it'll take a while just to get the place cleaned."

"I understand your feelings, even think you're right—as long as you don't feel rushed, and will be reasonable about the time you need to remain here. I might even help with getting it ready. Deal?"

Alex was overcome with emotion. He would never deserve a friendship like this. Earl was a good, generous man.

"Thank you" he stammered. "You know… I've searched for another word… I seem to be wearing *that* one out."

"You're welcome, Alex—have I made *that* clear? I'm very happy with all of this, and someday I may be asking a long list of favors of you."

He paused, looking down for a moment.

"Alex, I'm convinced *God* put you in my path, and for a reason. He knows what he's about."

Glancing at the clock and removing his feet from the footstool, Earl stood.

"Now if you've finished talking, I need a short nap. I have a meeting at six.

"By the way, I meant what I said about helping to clean the shop… if the situation works out… but I remain optimistic. When I have time in my busy schedule, of course… but the outhouse and dog house, they're all yours. No telling what's in *either* of them."

Laughing, he headed toward his bedroom and closed the door, anticipating a pleasant afternoon nap.

As Earl stretched out across his bed, he felt more clear-minded and satisfied than in a very long time. Before he closed his eyes, he prayed, "Lord, please work this out for us. And thank you for bringing Alex and Mike into my life."

Someday, Alex Nordin, you may understand what you've done for me.

His eyes closed to enjoy a peaceful nap.

❋ ❋

Monday morning the household of guys was full of excitement. Up before six, Mike was dressing, Earl making coffee and setting out milk and cereal, and Alex searching for what was needed for the day.

Mike was excited about riding the school bus, and Alex relieved because he wouldn't worry about the weather or his safety. Because there were only a few buses, each route was rather long. Earl's house wasn't far from the school, but the bus would be in route about twenty minutes with the stops.

The route and driver was the same for his house and the carpenter shop—if Mike were to be picked up at the shop, he would be picked up earlier and be in route longer.

Premature, he reminded himself... *this planning to make a home at the shop and checking bus schedules. Still... maybe.*

The morning's appointment with Mrs. Carpenter and her son was at eight-thirty at her home.

They drove into Mrs. Carpenter's gravel driveway promptly at eight-thirty. The large two-story frame house was beautiful, but not showy. It was painted in a pale yellow, with off-white shutters.

Alex's eyes were drawn to the heavy ornately-carved front door, which set the house in a category by itself. He was certain it had been the work of Mr. Carpenter.

Getting out of the car, the beginnings of spring were all around. In the fresh air was the aroma of new grass and budding trees, and a few crocus and daffodils peeked through in the immaculate lawn.

They turned at the sound of crunching gravel as Mrs. Carpenter's son, Joey, drove in behind them. It was rare for Earl not to know anyone in this town, but he was not acquainted with this family. They introduced themselves and walked up the steps to the wide wraparound porch. Joey was dressed in an obviously expensive brown suit, dress shirt, and tie.

He was tall, clean-cut, and appeared about Earl's age. Though he seemed a bit wary, he was cordial.

Earl also wore a suit, shirt and tie, though probably costing far less. Alex wore cotton work pants and flannel shirt.

Perhaps I should have asked Earl about my clothes. Don't have a suit anyway, so guess it wouldn't have mattered.

Earl had spoken to Ilene Carpenter on the phone the week before, and briefly when he stopped at her house to pick up keys to the shop. She'd been friendly and was clearly ready to sell—to have it off her mind. Earl hoped the son agreed.

Mrs. Carpenter greeted them as she opened the door.

In light of the impression the house had made on Alex, Mrs. Carpenter was not what he expected. She was dressed in an ordinary house dress, sturdy shoes, and no jewelry. She was not much over five feet tall, slight build, and her graying hair pulled into a neat bun.

Her bright eyes, however, belied her age and drew his attention. He sensed she was interested in, and paid attention to everything going on around her.

Her son gave her a hug as they walked inside.

She led the way through the spacious, immaculate, house.

"I thought we'd be more comfortable at the dining table to talk business. I have coffee already here and couldn't sleep much last night, so ya'll get the benefits."

She gestured to at a large tray of cookies and pastries.

"Yep, that's Mom... I call often wit concern about how she's sleeping. If she's not sleeping well, I know she's been baking through the night, and I come by more often," Joey laughed.

Earl joined the laughter. *Good start, relaxed, laughing, and with homemade pastries.*

Mrs. Carpenter began. "First off, I'd like you to call me Ilene. And call my son Joey. I know ya'll met outside. Okay, Joey?" He nodded.

"I already know Earl on a first-name basis. Mr. Nordin, you're Alex, right?" Alex nodded as she continued. "Don't want ya'll to think I can't get serious about business, but I'd like to discuss matters simply at first... and see how serious you are. Then if we agree on a few things, Joey and I have a friend who is a good lawyer. He could step in and work with us on details and legalities.

But I didn't want a lawyer involved yet, not until I got to know ya'll. Joey wanted a lawyer here all along—really wanted us to meet at the lawyer's office. He's Dan Lawson, by the way, maybe you know him. He has an office here and one down in Jessups."

Earl was enjoying the apple danish but was listening closely and beginning to think this might be going in the wrong direction. *Her manner is friendly and outspoken but she's very intelligent—she doesn't miss a thing and knows exactly what she wants.*

Unknowingly, his thoughts mirrored those of Alex.

Earl looked at Joey Carpenter. *Ilene made it clear this was not the way her son wanted negotiations to begin. Yes, Ilene knows what she's about.*

This could prove to be good or disastrous. I want a fair deal, for both sides, but I doubt I know anything at all about finagling a shrewd business deal.

"Mother is right, gentlemen. I wanted a lawyer present. However, I only want her to get a fair price for Dad's property and business.

"She's ready to sell, and it would be good to be finished with it. I don't mind saying that, but I want to be clear. She isn't in need of money. Bottom line, selling it would be good, but not necessary."

Alex remained silent. He could see this dream slipping away. They had agreed Earl would do the talking about the financial dealings.

"We're in agreement, Joey," Earl began. "I realize you don't know us. We don't know you either. I do know, and I've talked with Alex, about your Dad's good reputation. He established his business on fair principles. The location of the business is known in the community. A new owner would have to establish his own reputation, but I think the good feelings would be there to build on. It's part of the worth of the business."

He could see Ilene and Joey visibly relax.

"You don't know me," continued Earl, "but I bet you've checked me out.

"Of course I'm not a betting man, Joey, but I believe I'd be safe there." Joey smiled.

"Now we've gotten that out of the way, bottom line is how much you want and how much we can afford. To be truthful, I may not be able to afford to pay what it's truly worth. I'm not saying that to begin discussing a price, but to say I don't want to offend.

"If we come to a price agreement, I have a fair amount to invest, but will probably have to discuss a loan with my bank for a portion."

Earl continued. "In these negotiations, I'm the investor. Alex is the quiet type, well mostly, but he is the carpenter, the man with the know-how and talent, and the one to run the business. He's talented, honest, and a hard worker. I believe he could restore your husband's business to what it used to be. I think you would be pleased, Ilene."

Ilene smiled in agreement.

"If I may, we have questions before anything else—alright?" Earl asked.

Ilene and Joey agreed.

Earl continued. "We'd like a clear, written report of the exact size of the property itself, and whether there are markers at the property lines. We want to know whether everything in the shop will actually stay with it, whether the truck is included and if it is usable. Oh… and is there a dog to go with the dog house?"

Ilene burst out laughing. Joey looked puzzled.

"I can tell you something right now.

"If you want the dog to go with the dog house, I'd probably come down on the price just to get rid of the old dear!"

Alex spoke. "I have a young son, Mrs. Carpenter. The only real question he had was whether there was a dog. I didn't know Earl planned to make it part of the deal, but I guess it'd make Mike pretty happy."

"Write it down, Joey. They have to take *Sneaker*. And Alex—I told you my name is Ilene."

"Yes, ma'am."

After the laughter subsided, Ilene spoke again. "The land is about four acres and there were markers last I checked, small iron railroad stakes painted red, but it's been a while. It's registered at the County Land Office. I have a written inventory of everything in the shop. My husband, Martin, was very detailed, and updated the list every year, for himself and the insurance company.

"There's also a large tool box in my garage to be part of the deal—Joey has gone through it and took what he wanted of his father's, but a lot remains."

Alex leaned forward. "Would you allow me to keep the original name on the business... Mrs. Ilene?"

"I'd consider it... on down the road a bit. It'd be kinda personal to me, so I'll think about it. Do you mind if I ask you some personal questions, Alex?"

"No, ma'am."

Alex was uncomfortable, however, with the direction of the conversation.

He wondered whether she was aware of his being Russian, and how she might feel about it. And he was certain his past would not present a picture of dependability.

Ilene spoke kindly, but forthright.

"Alex, I know you are Russian—I have no problem with that. I heard you sent your young son here to stay with your sister until you could arrange your own papers and travel. I also know about your sister. I heard she was a fine woman. I was sad to hear of her death. You could say I've done some nosing around. You haven't been able to find a permanent job since you've been here, have you?"

"No, ma'am."

This, he thought, must be the way a person feels on the witness stand with no defense.

"Well, I know you've been diligently searching for employment. I even know about your job at the construction site."

She asked him to tell her about Mike, how he felt about schooling for the boy, and what he hoped for in their future.

She asked about his business in Russia, details about the type cabinets and other pieces he built, how he kept records, and what he did to build his business.

He answered the questions adding, "We brought pictures of many of the cabinets and woodwork I did in Russia."

She appeared satisfied. Alex breathed a sigh of relief.

"I do have one more personal question, Alex.

"You haven't mentioned a wife or anything about Mike's mother. *Is* there a wife, or something you can tell me about Mike's mother?"

Earl interrupted emphatically, "Ilene, you've asked a *lot* of personal questions, and he's answered. But this has nothing to do with our purchasing this business and property from you."

Joey appeared surprised. "Mother, I agree. This isn't *like* you—it's rude."

Ilene appeared deep in thought. "You're right. I can't explain really, just my feeling connected to my husband through this property, and the business he spent his life building. He loved it. And I want to know about the person taking it over.

"I guess you're thinking I wouldn't be *handing* it over, I'd be selling it for good money—but, it's how I feel."

She looked at Alex again. He saw the beginning of tears in her eyes.

He was stunned. "Mrs. Ilene... it's something I don't talk about... her." He glanced at Earl, then back. "I *was* married in Russia. She was wonderful, a good woman, and we were very happy. We'd been married about two years when Mikhail... Mike, he's called here... was born."

Choking up, he said finally, "Vera died when he was four weeks old."

He looked downcast—he wanted no more of this, business or not.

Ilene spoke quickly, giving no one else an opening, but her tone was soft.

"Thank you, Alex. I can see this was a deep love, and difficult to share. I'm sorry. I just felt I needed to know. I believe we're finished for now, gentlemen." She rose from her chair.

Earl wasn't sure where they were, nowhere as far as he could see.

Price had not been mentioned, not even a price *range*.

Good grief, I don't know whether the woman even wants to sell!

"Mother?" Joey asked, also confused.

"Alex… Earl. I believe Joey and I have some talking to do. I'll call you in the morning. Is it all right if I call early, before eight?"

Obviously dismissed, Earl was totally befuddled.

Alex felt queasy.

Earl answered, "Yessum, we'll be up."

Not a word was exchanged by Earl and Alex as they left the house, or on the drive home.

~ 17 ~

Returning from Ilene Carpenter's, Earl looked at the clock as he walked into the living room. "It's been a very long morning, and it's barely ten-thirty."

"Yes. It has."

"Alex, I don't know what to say. I've never seen anything like what happened this morning. I'm sorry she put you on the spot, though, completely unexpected and unacceptable. Not sure I'd want to be in a continuing deal with Ilene Carpenter. Whether she's even going to *sell,* I don't know.

If by chance she *does* offer a deal, I'll want to work through a lawyer of my *own,* through the bank, and be done with her."

"I don't know," Alex said thoughtfully. "She's not over the death of her husband, Earl, that's clear. Maybe she needs more time before selling his property. I know I have to find a job; I can't sit around until she's ready. We'll just have to forget it and *I* have to get on to another plan... quickly."

"If she calls in the morning as promised," Earl replied, "well, we'll just have to see. But if she says she needs time, I'll tell her we have to move on. I'm very disappointed, Alex. I feel badly about getting your hopes up so high," his voice began quivering, "for everything to fall apart."

"Don't apologize for trying to do something good. I'm sorry to see *you* disappointed."

Earl took a few steps toward Alex to put his arm around him. They stood together for a moment.

"Well, I'm not in the proper minister mind-frame, but I've got to get it together because I have visits to make this afternoon. One of the folks I'm visiting is seriously ill, and a couple of them have family problems.

"Think I'll make a stop at the park first. Being a bit chilly, there's probably no one on my favorite bench. I seem to gain comfort from the old trees, so it's one of my favorite quiet places. I need the Lord to help clear my head so I can go about his business."

Abruptly changing pace, he added, "Let's not talk about the property or deal anymore today. And... since you are a man of leisure for the rest of the day, and need to earn your keep, how about rummaging around the kitchen and figuring out something for tonight's supper?"

"Deal, Mr. Landlord. Maybe I'll surprise you. Might even be edible, but no promises."

As Earl left, Alex walked slowly to the kitchen. He felt the weight of life too much to handle. He'd *known* the possibility of Earl's being able to buy the business was just that—a *slim* possibility.

"*Why* did I let myself envision our living there, in the back of the shop... as before... it was an unrealistic dream."

He shook his head, as if to clear it.

And I'm talking to myself. Pull it together, Nordin—now.

Mike came running in from the school bus.

"Hey, Papa, where are you?"

"Here in the kitchen, waiting to hear about the bus ride and your day at school."

Alex had been busy and rather successful at clearing his mind… temporarily. He'd repaired the back door he'd noticed sticking, and found paint in the garage to do a few touch-ups around the door and back windows. He'd found a chicken in the freezer and put it out to thaw for supper.

"The bus was real fun. A lot of kids in my class ride the same bus. The bus driver is Mr. Sam and they call him *Mr. Sample Sam…* they explained if you have anything in your hand to eat, he always wants a little sample. He's nice, and funny. But he makes everybody stay in their seats and bragged that he ain't… I mean hasn't… lost a kid yet… but I think *he* said ain't.

"Whacha been doing today, Papa?"

As Alex thought what to answer, Mike was on to something else.

"I got homework tonight. I got to write a whole page about anyone I want. I can write about somebody I read about in books or somebody in my family or anybody I know. But it is supposed to say what he did to makes them special to you.

"I thought about writing about you, Papa, because you do so many things good, and you're smart and you always know what to do, and the answers to my questions.

"Then I thought about Brother Earl. He's important to everybody at church.

"He does *good deeds* like giving people rides, and a place to live... and he prays for everybody. Do you think I could write about Brother Earl? Would that be okay?"

Alex was trying to absorb the fact of his son saying he did many things *good*, was smart, and "always knew what to do." *How* could he think of him this way when he'd shuffled him around so much and still had no solid plan for their future?

"Writing about Brother Earl is a great idea. Are you going to tell him?"

"No, sir. If Miss Parker says it's good, then maybe I'll show it to him. Will you help me?"

"Sure 'nuff, Mike—is my Southern English getting better, you think?" They both laughed.

Alex managed to cut the chicken into fairly recognizable pieces though some appeared mangled. He'd found a jar of barbecue sauce, so would slather the chicken in the sauce and bake it for a while. He knew how to cook the rice he'd found. With loaf bread and heating a can of peas, it would be an acceptable feast for three guys.

Tuesday morning, Mike was ready to leave for the bus, but signaled Alex to come to the door with him. At the door, he motioned him to lean down, whispering conspiratorially, "Remember it's a secret about my paper—don't tell Brother Earl."

"Deal."

As Mike ran out the door, Earl raised his eyebrows. "What's with the whispering?"

"Well, *Brother* Earl, I have been sworn to secrecy."

The quietness of the house suddenly engulfed both men.

It was seven-fifteen. They wondered what to expect when Ilene Carpenter phoned. She'd promised it would be before eight. They were in agreement in believing they *would* hear from her. Otherwise, their thoughts rushed from one end of the spectrum to the other.

The phone rang at seven forty-five.

Earl answered. "Hello. Good morning, Ilene. Yes, he's here, too. Yes, ma'am."

For several minutes Earl listened. Then, "Yes, ma'am, I will sit, and I do have paper and pencil."

From Earl's tone of voice and what he heard from one side of the conversation, Alex had no idea what was happening, good or bad. For nearly ten minutes he said nothing. He listened and wrote notes. He never looked at Alex or changed his expression.

Finally, "Yes, ma'am... no, not what we expected. Yes, we'll talk it over.

Thank you. Good day, and God bless."

Exhausted, appearing pale, he hung up the phone. Alex was sure the news wasn't good.

"Alex, I *really* need a cup of coffee now. If I was a drinking man, I'd need a stiff drink," he grinned. "Would you mind bringing a couple of mugs into the living room? Then I'll fill you in. I can tell you, it's a lot to swallow."

As Alex walked back to the kitchen, the doorbell rang. It was barely past eight.

Who would come to the door at this time of the morning?

Pouring the coffee, he was surprised to hear Joey Carpenter's voice.

By the time he put the mugs on the tray with the cream and sugar and reached the living room, Earl was closing the door. He held a large plate covered with a napkin, and a thick envelope under his arm. "Guess we'd do better at the kitchen table, after all."

Alex turned back to the kitchen. Earl put the plate down and uncovered it to reveal a sampling of everything Ilene had served yesterday. He sat and began to open the package of papers, taking only a minute to flip through them before picking up his coffee.

A myriad of surprising developments had come about in less than an hour. He didn't know where to begin.

"If I can put all this in a nutshell, Alex, Ilene Carpenter likes us. She feels good about her husband's business being carried on by *you*, with my backing. She sees the business as an extension of her husband. She's willing to sell to us, but wanted us to fully understand she would have let it sit forever before selling to *just anyone*."

Ilene had explained. "My husband died more than two years ago and left a hefty insurance policy for me, more than I need for my lifetime. The money I get from the sale will go to Joey—now, not later. He's a good son and has reconciled himself to my decision. He wants me to be happy.

"I'm not hurting him financially—he's made his own fortune in recent years. Only telling you this so you'll know there'll be no hard feelings."

Joey concurred when he came by with the pastries and stack of records.

"Mother liked Mr. Nordin... Alex. She believes he is a good, honorable man who needs and deserves this chance. She could see he wasn't the kind to ask for hand-outs, so... in her eyes, this is the way for her *and* Dad—he's part of it, she says—to help make the future better for a good man and his son.

"She said something else that I honestly didn't understand, Earl. She mentioned that someone helped them out when she and Dad were first married. They never forgot it, but couldn't repay *that* person—so this, she said, was her chance to help someone else."

He shrugged his shoulders, indicating he knew no more.

With the plate of baked goods, Joey had brought copies of the inventory, papers on the truck, courthouse records of land measurements, and the original survey.

"Now, though, comes the *important* part."

Alex, a bundle of nerves, thought Earl seemed to have something to say that he couldn't quite get out.

"Alex, Ilene Carpenter has offered us the whole kit and caboodle for little more than half it's worth... in anybody's book. She is acutely aware of the worth, but this is what she has chosen to do."

"You mean… you can afford the investment—it's going to happen?"

They looked at each other and began to smile.

"Here's Ilene's written list. Mind you, this isn't a legal paper, but she spelled everything out.

"Right down to the bottom line where she listed, *Sneaker, the Dog—they have to take him with the deal*."

"Done!" Alex laughed heartily.

"Hallelujah!" added Earl, as they embraced and slapped each other on the back.

❀ ❀

The appointment at the lawyer's office was set for Friday morning, giving Earl time to finalize his business with the loan officer at the bank.

At ten o'clock they were all assembled in the waiting room of *Scott, Lawson, and Pearson*. A secretary ushered them into the office of Dan Lawson, the Carpenters' lawyer.

Ilene Carpenter and Mr. Lawson were quite a contrast as they took their seats at the head of the large mahogany table. She was dressed simply, though Alex did recognize the fine quality of her long black wool skirt, leather boots, and black and white sweater. She still wore no jewelry, but today he noticed her diamond wedding ring, which remained on her left hand. Her larger-than-life personality outshone anything she could have worn, but the executive business chair nearly swallowed her.

The remaining chairs were filled by Joey Carpenter, Alex, Earl, the secretary, and. Sam Nolen, the bank's lawyer.

Dan Lawson was quite at ease in this plush office, amply filling the large chair.

He was a huge, robust, man with wide shoulders, and a rather rough-hewn manner.

However, both Earl and Alex became aware of his approach with Ilene. He was softer, kind and caring, almost protective.

"Ilene, are you sure you want to sell at this price?" he asked, before opening the proceedings.

"I'm sure, Dan."

Later, going through the equipment inventories and land essays, he paused to look at her again. "Ilene, are you quite sure this is the *price* you want to agree to?"

Everyone was acutely aware that the only answer he received was a piercing look. He proceeded with no further questions.

In less than an hour, the agreement was complete. They shook hands, each one seemingly as pleased as the next.

Earl glanced at Joey. *He is true gentleman. More than likely still doesn't understand his mother's thinking, but seems satisfied to have it settled, no longer a concern—for either of them.*

"Now," Ilene said to Alex as they were leaving the office. "About old *Sneaker*. He's actually not old, maybe four or five. He was little more than a pup when he showed up at the shop. Martin, my husband, tried to ignore him. He didn't feed him for days.

"That dog continued to show up seemingly around every corner, still wagging its tail.

"Martin finally conceded—said when a dog was so starved its ribs were sticking out, but continued to be friendly, without begging, he deserved to be fed and given a name."

Alex sensed she was in the past, smiling at the memory of her husband.

She continued. "I've tried keeping Sneaker at the house, but he disappears after a few days, always ending up back at the shop.

"He's good with children, so I think he'll be good for your boy. Reminds me, I'd like to meet your son sometime when you see it possible. Anyway, just give Sneaker time. No doubt he'll show up there again."

"Yes, ma'am. Mike will want to meet you, too—the woman who gave him a doghouse and the dog to go in it. I can't thank you enough. You've been so generous. I'll try not to disappoint you, Mrs. Ilene. I can promise I'll run an honest business and do my best to live up to the name and reputation of your husband's shop and memory."

She was finally out of words, and reached up to hug him. He was surprised, and deeply touched. Then she turned to leave with Joey.

Outside, Alex turned to Earl, "*Now* I can't wait for Mike to get home so we can tell him the news. I will finally be working every day to build our future. Not to mention repaying you."

A separate agreement had been signed between them for Alex's eventual repayment of the loan, plus interest. The business would be transferred to Alex's name at that time.

They began laughing again, and celebrated with a Coke float for lunch. The full celebration would be later, with Mike at Seasons Moon.

"Alex, I thought of phoning Anna to ask her to join us tonight.

"She'll be so happy for you. It was just a thought. If you'd prefer just the three of us...."

"No, I'd like that," he answered sincerely. "Let *me* call her," he suggested.

Maybe this will be yet another beginning.

"Good idea—her number is in the address book on the phone table at the house."

❋ ❋

Mike was delighted. The most exciting aspect, not surprisingly, was the promise of a dog.

Anna eagerly agreed to join them for the celebration and wanted to know every detail.

"We have a lot of cleaning to do before we can actually move in and open it as a working business," Alex explained.

"I've decided to make the living quarters my first priority. The industrial-sized sink is at the back of the shop, so I plan to call that our kitchen. We have a table and chairs. The back room should work well for the beds, the one large chair, and our personal things."

Earl was enjoying just watching Alex, his excitement bubbling over.

"Hopefully, Mike can get into a routine with school while I'm in the process of getting the shop ready. Earl has someone coming over to take a look at the old truck and attempt to get it running—though *I'd* see it as a near miracle.

"There's so much to think about, my mind is reeling. But it's all so wonderful... thanks to your brother."

Leaving the café, Alex touched Anna's arm gently. "Thank you joining us, Anna."

"Oh, Alex, thank you for including me."

He took her hand, looking into her beautiful shining eyes.

Stumbling on his words a bit, he said in a lower voice, "I'll be engrossed for a while getting the shop ready, but I hope we can get together... do something... soon?"

Alex felt awkward, embarrassed to blunder over such a simple conversation.

"But Anna answered quickly, "Yes, Alex, I'd like that... very much."

~ 18 ~

A great deal was accomplished at the shop in the first week. Earl helped when he could.

The room that was to be their living area was spotless, including the windows, and it seemed roomier than Alex had thought. It would do nicely. He had cleared the spiders and webs from the privy out back, and swept it out. There was just so much cleaning you could do in a privy. Mike seemed to think it a fun idea—that would soon change.

He hoped to find a decent second-hand refrigerator at *Another-Time,* a store selling used furniture and appliances. He remained conscious of the fact that it was Earl's money he was spending. He would continue to cook on the little camp stove for a while and possibly add a regular stove later.

Earl, Alex and Mike were up early Saturday morning. Earl had a full day, consisting of a business meeting at the church office in the morning, a few visits after lunch, and a funeral at 3:00. He dropped Alex and Mike at the shop, telling them he'd see them sometime around dusk.

Mike ran through the shop, but was soon outside looking around excitedly. "Have you seen him yet, Papa?"

Sneaker. He asked the question every day.

"Not yet. Tell you what, though, his house isn't ready. That is *your* job today.

"Leaves and pine straw have blown in there over all this time. Clear all of it out. Be careful, though, could be spiders, even a snake in there."

Mike's eyes grew large with excitement and trepidation.

"Okay. How 'bout a bowl for his water and food?"

"Plenty around here, old cups, bowls and such in the cabinets." Mike was out the door.

Alex was expecting the installer from the telephone company, as well as a mechanic to look at the truck motor.

Before noon, Mike had the dog house cleaned, complete with a bowl of water, and another for food. Alex hoped the dog showed up soon, or he knew he would have to find one.

The mechanic, Ron, had been under the hood of the truck for a while, and the phone was being installed, when he heard another vehicle coming into the driveway. Thinking it was one of the utility companies, he headed outside.

Mike beat him there. "It's Anna! Hey, Anna, we didn't know you were coming… whatcha got in there? Did you know I'm getting a dog? He's not here yet but I got his house ready. You gonna help Papa?"

Anna was laughing and listening to Mike's long list of news and questions as she retrieved a large basket from her car.

"Hello. This is a surprise," greeted Alex.

His recent surge of confidence where she was concerned seemed to have disappeared. He quickly added, "A *nice* surprise."

"Well," she answered, "I not only brought lunch. I'm in my work clothes, and all yours."

She was dressed in jeans and a long white T-shirt with her hair up in a ponytail tied with a pink ribbon. She couldn't have looked nicer.

"Thanks. Maybe Mike can show you around first, while I check with the mechanic, to see whether he has any news about the truck."

Mike already had her by the hand, naturally taking her to see the dog house first.

Lunch was tuna salad sandwiches, chips, Mrs. Marshall's home-canned pickles and lemonade. They finished it off with home-baked *snickerdoodles*, which Mike and Alex both thought a humorous name for a cookie.

"I guess our appetites showed how much we enjoyed it, Anna. We barely left crumbs."

"Thanks. I'll tell Mom ya'll like her pickles. She'll be pleased. Looks like you're getting a lot done around here." She stood, brushing crumbs from her shirt. "Okay, where do I start?"

Alex hadn't given it a thought. He looked around, thinking everything too filthy for her to get into.

"Oh for goodness sakes, maybe you think I don't know how to get dirty. I see cleaning supplies and choices a-plenty. I must say I was thankful to hear Mike say you'd already taken care of the privy, which… honestly, I wasn't going to volunteer for anyway. I'll start where you left off with the cabinets."

Recovering, he replied with a smile, "I appreciate the help. In this case, it's worse than it appears."

"Mike's gonna help me," she said, winking at Mike. "He wants more snickerdoodles sometime, so I'm gonna make him work for them."

Obviously, Mike would help Anna with just about anything.

Earl drove up about six. Alex walked around the building to greet him.

"I see Anna's here. Not surprised. Hope everybody else showed."

"Come in and have a seat. The day couldn't have been better."

They came through the shop and Anna looked up from her place in the floor, cleaning a cabinet door. She grinned at her brother before turning back to the dirt at hand. Mike looked restless. Earl stopped to pat him on the back.

"Sneaker still isn't here, Brother Earl. I got his house ready."

Alex realized Mike had begun referring to "Brother Earl" rather than "Brother Marshall," which he wasn't sure was appropriate. He had mentioned it to Earl earlier.

"It's fine, Alex. He's probably heard it from a few of the teenagers. I see it more as a statement of their feeling comfortable with me, their preacher, so just let it go."

Now Mike looked at Earl as though he could handle any problem, even making a dog appear.

"I didn't think much about it, but on my way here I did see a dog. It was about the size Mrs. Carpenter described.

"I didn't notice what color he was, but he wasn't far away, walking in this direction."

Mike was already out the door, running full speed toward the road.

"Maybe I shouldn't have mentioned it. He'll be disappointed if it's not the one."

Anna stood, rubbing her back. "Well, he's been itching to get back outside anyway."

Mike, however, could be heard shouting, "Sneaker, you're here! Hey boy, yeah, you're my dog now. Hey boy... *everybody*... Sneaker is here!"

Rushing to the door, they could see Mike toward the back of the lot talking to Sneaker, who followed along with a wagging tail. He seemed to know he was home to stay.

He wasn't a bad-looking dog, a mid-sized male–what folks in the area called a *sooner*– "sooner be called one thing as another because he was a mix of so many breeds. His prominent color was brown, with a few spots of black and white.

"All is right in our world," laughed Alex. "He looks just right for Mike. And it isn't only the dog situation going right today, Earl. Ya'll sit down. You, too, Anna, I'm giving you a break. Or calling it quitting time."

"Ron got the truck motor to turn over. Tells me it needs a new starter and a few smaller repairs." Alex handed the parts list and prices to Earl.

"He apparently doesn't charge much for labor; all in all, less than sixty-five dollars total. According to him, the truck should be good for a long time and many miles."

"Doubt he's charging anything for labor. He said he owed me a few favors, and so he does. He's good at this, so if he says it'll be a good truck, I'm happy. What else?"

"Utilities checked out good and telephone is in. Oh, and the phone is a private line. The installer said I was lucky. I quote, 'not many get 'em, even businesses. Beings it's still listed under the Carpenter name... that helped' ".

Earl appeared amused. "Alex," a private line is good, but just *know this*—it doesn't actually mean *privacy*. The line should always be available to you, but does not prevent the operator from listening in. Trust your minister in this... I learned the hard way."

Laughing, Alex replied, "I'll take your word for it. Truth is, I doubt I could come up with anything else to want."

"How long before the truck's ready to drive?"

"Ron hoped to be back here with everything by Tuesday and hand it over the same day."

Earl stood. "Good end to a trying day for me. And thanks for feeding them, Anna. I was invited for a good meal with the Simpson family after the funeral today, so they'll have to scrounge tonight."

"*Tonight,* you say," Alex laughed, "*every* night.

"But we did eat a lot at lunch, and worked hard this afternoon. We'll most likely be ready to turn in for the night."

"Then let's head home. It's been a long day."

As they walked out, Alex turned to lock the door. Mike came running, Sneaker close behind.

"Papa, we going? We can't just leave Sneaker here. He won't know we're coming back... what if he leaves again? He drank a lot of water but he looks hungry and we haven't fed him." Mike looked alarmed.

Earl interceded, "Well, I can solve one thing. I do have a little food with me the ladies fixed up after the funeral. I'll share some of it with Sneaker."

Alex stooped down in front of Mike. "Mike, this is Sneaker's home. Right here behind the shop. You know I told you Mrs. Carpenter tried to keep him at her house, but he kept coming back here as he did today. He has a good house since you cleaned it for him, he has water and will have part of Brother Earl's food... which, I may add, he was holding out on *us*. I believe Sneaker knows you will be back. He has to stay here."

Mike began to cry. Though Alex knew he needed to be firm about this, he didn't feel strong about denying him anything.

Anna looked at Mike. In a quiet voice, she said, "Mike, you know Alex is right. Do you think it's fair for you to try to make him sad just to get your way?"

Mike looked at Anna. His tears slowed.

She'd gotten his attention.

"I really wish we could take him with us… but I guess he might get mixed up.

"Could we come out here before Sunday school in the morning and make sure he's still here and bring more food?"

With great relief, Alex answered, "Sure."

He looked at Anna as he mouthed the words, "Thank you."

He'd been glad she was here, for more than one reason.

In less than two weeks, the shop was inhabitable and they were almost ready to move in.

The phone rang before sunup. Alex heard Earl leaving the house shortly afterwards, which he'd learned wasn't unusual in the life of a minister.

He helped Mike get ready for school. "I'm going to take you to school and change your bus stop starting tomorrow."

"I hafta ride a different bus?"

"No. But, you'll ride the bus this afternoon back here to Oak Grove Street as you've been doing. We'll have our going-away supper with Brother Earl, and later go out to the shop and begin calling it home. In the morning you'll get on the bus there—but it's the same route and driver, just an earlier stop."

"Good. I've been telling everybody at school about it and I told Sneaker I'd soon be there *every* day—he'll be real happy."

As Ron had promised, the truck ran well. It rather *looked* like a wreck on wheels and was a bit noisy, but it did run well.

He'd come to agree with Earl about Ron's expertise with motors.

Returning from the school, he loaded it with the things left in in Earl's garage.

Earlier in the week Earl had helped him load and move the beds and larger items.

At the shop, he unloaded the truck, filled Sneaker's water bowl, and headed back to Earl's.

By the time Mike came running in from school, Alex had finished getting the bedroom cleared, changed the bed linens, and was doing last-minute straightening. He'd run the vacuum throughout the house, finished the laundry, and had begun supper for their farewell meal with Earl. He'd talked about it with Mike who was excited about "conspiring" to surprise him.

When Earl arrived home, he found the table set and pleasant smells wafting through the house. Alex noticed his friend's weary look.

"I heard you leave early this morning— tough day?"

"Yes. The Anderson boy had to be taken back to the hospital in Jessups. His lungs have gotten weaker and his breathing problems are frightening. He does *not* have tuberculosis, a huge relief, but he will have to be moved from the hospital to a special facility in Coalton."

Earl appeared deeply concerned. "They will be giving him treatments to strengthen his lungs and monitor his exercise and diet.

"The expense will be hard on the family, but they're hurting more because Coalton is nearly an hour away. They won't be able to be with him as much. Freddie Anderson is only ten years old—he needs family."

Earl realized Mike had come into the room. "I'm sorry guys, I've just been concerned. I've prayed with them, and they say they can get through anything to help Freddie grow stronger."

He glanced around, "But, I see ya'll have been busy. No dust bunnies around the house and supper cooking... must be your big celebration to move out, leaving me to fend for myself again."

Alex grinned. "Yep, you're right. You have time for a shower before supper. Tonight's treat is my first try at spaghetti. It's looking pretty good. I got your mother's recipe and a long list of hints."

Later as Earl sat at the table with Mike, Alex retrieved a small package from a drawer. "This is a little something to thank you and tell you how much your friendship means, Earl. A Rolls-Royce wouldn't be enough, but... well, here."

Mike couldn't contain himself. "I got you a surprise, too—you're gonna be real surprised with mine."

Earl was emotional as he took the package. Opening it, he lifted out an Italian leather belt with a small silver buckle and the initial "M."

"Alex, this is beautiful... thank you."

"I hope it's not overly showy for a preacher. I chose a less ornate one. Your belts are looking pretty bad if I do say so."

Earl held the belt as if it were a precious jewel. "It was a perfect idea—will make me look more respectable. Wasn't necessary, you know..."

"Ready for me?" Mike asked.

Earl was becoming emotional. Mike's interruption was well-timed.

"Of course. I cannot imagine what you have for me."

Mike stood. "Miss Parker had us to write a paper about somebody important or special. I wrote about you. Miss Parker said it was real good and I made an E for Excellent... and it was okay that it was two pages. I saved it for your surprise. That part was Papa's idea."

"I'm honored you chose me, Mike."

Mike grinned, observing Earl intently for his reaction.

"My Important Person, Brother Earl Marshall."

He'd written of Earl helping people at church, his visiting those who were sick at home or in the hospital, and his lessons in church and *vacation school.*

"Then, he started to be Papa's friend. He helped us move two times and then let us live with him. He even helped us find a carpenter's shop to buy."

Mike looked up from his paper. "Miss Parker helped me spell *carpenter*—that's a hard word."

189

He continued. "Brother Earl likes everybody and talks to them about God. And to God about them. He's a real good man.

"He can't cook good, but he can do lots of other things, *and* he's funny. So, I picked Brother Earl as my important person because he's the nicest man I know, besides my Papa."

Earl had been near tears. He was relieved when Mike finished with his comical note about his cooking.

He rose from the table and wrapped his arms around Mike. "You've given me the best gift ever—I love you very much."

For a few minutes the kitchen was quiet, the men emotional and feeling awkward.

Breaking the silence, Alex announced, "Anybody hungry enough to eat my spaghetti?"

Earl and Mike chuckled, and conversation resumed as they enjoyed their last evening together as one household.

~ 19 ~

In their own place again, Mike and Alex were up early the first morning.

Mike couldn't wait to see Sneaker. "I need to tell him good morning and remind him I'll be here every morning *and* afternoon now."

As he finished breakfast, he heard the school bus in the distance and ran out the door, waving to Alex as he climbed the steps onto the bus.

Alex was anxious to make more progress in the shop. He was also expecting his first delivery from the lumber yard. He'd ordered enough wood to make a few free-standing cabinets and ornamental items.

Earl had ordered an ad to appear in the local newspaper.

The *County Herald* newspaper office was in Jessups, and published twice weekly. Almost everyone in the county subscribed. Other than the radio, it was their only source for local news.

The owner was Harry Bledsoe, who bemoaned the fact that real news in this county was sparse, at best. People liked reading about a runaway cow at the fair and seeing their names in print; he thrived on actual *news*.

When Aleksander Nordin came to Mt. Seasons, Harry knew about it the first day.

He thought of doing an article on *the Russian* at that time, but decided to wait a while. He had a hunch the story might be more interesting later.

Harry was intrigued a few months later when he heard this guy had bought the old Carpenter property. *This might be the time for an article... a Russian buying a local business. What kind of spin do I want to put on the story? What was Ilene Carpenter thinking to sell to such a person anyway?*

Truth was, Ilene had a low opinion of Harry Bledsoe. Though he'd called ahead, she let him wait on the porch longer than necessary. She allowed a photograph, stipulating it be printed small, and answered yes or no to his questions, except for speaking glowingly of Mr. Nordin, further irritating him.

Driving to the carpentry shop, Harry rather dreaded the interview.

Nordin was just what Harry expected, towering over him—looking down on *him*, indeed. He didn't get much of an interview. Nordin had answered a few questions but had volunteered nothing.

Alex had attempted to focus on the carpentry and his experience, showing Mr. Bledsoe the book of sample pictures, but he seemed uninterested, rather preferring personal queries. Alex became uncomfortable.

Ending the interview, Harry asked, "And just how do you plan to fill Mr. Carpenter's shoes and keep the excellent standards... being a foreigner and knowing *nothing* about our ways?"

"I will do my best," Alex replied, humbly.

Harry sneered. "I think I have what I need, Mr. Nordin."

There will be more to come from this source—I'm almost sure of it. I'll just keep my eyes and ears open.

The new ad was published with the photograph of the shop and a rather mundane paragraph about the business re-opening and included the small photograph of Ilene. Harry had chosen not to ask for or obtain a photograph of the Russian.

'Carpenter's Carpentry' Reopens with New Owner
(Picture of Shop)
Many of our local citizens will remember "Carpenter's Carpentry," located on Woodson's Road. The business, established by Martin Carpenter, has been closed since his death. His widow, Ilene Carpenter, recently sold the business. Mr. Aleksander Nordin, a Russian immigrant, will operate and manage the business. Mr. Nordin was asked about his intentions to keep to the high standards of the original owner, he stated he would do his best.
(picture of Mrs. Carpenter)

❀ ❀

The ringing phone actually jolted Alex somewhat. Could it be someone wanting carpentry work already?

"Mr. Nordin? This is Susan Millbrook, from church. Earl gave me your number.

"Several of us are bringing supper tonight." Anticipating his reluctance, she continued without giving him a chance to speak.

"Now, Mr. Nordin, this is something we *do*. We like doing it and we want to make your transition easier. We're *bringing* the food—just say thank you." She was laughing now. Recalling her friendly face, Alex had relaxed.

"Thank you, Susan. Please call me Alex. Mike will be thankful for some home cooking. You will be our first official visitors."

At six, Alex heard a car pulling in. Going to the door, he heard several more. Earl was in the mix, along with his parents and Anna.

Alex had never seen anything like it. About thirty people crowded into the shop, all laden with food and wrapped gifts.

"Surprise!" Susan shouted, others echoing the sentiment. "First we'll eat—then you can open gifts."

Alex was overwhelmed. They had brought paper plates, cups, everything needed for the food, gallons of tea, and seemed to have planned everything from uncovering the food and serving, to clean up. When they'd finished eating, he and Mike were told to sit, and were handed the gifts.

There were dishtowels, cookware, dishes, a clock, sheets, towels, and a big box of canned goods and staple items for the kitchen.

Anna excitedly handed him the last package. "This one is from me and Mother."

He took the rather large package as Mike jumped up beside him.

He removed the wrapping, and held up large pieces of fabric.

Pam Marshall explained, "They're window curtains, manly enough, we thought. Anna measured, and we made them together. They're for your living and kitchen areas to make it feel more like home."

"You can make your speech now," interjected Anna cheerfully.

Alex stood. Looking around at the crowd of generous people, he wasn't at all sure he could speak.

He cleared his throat, attempting to summon courage. "Thank you. I've never experienced such blessings. We journeyed from another country to this town in America because my sister… Blancha… was here. She loved this town, and I see *why*. I've had nothing to give, but you all welcomed us…" His voice was getting weaker with each word. "Thank you."

Everyone applauded, a few saying "Amen!" Laughter erupted, putting Alex back at ease.

He looked at Mike. "How about you, son? You want to say anything to these folks? I'm sure they'd love to hear from you."

Never at a loss for words, Mike looked around the room, then nearly shouted, "Thank you, everyone!"

The group laughed and applauded, with a few shouting, "Bravo, Mike!"

Enjoying the attention, he decided to expand. "I like the curtains… now our room will feel more like Aunt Blancha's house.

"I like all the things for the kitchen—and I *sure* liked the food. Thanks."

By eight, almost everyone had gone. Anna, Pam, and Bill Marshall, who had ridden with Earl, were the last to leave.

About to go out, Pam said, "We almost forgot to tell you, Anna will give you a call and come over to hang the curtains in the next few days."

Pam was a small-built woman and, though tall, it was still necessary to reach to hug him. It was a touching moment. "We love you. We hope everything works out well with the business, and that you'll have a happy home."

"Thank you again, Mrs. Marshall. Your family means a lot to us."

Anna was the last to leave. She hugged Mike tightly. "See you soon, buddy."

She took a step and stood on tiptoe to give an unprepared Alex a kiss on the cheek, saying, "*You*, too."

For once, Alex didn't falter. "I will look forward to it," he said, touching her hand lightly.

I'll ask her out when she's here to hang the curtains—a good time, without people around. Her parents and brother like me… a good start.

After they'd locked up and headed to bed, Mike commented, "Boy, they sure like us, don't they? This was a good surprise."

"They are good people, Mike. I hope life always surrounds you with them."

~ 20 ~

The shop, with its living area, began to feel like home. Sneaker was a good pet for Mike, as well as a fair watchdog. Within the week they got into a routine with school and work.

When Anna called to set up a time to hang the curtains, he'd offered to help. *When we finish, I'll ask her out. It should be the perfect time.*

"Alex, I am in charge of this project—you can *assist,* agreed?"

It went quickly, Anna demonstrating her expertise and Alex dutifully obeying. By the time they finished, they had grown more comfortable with each other, teasing and laughing.

He helped her gather her hammer, measuring tapes, and leftover nails.

"Anna… would you go out with me one evening next week? Mike has a couple of school activities which will give me some free evenings… well, early evenings. Do you have any time?"

Man! I didn't mean to make a speech out of it… just stammered on and on…

"Of course, Alex. I thought you would never ask," she replied jauntily.

❈ ❈

Driving home from church on Sunday, Alex remembered his promise to Ilene Carpenter. He turned down the road to her house.

Knowing she had sold the property and shop to them, as well as being the previous owner of Sneaker, Mike was eager to meet her.

After introducing them, Alex stood back to watch, completely entertained as Ilene and Mike talked a mile a minute at the same time, noting it didn't seem to bother either of them.

They visited for over an hour.

"Well, we need to get home. Mrs. Ilene, I'd be pleased if you'd stop by the shop some time. I believe you'll be happy to see the work we've done. Of course the business itself isn't off the ground yet. It will take time."

"Thank you, Alex, I will. Mike is a fine boy and I believe old Sneaker found himself just the right one. Feel free to drop by here anytime, but I'll be seeing you before long. I'd like it fine to see the place all cleaned up and alive again."

"Yes, ma'am."

Mike suddenly turned around, going to her to put his arms around her waist. "*Thank* you for Sneaker, Mrs. Carpenter, and I really like living where your husband worked."

Mike seemed to have knocked all her props out, her expression being one of the happiest he'd ever witnessed.

The free-standing cabinet was beginning to take shape and Alex was ready to decide on stain and design for the doors. Pleased with the machinery and tools, as well as the work he'd done, he was feeling good about life in general.

After taking a break for a sandwich and cup of coffee, the phone rang. He was still not accustomed to *having* a phone.

"Hello, *Carpenter's Carpentry*."

After the conversation, he stood for a minute… grinning as if basking in sunshine.

He quickly picked the receiver up again to phone Earl at the church office.

"Earl," Alex began excitedly, "I just received a call from a Mrs. Maynard saying she has a house in the *All Seasons* area. She and her husband live there during the winter and generally rent it during the summer months. It isn't yet rented, and they are in town getting it in shape.

She said she heard I did beautiful work and wants the doors on her kitchen cabinets repaired or replaced. She's going to leave it to my judgement. I have an appointment at her house in the morning. A neighbor of hers will also be there, who may also want me for a project."

He continued, amazed. "She said *beautiful work*, Earl. I wondered where she would hear about me and my work and, for a minute wondered if she might have heard about Mr. Carpenter himself, but I didn't ask. It sounds as if I might have my first job, possibly another one from a neighbor. My first job, Earl! I hope I make the right impression in the morning."

Earl was laughing, equally thrilled. "That's the most conversation I've ever heard from you. First, don't ask where she heard about your work.

"After all, many folks have seen the folder with photographs of the work you did in Russia. And… I may have put a picture or two on the church bulletin board, the before and after pictures of *my* cabinet."

"What?"

"In *addition*… word is, last night and this morning, Ilene has been phoning around town recommending you for carpentry work."

Alex was dumbfounded. *Last night and this morning… after we visited her.*

"Alex, I don't know if you've heard a saying we're fond of, 'Don't look a gift horse in the mouth.' It means just accept, don't question it. Go see Mrs. Maynard in the morning, be your own charming self, and get a signed contract."

"I *do* have a charming side, don't I? I'll let you know how it goes."

Before the work for Mrs. Maynard had been completed, Alex had three additional contracts lined up in the All Seasons area.

He was feeling useful again. They were building a good life, thanks to a lot of people. He thought he would soon be able to begin making payments to Earl.

They were attending church regularly and getting involved in the activities, as well as being involved in life in general in Mt. Seasons.

By the end of April, Alex and Anna had been out several times.

Time had passed quickly, Alex thinking surely no one had as many changes and ups and downs as he'd had in the past few months.

He had taken Anna out to eat on their first date, afterwards enjoying leisurely window-shopping on Main Street. She always asked about Mike—her consideration of him was one more thing that made their relationship so comfortable.

Anna cooked for them one evening, bringing bowls and pans of food to the shop, and a game to play afterwards.

Everything was delicious. After putting leftovers away and turning the radio to country music, they played, *Uncle Wiggly.* "This is one of my favorite board games," Anna declared. "I'll help you with the words, Mike."

Other evenings they had attended a local exhibit, gone for ice cream sodas, and even took pleasure in the local taxidermy display, termed *wildlife museum* in a town this size.

When a school friend invited Mike to spend the night, he called Anna to ask her to the picture show to see *The Egg and I.*

"Fred McMurray is one of my favorite actors," she chatted, "but I *especially* enjoyed the old couple, Ma and Pa Kettle, in this one." They had laughed throughout the show. Walking her to her door that night, she put her arms around him, kissed him on the cheek, then pulled back to look directly into his eyes, "I had a great time, as always, being with you."

"As I do with you," Alex agreed.

He leaned in to give her a proper good-night kiss.

"Good night, sweet Anna."

Driving home, he realized how much he enjoyed the brief feeling of his lips on hers, and the warmth of her in his arms. She was perfect.

But… why don't I feel I'm quite ready?

※ ※

Alex was staying busy. He determined a schedule during the school week. If working at a customer's home, he quit at 5:30 to be home by six.

Mike didn't mind getting the key from an abandoned bird house in the yard and coming in to the shop alone. He would give Sneaker a treat and play a while before beginning homework. If Alex was working in the shop, he'd stop work briefly to hear about Mike's day, and then continue until six.

Things were going smoothly.

"If everything in your life is going well, watch out for bumps in the road ahead." Alex had heard the saying, but was nevertheless unprepared.

Finally, a contract for new cabinets. The kitchen wasn't large, but Mr. Sims wanted to update. He looked through Alex's book of prior projects, including those in Russia. Alex had included other photographs from Mr. Carpenter's books, clarifying which were actually his work, and those he had not done, but could duplicate.

Mr. Sims turned the folder toward Alex. "I think this design would be perfect, elegant but not overdone, and maybe a little lighter stain. What do you think?"

"Good choice. The design on this one is one of the simpler to do, so will cut down on your cost considerably," replied Alex.

"This is why your business will continue to boom, Alex. Do you know why you received so many calls after beginning the work at Mrs. Maynard's?"

"Honestly, no. I'm thankful, and I've been a little afraid to question it. Folks around here are awfully nice, though. I figured they talked with each other and like dealing with a local business."

"May have been the initial reason Martha Maynard phoned you, but it could have ended there. She had no idea whether to tear out the old cabinets or repair, told me she expected any carpenter to suggest new ones. After all, the cabinets were the originals, over fifty years old and in bad shape.

"Yet, *you* told her it would be a shame to get rid of good, solid wood. You told her you could repair and refinish them for half the price. Correct?"

"Yes, sir. But I simply answered her question—my opinion of the best option."

"Well, don't change your way of doing business, it's the *real* reason you're doing well. You gave Mrs. Maynard an honest answer when you could have gone in the other direction and charged more. *That's* the word that got around... and the exceptional work."

"Thank you." After a pause, he continued. "I have one job to finish, but can begin work on your cabinets by the middle of next week.

"I believe I can have them installed in about two weeks."

So kind. I feel more at home in Mt. Seasons each day.

Alex and Anna had a date to attend a party Saturday night. Mike was invited to a birthday sleep-over.

Alex took Mike to Sammy's house. He'd carved a small truck as a birthday gift, and Mike had helped with the painting.

"Have a good time. Don't forget to mind his mother and thank them for the invitation."

"Yes, sir. I hope James is here," he called out, running up the walkway.

James had not yet moved—Bob J. had decided to wait until school was out to move his family to his new work location, and was able to be home most weekends.

Alex smiled thinking of Mike's happiness. He, too, was looking forward to the evening with Anna and a good group of church friends. It was to be a surprise party for Myra Greer.

He had no inkling of the surprises in store for *him*.

Myra was scheduled to be at the church fellowship building at six-thirty. Alex picked Anna up, and they arrived at six, as most others.

Anna had told him she'd purchased a necklace for Myra as their joint gift.

Before they arrived at the building, she signed the card and handed it to him.

Seeing their names together signaled something of a step in their relationship. A small step… but it suddenly loomed large——he didn't understand what had brought on his misgivings.

He looked at Anna as they entered the building. Really *looked* at her. She wore a slim-fitting emerald dress with matching earrings, which brought out the tiny green specks in her brown eyes.

I've never seen her without a smile, always full of joy. She usually wears something pink, but tonight I see it only in a touch of lipstick. She always looks great by any standards. With her loving, happy personality, she is quite a package, the whole *package I'd say.*

Get a grip, man, you could not be luckier!

I don't understand my own feelings. But… my heart seems to be holding back.

The group around them was discussing a house being burned to the ground, still smoldering, but gone. "No one was living in the house, but the owner was understandably upset—he lost everything."

Someone asked, "Whose house?" About the time he heard the answer, "Snider," they began whispering that Myra was about to open the door.

Could it be Blancha's house, the one owned by a Mr. Snider?

There was no time to ask. After the party began in earnest, he forgot it.

When the excitement of the surprise died down, they headed toward the heavily laden food table, with Myra commenting cheerfully, "Looks as if I'm forced to delay opening gifts until everyone eats." There was always an enormous spread, but tonight there was the addition of a huge birthday cake.

Alex spotted Earl coming toward him, with his arm around a lovely, auburn-haired woman. They must have just arrived. He had not seen the woman before, but she was stunning. The look in Earl's eyes, the happy face and wide smile, told him Earl thought so, too.

She looked a little younger than Earl, tall, maybe five-eight, wearing a dark gray skirt and soft blue sweater with a gold necklace and dangling gold earrings.

As they came closer, he saw that her hair was long, several inches below her shoulders, the auburn color being a perfect frame for her smooth, creamy skin, perfect red lips and eyes of blue. He felt engulfed in her eyes as she looked toward him.

Earl has finally found someone. Past time. But where, in this small town, could he have met her?

"Alex!" Earl exclaimed. "Hey, Anna, this surprise is for you as well. No scolding from my little sister—I didn't know she was coming in today."

So, she's from out of town.

The woman stood close to Earl as they laughed together. Anna joined in, smiling as she attempted a bit of a scolding look.

"Hey, Mary, if I'd known you were coming, I might have helped clean your house."

The women hugged tightly, talking and laughing at the same time.

When they drew apart, Earl turned to take the woman's arm again, looking toward Alex.

"Mary, this is Alex Nordin, the guy you've heard so much about."

"Alex, this is Mary… my other sister."

She took his hand, then reached up to hug him. "I feel we're already friends."

His sister. Not a girlfriend.

Sunday morning, Anna and Mary came into church together, and came to sit with them. "Mary doesn't like the front rows either," Anna whispered, indicating her parents on the second row.

Alex was well aware of sitting with the two best-looking women in church, probably the county. He wondered if people were speculating as to what they were doing with him—*he* certainly was. He couldn't help glancing toward Mary occasionally, feeling unreasonably drawn to her.

Mid-service, Anna's gaze caught his eye. He was dutifully "flustered from top to bottom," Blancha would have said, with one of her unusually Southern sentiments.

The attraction to Mary… more a curiosity… is due to my friendship with Earl and Anna, and the fact that I didn't know about her until recently. That's all it is.

After the service, a group decided to go for hamburgers.

Alex had thought he'd spend this afternoon with Mike, but Mike begged to go, and was being encouraged by several friends.

"All right, but you have reading and other things to catch up on when we get home."

At the restaurant, Earl sat with Alex. "Better get a seat by you before both my sisters claim it."

He suddenly appeared solemn. "Alex, I'm glad we have a minute alone."

"Is something wrong?"

Earl looked around. "I'll get to it. A man stopped by the church office Friday asking questions... about *you*. Not a local guy; maybe a detective, plain clothes—he flashed an ID, but I guess I wasn't focused. He had your address but had been by and you weren't there. His demeanor was all business, very serious, but wouldn't tell me anything. I wondered if you might have an idea of who he was, and wanted to forewarn you to expect him."

Earl's expression was questioning, as if Alex might have a simple explanation.

Alex was dumbfounded. "Police? Detective? I have no idea."

The conversation ended as others joined them. The lovely Mary sat across from him. He *was* curious, and wanted to get better acquainted. But he wasn't sure he even made polite conversation. Anna was by his side chattering away as usual. Mike was at a table with the other boys.

Alex had lost his appetite.

~ 21 ~

The school bus rumbled up the rough road Monday morning. Alex opened the door and gave Mike a hug before he ran to the road.

Something caught his eye… up the road. It wouldn't be easily noticed parked off the road, but he was sure it was an official car of some type. Alex felt sick, a foreboding he couldn't explain. Where he came from, any *official* meant trouble… regardless.

He walked back inside and poured a cup of coffee.

Will the man sit out there and observe my activities, or will he come to the door?

He needed to get to work. Thankfully, he had work lined up for a month and promises made for the next. But the knot in his stomach indicated a fear he'd not felt since he'd been in this country. Not even when Blancha died or when he was without a home or job.

When he heard nothing and finished his coffee and toast, he thought it best to get on with the work at hand. Work generally cleared his mind.

By eleven, he was well into the planning of his next order. After having lunch, he'd go over to the house on Green Valley to keep his appointment to finish the last of the hardware and collect final payment.

He'd been successful in pushing the earlier fear to the back of his mind as he worked.

As he gathered his supplies, Sneaker began to bark loudly.

Bam! Bam! Bam! Not a *knock* at the door, more of a pounding.

He'd never heard such authoritative barking from Sneaker.

The dog did not disappoint. He was standing up against the door barking and bearing his teeth as Alex opened the door. He realized the man must have leaned *over* the animal in order to knock, maintaining a cautious eye.

"It's okay, Sneaker. Back down, boy," Alex commanded. The dog's ears straight and stance firm, he turned his head momentarily to him, then back at the man who was holding out identification.

"I said it's okay, boy."

To the visitor, he asked, "May I help you?"

"I am Chief Autry," he answered, continuing to offer his identification Alex now recognized as a badge. But he was confused as his visitor wasn't in uniform.

"Are you a detective, or with the police here?"

"Are you Aleksander Nordin, formerly of Russia?"

"Yes."

"I'm from the FBI in Washington, the *Federal Bureau of Investigation*, Mr. Nordin. I have questions, which may take a while. May I come inside?"

"Yes, sir. I have an appointment this afternoon, though, and need to leave shortly."

"I need about an hour. I suggest you give it to me."

There was nothing in the man's demeanor to quell his fear.

He was not tall, certainly less than six feet. His skin was very light, pale in contrast to the dark, nearly black hair and eyes.

His clothing completed his harsh appearance. He wore a somber black suit, starched white shirt, plain black tie and black shoes.

From a distance, you might assume this man was a weakling. A closer look, his eyes, strong stance and movements contradicted the thought. This man's strength wasn't physical, but his determination and confidence, along with the authority in his voice, would be difficult to dismiss.

"I'll answer anything I can, but I need to make a phone call to let my customer know I will be delayed."

"I'd prefer we get to it, Mr. Nordin, with*out* delay."

Alex hesitated. Then he straightened to his full height and looked directly at him.

"Sir, if you will have a seat at the table, I'll be less than a minute. My customer is expecting me and I will phone to let her know there will be a delay."

Alex strode to the phone. The man continued to stand, perhaps wondering whether Alex might dash out the door.

As promised, Alex made his conversation brief.

Chief Autry... from Washington... the FBI.

Within a half hour, Chief Autry had presented a frightening scenario of a theft in Russia and a politically complicated involvement.

"Ten miniature portraits of a Russian emperor and empress and their family were stolen. They were painted by a well-known artist from the last century, which makes them extremely valuable monetarily *and* historically."

The Chief glared at Alex, expecting a reaction, but continued, his voice seeming to roar in the shop. "The paintings were shipped across country intended for the *Winter Palace,* a part of the large *State Hermitage Museum.*"

After emphasizing the Russian locations, Autry paused confidently.

"I imagine you are *familiar* with one of the most well-known places in Russia, though. One stop along the route was near *your* village, Mr. Nordin. We believe they disappeared somewhere close to that point and were later smuggled into the United States.

"If this proves to be true, the political turmoil will be great, as well as the punishment of the guilty party or parties."

Alex was horrified, but could not think why this man's search had led him here. He had no idea how to respond.

"Mr. Nordin, you would be wise to tell me anything you know about this—*any*thing."

Alex was growing queasy, trying to find his voice.

"I know *nothing* of this—honestly, Sir.

"I suppose you expect denial, but I have no idea what you are talking about. I've *never heard* of the paintings. Doesn't matter if they were known throughout Russia.

"I was, and *am* a working man. My family didn't visit museums. We barely left our village."

He knew the chief didn't believe a word and, in fact, was barely listening.

"Chief Autry, may I ask why you have come to *me?*"

"Mr. Nordin, we were given your name specifically, along with the name of your town and the street address. Turned out you no longer lived at that address—strangely enough, the *house* was even gone, almost the entire lot burned to a crisp... but it was easy to track you in this small town. Pity for *you* that you didn't keep moving."

Alex was growing more confused. "Who gave you my name?"

Chief Autry was shaking his head.

"If you checked up on me, Chief Autry, you must have found I was practically homeless shortly after my arrival—with a young son. I looked for work without success. Had it not been for the local townspeople, I'm not sure how we would have lived. Does that sound like someone with valuable paintings stashed away?"

Without acknowledging the question, Chief Autry said curtly, "Mr. Nordin, I can't arrest you now, but it may not be long. You'll be watched.

"It appears to me you are doing alright *now*." He scanned the shop and equipment as he spoke.

"If you try even to leave this *county*, you will make your problem much worse."

He'd been there less than an hour as he stood and began walking toward the door.

"For my part, I don't care what happens to you, Mr. Nordin. My information tells me you are a thief who has fooled a lot of people.

"I'm obligated, however, to tell you if you cooperate and give full information on the whereabouts of the paintings and names of anyone else involved, it might save your life. I'm also obliged to advise you to attain a lawyer."

He handed Alex a business card and was out the door. Alex heard Sneaker bark twice, as if reminding him he was still there.

He sat down, shaking. How could he fight back when he didn't know who to fight? Every single fact Chief Autry had presented was news to him. And he could think of no one who might have implicated him in such a thing.

Though Alex was in in bad shape mentally, the job on Green Valley Avenue in All Seasons had to be completed. Thankfully, only the hardware was needed. The lady of the house was busy and didn't have time to talk with him or stay in the kitchen as he worked.

If she had, she would most likely have observed his bloodshot eyes, and the fact that he couldn't communicate well.

She rushed in, repeated she loved it, and gave him the final payment. He quietly thanked her, and left.

He had no time to do a better job of pulling himself together. Mike was home when he returned, full of school news and, for once, didn't pick up on Alex's mood. He talked on and on about Miss Parker, a new girl who had moved here late in the school year, and Brother Earl's sister, Miss Mary.

"What do you mean, Mike, about Mary?"

"When we were in the library today, she was there talking to the librarian, Miss Thornton. Most of the kids call her 'Miss Thorn' because she's all prickly—fussing at kids all the time and never smiling. I *know* it's not nice, Papa, but she really is that way and it's funny.

"You should have seen her when Janie Johnson bumped into the book cart the other day. It was stacked way high with books and almost all of them fell... and everybody yelled because they didn't know what happened. Books were everywhere and Janie was in the floor crying... Miss Thorn was running all over the place yelling."

"It sounds as if Miss *Thornton* has a difficult job attempting to keep order. But you said you saw Brother Earl's sister, Mary?"

"Yes, she came over to talk to me and said Brother Earl told her a lot about us—me, *and* you, She was there to see Miss Thorn... Thornton, about maybe helping get more books donated to the library. I really like her. She's nice... and, I like her kinda-red hair.

"She said she'd be seeing us at church a lot. She sure smelled good, too."

Alex agreed with him about Miss Mary.

"You know, Mike, I'm pretty tired this evening. I was thinking about going to bed a little earlier and listening to the radio for a while."

Mike considered it a treat to listen to the radio after they'd turned out the lights. After an early supper, they climbed into bed together to listen to the *Grand Ole Opry*.

❊ ❊

The following morning, Alex worked on cabinets for Mr. Sims. He had prayed for facts to come to light, and authorities to realize he'd had nothing to do with the theft or smuggling. He didn't think he should get a lawyer when he had nothing to tell anyone. He could only continue with his work.

He'd barely begun when there was a knock on the door. Strange, he hadn't heard Sneaker. Now he heard him bark halfheartedly a couple of times, almost as though he didn't mean it, nothing like the day before.

He opened the door to find Mary Marshall leaning down patting the contented dog.

"Good morning, Alex. Remember me?

"Hope I'm not interrupting too much, but I've been curious about your place. I heard much of the ongoing saga of the shop purchase before we met."

He was surprised at her showing up unannounced.

"Sure, come in. Hope you have an idea of what to expect from a working carpenter's shop."

As he held the door open, she took a step inside.

He watched her every move, fascinated.

Walking slowly around, she seemed surprised, "Looks clean for a work area."

"I guess I'm neat, for a guy—I work better when I clean the mess as I go. I don't know how to show you around—you can pretty much see everything from where you're standing," he laughed. "Except for our room at the back, the one we call home."

Mary turned to face him. "Want the truth, Alex Nordin?"

"Generally."

"Oh, it's not sinister," she laughed. "I told the truth. I just didn't add I wanted to get to know you without my brother, sister and parents around… and I had nothing else to do."

"Would you like a cup of coffee? I make lousy coffee, or so your brother says. I don't cook much so have only cookies from the grocery… they might help the coffee go down easier, though."

She sat at the kitchen table. "Thank you. *You'll* learn right away I'm not like Anna. I cook, but rarely bake. I was well aware a proper woman would have brought a plate of home-baked goods, but I didn't want to start off with false pretenses," she grinned.

She was easy to talk with, and didn't seem to stand on ceremony.

She knew about the death of his wife, and asked how Mike was dealing with not having a mother. She didn't dwell on the subject, changing the topic by asking about his work progress.

"This shop is a dream-come-true for me—all due to Earl, as I'm sure you know.

"It's going very well, though still in early stages. It will be years before he sees a profit, but I'll do what it takes to keep him from ever regretting it."

He paused, looking at her before asking, "Tell me about you, Mary."

"I grew up here in Mt. Seasons. Life in a small town is great for a child; I can't remember a time of unhappiness. But when I studied other parts of our country and the world, I wanted to see some of them. Most of my classmates said the same, but the vision never faded for me. I was fortunate, blessed, to have accomplished that dream.

"I've been able to travel to many different states. I marvel at the different beauties in each one, and the diverse lifestyles—yet see how much we all have in common. I've only been out of the country once, though. I traveled with friends to Italy on vacation."

She paused. "I've loved living in Chicago, seeing other places, and meeting so many people. But I'm not sure I want it for a lifetime.

"Home just feels good. I suppose you could say I'm at a crossroads.

"I'm in a position of being able to choose whether to stay in Chicago, move to another city, or return here and possibly open a dress shop nearby.

"I have good contacts to make it work. I've taken a leave of absence from my job to give me time to consider my options."

She smiled and continued, "I've talked too much about myself. I'll leave and let you return to your work. I'm sorry for the interruption."

With a mischievous twinkle in her eyes, she added, "Well, not so much that I'd take back the time getting to know you."

He accompanied her to the porch. "Alex, thank you for showing me around."

"My pleasure, Mary."

"Alex, would you have time to come by *my* house one day? I have a few areas I'm considering remodeling, actually repairs, I suppose, but I need advice. Do you have any time available this week?"

"Of course. I'll have to let you know later about an exact time."

"Good. Phone to let me know when to be home. Any day or time, really, I'm working from home only a little, and have *no* social schedule."

He watched as she walked down the steps to her car, turning to wave before she drove away.

She'd been here about an hour, which seemed five minutes. He'd felt immediately at ease with her—unsure of the reason.

Certainly they had nothing in common. She was a highly educated business woman, owned property, and had traveled extensively.

She takes my breath away... which shouldn't be... and why do I continue to stand here on the porch gazing at the road?

He sighed, trying to clear his thoughts, but returned to work with renewed energy.

~ 22 ~

Mike's first few minutes after school were always spent with Sneaker. The dog ran out to sit by the road as soon as he heard the bus in the distance. After Mike checked the water bowl, he hurried through the shop, shouting, "Hi Papa, I'm home!" then out again with a snack for his pal.

Only after this routine did he return to tell Alex about his day.

Today he seemed to want to talk, returning inside to sit on the tall stool as Alex sanded a piece of wood.

"Let me wash my hands, Mike. Then we can sit down with a glass of milk for a few minutes. Got something on your mind?"

"Did I tell you Miss Parker is getting married? She told us she will be *Mrs. Guthrie* next year. Her husband... when they get married... is a dentist. He seemed nice, Papa. He came one morning and she *introducted* us to him.

"Everyone in the class is invited to their wedding in July at a big church in Jessups... she doesn't want any of us to get her a present... she said it would be enough just to see all of us there..."

He had to pay attention when Mike began sharing news. But he thought he was about to ask whether he could attend the wedding.

"Papa, Miss Parker is real nice."

"You've liked her from the first—she's a good teacher."

"She dresses nice and smells good."

Now, Alex wasn't at *all* sure where this conversation was going.

"Papa? Miss Parker said some of the ladies are giving her a shower next week... she seemed glad. Why are other people giving her a shower?"

Just when Alex thought he understood English, even Southern English, something came up he didn't understand—a word, custom, even a way of viewing life.

"Well, Mike, I don't quite know. I guess this is a question for you to ask Anna... or Mary... maybe it's a custom here for brides."

"Okay. It just sounds... well, funny. I didn't want everybody to know I didn't understand about showers for ladies, though, so I just acted glad."

Alex got back to work and Mike settled down to homework. A half hour later, they heard a car in the driveway. Seeing Ilene Carpenter as he looked out, he hurried to open the door and step out onto the porch. Mike followed closely behind.

"Welcome, Mrs. Ilene. Glad you stopped by."

"Right happy to be here, Alex. Even from the driveway, I could see you've done a lot of work. I have driven past a few times, as you probably guessed. Hello, Mike—and there's old Sneaker coming to greet me, looking mighty happy."

Alex hurried down the steps to escort her around the outside of the shop first.

Mike became involved with throwing a stick for Sneaker.

Entering the shop, Alex waited as Ilene wandered around. She looked closely at the equipment, all of which had been cleaned, the cabinets in progress for Mr. Sims, and the kitchen area. She appeared pleased.

He walked toward their living area, opened the door and motioned her inside.

"I'd like you to see *this*—I think it's just right... for two guys, anyway, and not unlike where we lived in Russia."

Again, she walked unhurriedly around the room, touching the curtains, the full-size bed, the smaller one, and a lone overstuffed chair. She paused at the desk of her late husband, appearing emotional.

Alex said kindly, "It's a great old desk—you know, if you'd like to *have* it now, I'll move it to your house."

She looked at him, recovering. "No... it's where it belongs. Everything looks great, a good place to live and work. I'm proud for you. My husband... Martin... would've been real pleased to see it like this."

"Thank you, ma'am."

Mike suddenly burst back inside as they came from the living area back into the shop.

"Mrs. Carpenter, you're a lady, aren't you?"

They looked at him questioningly. Alex was about to caution him, but there was no stopping the roll he was on.

"I asked Papa and he didn't know and he told me to ask a woman and you're one and I bet you know all about lady-things."

"...Mike," began Alex. To no avail.

"Mrs. Carpenter, you know my teacher Miss Parker... well, she was an un-plucked bloom or something, but now she's gonna get married so I guess she's plucked now, but she told us the ladies are going to give her a shower, maybe more than one..."

Mike took a short breath. "I didn't know why they'd have to do it *for* her... she's clean and smells good every day at school... Mrs. Carpenter, why do other ladies hafta give her a shower before she can get married?"

Alex was beyond embarrassed, but Ilene burst into an uproarious laughter, tears rolling down her cheeks, so he smiled and decided it best to let the conversation take its course.

Mike wasn't sure what was so funny, but since he'd already thought the idea of ladies giving one another a shower was strange, he joined in.

When Ilene caught her breath and calmed herself, she sat in one of the kitchen chairs.

"Come here, Mike." Obediently he came to sit beside her.

"Honey, I gotta come visit you more often. You make me feel good." Mike grinned.

She looked at Alex before turning back to Mike. "I do know about these things, and it *does* sound strange, funny even, when you *say* it. But it's not the way it sounds."

"You ever heard of 'showers of blessings' in church, or being 'showered' with compliments?"

Mike frowned, shaking his head.

"Well, let's see… sometimes when it rains, but not hard, we say we had a shower.

"But if it's a hard rain we might say it poured, right?" Mike nodded.

"Don't think I'm doing a very good job explaining, but what your teacher meant was the ladies were giving her a kind of party, a different kind for a bride.

"It's called a shower, actually a 'bridal shower,' because they 'shower' her with gifts—just means there's lots of them—gifts like dishes, tablecloths, sheets and pillow cases, anything to use in the house."

"And curtains?" asked Mike.

"Could be."

"People came to give us a party after we moved, with lots of gifts for our kitchen, even curtains. They said it was kinda a welcome home, but that's like a shower too, isn't it?"

"You're right, Mike. We seem to have lots of names for different times and things, and maybe they don't all make sense to you. Sometimes not to us either, we've just grown accustomed to doing or saying it that way.

"When a lady is going to have a baby, they give her a baby shower before the baby is born. They give gifts for the baby—clothes, little gowns, diapers, diaper pins, bottles, anything for a baby. So I 'spose a shower does have several meanings.

"If you haven't already heard it in church, you will some time—they'll say there are 'showers of blessings,' meaning God sends lots of them. If I say I 'showered' her with flowers, it means I gave lots of them. Does this make more sense now, Mike?"

Looking to the side, she asked, "Alex?"

"Yes, ma'am," they answered. Alex adding, "Thank you."

"Well, I 'spect I've been here too long, but I might be coming by more often... just in case you have more lady-questions, Mike."

Mike finished his homework while Alex worked another hour.

Later, as he lay in bed, Alex thought what a full day it had been. It began terribly... with Chief Autry's visit and accusations. Then the *delightful* visit from Mary Marshall, and ending the day pleasantly with Ilene.

Lord," he prayed, "life has been so good this past month. Please help us. I don't know how to stop this trouble about a theft in Russia. Please, *please* show the authorities the right answers."

The visit from Chief Autry was foremost in Alex's mind the next morning. He had to talk with Earl.

This explained the visit and questioning Earl told him about. It didn't explain why authorities suspected *him*, but apparently he was their number-one suspect... of theft and smuggling! He could not absorb it.

He couldn't talk about it over the phone. Even with a private line, Earl had emphasized conversations weren't guaranteed private.

This was far too personal, anyway. He decided to go to the hardware store to pick up an order. By that time Earl should be in the church office. His stopping by there would be nothing out of the ordinary.

"No, Alex, Brother Marshall is actually out of town for two weeks. He left early this morning for a seminar in Nashville for a week. When he leaves Nashville, he will be going to speak at a revival in Clarksville, near there. I have phone numbers in case of an emergency, but it would probably take a while to track him down."

"No. Thank you, Edna. It'll wait."

Two weeks? A long time before I can share this bombshell. I could not possibly talk with anyone else.

Pulling out from the church, he had an idea. Spotting a phone booth, he stopped to make his call. As he climbed back into the truck, he felt pleased with his new destination.

Mary opened the door before he reached the porch

"I'm so glad you phoned. I'm brewing a fresh pot of coffee. I *do* make good coffee," she laughed. "Lucky for you, I stopped at the bakery yesterday."

They walked through the house room-by-room as she showed him projects she had in mind. Refinishing the solid oak kitchen cabinets would be the biggest job.

Additionally, there were two bedroom doors that needed to be replaced, some painting, and other smaller repairs.

"Oh, I almost forgot one of my major concerns—the front door."

Having lived in the house with Earl, he was familiar with it, and knew about the door. I, too, was solid oak, six or eight inches thick. Obviously it had been beautiful when built, but time had brought hairline cracks, peeling, and obvious holes from perhaps a hanging wreath, children, or a myriad of other possibilities.

"This can be refinished and repaired, Mary. The holes can be filled in. I'll sand the whole thing down and re-stain it. The hardware is unique and still perfect. When it's all cleaned and has a layer of protection on it, the door will be gorgeous again."

In spite of taking detailed notes, they finished in barely thirty minutes. She brought the coffee and Danish to the living room and they began talking. Two hours later, he glanced at the clock.

"I really have to go," he said. "I had no idea I'd been here so long. I'll get the figures together and talk with you sometime next week. I have a job to finish before I obligate to anything else."

"Sure. Call when you get the information together. I'll take you to my favorite spot to eat and we'll go over it afterwards. Sound okay?"

The way she'd put it didn't leave much choice, exactly what she intended.

❈ ❈

There was a visiting speaker Sunday morning. Just before the service began, Anna leaned over to whisper, "Earl said he forgot to tell you he'd be out of town."

Afterwards, Alex asked about Earl's trip.

"Well, I left his house Sunday night about ten. "The three of us sat around all evening catching up on family news. I was leaving when he realized he hadn't mentioned the trip to you. Plans weren't final until a couple of days before. He laughed and said he knew you could handle the shop without him." Anna was smiling, moving her hands vigorously in an attempt to mimic Earl's voice and dry humor.

Another week. This knowledge is eating me alive.

The following week Alex completed installing Mr. Sims cabinets.

"Here's the balance due, Alex. Beautiful work. If you ever need a reference, I'll be happy to furnish one, but I doubt you'll need it around here."

"Thank you. The choice you made in size and design was good, just right for this kitchen." The two men shook hands as he left.

He stopped to pick up a loaf of bread and sandwich meat at the local deli. It was family-owned and managed, and they were nice folks.

With a few small tables at one side, they seemed to do a steady business preparing made-to-order sandwiches for a quick lunch.

Opening the door, he saw Mary.

The effect of seeing her was… something he didn't understand, and couldn't have described.

He didn't even know her that well, having seen her only a few times.

Having heard the bell as the door opened, she turned and waved him over to the table. Her open smile made him feel she was happier to see him than anyone else in the world.

She was dressed casually in loose-fitting tan slacks and a lightweight peach-colored sweater. The sweater perfectly complimented her auburn hair, which was pulled back loosely with a large barrette at the nape of her neck.

After a few comments about the weather, and noticing she had only a coffee cup on the table, he found himself asking if she had time for a sandwich.

"I have all day—I'd love to have lunch with you," she replied.

Why didn't I just speak and go on my way? What's wrong with me?

They ordered sandwiches and Cokes, and began talking.

"What about a piece of one of their home-baked pies?" he asked. They decided on the coconut.

She was easy to talk with. She asked about the difficulty of adjusting to another country and he found himself talking about growing up in Russia and the differences between the countries, the terrain, weather and lifestyle.

Finishing the pie, they decided on another cup of coffee. Still, he wasn't ready to leave.

But this was as far as anyone could stretch a simple lunch.

~ 23 ~

After the impromptu lunch with Mary, Alex worked up figures for the work she wanted done.

The following morning after Mike left for school, he looked through wood samples and stains and selected a few for her to look over. As he dialed the phone, he wondered whether she would have the same enthusiasm today.

"Good morning. It's Alex. I'm at the shop and have figures for the work you were interested in having done. I can give you a good estimate and have stain and paint samples for you to look over; just wanted to schedule a good time for you. I do have appointments all day tomorrow, but that's my only full day, so whatever works otherwise."

"Alex, I told you I have no social life. I'm working on a few projects from home, but I make my own schedule. Could you pick me up in about an hour? I told you I wanted to take you somewhere. We'll eat and discuss business afterward… if we have time."

She's good at this, telling you what to do and leaving no open ends for discussion.

He didn't mind at all.

"Give me an hour and a half and you've got a date, okay?"

Why did I call it a date? Well, it's already out there—maybe she won't think anything about it.

When he drove up, she was waiting on the porch. Giving him a wave, she skipped hurriedly down the steps to the truck. She had a large basket with her, which she tossed into the back of the truck.

Directing him to a little country store just outside of town, she asked him to wait as she took the basket inside. Returning, the basket had been filled and was covered with brightly colored napkins.

"Okay, we have our lunch. Now drive down this street one block. There's a dirt road off to the right. Turn there."

"Not telling me more?" he asked. She responded by cocking her head as she smiled at him, her smile having an overwhelming effect.

Didn't Anna's smile have an effect as well?

After driving a few minutes on the dirt road, she said, "Roll down your window," as she did the same.

He began to hear and smell the freshness of rushing water and knew there must be a creek nearby—then he saw the waterfall. It wasn't especially big, but the combination of the natural boulders below and the surrounding wild ferns and flowers, its beauty nearly took his breath away.

"Our destination?"

Looking delighted and satisfied, she replied, gesturing with her hands. "This is it. Park to the left of those trees. I have the basket, so grab the blanket from the back of the truck."

There was only one picnic table, but numerous nice spots for a picnic.

From this vantage point, with the sun glistening on the water, the fresh smell of surrounding grass, and the water splashing below, Alex couldn't think of a better place to be.

She covered the table with a cloth and placed the basket of food and paper goods on it. "Let's take the blanket closer to the falls," she said, as she put her arm through his.

The path was short and only slightly overgrown.

Mighty oaks and tall pine trees towered over the area, moving only slightly with the gentle breeze, as a multitude of wild flowers bloomed below. The relaxing silence was broken only by the sound of the waterfall. Alex noticed one fallen tree, an enormous oak evidently broken by the strength of a storm years before.

Another gentle, pleasant breeze must have turned into a ferocious storm to have downed a tree such as that.

"Isn't this a great place?"

He smiled, taking in the view. "It's beautiful. I love being surrounded by nature."

She took the blanket from him. "Let's spread it here."

They sat quietly on the blanket looking at the water. The day was chillier than usual for the time of year and the area was mostly shaded. They'd worn light jackets, but Mary sat close and leaned slightly against his shoulder.

Unwillingly, Anna came to his mind. *What would she think of this scene? Not hard to figure out, she wouldn't like it. But I feel so content… here… with Mary.*

After a few minutes, Mary stood and stretched as she looked around, then put her hands on her hips.

"Stay put," she said, motioning with her hand. "I'm going to bring the basket here. I like the blanket much better than sitting at the table."

Returning, she brought out fresh baked bread from the basket, roasted chicken, fruit salad, and sliced goat cheese, all from the deli. From the last bag, she pulled out a small bottle of wine and two glasses.

"Everything was freshly made this morning... except for the wine, of course.

"I drink it rarely. but thought it would be just right with these foods and this beautiful place."

"Sounds good—I enjoy a good glass of wine occasionally. Many people in Russia consider it a part of the meal, but I somehow never developed the preference."

They spent several hours talking. She talked about her parents, as well as Anna and Earl.

He told her more about his parents, and Blancha, whom he sorely missed. He mentioned Vera briefly, and shared more about the years after Mike's birth.

He realized he was comfortable sharing things he'd been reluctant to talk about for years.

She put the foods away as he folded the blanket. "Mary, we have not once discussed the work you wanted done at your house. Are you actually interested in doing it?"

"Yes, of course." She grinned, "Probably wouldn't have thought about it for another five years, though, if I hadn't laid my eyes on the man I wanted… to do the work."

Alex felt himself blushing. *Blast!*

Only slightly recovered, he paused a minute before replying. "Do you want me to leave the figures with you to look over?"

"You can give them to me, but I *want* you to do the work. I have no need to discuss the figures; I know they're fair." As they climbed into the truck, she added, "You did mention choices of stain and paints, though. Show them to me and tell me what you think."

He complied, giving his opinion, and she concurred, all taking about five minutes.

"Start anytime you want, Alex, but do any other jobs first. I'm in no hurry and I don't want you to lose other contracts. Besides, when you're at *my* house, I'd prefer you not to feel rushed."

They drove in comfortable silence back to her house. He got out, going around the truck to open her door, and helped gather the basket of leftovers and the blanket.

Walking her to the porch, he said, "It was a *very* nice day, Mary. I enjoyed it."

She opened the front door. "So did I. Would you take everything to the kitchen?"

She walked with him, holding the half bottle of wine. After they put everything on the table, she turned to him, reached up and wrapped her arms around his neck. Standing on her tiptoes, she kissed him.

His response was immediate and involuntary, leaning down slightly to wrap his arms around.

He pulled her closer, opening his lips to cover hers. Feeling her warmth and the sweetness of her in his arms, nothing was on his mind but this moment and the passion he'd thought was gone. Warmth and desire surged through him, and it was apparent neither wanted to slow down.

"Rinnnng… rinnnnnng… rinnnnnnng!" The phone. Rinnnng… rinnnnnng… rinnnnnnng!" Again and again… for an eternity… *Why didn't they hang up?*

Mary reluctantly pulled away, sighing. She walked to the phone, answering in a somewhat hoarse voice, and keeping the conversation short. Alex's emotions were in turmoil, his body sympathizing.

As she replaced the receiver, she turned to him. "I had to answer it. I'm sure you know I didn't want to."

Alex nodded, looking at her with longing.

She continued, looking into his eyes as she spoke quietly, "Before Earl left, he told me he was expecting someone to call here to confirm dates for a conference… later in the year, but it was important that he confirm his attendance."

He took a few steps to her, leaned in to kiss her again, but this time less urgently. He had his hands on her shoulders, not wanting to pull away at all. He wanted to hold on to the feeling of the embrace, the warmth of her body, and the feelings stirring within.

But, he pulled back.

"I need to go, Mary. We need time. To think."

"I have strong feelings for you, Alex. Obviously."

"I have feelings for you, too—more than I should. We've known each other such a short time."

"Anna. It's Anna, isn't it?"

"Yes. We have no agreement, but we've been dating and becoming closer. This isn't the way I do things, seeing two women at the same time, certainly not sisters. Anna will be hurt, I'm sure. And she's a good friend."

"A *friend*, Alex. That's what I saw between you two. At least from your side. I'll tell you something… when I came to your place that day, it was to get better acquainted, to see whether I thought you were right for my little sister."

Mary paused briefly. "Really. She and I are only two years apart, but she's still the youngest. I'd been with you only a short while before fearing I was checking you out for myself.

"Then I decided I was all right with it-- *because* I realized I'd seen no more than friendship in your eyes for Anna. If my feelings for you turned out to be mutual, then it was the right thing. I think it's turning out to be mutual."

She looked at him questioningly.

"You're right. But we still need to take a step back."

Near the front door now, he looked at the clock. "It's nearly five and I always make a point of being home by five.

"I have a child, Mary. You know that, of course, but it's something for you to think about.

"He's a big part of my life. Right now I'd say he *is* my life."

As he put his hand on the door knob, she exclaimed, "Oh, wait... I have food for you to take." She hurried back to the kitchen and returned with several bags.

"I ordered more than we'd need with this in mind. It'll be plenty for supper for the two of you. Tell Mike I said hello. He's a great kid—and you are a great father. It's one of the traits I admire and... like... about you."

"Thanks. I'll tell him you sent the food and a hello."

He opened the door. As they stepped onto the porch, he turned to her. He wanted to kiss her again, as she was well aware.

But as he began to turn back toward the steps, she took his arm, stood again on her tiptoes and kissed his cheek.

"Good night, Alex. Sweet dreams."

~ 24 ~

The Marshall Family

Earl, Mary and Anna grew up in Mt. Seasons with their parents, Pam and Bill Marshall, who had lived there all their married life.

Bill was a salesman. Pam enjoyed being a full-time wife and mother. They made a striking couple, both tall, though Bill claimed at least two inches on his wife.

In another view, they were a study in contrast. Bill's eyes and hair were dark brown, and he tanned quickly in summer. Though he had strong beliefs, he was a quiet-spoken man, choosing to listen until there was a definitive reason to speak, the "strong silent type," Pam called him teasingly.

Pam was an outgoing, bubbly blonde, with light blue eyes, and fair skin, which had a tendency to freckle.

Pam knew people thought she made the decisions in their marriage. Neither she nor Bill cared one wit—but it was Bill to whom she acquiesced, gladly and lovingly.

He teased her about being a full-time volunteer—for the PTA, food programs, and home-room mother for three classes.

They were a happy family, and lived comfortably.

When Earl began high school, he expressed the desire for a college education to his father.

"Son, there's no way my income could be stretched to pay for further education. If you're serious, I advise a part-time job, a good idea in any case. And keep up your grades."

Earl earned a small scholarship to the community college in Jessups, and continued to work as much as possible. Finally sure of his desire to be a minister, he earned a scholarship through the church to enroll in divinity school.

Though Mary had a happy childhood, she wanted to see more of the world.

Females were not expected to have college ambitions. In time, though, she followed in her brother's footsteps to the community college.

Mary attended two years, managing to also work almost forty hours a week in a dress shop. After two years, she won a scholarship to a design school in Chicago, Illinois, and was on her way to fulfilling her dreams.

Bill and Pam were not happy to see Mary move to a big city, but were further dismayed when Anna graduated from high school and received a partial scholarship to a nearby teacher's college.

"Whatever happened to young ladies who finished high school, and began planning a wedding and family?" Bill asked, frustrated.

After Anna's first year at the teacher's college, Pam was diagnosed with cancer.

Anna volunteered to postpone her education.

She would be with her mother for surgery, doctors' appointments and treatments. Bill's keeping his job and insurance was critical.

No one said it aloud, but Anna knew she would postpone everything until her mother was well… or until the end.

Two years later, Pam Marshall was declared cured.

The family had quite a celebration.

Anna could now happily continue her education.

While home, Mary heard of a local house for sale. She'd remained in Chicago with a job including travel, but it had not taken long to think she might want to return to Mt. Seasons someday.

God works in mysterious ways.

Earl, too, returned home for the family celebration.

Local church board members spoke with him about his ministry in the large Birmingham, Alabama church, and offered him the ministerial position in Mt. Seasons.

Earl had actually been contemplating a move, though never dreaming of returning home.

Therefore… Earl returned to Mt. Seasons to live in the house his sister had purchased.

~ 25 ~

A loud commotion began the morning—
Sneaker barking as someone knocking at the
door nervously attempted to calm the dog.

Mike was barely out of bed, and Alex had
just put on a shirt and started a pot of coffee.

"Who's at the door?"

"Don't know, Mike, going to see." He
opened the door to a man in a uniform—neither
of which he recognized. He did notice, though,
Sneaker had barked to announce the arrival of a
stranger and was positioned by the door, but
lacked the aggression shown Chief Autry just a
few days before.

"May I help you?"

"Are you Aleksander Nordin?"

"Yes. And you?"

The man held out an official ID and badge,
saying, "My name is Aaron Hall. I'm an
investigator for the County Fire Department.
I'd like to talk with you."

"Well, Mr. Hall, it's pretty early. Come in,
but I have to get my son's breakfast, and get
him ready for school before I can talk. I
haven't had coffee yet either, and I don't
handle my day well before coffee."

"Understood. I honestly thought it would
take me longer to get here and find your place,
so I apologize for the early hour. Once you get
the coffee going, could I pour myself a cup?"

Mike came running from the bedroom,
dressed and looking for a book.

"Hey, Papa, I can't find my spelling book. It's red. I had it in the bed last night I think... you were helping me with my words, but it's not in there...did I put it in here? No, it's not on the table... have you seen it? Oh, hi, Mister. You wanting new cabinets? Papa does the best anywhere."

Mr. Hall stood. "Good morning, young man. I just need to talk to your Daddy a while. But I'm going to have a cup of coffee while ya'll finish breakfast and you get off to school."

"Okay... sir. If you see a red book, I'm looking for it. I'm having a spelling test today and I'll lose five points if I don't have my book."

Mike sat to eat his cereal, but continued to look around as he ate. Alex walked back to the bedroom, then out again into the shop area. Finally he walked to the kitchen counter and lifted a dishcloth, revealing the book.

"Here it is. You came back in here for water last night. Guess you had the book in your hand. Anyway, problem solved." Looking at the clock, he said, "Bus here in five minutes. You gotta get out the door."

"Yes, sir." Alex leaned down to give him a hug. Mike returned the hug and added a wet kiss on his cheek.

"Bye. Love you!" he yelled as he ran out the door.

"Okay, Mr. Hall, all yours." Alex turned to see the man smiling toward the door.

"Nice boy. Don't think I'll need much time. I hope you have answers for me. Maybe we can do this over another cup of coffee."

"Sure."

Alex poured the coffee and sat at the table.

The investigator was pleasant. But he was to deliver another shock to Alex's world.

"Mr. Nordin, were you aware the house you lived in with your sister, Blancha Aldredge, had burned to the ground?"

"No."

"The house was owned by Abraham Snider, better known as Abe. Thing is, the fire has been determined to be arson. Where were you on the evening of Saturday, May third?"

The night I met Mary. Why would that be what I thought of first?

"I know exactly where I was. And I *did* hear about a house burning, but didn't realize it was the one Mr. Snider owned, and I'd lived in."

Something like a shockwave went through Alex's body at that moment as he suddenly recalled Chief Autry's conversation... *the house was even gone, almost the entire lot burned to a crisp* It had not even registered with him at the time! What was wrong with him?

His speech faltering, he continued, "I heard about it... at a church birthday party. I picked up my date, and we arrived at the church at six o'clock. We were there all evening, so that should clear that up."

My date was Anna.

"Sorry, Mr. Nordin—won't do.

"We think the fire was set somewhere between five and five thirty. It was a slow start, probably been smoldering a while before bursting into flames and engulfing the house. Gave you plenty of time."

"Not only would I *not* do anything like that, I had no reason to do it."

"Mr. Snider says you do."

The investigator flipped pages in a notepad. "Snider said you're Russian, and came to Mt. Seasons with a chip on your shoulder. He stated you were very angry when you had to move out of the house after your sister died. Told me he felt bad about it, but you were quite nasty to him and promised he would be sorry. He said you made remarks about having plenty of money soon, and you'd *show* him, but he didn't know what you meant."

Incredulous, Alex hardly knew how to respond. He stood, walked to the window, then back.

"Mr. Hall, my word may mean nothing to you or anyone else, but there's only one thing true in his entire statement—I *am* Russian."

"What else can you tell me, Mr. Nordin?"

"Of course I was upset at his asking us to move… on the actual *day* of my sister's burial. He didn't ask, he told us we had to move, and gave me a short deadline. I was upset and maybe a little angry, yes. He was *not* sorry, I can assure you. He was very rude. But I wasn't ugly to him and I said none of the things he told you.

"I had no idea of where I was going from there and had no job, so I couldn't have 'shown' him anything."

Mr. Hall stood and moved toward the door.

"That's all for now, Mr. Nordin. I'd like to think this would be the end of it, but the investigation is just getting started. And Mr. Snider is talking loudly to a lot of people about your being responsible."

Alex opened the door for him.

"Good day, Mr. Nordin."

Good day?

If things continued as they were, he could foresee having his papers revoked and being sent back to Russia. Life would be over for him and far from as good for Mike.

※ ※

The morning after the fire inspector left, Alex attempted to absorb everything that was happening. He felt he was watching a drama from afar—not happening to him.

It can't be me *accused of such horrible actions.*

Unsure how long he sat staring ahead, seeing nothing, he eventually pulled himself from the chair. He still knew nothing he could do. He would continue his work—what other choice was there?

The task at hand was building new kitchen cabinets for a Mrs. Bennett, who lived in town. He'd done the measuring weeks before, giving her an estimate and an approximate start date.

Paying the deposit, she'd exclaimed, "I am *thrilled* to get you, Mr. Nordin.

"I've seen your exquisite work in several of my friends' houses."

He sat at the table now with a third cup of coffee, pondering the word *exquisite,* and reviewing the list of materials he'd need to purchase.

Rinng, rinng, rinng.

The phone interrupted his thoughts.

"Yes, good morning, Mrs. Bennett. I was just on my way to buy the materials to begin your cabinets."

She began to talk, rambling really—and finally came out with it—she was cancelling the order and demanded refund of her deposit.

"Mrs. Bennett, we can work out some kind of payment plan if you can't pay the entire amount as agreed. Or if this is a family emergency or something else, I can put your project on hold for a while."

"No. I've changed my mind."

"You know the agreement states the deposit is non-refundable."

She became more agitated. "What kind of person *are* you, trying to fool everyone with this image you present? You just can't get away with it around here!"

She wasn't making sense.

"Wait a minute, Mrs. Bennett. I gave you an honest estimate, and intended to get everything done on the schedule you requested.

"However, as you seem adamant about cancelling, I will refund your deposit to keep a good community relationship. I'll bring it by this afternoon."

"I do *not* want you at my house again," she nearly shouted. "Mail a check to me. I'll expect it within a few days."

He stood holding the phone, realizing she'd hung up. He couldn't understand what had just happened. He thought about everyone he had done work for or dealt with in any way, and could recall no problems. She'd left him no recourse but to return her money... by mail.

He had several tentative contracts, but nothing promised for the rest of the month, thinking he would be busy with Mrs. Bennett's project.

After a few minutes of reflection, he decided to begin the work for Mary. She had said nothing was urgent, but it was what he wanted to do. He tried to convince himself it was because of his friendship with Earl.

But he knew he wanted to see Mary, and this was a convenient excuse. He could get a few of the smaller repairs done for her, and still call his next client to give them good news about getting an earlier start.

He was humming to himself now as he picked up the phone to dial, shutting the irrational woman out of his mind and thinking of the more pleasant subject—Mary.

There was no answer. He realized he'd continued to let it ring for much longer than reasonable, and recognized his disappointment at not hearing Mary's voice.

Nevertheless, he decided to go, hoping she might return.

He let himself in, but left a note on the door so as not to startle her if she came in without noticing his truck outside.

He began working in Mary's house, the one he'd always thought of as Earl's.

After an hour, he'd lost his enthusiasm. He realized he could get back home about the time Mike arrived from school. They needed more time together. Maybe they would go to the picture show and call popcorn their supper. Alex hadn't been to the show here and only twice in Russia. This would be a real treat.

The show was a good idea. He'd called the Ritz to see what was showing. They had a new one every week or two and this week was *Tarzan and the Huntress*, a perfect choice for Mike.

"Boy, Tarzan is brave," Mike chatted on the way home. "I liked when he did that loud yell, and all the elephants came running."

They were home by eight, Mike in bed and asleep by nine.

Alex was turning out the shop lights when the phone rang. It was almost ten o'clock. Who could be phoning this late?

"*Carpenter's Carpentry,*" he answered.

"Alex—it's Mary. I know it's late, but I just noticed you'd been working at my house today."

"Yes. I phoned, but you weren't there. I was at a bit of loose ends and decided to come on over. I hope that was all right.

"I won't be getting to everything, but I had a cancellation so decided to get a couple of the smaller items on your list completed."

"Alex," she said, interrupting his flow, "I was disappointed not to see you.

"I *just* saw the evidence of your work." Talking fast, she seemed upset. "Will you be back tomorrow?"

Quietly Alex answered, "I don't want to be a hindrance, Mary. Maybe you can think about it, and give me some kind of schedule as to when would be best for me to be there."

"Alex Nordin—I am *not* that busy." More calmly, she added, "If I *were* busy, I'd cancel anything to see you. Didn't I make that fairly clear?"

There it was—that knot in his stomach. It was different, anxiety and relief combined.

"I was disappointed not to see you today, too. Then I thought perhaps I was building things up in my mind."

"Alex, will you be here in the morning?"

"Yes… I can probably be there by 8:30."

"Good. I will be here."

Then, softly she said, "Good night, Alex. I wish I could kiss you good night, but I'll wish you sweet dreams anyway."

~ 26 ~

Before eight that morning, he was ready to go. Like a child, he didn't want to get to Mary's earlier than expected.

He was pacing, looking for something to do for a few minutes when the phone rang. He hoped it wasn't Mary saying she couldn't be there.

Another client for whom he had lined up a kitchen remodel next month. Cancelling the order. The contract hadn't yet been signed, but he had given them a tentative start date.

"May I ask why, sir?" He would not give Alex a reason. He was rather blunt, though not as rude as Mrs. Bennett.

He knew money was tight. But two cancellations so close together told him there was another reason. He was afraid now. But of what?

Two cancellations, one right after the other. Something was wrong.

But Alex headed out to Mary's house.

It was a beautiful, cool morning, sun shining, and signs of spring everywhere. He'd been pleased to see a sprinkling of wild flowers blooming on the edges of the shop property he hadn't cleared, and two dogwood trees budding.

His conversation with Mary last night made him more anxious to see her.

Again, she was waiting at the door, opening it before he was out of his truck.

Her broad smile made his worries melt away. Seeing her seemed to fill him up. His steps light and his mind clear of all but Mary, it took only a minute to hurry across the yard, up the steps and inside. She closed the door, and gave him only the briefest second to set his tools down before embracing him.

Even as he returned the emotion and recognized how little control he had, there was no better feeling.

Finally she pulled back. "Could you just take today off? We need more time together. I realize that—more time to be sure of what I believe we're both feeling."

"Mary, of course it's obvious I have feelings for you. But we haven't known each other long. I just don't want to skip the important steps necessary for a solid relationship."

Her laugh was actually a relief. "My, that sounds pretty formal, Mr. Nordin... important steps?"

Laughing again, but more seriously, she continued. "You're right and that's exactly what I meant... I think. How about spending the morning *here*? I can turn on some music, and we can relax and go through family picture albums. You can get to know me better. It will even include Anna. I'll make cocoa... how about it?"

"Sounds good. About the music... something lively, okay?"

"Well, if you insist."

"Could I take you to lunch later?"

"Oh, *yes,* I was actually counting on that."

It was a lovely morning. She pulled out several photograph albums.

The photographs were of Mary's childhood.

"When I put the albums together, naturally I was only interested in myself," she explained with a grin.

"There *are* some of my parents' in their younger years, but only if they were with *me*! Same for Anna and Earl.

"That's the point, of course, for you to see how wonderful I have always been. Well, except for the year of the horrible permanent wave in my hair."

Just being with her was good. They enjoyed many of the same things, and could share laughter as well as serious moments.

She brought a tray from the kitchen with two large mugs of hot cocoa. As she handed one to him, she placed a box of chocolate candy on the coffee table. "You can never have too much chocolate."

Looking through the years of her life painted a picture of Mary as a lively young girl, playing softball in junior high, and making an attempt at tennis. "I didn't have the coordination for it," she admitted.

She was in the math club and the school chorus. Some of her elementary school pictures were *so* cute, and others made him laugh.

"Really bad hair that day in the ninth grade," she laughed, and he could not disagree.

"Hmmm, you were in the Math Club, involved in sports, and also sang.

"Brains, brawn, and harmony. So, after you conquered the big hair, you were a rather complex combination, especially when in such a gorgeous package."

She hit his arm playfully. "Now you're making fun. Not fair since I can't see *your* growing-up years."

He looked at her seriously. "You *are* all that... and I'm not kidding at all."

He did feel he knew her better after looking through several albums. He had enjoyed seeing Earl as a boy and Anna as a toddler, and was pleased they'd taken the time to become closer in this way.

He put his arm around her. She put her hand up to gently touch his face.

He leaned in to kiss her. As she pulled closer, his heart soared with tenderness, the myriad of emotions when your mind becomes a total blank—of everything but the moment.

All the clocks and music had ceased, the world had stopped turning.

There was only Mary, sweet, soft, loving Mary.

I have to return to the moment... to reality.

He relaxed his arms and pulled back slightly, looking into her eyes.

"Alex..." she whispered.

"Mary. I wish I could put into words all I'm feeling. On the other hand, I'm sure it's better left unsaid just now." He stood.

"I think it's a good time to get some air. I have an idea for the afternoon and lunch.

"How about touring a cavern down the mountain a few miles? I saw a sign for *Wonder Cave,* and thought it sounded interesting."

"Oh yes, I haven't been there in years."

Just before reaching their destination, they stopped for a hot dog.

"Well, you're getting by pretty easy for a lunch date," she laughed.

"I'll be spending big bucks to take you into a dark cave, lady. You can't expect everything on a second date."

"*Second* date? You're counting our picnic as the first?"

"I might not have, but the way it ended I think it definitely counts."

She laughed, that wonderfully contagious laugh. "Yes, it counts. Glad to know you hadn't forgotten."

The cavern was fascinating, *wondrous,* as its name. They had a private tour guide as they were the only tourists at the time. The silence, smell of dampness, and occasional drop of water from a stalactite captivated Alex.

They wound their way through the sometimes-narrow passageways with the only light being the lantern carried by the guide, though occasionally turning on a large flashlight to shine upward to point out the bats at the highest points.

"Some of the beautiful formations you see are stalagmites," he explained. They grow upward, *mightily,* from the floor of the cavern.

The stalac*tites* grow down from the ceiling like icicles and *hold tight.*

They were produced by precipitation of minerals dripping from the cavern ceiling.

The growth of only an inch takes more than a thousand years."

With his delight in everything so evident, Alex was a tour guide's dream.

As they exited the cavern, Alex was about to thank the guide when the guide instead turned to *him.* "I enjoy watching someone appreciate the wonder of creation. It has truly been *my* pleasure to escort you today, sir."

Mary had also enjoyed watching Alex as he absorbed this new experience.

"It was as if I were seeing everything for the first time, through your eyes. It's been a while since my fifth-grade tour, but I have a new appreciation."

They returned to her house about five.

As they walked up the steps to the porch, he remarked, "It's been a *wonderful* day, one of my best ever."

"It isn't even dark yet. Come in for a while."

"It's nearly five, and you know I always try to be home for Mike by then."

"Yes, of course. I'd never try to come before Mike. I think *he's* pretty wonderful, too."

This time he initiated the embrace, kissing her and holding her tight. It was difficult to let go, but holding her at arm's length, he said softly, "May your dreams all be good, and include me. Will you call me in the morning?"

She promised, and he was down the steps and driving away before his mind reluctantly let go of the warmth of their embrace.

After supper, Mrs. Carpenter phoned to ask if he might have a day available to do a few tasks around her house.

"For you, Mrs. Ilene, anything. As it happens, I could be there day after tomorrow, if you don't mind my bringing Mike. He's used to tagging along when I work. He might actually *do* a few things for you."

"Oh, Alex, having Mike here would be icing on the cake. See you at seven on Saturday. Bye now."

Ilene didn't believe in wasting time, on the phone or otherwise.

Mary phoned at eight the next morning. "Alex, will you come over? I know it's ridiculous to say aloud, but I miss you. I've thought of nothing else since you left. I loved every minute of our day together yesterday."

"I can be there in about thirty minutes. I've missed you, too. But, Mary, I have to work, you know. I'm barely getting started and already there are problems to work out."

"What problems?"

"Oh, just business," he said offhandedly, "but business is important. It's building a future, especially for Mike, and, of course protecting Earl's investment.

"I'll be over, but I insist on finishing at least two items on your list today. Tomorrow I've promised the day to Mrs. Ilene.

"I also need to begin work on another of my bigger projects next week.

"Mary… you and I need to be level-headed. Part of that is what I have to do to make a living. You understand, don't you?"

"Right now, this moment, with the phone lines between us, I understand.

"Oh, I know you're right; I'll work on being level-headed. Funny, I've been level-headed all my life, very focused. I seem to be veering off course… and I don't much care.

"By the way," she added, "Earl is still out of town."

They didn't speak for a moment.

"I see."

Another brief silence. At almost the same time, they began to laugh.

"All the more reason to maintain focus. You have the list ready, and decide what you want taken care of first."

As agreed, he did several of the smaller repairs in the house, before sharing a sandwich and a glass of tea for lunch.

"It's been a good morning with especially good company," he said. "I'm going to make a few customer calls this afternoon before Mike gets home."

"Well… I'll just have to live with the fact if you *must* work for a living."

She walked with him to the door. Before opening it, he embraced her. She came into his arms eagerly as his mouth covered hers. "Oh, Alex…" she whispered.

As he pulled away, he said hoarsely, "I know. I thought I'd never feel this way again… but… I'll see you soon." He kissed her forehead lightly, and was out the door.

~ 27 ~

After the initial grumbling from Mike Saturday morning, they were on their way to Ilene's before seven.

"I *do* like her Papa—a lot. Just, I'd like her better at *ten* on a Saturday." He looked at Alex with a grin.

She was waiting for them, obviously thrilled to see Mike.

"I baked cookies 'specially 'cause you were coming, young man. So you're obligated to eat at least a half dozen before you leave or you'll hurt my feelings. Of course I got a plate full for you to take home, maybe share one or two," she winked.

Walking to the hallway, she began to show Alex the repairs needed.

"This crack in the bathroom door is plumb driving me crazy."

Observing the hairline crack, Alex asked, "How long has it been there?"

"About twenty years. Makes no never-mind... 'cause I can't stand it now."

After showing him the other items on her list, he could see nothing amounting to much. Certainly nothing that had not been the same way for a very long time, other than perhaps one small broken window.

"I can get everything done today, Mrs. Ilene. I'll go back to the shop and pick up a few things and be right back. Come on, Mike."

Mike was happily working on the cookies, but stood to go with him.

"Oh, no, you don't," Ilene interrupted. "He's staying right here with me. I need to find out how Sneaker is doing and a few other things, and whether there are more questions I can answer."

Alex didn't have to ask Mike, as he'd sat back down, nodding and grinning.

Alex had completed everything by four, and she asked him to sit with her for a few minutes. Mike was in the back yard checking out the blooming fruit trees and bee hives. She was about to hand him an envelope, which Alex was sure held cash.

"Mrs. Ilene, you have done so much for me. I was happy to do for *you* today—I have no intention of ever charging you."

"Don't think I didn't figure on that, Alex," she laughed. "But you're taking this because I want you to have it. You're a good man. I know it. A man can't be the kind of father you are and not be a good, honest man."

He wasn't sure what to make of her statements, but answered, "Well, thank you. I'd like it, though, if you would call on me when you need something, just as a friend."

"All right. I want *you* to know you can count on me to be your friend, *no matter what.* If you need somebody to talk to, I'll be right here."

Alex was puzzled.

She sounds so serious. Must be other concerns on her mind.

"Meant to ask, did Mike have a list of questions for you today?"

Ilene's whole demeanor changed and she began to laugh again. "*Indeed* he *did*. He is a great kid. Nothing important, mind, just a few questions."

He rose to leave, but she clearly wasn't ready to say good bye.

"One of his questions was about sex."

Alex's eyes grew large as he slowly sat back down.

"What?!"

With a twinkle in her eye, she replied, "Yeah, I figured that would postpone your rush to leave. I answered him too, real plain."

"This is fun," she thought, looking at Alex's expression. She paused for dramatic effect.

"He said they talked about it all day at school yesterday... *sex this, and sex that.*" Mike told me he understood a lot of it, but asked me to explain more about the word."

"Mrs. Ilene... I'm *sorry*. He should have asked *me*."

She couldn't hold it in any longer. "Oh, Alex, I'm teasing—it wasn't really that at all," she laughed, "It was what I *thought* he said. My stomach was churning as I thought about what to answer, and what I would say to that teacher and the school! First grade, of all things.

"But, then he started talking about flies, roaches, crickets and such. He said Miss Parker told them they were all *sects*. Thing is, Mike had only picked up the last part of the word— S.E.C.T.S.

"Miss Parker was teaching them about *in*sects. I thought he was actually wondering about sex. Shook me up pretty good, I'll tell you."

"Ilene Carpenter, you have a mean streak!"

"Well, Alex, you might want to know that I had a real good answer after I figured out what he really wanted to know. First thing, I made sure he would say it right next time, '*in*-sects.' They look very different from each other, sizes and colors and some can *do* different things, like flying, and some live in the ground, some build mounds or nests.

"Then I told him it was kinda like people, though we don't have all the differences of insects. We are all people, but different colors, sizes, personalities, and people have different *talents* and can be *better* at some activities than others. Basically, though, God made *us* pretty much alike as far as our bodies, two legs, eyes, those things.

"Not the very best explanation, but I thought it'd do all right for now. I guess I forget Mike still has some English to figure out."

"Yes, ma'am, we both do, and you did just fine. However, you've caused *me* to lose a few heartbeats."

Mike came around the house at that moment. Perfect timing. Another interesting day.

❈ ❈

After their pleasant day with Ilene, Alex was heating canned soup for supper… again, and feeling guilty.

"Rinnnng! Rinnnng! Rinnnng!" He cringed, fearing the phone call would bring another cancellation.

Mike answered, "Carpenter's Carpentry." Pleased, Alex liked the sound of the phrase coming unrehearsed from Mike.

Obviously happy to hear the voice on the other end of the line, Mike replied excitedly, "Hi! I've missed you too."

After another few seconds, "Sure, we're not going anywhere. Come on over... okay, I'll ask."

"Papa, it's Anna. She asked if she could come over and I said sure, but she wants me to ask you."

"Of course. It'll be nice to see her." But he was ashamed. He had not contacted her in weeks. They'd seen each other only at church. Yet, what could he say?

She was there in about thirty minutes and, as usual, a delight. She brought the board game, *Monopoly*, and a plate of freshly-baked snickerdoodles.

"You've never heard of Monopoly? You know, I sometimes forget you haven't always been here." She looked at Alex, adding more seriously, "You had a whole *life* before we met."

Returning to her usual bubbling conversation, she explained, "Monopoly is our family's favorite game ever, and snickerdoodles our favorite cookie."

They had a great time learning and playing the game.

Mike caught on quickly, though needing help with counting the play money, which would help in school later on.

Alex, being slower to catch on, explained, "I'm having trouble taking a game seriously when the houses are so poorly built," bringing screams of laughter from Anna and Mike.

Anna was declared the winner. "I did have an advantage on you two, but next time, no excuses."

After Alex told Mike to get ready for bed, he had misgivings about sending him from the room, leaving him alone with Anna.

She was a wonderful woman, as well as being so attractive. She was a good friend and fun to be with. There were no negatives... except he didn't have the same feelings as when he was with her *sister*. She would hate him, and there was no defense.

He made small talk about the day at Ilene's, though not everything, and how generous she continued to be with her kindness and friendship.

He found himself telling her about the two cancellations and his concerns. Another one of Anna's positive traits was being easy to talk with, a good listener, *and* compassionate.

She seemed thoughtful. "I don't know, Alex. That horrible Abe Snider is talking about you around town. He's still saying you started the fire that burned his house down. No one who knows him pays any attention.

"Folks who live here just *part* of the year may have heard it as well. I'd hate to think so; maybe it was just coincidence."

"Maybe," he replied.

She pulled her chair closer, turning to him. "Alex, why haven't I heard from you lately? You've just told me the work you had scheduled for the week has been cancelled. Is something wrong between us?"

"Anna," he answered softly. "Nothing is really wrong. I... don't know how to explain."

She put her hand on his. "I'm not in a hurry, you know. If you just need time to build up the business, I understand."

"I do have a lot on my mind, but..."

She moved her hand up and to the back of his neck, then kissed him on the cheek—slowly... intimately and personal. He was about to move back, to stop this, when she withdrew and leaned back again.

"Alex, I care for you."

He could see her embarrassment—and he was struggling not to say or do anything insincere.

Quickly lightening the mood, she rose quickly, beginning to gather the game pieces. "Maybe you won't come in third when you play again. Should I leave it so you can practice?"

Mike returned in his pajamas, smelling of toothpaste.

"Please, please, can she leave it so you can play with me when I don't have much homework?"

Anna answered, "Exactly what I thought, Mike. Well, I've got to get home." She looked at Alex and asked, "Shall I save you a seat at church in the morning?"

"Yes, we'll be there."

As he got ready for bed, he thought about what a mess he was in.

He didn't like dishonesty in *any*one, but that's clearly what he was. As well as being a coward.

I'll call Anna next week... Monday... no more delays. I'll arrange a time for us to talk, and be straightforward.

Alex and Mike had grown to look forward to Sundays. Mike liked Sunday school and church, and was pleased that Alex didn't work in the shop. Alex felt the same.

Earl was to have returned late last night. He would finally get to talk with him. Still, probably not before Monday. A minister's Sundays were always full—more so, after being out of town two weeks.

Entering the building, he immediately spotted Earl. Joy welled up inside him—he had missed his friend for so many reasons.

Walking hurriedly to him, he waited for a space between others, eager to welcome him back. He happily embraced him, slapping him on the back. "Earl, I'm *so* glad you are home!"

Earl returned the embrace, but it felt stilted. He nodded and replied he was glad to be back, saying no more.

Something feels off. What could be wrong? I've been so anxious during this two weeks, missing him, and anxious to talk.

He walked slowly into the sanctuary.

Anna and Mary came in together to sit with them, Anna beside him, and Mary by Mike. Alex had a difficult time focusing on Earl's lesson.

Often they would go out to eat with a group after the Sunday morning service. They didn't always join them, as he was mindful of his spending.

He decided not to agree to lunch with *any*one. He couldn't handle much more tension, though it was possible he was the only one feeling it.

Mary was aware of his concerns about Anna, of course, but didn't seem worried.

Earl! That's it!

Suddenly he knew. His attitude toward him—Earl knew Alex was seeing Mary and that Anna thought he was interested in *her.*

I'll talk to Anna on Monday as I'd planned—be honest and break it off. She will be hurt, probably angry, with every right. It may even ruin any possibilities with Mary— there is no other choice.

I'll try to talk with Anna in the morning, then see Earl and clear this situation. Then I can finally tell him about the real bombshells— the FBI, and the fire investigation.

As the service ended, the usual hum of voices throughout the sanctuary began, softly at first, growing louder. People were talking with each other as well as making efforts to speak to visitors—it sounded like a big family reunion.

Anna was surrounded, as usual, but he was able to catch her eye. As he walked over, he touched her arm. "I really need to talk with you.... privately. Do you have classes tomorrow?"

"No," she replied, obviously pleased. "Call me in the morning."

"I will."

As they were about to leave, Earl motioned to Alex with a look of solemnity.

"Alex, the family is going out to eat. Would you let Mike go with them? I've already spoken with Mary and she can bring him back to the house when they've finished. You and I can pick up burgers and go to the house to eat. I need some time with you, just the two of us… to talk."

"Of course," Alex answered, grasping to feel some warmth, but glad nonetheless.

He told Mike he and Brother Earl had business to discuss. Mike was naturally happy to go out to eat with some of his favorite people. Alex was surprised, though, when Mike stepped over to take Mary's hand, though Anna and Mary were standing together.

Well, here it is. I'll tell Earl I'd already made up my mind to clear the air with Anna. I pray this will not permanently affect our friendship. Truth is, though, I'm planning to break up with one of his sisters and unable to deny having serious feelings for the other. How would any brother react?

There seemed to be no realistic way to repair the situation. He simply had to take one step at a time. He feared he would lose any chance with Mary. This thought hurt deeply. His feelings for her had grown quickly, and he'd thought… dreamed… of more. This might very well end everything.

He was also aware he was pushing the serious issues with the law aside.

But I don't understand those issues—my hands are tied. I can only deal with the issues with which I might have some control… my feelings and behavior with Earl's sisters.

As it turned out, this was the least of his problems.

※ ※

The two men ate almost in silence. There were a few mundane statements such as the burger being good and the attendance at church being up today. But there was none of the comfortable banter and laughter Alex had come to enjoy so much.

Earl pushed the wrappers to one side. Alex began gathering the trash.

"Leave it, Alex!" His tone was so abrupt, it startled Alex.

"Earl… okay… look, I think I know what you want to talk about. I've been thinking about it a lot, and know I have to do something. I never meant to complicate things. There was no real commitment, no promises… but I know it's not right."

"Are you talking about Anna?"

"Yes, isn't that what you wanted to talk about?"

"Alex, I'm not happy that you seem to have an effect on *both* my sisters. With Anna, I was okay with it, but now…"

"I know. I'm going to talk to Anna right away, tomorrow in fact. I told her this morning I would call her. I don't want the friendship between us, *you and me*, ruined because of this."

"Alex. I think at the moment I have to tell you to just shut up. I am indeed unhappy to see that you are about to upset my sister.

"Perhaps you will upset *both* sisters, but that isn't today's biggest problem."

"Then *what?*"

"When I said to shut up, I meant listen. I never thought I'd be talking with you in this way."

Alex had never heard this tone from Earl. It was scaring him. He'd never even heard him raise his voice. For anyone else it wasn't loud, but Earl? U*nheard* of.

"Just listen, please, Alex… then I have questions… and I'm asking for the truth."

Alex sat quietly, more concerned than he'd been since leaving Russia and traveling to the United States, the land where dreams come true.

Earl continued in a slightly lower tone. "I told you about the man who came asking questions about you. You insisted you had no idea what it was about. I know now he's been to see *you.* Yet, you didn't mention it to me."

"Yes, Earl, that's the other…"

"Don't interrupt. He has been *back* to see me and I think he has been talking to a lot of people. He is with the FBI—that's as serious as it gets."

Alex wanted to tell him again that he still had no idea what the authorities were talking about, and he had done nothing they mentioned. But, as Earl requested, he remained silent.

Earl continued. "He was waiting in his car outside my house when I returned home last night. It was late.

"He'd waited, though… at my *house,*" he emphasized. "We talked in the living room and Mary assumed it was a church problem, so I allowed that impression.

"He asked about miniature paintings which had been stolen from Russia. They believe they were smuggled into the United States. And they have strong suspicions this was accomplished by *you.* Now, tell me about it… everything."

Alex spoke softly, "I know nothing about it. Please don't doubt me. I had never heard of the paintings, barely about museums in my country—I rarely left our village. Surely you know I am not capable of being a thief… or a liar."

"*Right now*, Alex, I only know you are in a lot of trouble. I'm not sure you realize it. Maybe you thought it would just go away.

"Abe Snider continues to talk to the *local* police about your setting his house on fire. Somehow, he heard about authorities higher up questioning you about a crime in Russia.

"Come to think of it, they probably talked to him, since he was your sister's landlord and you lived there before her death. You're being accused of *two* crimes, Alex."

"I am not a thief or a liar, Earl!"

Trying to remain calm, he added more quietly, "Or an arsonist. I wanted to tell you about Chief Autry's visit to me right away, but you'd just left town. And it was the first I'd heard of the theft from Russia, or smuggling. Surely you believe me."

Earl looked hurt, as if he had been slapped. He did not respond.

"The same is true of the fire investigation, Earl. He also visited me after you left town.

"I didn't know what to do, *any*thing to do. I didn't want to talk to you about the accusations over the phone... even if I could have gotten in touch with you." Alex dropped his head, his emotions spent.

"Alex, you remember my helping you pack when you moved from Blancha's house, don't you?"

"Of course. What has that to do with it?"

"Alex, a person could not forget such a painting."

"Such as *what?*"

"In the box... the blue box. I saw it."

"What blue box? I don't know what you're talking about."

"I mentioned the box to you as we finished in the house. It wasn't especially large. Did you unpack everything when you moved into the shop?"

Alex nodded, trying to remember a blue box.

"*Every*thing... you're sure... and you don't remember a small blue box, ornate, fancy designs or such?"

"No."

He saw Earl's expression. His best friend didn't believe him.

Mary and Mike returned from lunch, coming into the house, talking excitedly.

Alex quietly rose from the table.

"Hey, Mike, glad you're back, but we need to get home." He took him by the hand and led him out the door to his truck. Mike was telling Earl and Mary goodbye, and they'd returned the greeting.

Mary had given Mike a quick hug at the door and looked at Alex questioningly, but he looked away. He wondered if Mary had really known what Earl talked with him about... there could be a lot of talk by now.

Can she, too, think I'm capable of stealing and lying?

Everything he'd been thankful for a week ago, everything he valued—his reputation, work, the future he wanted to build for Mike, his friends, maybe even the woman he could love and have a future *with*—all seemed to be dissolving before his eyes.

Thankfully, Mike was tired. After a brief time outside with Sneaker, he only wanted to lie across the bed with his books.

Alex was glad tomorrow was a school day. He didn't want to face Mike while carrying this load of worry about Earl's doubts and everything about the situation. What charges might actually be brought against him?

There is only one thing for which I feel guilt—Anna and Mary. I'll call Anna in the morning and set a time to meet and talk.

He was too heartsick to think beyond that.

What was to happen to his relationships with the Marshall family, the family of which he'd felt so much a part?

~ 29 ~

After the school bus pulled away Monday morning, Alex looked around their living area and shop, trying to remember or spot anything he had not unpacked. He should have asked Mike if he'd seen a blue box. He'd do that this afternoon.

It was early to call Anna. He'd wait until around nine-thirty, a knot forming in his stomach thinking of what he had to say to her.

He didn't get the chance to do either.

At eight-thirty, he was working up figures for a job he prayed wouldn't be cancelled, when he heard vehicles pulling into the driveway. Going to the window, he *knew*. There were loud voices and he heard someone running to the back of the shop. It was the police, FBI, or whoever they were.

Alex opened the door before they reached it. There were three parked cars, one with some type of emblem, the others unmarked.

Stepping onto the porch, he shouted, "What is this about?"

Then he recognized Chief Autry stepping out ahead of several other men, all dressed in black suits.

"I think you know, Mr. Nordin. I have federal agents with me. We have come to arrest you, and search the premises. We have a search warrant. You are allowed one phone call, if you wish. I'd advise it be to your lawyer."

Alex couldn't breathe, much less think. He had no idea who to call or what to do.

I don't have *a lawyer. And I can't call my best friend... he seems to have lost trust in me. Who? Mary? She would come, but it wouldn't be fair to her. I'd hoped beyond hope to clear this up before I had to see questions in her eyes.*

Mentally going through his list of friends and acquaintances, he thought, *Anna... sweet Anna. No, that's out of the question—I'd already planned our breakup. The people I've done work for who shook my hand and told me how they appreciated my honesty and good work? No solid relationships there.*

There is only one *person.*

As Alex returned inside, two of the men followed closely, standing by his side as he made the call.

"Thank you," he said. He placed the receiver back in its cradle.

"Sit there," one of them demanded, pointing to a kitchen chair, "and put your hands behind you."

He did as directed, wincing as they handcuffed him. Cruelly, he thought, they began searching the place, with one of them standing close, watching him.

His precious tools were being thrown aside or dropped onto the floor. He wanted to scream, but felt more like crying. He was humiliated and afraid, but at a loss to understand.

He heard another car—someone on *his* side... someone who would know who to call.

Ilene Carpenter got out of her car, glaring at the men as she came straight inside to Alex. As she came closer, tears began to stream down her face. In further humiliation, he felt his own eyes filling.

"Alex, who's in charge here? I need to talk with him, and get some facts."

He looked at Chief Autry, nodding his head in his direction.

"It's Chief Autry, with the FBI. Mrs. Ilene. They're accusing me of a theft back in Russia... arranging for paintings to be smuggled to the States. I don't know what they're talking about. I hope you believe me. I'm sorry to have had to call you."

His tears had dried as he lowered his head. "I had no one else."

She patted his knee and pulled out a handkerchief to blow her nose. Turning, she straightened her back and walked straight to Chief Autry, looking as though she could eat him with one angry bite.

❋ ❋

Sitting in the local jail, helpless, his greatest concern was Mike.

Ilene's first action had been to call her lawyer. Afterwards, she reassured Alex. "Don't worry about Mike. I'll wait here at the shop for the school bus."

A local being arrested in a small town, citizen or not, *by* out-of-town authorities—is news that travels faster than anyone can imagine.

Within the hour, practically everyone had heard about it. Someone called the church secretary, who told Earl. Bill and Pam Marshall received a phone call from a friend, and told Anna, who had slept late since she had no classes. Mary heard it in the grocery store.

Abe Snider heard about it when he arrived at his office—his secretary could always be counted on for the latest gossip.

Walking into his private office, he closed the door before beginning to smile.

This would surely help in his effort to bring charges against Alex for burning his house.

Mary phoned her friend, Marian Thornton, the school librarian, and asked if she could find out whether anyone had picked Mike up from school.

"No one has picked him up, but we've all heard about the arrest. Well, the teachers and administrative staff have heard. I don't think any of the children know about it."

"Marian, do you think Mike could have heard?"

"I don't think so, Mary. I really don't think any of us would mention it."

After they talked, Marian went to the office and learned someone had phoned to say Mike would not be alone when he arrived home.

Marian called Mary back to give her the information—*someone* would be there.

All this was possible in a small town.

Mary headed towards Alex's shop to await the bus with whoever else was there.

At the same time, Earl left his office to do the same thing. And Anna left her house, against her parents' advice, also to be there for Mike.

When the three siblings arrived, they found Ilene waiting. They had only a brief while to talk before time for the bus. They decided Ilene would tell Mike what happened, but as little as possible. Each of the women wanted to take Mike to their home, so they eventually agreed to leave the decision to Mike.

The bus rolled up and came to a stop. Mike hurried down the bus steps, and turned to wave at Mr. Sam before heading toward the shop.

He was running to see Sneaker, who was at his usual place near the road under a large tree, tail wagging. About the time Mike leaned down to grab Sneaker around the neck, saying "Hey boy, hey boy," he noticed the four on the shop porch.

"Come on, boy, we got company," Mike shouted as he ran to the porch, Sneaker following closely.

Clearly, he'd heard nothing of the day's events.

When he got to them, though, he knew something was wrong. No one smiled. He looked from one to the other.

Ilene spoke, "Hi, Mike. I know you're wondering why we are all here. How 'bout we go in and sit for a minute?"

"Is Papa okay?" he asked, as Alex was the one missing from the crowd.

Though it was not uncommon for him not to be home until around five, he knew things weren't right.

They walked inside. Ilene pulled out a chair for Mike to sit at the kitchen table, and she pulled a chair close to sit beside him.

"Your papa has been taken to jail, Mike."

The others gasped at the fact she had chosen to *open* with that statement.

※ ※

"Now, Mike," Ilene said, putting an arm around him, "I told you the worst first. You know I'm always straight with you. The men who arrested him think he did something bad in Russia, before he came here. They think he stole something of great value. He has a good lawyer, one I trust, and we're going to try real hard to see that your papa doesn't have to stay there long."

Mike began to cry, though obviously attempting to control it. He looked around at each of them.

Ilene continued more softly. "We're all here because we love you. I'm sure you know that. You can go home with one of us tonight, and stay as long as it takes to get Alex home. We *all* want you, honey, but it's up to you…"

Looking from one to another, Mike sobbed, "Papa is *good*. Do you think my papa did something *bad?*"

Anna looked puzzled, but was about to say she didn't think so. Earl looked straight ahead, praying silently that it not be true.

While they hesitated, Mary answered emphatically, "*No,* Mike." Then quieter, "Alex did nothing wrong, I'm sure of it."

Ilene agreed vehemently. "Of *course* your papa is not bad. Alex is a good man—of that I'm *very* sure."

Mike got up to go to Mary, wrapping his small arms around her waist, crying harder.

Anna came closer. She put her hand on his shoulder. "Mike, honey, I'd like for you to come home with *me*... until Alex is home again." She smiled at him and continued, "We've been buddies ever since you moved here. We have an extra bedroom... how about it? We'll get a few of your clothes and go, okay?"

Mary had released her arms from him and was all right with his going with Anna. Her heart was breaking for this precious boy, as well as being torn thinking of Alex in jail. Mike had long known Anna as a friend and would be comfortable with her.

But he looked up at Mary. "Can I go home with *you*... please?"

She leaned to pick him up. "Honey, I'd like nothing more. Let's get some of your clothes. Maybe Anna will help us."

Mary looked at Anna, hoping to have no hard feelings over this. All she wanted was for Mike to feel as protected and safe as possible.

"I hear you and Alex lived in my house for a while, well, kinda Brother Earl's house then. You can stay in the same room."

Mary finally saw a small smile. She glanced at Earl as he gave her a thumbs-up.

❁ ❁

Ilene stayed in close touch with Alex. The lawyer she'd hired was Dan Lawson, who had handled the sale of the shop.

"Dan is more than qualified. He can *handle* this, Alex," Ilene assured. "This is actually more in his line of work now. He hasn't done the small stuff, like our property deal, on a regular basis in a long time. He did the sale for me 'cause he's been our lawyer since he was a brand-new lawyer, and new in town."

She'd had no qualms about visiting the jail. Alex thought nothing intimidated this woman. He was not only glad to have her on his side, he was more thankful than ever to have her as a friend.

"I don't want Mike here, Mrs. Ilene. Be sure everyone is clear on that. I miss him terribly, but his visiting a place like this would be upsetting, and cause him more worry. I'll be allowed a phone call each evening, and I'll talk to him then."

"Done. I'll tell him children aren't allowed to visit. 'Matter of fact, it's probably true."

As much as Ilene wanted to believe charges would simply be dropped, the situation had grown worse.

One of the miniature paintings had been found in Alex's living area at the shop.

"Why will they not agree to bail?" she asked Dan.

"There is a secondary reason, Ilene," he explained. "Abe Snider has accused Alex of setting the fire that destroyed a house he owned. He created such a ruckus that Alex has become an official suspect, the *only* suspect I know of."

Ilene updated Earl each day. He would pass it on to Mary, Anna, and their parents.

Mary had Mike's bus stop changed again, and was always home when he got off the bus. Mr. Sam's being the driver for both stops on the same route helped greatly.

She didn't know what to tell Mike. She wanted to be honest with him. Often, however, the honest and safe answer was that *she didn't know what was going to happen.*

There were plenty of speculations. Truth was there seemed to have been nothing to point to Alex's *innocence.*

Yet, she believed in him, as did Ilene.

Mary wasn't sure how Anna felt. She had certainly had feelings for him and possibly *thought* she was falling in love. She loved Mike, and Mary knew she was hurt when he had not come to her in the crisis. But surprisingly, she had not asked about the possibility of visiting Alex, or Mike for that matter, and knew only the information passed on by Earl, asking no more.

Earl was a puzzle. She knew he and Alex had become very close. He'd had enough trust, and faith, to invest his financial savings in him.

Earl loved Alex as a brother. She'd seen that for herself. She'd felt it when she first heard about Alex from Earl, and then confirmed the feeling when she saw them together. Alex had somehow filled some gaps in for Earl.

Something about him had helped Earl's healing about his own past.

But now? She saw Earl distancing himself. She'd had the feeling when he suspected she and Alex had feelings for each other. She'd thought it was because of Anna. Now she wasn't sure that was the reason—or not the only one.

Mary visited the jail the third day after the arrest. Official charges had not been made, but appeared imminent. She wasn't even aware of all the details of the accusations.

She knew Alex was accused of taking valuable paintings in Russia, and smuggling them into the U.S. She was shocked to learn they'd discovered one in his shop. Still, she knew there was an explanation.

What does one wear for a jail visit? What a ridiculous concern.

But she finally decided on what she'd worn the day she'd seen him that day in the sandwich shop. It was a sweet memory. They'd lingered there, adding excuse after excuse not to part, neither of them admitting it.

Ushered into the visitors' room, her heart seemed to catch in her throat.

She thought she hurt for him *before* visiting this place, but when he came into the room, she felt genuine physical pain, aware of her own quick gasp.

He sat down across from her, thankfully without bars between them, only the table.

They grasped each other's hands as Mary tried not to cry.

He hadn't changed physically—he was still the same wonderfully sweet man with the kind, shy, eyes, full of love. But now there was also fear. She so wanted to go around the table to hold and kiss him, but they were limited to the touch of hands, and watched closely.

"You wore the peach sweater. I remember it from our day at the sandwich shop. A good day. I felt so inadequate, but still couldn't pull myself away from you. The color is beautiful on you. *You're* beautiful. Thank you for visiting... but I also hate your being in this awful place."

"I had to see you in person. To touch you and somehow reassure you."

His endearing smile reassured *her,* as he answered, "It means everything to me, Mary."

They didn't talk a great deal about the accusations. She told him how well Mike was holding up, though missing him greatly. She tried to lighten the mood by recalling funny things Mike did and said. They laughed as they agreed he supplied ample material, even though the mood was more somber for everyone right now.

As their time was nearing an end, he told her what he knew about the accusations, reaffirming he'd never heard of the paintings.

His concern, as she'd known it would be, was for Mike. He worried what this would do to Mike's life, how his friends, even teachers, would treat him. He worried about what he thought. He knew Mike would trust and defend him, but...

"How *long*? Mary, he's so young. If I'm imprisoned for years, which is what this offense would demand, what will happen to Mike? That's what terrifies me—how will it affect Mike?"

"Honey, I…"

"I know he can be taken care of physically! But, mentally, his feelings of security, belonging, being a happy, carefree child, as he deserves, and has been *most* of his life. But that would be torn apart."

Mary squeezed his hand. "I would do *any*thing for him—at least know that, Alex."

He calmed somewhat, regretting his outburst. It was honest, yet he hadn't meant to burden her with it.

"I'm sorry. I know what you are doing for him, Mary. I haven't sufficient words to explain what that means to me."

He squeezed her hand. He knew their time was up. The guard had been lenient. perhaps he would continue to be so.

Alex leaned across the table only slightly, Mary taking his cue as she leaned in to meet his lips… briefly… tenderly.

"Sweet dreams," they each whispered.

As she left, her faith in him was stronger than ever.

She drove to Ilene's.

"Is there any news on the case against Alex? I suppose I mean what is the lawyer *doing?* Is there something I... or *any*one can do?"

"I believe in him, Mary, no matter what.

"But I'm beginning to fear his innocence can't be proved. His cousin accused him, and the fact that one of the paintings was actually *found* at his place gives her story credence. Adding the suspicion of arson doesn't make him look any better."

"A *cousin* accused him of the theft and smuggling?"

Ilene shrugged her shoulders. She didn't know anything more.

"The painting being found at Alex's place is the most worrisome thing and the biggest mystery. I *know* he's innocent. Ilene, do you think it possible Alex has some kind of explanation, but a reason for not giving it?" Mary pleaded.

"I've thought of that, but I don't think so. I've seen no indication."

Sniffling, trying to hold the tears, she spoke her greatest fear aloud, "Mary, I'm so afraid we *can't* save him, no matter how much we do, or want it. I love him as a son."

~ 30 ~

*T*he *County Herald Newspaper* morning headline…

RUSSIAN SUSPECTED of THEFT and SMUGGLING— NOW ALSO ACCUSED OF ARSON

"Of course it's horrible, Mary, but it was to be expected—it's news."

"Earl, you changed about him a few weeks ago. Did you know something about this before we did?"

"I knew they were asking questions. They questioned me. I told Alex about it immediately. He assured me he knew nothing about it."

"But there's more," she insisted. "I know you. You were cool to him after you had the impression he might be interested in me, which is true, by the way. For the record, I made the first move—I'm in love with him."

Earl appeared surprised, but didn't comment.

They were sitting in the kitchen. She moved her chair closer to his, to look at him more directly, gaining his full attention.

"Alex is a good man. He is still the man you *thought* him to be, honest, kind, thoughtful, a faithful father and friend. I think he is in love with me, too, Earl, but he's been very concerned about hurting Anna.

"He treasures Anna's *friend*ship, and Mom and Dad's—but especially yours."

Earl sat quietly as Mary leaned back, saying no more. He was hurting. She could see it.

❋ ❋

Harry Bledsoe had relished seeing the headline in the *County Herald*. After all, he was the one who made certain it was front page.

Harry was not only the owner of the Herald, but editor, reporter, and salesman. In addition to delivery boys, he employed several other employees. The Herald was a bi-weekly newspaper, and he made a good living from it.

He was rather short, no more than five-five, even with the thick heels he'd had added at Carter's Shoe Repair. He had many nicknames referencing his height, and his attempt to compensate by being arrogant. He had always been a little overweight. At age fifty, he was also losing most of the red hair which had always been in sparse supply.

The paper's profit depended on advertising, and new ads were getting scarce. At the first hint of a new business, he was their first caller, convincing them of the value of placing an ad.

Harry gloated as he remembered his meeting and brief interview with Aleksander Nordin a few months ago. His hunch had proven correct. Yes, indeed, he enjoyed publishing the news of his arrest.

Harry wasn't alone in taking pleasure in the arrest of *the Russian*.

In the town of Mt. Seasons, which Alex had deemed full of good people, Abe Snider smiled as he read the article. He poured himself a celebratory drink.

Abe looked around his office, rather satisfied. It could've been bigger and somewhat more posh, though. Perhaps he'd soon make it so. Business was going well and growing, he thought, stretching his long legs out to rest on his fine mahogany desk.

The Snider Real Estate and Investment Company, begun by his grandfather, George Snider, had grown larger than any dream ol' Grandad ever had. Abe's father, Lincoln Snider, joined his own father in the company when he finished college, and together they built it into a larger corporation. The investment company had grown from three to twenty people, and the realty office from five to twenty-five.

Unfortunately, George had died suddenly when Lincoln was only forty-six. And Lincoln was killed in a freak accident the following week, leaving the entire corporation to his son, Abraham, long known as "Abe."

At twenty-four years old, Abe was fresh out of college. He made a multitude of changes in his first years as head of the company, gratified he'd completed enough business courses to figure it out quickly. Though he lacked the caliber of character of his father and grandfather, he added, "Honest Abe," as a byline on all company papers.

Finally, he decided to add a construction company to the corporation.

He would not only make money, but would save what they'd been paying other contractors.

Some people just couldn't stand change, he thought. He had lost nearly forty percent of his employees when they didn't agree with his vision. He'd build it back, though, with people who thought his way.

His concentration was now on the construction company and it was well on its way.

The construction company headquarters was in a nearby town, under another name--Abe not quite ready for the unveiling.

He had plans for a particular block in the little town of Mt. Seasons. It would make him a small fortune. Blancha Aldredge had held him back, but she was finally gone.

How conveniently the awful little house burned to the ground.

Not only will I get the insurance money, it will cost less to have the property cleared.

I'll leave the burned remains long enough to cause the owners of the neighboring houses to think they might have to look at it for the rest of their days. They'll see the neighborhood going down quickly and be more anxious to sell.

He would enjoy seeing the Russian go to prison. However, the fire investigation had come to a standstill. The evidence of arson was solid, but they had only Snider's accusations as to who was responsible.

Hmmm, the arrest of Nordin on charges of theft and smuggling... that will make it easy for them to accept what I've said. His dishonesty and bad character is obvious.

The local fire chief contacted him with the information of a state investigator being called in. He could not have been more pleased.

Everything is falling neatly into place.

"Honest Abe" might be proven wrong.

✽ ✽

Other than praying for a miracle, which he did, Alex could only sit in the jail cell. The guards treated him well enough, though he felt as if the word "thief" was written in indelible ink on his forehead.

Thief, smuggler, liar. And arsonist? How could a person get into such a mess and have no understanding of how he got there?

Mike sounded well each evening when he talked with him by phone, but he knew his son was trying to be brave. He told him about school work and grades. It was obvious Mike was growing closer to Mary. That pleased him. He sometimes had a minute or two to talk with her. Just hearing her voice gave him strength. Amazingly, she'd shown not a moment's doubt in him.

He could see how things looked. The facts and circumstances were stacking up higher against him.

✽ ✽

Finally, Earl visited.

Earl had been praying fervently for Alex, for himself, and for the truth. Being a minister had its privileges, especially in a small town.

He was known here, and was granted a visitor's pass with no time limitations.

The guard would remain present and they would be seated across from each other at the table. Regulations stated that no embracing or touching of any kind be allowed, other than possibly touching hands across the table.

Both Alex and Earl were apprehensive. Alex still felt the depth of hurt that came when he realized Earl doubted his innocence. Earl had been hurting, wondering if he might have made a grave error in judgement of the man he'd chosen to trust with his friendship, money, and home.

Alex was seated at the table when Earl entered, but he stood, wanting to feel the assurance of a friend being here to share his pain.

Earl's manner gave no clues. There was an ordinary handshake before they were seated to look at each other across the table.

Alex began. "Thank you for being here— and for taking Mike in. I know he feels more at home there than anywhere."

"I'm glad to have him. It was Mary, though. He *chose* Mary out of all of us... to trust, I guess, and to be with.

"He's such a delight, as you know. I can only imagine how it's hurting you to be away from him."

"How do *you* think he is doing?"

"He's in a lot of pain and misses you terribly, but doing as well or better than anyone could expect.

"He keeps his school work up, and mentions often that he'll be able to tell you when you're home again.

"We haven't told him a lot, Alex. I've been thinking maybe we should share the few facts we know. What do you think?"

Thoughtfully, Alex replied, "He's smart. I think you should tell him everything you know... and everything people are saying. If you don't, eventually someone else will do it."

"Alex." Earl looked about to break down, but Alex didn't know what to do. He couldn't embrace him and didn't know what to say. He wasn't sure what was going through his friend's mind.

Finally, Earl looked at him with a small smile.

"Alex, I have loved you... like a brother, really. I trusted you as I haven't trusted anyone in a long while. With everything. Everything I had, as well as my heart. Once I asked you to listen, and not interrupt. I'm asking this again... now."

"All right—don't hold anything back."

"It's probably not what you're thinking. I told you once or twice *you* were helping *me* as much as I was helping you... I know you remember." Alex nodded.

"But you didn't understand what I meant. There's something I didn't share with you... so perhaps I can't truthfully say I trusted you with everything. There was one very important thing I didn't tell you."

Alex looked baffled.

After a pause, and with difficulty, Earl continued, "I never told you I'd been married."

As expected, Alex was astonished. He repeated weakly, "Married?"

"Yes. My family doesn't mention it because it causes me so much pain. Sound familiar?"

Alex was too much in shock to respond.

"Alex, when I met you, I liked you immediately. I'd met Mike, of course, and saw him several times at church. Also, Anna had told me a lot about him.

"I'd been acquainted with your sister, Blancha, for several years. She was a fine woman. Years ago, she was sick with influenza and was out of church a few weeks. I visited her several times, and one day our conversation turned to her family in Russia.

"She told me about you. It was on her heart that she hadn't been there to help with your parents, and again when your young wife died, though she'd never seen either of you.

"She told me a lot over time, but asked that I keep it in confidence. She reminded me of that when she found that your boy was coming to live with her.

"She was so pleased Mikhail would be here, and that you would soon follow.

"Our both losing our wives at a young age, Alex—perhaps it was the reason for my feeling closer to you even before we met." Earl was choking back tears.

He saw Alex's look of shock, but held his hand up to stop him from speaking.

He continued haltingly. "We'd been married for two years. Susan, my wife, was expecting our first child. We lived a few hours from here. The church was fairly large, and the people were wonderful.

"There was a serious influenza epidemic. Susan was about four months along when she became ill. Eventually, she was hospitalized with an infection. She grew weaker every day. After about a week, the doctors said they had done everything they could. I sat with her... she lasted a few days. I held her hand as she breathed her last breath.

"After she died, I was asked whether I wanted to know the sex of the child she was carrying. Our child... was a boy.

"So... I understood your pain of losing a wife, and you had a young son, who *lived*. I sometimes pictured myself raising a boy alone. But I could never bring myself to talk about it. As time passed, I felt closer and closer to you. Of course, my family already loved Mike.

"I enjoyed being with you and admired the spirit you had. You never looked beaten. You maintained an inner strength it even when homeless and seemingly hopeless.

"I prayed for you and felt led to do more. Truthfully, I didn't want to lose you from my life. And it remains my firm belief that God put you and I together."

He lowered his head, completely spent. Alex reached across the table and took his hands. They sat in silence for several minutes.

"Earl. I wish I had known, but of course I, of all people, understand. I'm so sorry, but I'm glad you could finally tell me."

Alex hesitated before continuing.

"I know there isn't a single fact to support my innocence, Earl. *I* believe I will be convicted." Alex said it as a matter of fact, without emotion.

"I want you to understand... your friendship sustains me. Thinking it might be lost hurts almost as much as anything in my life. But I say again, I did not know anything about the paintings. I did not steal anything. And I did not start a fire to burn Snider's house. I give you my word... as a Christian... your friend... and your brother.

"But I have no explanation."

Earl rose from the table. He walked around to him.

Alex glanced at the guard who had not moved from his spot. As Earl came to him, he put his arms around him and began to sob. He and Alex stood embracing and crying together for several minutes.

When Earl finally pulled back, Alex looked at the guard again, and at Earl with a questioning expression. Earl smiled, a welcome sight, and whispered, "minister privileges," as he walked back around the table to sit across from him.

"Alex, I believe you. I'm sorry I ever doubted. I'll help fight for you, though I don't know in what manner.

"One thing I can promise—you need never worry about Mike's being well-cared for and loved... no matter what happens."

Standing to leave, he added emphatically, "I'll be seeing you more often. You are *not* alone in this. I pray for you every day, and many others are doing the same.

"*God* has not left you, either."

Before Mike returned from school that day, Earl had a long conversation with Mary. They agreed to talk with Mike together, tell him everything they knew, and give him a chance to ask questions.

This would prove to be a fruitful conversation—one they could never have predicted.

~ 31 ~

Three days without visitors.

Even the guards noticed.

He was still allowed to call Mike each night, but the time had been cut down, the guards explaining there were more in-house prisoners.

He had only time to ask about school and tell him how much he loved him. Mike seemed hesitant in talking with him, but he attributed it to passing time, and his being more unsure of what was happening.

He missed him so much. He wanted to see him off to school in the mornings, and watch him bounding through the yard with Sneaker. He wanted to kiss him good night.

"Papa, Mary takes me to check on Sneaker every other day, and she goes other days to be sure he has food and water."

How wonderful she was for Mike. He yearned to hold her again, but became more convinced each day it wasn't going to happen.

Why hadn't *any*one visited? Mary had been there regularly until now, and Earl had been adamant about visiting often.

Has something happened to convince them of my guilt after all?

"Please, Lord, even if I am convicted, let Mary and Earl continue to have faith in my innocence."

The fourth day, Chief Autry made another visit. He repeated questions and asked a few new ones. About his cousin Arta.

"I actually knew little about her... as I told you before. But my aunts did, and felt sure Mike would be safe with her. She was my only way to get Mike to the States."

"What did the *boy* have to say about her later... to your sister or you?"

"Almost nothing."

"What about Blancha, what did *she* say about the girl dropping Mike off at her house?"

Alex thought for a minute. "She only said that Arta seemed ready to put him in someone else's hands. My sister was a kind woman, so when she said Arta didn't even come inside when she deposited Mike, I realized she had pretty much dumped him and gotten away as quickly as possible. But Blancha said Mike looked good, and it seemed he'd been given everything he needed on the trip. I couldn't have expected more. She kept our agreement.

"...No, we never heard anything else from her and I have no idea where she went or where she might be now. She hadn't told me her destination after she arrived in the States. I did think perhaps it was the Southern part since she didn't argue about where she was to leave Mike, but I didn't know.

"Didn't you pay her to bring him here?"

"Yes. But it wasn't a lot, only all I had."

Chief Autry's demeanor seemed different, not as threatening.

But he offered no hope.

Another day passed without a visitor. When he phoned Mike later, Mary answered.

"He's gone to a party at church. I hope you don't mind, Alex. He was concerned about not talking with you, but I told him you would want him to have a good time."

"Sure," he agreed, but was sorely disappointed. "Mary, are you all right?"

"I'm good, Alex, but we have *all* been very busy these last few days."

She sounds nervous. I can't ask anything more of her, I have nothing to offer—but I miss her so much.

"I understand… will you give Mike an extra hug for me at bedtime?"

"Of course. Alex… I'll see you soon. Good night."

Alone in the house, Mary put the phone down and sat in the recliner. She'd wanted to comfort him, to assure him all would be well. But she could tell him nothing. And she was afraid.

She began to cry. Her crying grew into sobs, then loud screaming sobs, her body wracked. She heard the sounds, from afar it seemed. She cried until she could cry no more.

After Alex was escorted back to his cell, he lay down on the cot. He had cried the first night there.

Tonight the tears came again, harder, from deep inside. Feeling like a lost child, he cried himself to sleep.

❋ ❋

The next morning, a guard brought Alex breakfast as usual. But today he also brought a newspaper.

"You might *enjoy* the paper today, Mr. Nordin."

Alex doubted it, but thanked him. The coffee wasn't bad here, no worse than his.

Breakfast was the best meal of the day, and generous servings. He finished the eggs and toast, waiting to read the paper with the second cup of coffee they'd been kind enough to include.

As he opened the County Herald, the headline nearly jumped out at him...

SNIDER IMPLICATED IN SETTING FIRE TO HIS OWN PROPERTY

Snider? This made no sense at all, but he eagerly read every word. The article actually gave little more, only that new evidence had been found. Abe Snider had refused comment. According to unnamed sources, he had been warned not to leave the county.

The guard returned to take the tray.

Alex asked, "Have you heard anything more about the Snider case, other than the newspaper reported?"

"No. Pretty much common knowledge Snider isn't well-liked around here, to put it mildly. My sister worked at the realty office when he took over, and she quit after a year. Said she'd rather starve than to do business the way he wanted.

"I don't know anything else about the story, but anybody who knew him probably wouldn't be surprised."

Could this be a sign of more good to come? At least one thing on the negative list might go away. Thank you, Lord.

He had nothing to do, so he read and re-read every word in the paper, not only the articles but every ad, announcement and caption under the pictures.

The lunch tray was brought to the cell, then a brief time allowed outside in the small area with the high fences and barbed wire.

After the time outside, it was time for supper. The supper tray usually came around five, but it was past five-thirty and he hadn't seen anyone.

Another day without visitors.

Finally, the guards were coming through with the supper trays. He'd grown to hate the sounds of the cell doors opening and closing, so loud and final. But when his guard came to his cell without a tray, he stopped. "You aren't to be served tonight, Mr. Nordin. I wasn't given a reason."

Before all the trays had been delivered, another guard came to his cell and unlocked it, pulling it open and motioning him out. "Come on out, Mr. Nordin. Seems you're a privileged character tonight—they want you in the dining room."

Alex did as told, though puzzled, wondering whether this was good news or bad.

Could it be my last meal, *so to speak? Could they be transferring me to another, more secure location?*

They walked down a hall and into the small dining area. He sat where the guard indicated. The side door opened and Mary came in with a large picnic hamper.

He jumped up, exclaiming, "Mary, what's going on?"

Mary smiled and hurried to him, setting the basket down. She wrapped her arms around him and began to smother him with kisses.

What an amazing feeling. I'll cherish her nearness as long as I can.

When she finally let go, there were tears, but the smile remained.

"My brother," she explained, "well-known trusted minister and *your* best friend, and Mrs. Carpenter, who has influence none of us understands... well, they arranged it. For privacy and my bringing you a home-cooked meal... my love."

He embraced her, never wanting to let go.

"There's no better feeling than having you in my arms," he whispered.

After reluctantly ending the embrace, they sat at one of the smaller tables as she began to take the food out of the basket.

"Lest you get the wrong impression, I cooked very little of this. It was kind of a combined effort—partially me, mostly Seasons Moon and... you'll like this... Mike helped make the cookies. He knew I was bringing a meal and that children can't visit.

"He was excited I was going to eat with you, though, and would tell you he'd helped with the cookies. He was making visits with Earl this evening. We thought you wouldn't mind if he wasn't there to talk with you tonight. He can cheer some people up."

He briefly wondered about not being able to talk with Mike two nights in a row, but if Mike was happy… and Mary was here with him… he'd count his blessings.

The food was so good, nothing like what he'd had all week, but it was the companion he cherished.

"I do have additional news about Snider's fire," Mary began. "The investigator was curious about a key found in the yard. It would have been fairly close to the house, but outside nonetheless. It looked to him like a fairly new key and it was alone on a little chain but in some kind of key holder with *PPC* on it. The investigator tracked it down to the town of Oakcrest and a construction company called *Professional-Progressive Construction.*

"It took longer to verify Abe Snider's ownership of the company. They're in process now of verifying the particular key. Generally there are two original keys, they said, which can be easily identified. When copies are made, each one usually has a defining number cut into it. They hope to prove this particular key was issued to Abe Snider, personally. Fairly concrete evidence."

"He'd burn a house he *owned? Still* doesn't make sense."

"It seems he had been checking on having it torn down. He had bigger plans for the property, and this would save the expense of tearing it down. As a bonus, he'd get the insurance money. He thought win-win. The investigator seems to think the idea may have come to him after he heard the accusations about you and the theft in Russia. He thought you would already be regarded as dishonest, and it would be easy to blame on you."

"At the very least, I think they'll allow bail now, Alex. Ilene is checking. I couldn't wait to share a bit of *good* news with you, and I can't help but believe there will be more to come. But now... our time is limited, after all; let's change the subject."

"Mary... I don't deserve you..."

"Dear man... you don't even know the real me, all my terrible faults, but I expect you will ... one day. I know we'll have plenty of time."

"I hope so. I want to know everything about you.

Though generous under the circumstances, their time together was too brief. They embraced as they said good night.

"I'll go on and on to Mike about how much you enjoyed the cookies," she told him.

As she was almost out the door, she said, "Oh, I won't be here tomorrow, but I promise I will see you in a couple of days. I'm going with Mike's class on a field trip tomorrow afternoon. And we'll probably be a little late, so I doubt you'll get to talk to *him* tomorrow either."

She was talking faster than usual. "I'm sorry, darling. If Earl doesn't get here tomorrow, make him your evening call.

"He'd like it. Of course, I don't ever know his schedule for certain."

After Mary left, Alex felt uplifted and hopeful. For a while. Then he began to wonder about her saying he wouldn't be able to talk with Mike again tomorrow. *Three days in a row.* Was something wrong with Mike?

❊ ❊

The truth about Mike was that he couldn't be trusted to keep information from Alex. And they didn't want to give false hopes, though Mary and Earl were extremely hopeful.

Mike was so excited to share his surprising revelation, there was no way he could talk to Alex and not tell all. They hoped they could soon give Alex good news without doubts and misgivings.

The night Mary and Earl sat down to talk with Mike, things had turned out much differently than expected.

After they shared what they knew, they were about to ask if he had questions when he blurted out excitedly, "I knew about that painting—I saw it and knew where it was... why didn't somebody ask *me*?"

Mary and Earl were dumbfounded.

Mary felt a lump in her stomach. *Oh God, let this be good, please let it be good.*

She attempted to remain calm.

"Mike, it seems you have more to tell us than *we've* told *you*, honey.

"Can you tell us all about it… where it came from, who showed it to you… why it was hidden? *Any*thing?"

So Mike began in his hurried way of talking when excited, running his sentences together, and barely taking a breath. But he knew a great deal.

"When I was getting ready to come here from Russia, Papa packed one bag for me… not big… he said I wouldn't be allowed much, and he wanted *me* to keep up with it. I begged to bring my old book bag, so I could have books and pencils, and drawing paper… he said I could 'cause it would help me have something to do on the long trip. I was glad—I had lots of drawings to show Aunt Blancha when I got to her house. And I liked reading my books… and she read them with me."

Earl and Mary exchanged glances, wondering where this was going.

"*Any*way… after Papa left me with Arta, she said she'd brought a surprise. It was a brand-new carrying case, a little bigger than my book bag, but not big—I really liked it… she said I would have a little extra room in case I got a souvenir or anything on the way, or could put my sweater in it. She thought we should throw out the old book bag, and I thought it was okay, 'cause the new carrying case was lots better."

Stopping to think for a minute, he added, "That was about the only time Arta was *real nice* to me, you know, as if she liked me, and was happy. On our trip she didn't talk much.

"When I got to Aunt Blancha's, she let me put my own things away in my room.

When I finished, she came in and picked up the little suitcase Papa had sent, and the carrying case Arta had given me... she was going to put them in the closet." Mike was nervously excited, relaying all he remembered.

"The case Arta gave me came open when she picked it up. She said the lining seemed to be coming loose, maybe she could mend it."

Mike stopped for a minute, thoughtful. "Then she got kinda quiet and pulled something out and asked, 'What is this?' She was holding a little framed picture she called a painting... I told her I didn't know 'cause I hadn't seen it before. Then she asked about the bag 'cause she noticed it looked newer than the other, and I told her about Arta surprising me with it. She didn't ask anything else. I guess she put both cases in the closet... I don't know if she sewed it."

"Mike," Mary began hesitantly, "this information might really help Alex. We're not sure, but if you remember anything more, we want to know about it... *any*thing."

"Can I *call* him now and tell him?"

That's when they decided to stall Mike's speaking with Alex until they learned more.

As an afterthought, Earl asked, "Mike, do you ever remember a small blue box—you might say it was a little fancy? Could you have seen it when you moved into the shop?"

Mike put his hands and fingers up, forming a shape. "About this big?"

"Exactly. Did you see it?"

"Yes… one day after we moved to the shop. There were a couple of boxes in the closet we hadn't opened.

"The boxes had "Blancha" printed on the side… they weren't big… but I was trying to get a jacket off the shelf and knocked one off.

"It came open and didn't have much in it, just a few books and a blue box.

"So I put the books and the blue box on the shelf in our room 'cause it already had lots of other books on it. Papa keeps some books by his bed, Aunt Blancha's Bible and a book for ordering tools, but most of the others were on the shelf. I took the empty box outside and tore it up to use in the bottom of Sneaker's house to make it would be nicer for him."

Mike was sensing the tension in the room. He looked at Earl, then at Mary.

"Was this something Papa needed? I didn't think he'd care about my putting things away."

Earl saw the apprehension in his expression. He put his arms around him, hugging him tightly. "This is only something we needed to know, buddy, and something else that *may* help your Papa. You have done everything right. Soon, I hope everyone will know your *Papa* did all the right things."

After Mike got ready for bed, Mary listened to his prayers and tucked him in

Then they phoned Ilene. She called Dan, who got in touch with Chief Autry early the next morning. Everyone was excited, but almost afraid to hope this might be the answers needed.

~ 32 ~

Three days had passed since Mike's revelations.

Alex knew nothing of the new disclosures.

He was waiting for the lunch tray.

One of the events of the day, There's breakfast, lunch and supper, maybe a visitor, and my phone call in the evening—a pathetic life. No, not life, just pathetic.

He glanced up, surprised to see his lawyer. The guard unlocked the cell door, pulling it back with loud clatter. He didn't see the lunch tray, and it was customary to bring him out to the visitor's room to see anyone. He was apprehensive.

"Got bail for you, Nordin," Dan reported. "You're out on Earl Marshall's word that you won't leave town. You will be allowed to work at your shop during the day if you like, but you must report to Mr. Marshall every night, and spend the nights in his home. Agreed?"

"Of *course*."

After Alex gathered his meager belongings, they walked through the building.

"One more thing, Alex," Dan said, less stiffly. "I talked with Chief Autry this morning. I agreed the authorities could search your house and premises again, this time authorized with my signature. It takes time to obtain another search warrant, and we all felt it necessary. Agreed?"

"I don't understand, but if you thought it best… I guess it is."

Suddenly Alex halted, reached out and slammed his hand hard against the wall.

"They go through everything I own, everything, and said they found what they were looking for, which is still a *disastrous* puzzle to me!"

Angrily he asked, "What *else* do they expect to find?"

"Look Alex, there's a reason, and we'll talk about it tonight. Now, however, is not the time to lose your temper."

There was no further conversation until they reached the front desk. After the release papers were signed, Alex assumed he would be driven to Earl's.

As they opened the main door and stepped outside, Mike was running to him. Earl and Mary stood happily beside the car.

"Papa! I'm so glad to see you… not just talk on the phone…. you're coming to Brother Earl's… and Mary's… we can't wait for you to get there… we've been cooking… I'm gonna sleep in the bed with you… and I knew all about it but they didn't want me to tell you… and I liked making visits with Brother Earl…"

Taking a short breath as Alex lifted him up into his arms to hug him tightly, he said, "Papa you've loving me so hard I can't breathe…," then laughingly continued, "I don't care though… did you know about the bag Arta gave me?"

Alex heard almost none of his words. "Mikhail, my sweet boy, how I've missed you."

They were all crying by now. He didn't know what would come next, but for now he was surrounded by the people he loved most in the world. It was difficult to let go of his son, even to get into the car.

There was a genuine homecoming at the house. Though Alex was well aware of remaining under an enormous dark cloud, and the possibility of this happiness being taken away quickly, this was a day in which to rejoice. He walked inside and sat in the biggest overstuffed chair. Mike climbed into his lap and laid his head on Alex's shoulder, content—his conversation ceased, satisfied just to be close again.

Mary returned from the kitchen with a cup of coffee for Alex. "Lunch will be ready soon."

"You cooked?" he asked, good-naturedly.

"Indeed I did, Mr. Nordin, and you darn well better say it's the best roast and potatoes you ever had." They all laughed before she added, "It's one of my specialties, the other being take-out."

"Since we have a little while," Earl suggested, "Alex, we need to fill you in… update you, I suppose, on your case. Dan is coming back later this evening to go into some of the legal details, but he left to give us time together, first. Ilene will be here later, too."

They sat in a tight circle, Mary, Earl, and Alex, with Mike in his lap.

Earl told him what they'd learned from Mike, and of contacting Chief Autry with the information. They felt he believed them.

"The chief paid me another visit in jail. I had an odd sense of a change in attitude, though he said nothing of any developments."

"There are no more hard facts," Earl explained, "but we've been told the search is on for Arta. Facts of when and where the crimes were committed are implicating her more and more."

Mike remained silent, but finally raised his head, his expression troubled.

"Papa, I forgot about the little picture—I didn't know what Aunt Blancha did with it."

"Of course. You did nothing wrong, Mikhail. I'm glad they finally told you what was happening so you could explain the facts to *us*."

Mary noticed Alex reverting to his son's proper name in this emotional turmoil. She smiled at the closeness of the father and son, and prayed nothing would separate them again.

"It's almost time to eat. Mike, how about helping me get the food to the table?"

Anna arrived with a cake. "You're not having this celebration without me!"

After placing the cake on the buffet, she walked to Alex, giving him a hug.

"Thank you for being here," he said sincerely.

"I wouldn't miss a celebration for a friend."

From the kitchen, Mike was heard to ask, "Hey, Mary, what's the difference between a girlfriend and a girl that's your friend?" They all listened but heard no answer.

Then Mary called out, "Time to *eat*. Everybody get in here."

As they gathered around the table, Earl led them in a prayer of thanksgiving for having Alex with them again.

"And Lord, please oversee this investigation, guiding authorities to evidence proving Alex's innocence—to show the truth."

His "amen," was echoed emotionally around the room.

After the late lunch, which Alex declared *was* the very best roast and potatoes he'd ever eaten, they agreed to delay Anna's cake until later. Mike didn't appear to agree, though he didn't argue.

Anna scooped a spoon full of strawberry icing from the cake and handed it to him. "This can tide you over till you get cake to go with it, honey."

"The icing is piled on so thick, that spoonful won't even be missed," declared Mary.

They walked toward the living room, leaving the dishes for later.

"Alex...," Anna began, "would you go for a walk with me?"

Looking toward Mary, she asked, "Okay if I borrow him for a little while?"

Mary nodded.

Mike jumped up. "I'll go with you."

Earl interrupted. "Mike, I know you don't want Alex out of your sight, but Anna and Alex haven't gotten to talk in a while. Besides, I'd really like you to tell Mary about our visit to Mr. and Mrs. Harper the other night. Remember, the older couple who had ice cream for us?

"Mary had asked me how they were doing. You really liked them, so you could tell her what you thought."

Not totally convinced, Mike looked at Alex and back at Earl. Alex put his hand on top of Mike's head. "We won't be long, son... all right?"

"Okay. Hey, Mary, you shoulda seen Mr. and Mrs. Harper's little dog... his name was Scamp... they said it was because he always got into things... they were nice... Brother Earl told me they'd been sick a lot, but they were laughing and smiling—they didn't even seem old..."

Mary winked at Alex, and waved them out.

Though nearing summer, a cool breeze caused Anna and Alex to button their jackets as they walked. It was a great old neighborhood, sidewalks on every block, and large trees hanging out over the streets.

The streets were completely shaded for the summer, but colder during the winter months.

The neighborhood had been well kept. Many homes were still inhabited by the original owners, or the next generation of the family.

They strolled in silence for a few minutes in the peace of late afternoon. There was little traffic in the area, no one out, the only sounds being the rustle of dry leaves and crunching of acorns underfoot.

"Anna, I've wanted to talk with you. "I'd planned to do so on the day they came to arrest me. I haven't done right by you, and I'm truly sorry."

"Well, Alex, I wanted this time alone with you to clear the air… to tell you it's all right. I'd pretty much figured out why you wanted to talk with to me on Monday.

"I don't deny rather *pursuing* you. We had some nice evenings and I thought we might get more serious. We didn't, really… I just didn't want to admit it.

"On the other hand, yours and Mary's attraction to each other was obvious almost from the beginning. I could see how she felt about you over a month before your trouble began. I refused to look to see how *you* felt, but I believe you feel the same about her. You're good together."

They continued their leisurely stroll, Alex keenly aware of breathing the fresh, cool air, looking up to the blue sky, and knowing he would shortly return to the comfort of home, friends, and Mike.

I will never again take these blessings for granted. Lord, please protect us, as only you can.

"I felt dishonest, Anna. You were such a good friend to Mike, and you and I had some nice times… and evenings.

"But I felt differently about Mary—yes, almost from the first time I met her. But I didn't begin to know how to sort the situation and feelings out. Still, it was a cowardly way to handle it."

"I can't honestly say I've been in love with you, Alex. I was interested, you know, and fascinated. We've been good friends. Do you think we can keep our *friendship?*"

"That's my hope."

He smiled and took her hand as they walked.

Anna continued, "To Mary's credit, she did mention her feelings for you a while back."

She was aware of Alex's expression of surprise. "I guess you could say she wasn't really going behind my back. I responded to her by saying you and I were dating before she'd ever *met* you. She agreed, but said she had not sensed anything serious. What she'd seen was my *infatuation* with you, and your view of me as a friend. Quote, *beautiful female friend, but friend nonetheless.*"

Alex didn't know how to respond. *I'm letting her down again. Are there any right words? I can't deny anything—Mary's conclusion was correct, on my part.*

"Alex, I didn't mean to put you on the spot, but I see I have. Let's just conclude that I agree—Mary was right. I denied it, but she was right. I am more than okay with your being in love with my sister now, and that someday you just might be my brother.

"Furthermore," she grinned, "I had a date with Jimmy Greenwood last week.

"You probably know him from church and the hardware store. I've known him a long time, and I like him... a *lot*. Maybe it could get serious—it's too early to tell, though Jimmy has already thrown out some hints along those lines. So, Mister, you've been *replaced*."

She turned to him with her sweet smile.

"I know I'm talking too much, but I've been storing all this up. I confess I had to sort out my feelings *for* you and *about* you after your arrest. But I *have*. I care about you and believe in you in a strictly *friend*-relationship. And I'm not just saying that about Jimmy for effect—I do seriously like him."

He saw tears in her eyes. "Alex, you know how much I love Mike, and he loves me too—we're buddies. But, do you know who he went to when he wanted more than a buddy to wrap his arms around and hold him? *Mary*—he wanted Mary.*"

She paused. "So... you and Mary move on in your relationship with my blessing. I think you'll have a wonderful future together.

"Now, let's cross this street and head back to the house."

Alex smiled as she finally took her hand from his as they walked to the house.

"Thank you, Anna. You're very special to me. I've let you do most of the talking. But I do take the blame for the situation. I let you down.

"I liked you so *much*—still do, of course. And I thought perhaps those feelings would grow into something more.

"When I met Mary, though... everything changed. My feelings were different for her.

"I tried to deny it. But I couldn't. And I let the situation continue. I felt guilty, which tells you I knew I wasn't doing the right thing. I want you to know how truly sorry I am."

She put her hand on his arm, squeezing it. "All right, we've cleared the air, and still love each other… platonically," she laughed.

"I'm not a free man, only out on bail. The most serious charges are still out there, Anna. We're all excited about the new information. We think now *we* finally know what happened. But it's not *proof*. I may still be convicted and go to prison.

"I'll not be planning a future with or for anyone until I know I have one. Right now I'm only worrying about Mike's future."

They were within sight of the house and they could see Mike at the window. They both laughed and began a faster pace. Going up the steps, Anna said, "One worry you do not have is Mike's lack of people who love him."

As Mike opened the door, she heard his reply, barely above a whisper, "Yes, but he needs *me*."

After Anna and Alex, returned from their walk, Anna suggested, "Hey, Mary, how about we do the dishes now and have sister time?" For Mike, she added, "Then, strawberry cake."

Ilene Carpenter arrived with Dan Lawson as the women finished in the kitchen. Ever the lawyer, Dan seemed to scope the room before carrying his over-filled briefcase to the sofa. He sat down, retrieving a large stack of papers, as Mary and Anna returned to the living room.

Dan studied Alex. He directed the conversation to him, speaking loudly enough for all to hear.

"Alex, what we need to discuss is very personal. Ilene has agreed to step out of the room while we go over it, and I'd like to request the same of the others. Or you and I can go into another room."

Everyone except Mike, who had reclaimed his spot on Alex's lap, stood to leave.

Without hesitation, Alex replied, "No. Everyone will stay.

"With respect, Dan, I know you want what is best for me, as your client. But everyone in this room has invested in me.

"My son trusts me with his life. Earl has trusted me with his friendship, confidence, home, and a great deal of money.

"Ilene…" he paused, fighting tears, "Mrs. Ilene has trusted me with her good husband's name, took a financial loss for me, and stands by me even though others say I'm a criminal. She's even paying *you*. As for the ladies, Mary… and Anna… they have invested in me, too. I want nothing kept from anyone here. Everyone just sit back down."

They all took a seat. Noticing Alex whispering in Mike's ear, they were sure he was promising cake still to come.

First, Dan recounted the surprising information obtained from Mike.

"The authorities are at your house now, Alex, searching for the bags Mike brought from Russia. They hope to find more evidence of the paintings having been hidden there.

"On *our* part, we could hope it would prove they were hidden there, but not by Alex. But they may just inquire about the location of the others."

From the large stack of papers, Dan looked through and pulled out a photo of the painting found on Alex's premises.

He held it out, asking, "Has anyone seen this before?"

"Yes, sir," Mike answered. "I remember the little flower in the corner."

Earl spoke, "I believe it's the one I saw as I helped pack Blancha's room before they moved out. It was in a blue box."

Everyone else leaned in to take a closer look, but shook their heads, including Alex.

"Arta Nordin is listed on an all-points bulletin as being wanted for questioning. She seemed to disappear after the initial accusation, Alex.

"This will not only be a federal crime, but an international one, as well as a political scandal. I'm trying to advise you of all the facts. We'd like to find that Arta did everything, and proof of it, but it's shaky right now. There's no real evidence against her."

Sighing, he continued, "Bottom line, Alex, if things come back to you and you're officially charged..." Dan glanced at Mike, hesitating before adding, "it is as bad as anything you can imagine."

The atmosphere was somber. The ringing phone broke the silence. As Earl went to answer, everyone began moving around.

Mary announced, "Now we've having cake, and I'll make coffee for anyone who wants it."

Mary expected Mike to come bounding out of Alex's lap. He didn't move. He remained still, quietly laying his head on Alex's shoulder again. It was the saddest thing she'd ever seen.

"Dan, the phone is for you." Earl waited for Dan to take the receiver. The caller had only identified himself as being from police headquarters.

As the cake and coffee were brought in, Dan finished the conversation. Alex eased Mike into another chair for the cake. He took a mug of coffee from Mary, touching her hand, letting it linger for a moment.

Among the happy sounds of everyone enjoying the cake, Dan returned to the room.

"The phone call brought good news... we *hope*. Arta has been located, along with an American boyfriend she met in Russia. They have them in for questioning... just questioning... don't count too big on this," he warned.

~ 33 ~

"**I** don't *want* to go to school today. You've been *gone*, Papa, I want to stay with you."

It was uncharacteristic for Mike to argue, and he was convincing. Alex was tempted. He would love to have him all day… especially being unsure of how many free days he had.

"Tonight is parents' night, Mike, and you have things to finish at school. You will have only one more day after today, and I don't want you to miss anything. You can get off the bus at the shop, though, how about that?"

Reluctantly, he answered, "Yes, sir."

Alex had misgivings about attending parents' night, unsure of how he would be received. However, parents were invited to see the final art and other projects of the students, as well as being present as certificates of passing were presented.

The next day would be a "going-away-for-summer" party. Alex had written it on the calendar and had carved a "Perfect Teacher" plaque for Mike to give to Miss Parker.

Finishing his coffee, Alex realized Mike remained at the kitchen door, as if waiting for something more.

"I finished the plaque for Miss Parker last month. I'll get it from the shop today. Is there something else?"

"Well… most kids will have two parents there tonight… and I know my Mama is in heaven, but… could Miss Mary come with us?

"I already asked Miss Parker. She said I can invite anyone I want."

Alex was overcome with pride in the abundance of love and caring in Mike. He prayed it would never be replaced by anger.

"Know what? You have about five minutes until the bus. I know Mary is up. Why don't you knock on her door and invite her?"

Alex couldn't stop smiling as Mike ran to Mary's door, banging on it as if there were an emergency. He heard her open the door and say, "Come in, Mike."

In a few minutes, Mike yelled, "She said *yes*, Papa... I hear the bus... bye, see you later!"

Mary walked into the kitchen with tears in her eyes.

"He wants me to *repersent* his mother tonight."

Going to the window, Alex waved to his smiling son as he climbed the steps into the school bus.

He returned to the kitchen. Earl had left earlier for the office.

Mary was pouring more coffee.

He went to her and kissed her cheek as he ran his hand over her back. He felt he was living a dream to have this incredible woman in his life. "Nice sight... to see you here in your robe, with sleep still in your beautiful eyes."

"Good to have *you* here this morning. You're quite delicious, you know that?"

Changing pace, she asked, "What shall we do today? Or do you want to stay here and just relax?"

"I'm going to the shop to see what kind of mess they made *looking through everything.*"

She hadn't seen him angry before, but she saw it in his eyes for a moment. He certainly had a right to feel this way.

"I told Mike I'd be there when he got off the bus there today. I'm sure there's plenty to do."

"All right. Finish your coffee. I'll be ready to go with you in about fifteen minutes." She left the kitchen, realizing he'd put up no objections.

Sneaker greeted them happily, wagging his tail, running around in circles, and barking. He ran to Mary, who reached into her pocket for doggie treats. He took them greedily and ran back to lie in front of the doghouse.

"So… making friends with the dog to get to its owner, I see," Alex teased.

"*Mike* is his owner and I'm in pretty good standing with him already… but I have other ideas in mind for you, sir."

She moved toward him. They embraced, holding each other, relishing the closeness, and a long kiss.

"It's so good to have you in my arms, warm, loving…" Alex looked into her eyes tenderly. "*But,* if I do have any good reputation left, you're going to ruin it standing here in broad daylight attempting to seduce me."

"Oh, you're right," she answered coyly. "Let's go inside then… to clean up the *shop*."

Everything was indeed a mess. Every drawer in the shop had been pulled out, shelves in disarray, and items pulled from the cabinets.

Much of it had been strewn about on the floor.

The living area was worse. Mattresses had been taken off the beds, every piece of clothing pulled from the closet and the drawers… which at least they'd laid across the beds and not left on the floor. Every single book seemed to have been examined.

As far as Alex could see, only three items had been taken—the small suitcase Alex had packed for Mike, the case he'd gotten from Arta, and his own suitcase. He wondered if they were taken on the initial search, or just yesterday.

Mary looked around the living area, dismayed. "I'll work in here. You start in the shop."

Alex walked slowly back into the shop without a word. She knew he was emotionally ripped apart, but she had such admiration for the way he'd handled this nightmare situation. She'd never doubted him. Now, with every passing day, her resolve grew stronger and her love deeper.

She began getting the clothing off the beds and back into drawers and closet. Clean sheets had to be put on the beds. When she finished, she tackled the books and everything else strewn about, finally returning to the shop area an hour or so later.

Alex had returned tools and equipment to their proper places, pretty much ignoring the kitchen area.

He'd wiped down the equipment and work tables. His back was to her as he stood in the center of the shop, slumped and quiet.

She walked up behind him, slipping her arms around his waist. He didn't move. He finally reached back to hold his arms around hers, continuing to stand quietly with his back to her. She laid her head on his upper back.

"Alex?" He dropped his arms. She released hers.

"Alex, please turn to look at me."

He turned to face her... pale, as if life and hope had been drained away.

Quietly, looking into his sad eyes, she begged, "Don't give up."

"I believe I will go to prison—I truly do."

"Mary... I'm wondering about the decision I made to send Mikhail here. In Russia, he would have had *me*.

"But... he wouldn't have had the opportunities he can have here, hope for a better life. Maybe it was right... if he can get through having his one parent a criminal in prison."

"Do *not* give up, Alex Nordin! Not on yourself and not on *us*... I'm counting on there being an *us*—I am completely head-over-heels in love with you."

He hadn't seen her truly cry throughout this ordeal, but tears were flowing freely.

He took her in his arms, pulling her close and caressing her hair. "Mary, I think you *know* I love you. I haven't said the words, and don't have the right to say them now. But I do love you.

"I am deeply, with all my heart, in love with you.

"My *fear* is deep as well. I fear it is not to be… that I cannot have you and love you the way I want, and the way you deserve."

Again they stood together silently, holding each other.

"Alex, I will not give up on you… ever."

The moment was broken by Mary's stomach growling. He stepped back as they began to laugh.

"Lady, you are noisy when you're hungry."

She took his hands and looked down at them. "Ugh, we're both filthy. We need a break. Let's wash up and go get a burger and take it to the park to eat. Then we'll come back to finish up before time for the school bus."

When they returned to the shop, Alex had pulled himself together well enough to greet his son with a smile.

Parents' Night went smoothly. Though Alex thought there might have been a few sideways looks, Mike showed no signs of intimidation.

Most of his classmates had both parents there, but Mike was delighted to introduce his Papa, and Miss Mary, his special friend.

❅ ❆

Mary slept later than usual the next morning.

After Mike left for his last day at school, Alex returned to the kitchen. He'd had coffee, but wanted eggs.

Earl was at the table reading through his notes for a sermon.

"I'm going to scramble eggs. Shall I do a couple for you?"

"No, thanks." Earl put his papers aside. "I know we're all anxious every minute for news on your case, Alex. How are you doing... really?"

"Not good, I nearly fell apart yesterday. Mary threatened me and put me back together."

"You stayed solid and strong while in jail. I think you feel you can relax, be yourself here... it's good for you. You're not in it alone you know. In fact, your corner is getting rather crowded. I am wondering if we might need to give you more space. You're required to be here at night, but you don't have to have one of us looking over your shoulder all the time."

"I appreciate it, but I haven't felt closed in. I'd be lost in every way without all of you. I may get away a little today for some alone time, though. Unless Mary doesn't agree," he smiled. "If she feels strongly about looking over my shoulder all day, I expect I'll let her have her way. I care deeply for her... as I'm sure you know by now."

"Yes, and I was glad to see you and Anna had cleared the air. I actually think she's interested in this guy Jimmy, at church."

"Jimmy Greenwood. She mentioned him to me."

"He's a good man. They're a good match and I hope it works out."

Earl began to grin as he had earlier in their friendship. They were finally relaxed together again.

"I might have some news of my own, you know. Do you remember meeting Carol Hall?"

"No."

"She was the secretary when we signed the final papers for the purchase of the Carpenter property."

"Oh," Alex replied. "I do vaguely remember a young woman being there, but not much else. What about her?"

"Well, I guess you could say she made more of an impression on me. I called her a couple of weeks later and asked her out. She remembered me very well; though her memory of you was vague," he laughed.

"We've being seeing a lot of each other and I'm getting more serious about her. I think she feels the same."

Alex grinned. "I guess you want to tell me about her, huh?"

"Yes. She's about a year younger, never married. She lives in Jessups and has been working at the law office about two years. She has the prettiest brown eyes I ever saw, short, dark hair, laughs all the time. We've been out to eat, to some shows, and she's cooked for me a couple of times.

"Alex, I'm really happy. You know, as only a woman can do for you. She understands when I have to change our plans because of church business. She's a good woman, and strong in her faith. It feels right."

He shrugged his shoulders, raising his eyebrows in question.

"I'm thrilled for you. When can I meet her?" His expression changing, he stopped short.

"Wait... what does she think about your harboring a criminal? I'd think it might be a burden on a new relationship."

"She knows all about you and your situation. Contrary to what I said before, she remembered you quite well from the day in the law office. She had a good impression of you, thought you were humble and appreciative, and... kind. Also, she said if Ilene Carpenter thought you were a good guy and I agreed, she'd be in your corner with us. I hope you can meet her soon. The time isn't right now—too much going on."

"She sounds great. I'm happy for you."

Mary came into the kitchen yawning, and hair in disarray.

"Yikes, Mary! Did you forget someone else might have to look at you this morning?" Earl laughed.

She reached up to smooth her hair and put her hand over her mouth to stifle another yawn. "Not really, smart-mouthed brother, but he might as well know what life is before coffee."

Alex got up, poured her coffee, and motioned her to the table. "Sit and let me watch the transformation."

When she sat, gratefully accepting the coffee, he bent to kiss her cheek.

"Going to get dressed... I'll return after you have time for *two* cups."

Earl gave him a thumbs-up, and left the table to head for the office.

Days are long when waiting for news. It had been only a week since Alex had been released on bond, but each day seemed as two.

He tried to stay busy and useful, nearly impossible in his situation. Mary had told him about a charity craft fair coming up soon. He decided to make a few pieces suitable for the sale from scraps of wood not large enough for use in cabinets or other projects. *If* he ever *had* other projects.

Still, working with wood seemed to clear his mind.

Mary attempted to give him more time alone with Mike since school was out, but made it clear she was always available. She was seriously looking into opening a dress shop, either in Mt. Seasons or another nearby town. She wanted to move home—and had decided this even before she was sure of her feelings for Alex, and his for her. She wanted a future in her hometown.

She could no longer envision her life without Alex. But the possibility in the back of her mind, the thought she didn't want to admit —she wanted to be there for Mike if the worst happened.

They'd gone in separate directions for a couple of days, seeing each other only briefly in the mornings and at night. The third day, Mary phoned the shop shortly before noon.

"Hi, would you mind a little company this afternoon?"

Alex brightened, saying, "If it's you, I'd welcome it. When can you be here?"

"Would you like for me to stop at the deli on the way, or do you want to get out for a while?"

"The deli sounds good. Rather just be the two of us, I think, if you don't mind."

He added, "Mike's here, of course, but spends most of his day in the woods with Sneaker, or on his bike. I have some things to show you I hope might be good for the charity sale."

When she drove up, Alex was waiting with the shop door open. She collected a kiss at the door and walked to set bags of food on the table. She was about to ask what he'd been doing to keep busy when her eyes were drawn to his work table.

"Alex. They're *beautiful*—have you done all this in only a few days?"

"Yes—some don't take long. Do you think they're right for the sale?"

Mary picked up carved birdhouses, small wooden animals, towel holders, carvings of houses, short sayings, and other items suitable for hanging. He had one large wooden bin with "Laundry" carved into the front.

"Honey, you could make a good *living* doing this. They're wonderful, and perfect for the sale."

~ 34 ~

Morning newspaper headline…

ABRAHAM SNIDER INDICTED— CHARGES OF ARSON AND INSURANCE FRAUD FILED
He will no longer be known as 'Honest Abe.'
According to authorities, who spoke only with
assurance of anonymity,
there is little doubt of conviction.

One chapter closed. There was evidence of Snider's ambitious plans for the property where Blancha had lived. He had been one of the first people Chief Autry questioned about Alex and the possible theft in Russia—this appeared to be what gave him the idea to burn the house and place blame on Alex Nordin… whose reputation would already be in question.

❋ ❋

It had been almost three weeks since being released on bail, with no further word from anyone regarding the theft and smuggling charges.

Mike was at a friend's house for the day and would spend the night. Alex had seen his hesitation at being away from him, but he did want to go.

Alex reassured him, "Of course you should go. Your alternative is going to the charity sale."

Alex and Mary drove to the school late in the afternoon to deliver his items and help set up.

The sale was to begin at eight the next morning.

As they began unloading his truck, others came to help, Marian Thornton among them.

"Marian, this is Alex Nordin. You know his son, Mike. Alex, this is my friend Marian Thornton, the school librarian."

The two shook hands.

"You probably know me as Miss *Thorn*."

Seeing his surprised expression, she continued, "Oh, yes, I'm well aware of my nickname. I simply accept it as part of the job," she laughed good-naturedly.

"Well, Marian," said Mary, "you and the committee decide pricing since you've done this before. We'll take the ten to noon shift tomorrow, if that's okay."

"That will be perfect," replied Marian.

When they arrived shortly before ten the next morning, Alex scanned the area for his items.

"Mary, do you see anything we brought yesterday?"

She looked around as they got out of her car. "No, they must have moved them."

As they stood, puzzled and looking around the area, Marian Thornton saw them and ran to them excitedly. "Mary! All the woodwork you brought in has been sold. Everyone is talking about it… and wanting more."

"That quickly… *all* of it?" asked Mary.

Marian was nodding enthusiastically.

"You wouldn't believe it," she continued. "The prices had barely been assigned when the volunteers started purchasing last night. You know our rules—if you volunteer, you get first pick, but no discounts since it's for charity."

Mary hugged Alex, who looked baffled, but pleased.

"See? I told you they were wonderful."

Marian added, "There were only a few items left by the time we opened this morning and they were sold first thing!"

"I made everything from scrap wood, Mary… *scraps*."

She could see he was beginning to beam. During their two-hour shift, people begged him to take orders for items they'd seen purchased by other people. At first he declined, but Mary began making a list of names and items requested, explaining, "I'll let you know if he has time to do more."

She had two pages of requests when they headed home.

Ilene was waiting at the house with news.

"I talked with Dan. He's gotten word Arta is finally talking. She was adamant about your theft of the paintings, Alex, though she said she doesn't know anything about how you did it. She said if they found one, you must have the others hidden, or had already sold them.

"However, she couldn't get around the evidence of at least one having been brought here in the bag she gave to Mike, which *you,* Alex, never knew about.

"Because the paintings are miniatures, the space is large enough to have held all of them at one time. They have a good lead on the man she's been seen with, and Dan said he'd been told she was wavering on her story more every day. They believe when they find the guy, she'll crumble, giving us more answers."

Dan had agreed it was all right for her to give him the good news, or at least hope of it *becoming* good news.

❋ ❋

Newspaper headline…

NORDIN APPEARS GUILTY
of Theft and Smuggling of Russian Paintings.
Sources Reveal
More Than One Nordin in the 'Picture.'

"*Who* will read the entire article?" exclaimed Mary. "Most will only read, *Nordin appears guilty.* What are they doing to him, Earl?"

Alex had left with Mike before the paper had been delivered. He was dropping Mike off at the school for a day called *June Fling* for the first, second and third-graders. The bus would run its regular afternoon route, so it would not be necessary to return for him.

Mary was very upset about the headline. "Alex was so happy last night, thinking the case might be breaking. He was eager to work on more of the craft items as they were such a success."

Earl was shaking his head, personally wondering whether this cloud would ever go away.

It would become worse.

Mike got off the bus at the shop that afternoon. Mr. Sam had been cooperative about all the changes they'd made concerning the bus stops. Today, he simply asked Mike which stop was his.

Again, blessings of small town life.

The bus rumbled down the road noisily, each stop announced with the screeching of the brakes.

Alex smiled, knowing Mike would first greet Sneaker before crashing through the door with news of his day.

He heard Sneaker's usual excited barking but nothing more. He was working on another laundry bin, using the last of the bigger pieces of scrap wood.

Alex continued working for a few minutes before sensing something being wrong. He'd heard nothing more from the yard. Even Sneaker was quiet. He looked out the window to see Mike sitting on the ground quietly petting his dog. But he was crying.

Alex was out the door quickly, running to him, "Are you hurt? What's happened?"

Mike barely raised his chin, his eyes filled with sadness and streaming tears.

He did not appear to be injured. Alex sat down beside him. "What's wrong, son?"

Mike began sobbing in earnest and worked himself up into Alex's lap, putting his arms around his neck.

His sobs grew deeper and louder. Alex would have to wait until he was able to talk, so he sat with his head down on top of Mike's, gently rocking him back and forth.

They sat there in the dirt until, finally, the sobbing subsided. Still, Mike didn't look up and he continued to cry more quietly.

"Mikhail... I love you so much. I need to know why you're hurting. Please tell me what's wrong."

Mike raised his head and pulled himself up to stand.

"Are you ready to go inside?"

"Yes, sir," he answered, his voice barely audible.

Alex stood and picked him up, carrying him inside, through the shop to the larger bed, and lay across it with him. He put his arm over Mike... to wait. It was nearly an hour before Mike spoke.

"Papa... you always tell me the truth, don't you? Since we talked about Mama, you promised you would always tell me everything."

"I will always tell you the truth. Now, there might be things I don't tell you because I don't want you to worry, or maybe something just might not be important for you to know..."

He was trying to cover all the bases, having no idea what was on Mike's mind.

"For instance, I didn't tell you I kissed Mary at the breakfast table today, and it wasn't the first time I'd kissed her."

Finally, a faint smile on Mike's face.

Oh God, I hope it's something so small.

"I knew what they said about you setting the fire... then they found out the man with no heart, Mr. Snider, did it... and I knew they thought you had stolen something from Russia, but when I told about the little painting, I thought it would help show them you didn't do it."

"Yes, all correct."

"Some kids today were saying you *did* steal things and the newspaper reported Arta just helped you get them to America. They said she told the police all about it and you were going to prison... forever.*"*

It was difficult for Alex to speak. He sat up on the bed and pulled Mike onto his lap again.

"Mikhail, I will *never* lie to you. I didn't steal the paintings. I've never stolen anything in my life. But... honestly, I cannot promise I won't go to prison—I have to prepare you in case it happens. I didn't do it, son, but sometimes the police believe the wrong people."

Mike had ceased his crying, but watched Alex intently.

"I don't want to be without you... *ever* again!" This cry sounded of anger, which Alex thought worse than hurt. So he waited a minute.

"Mikhail, the truth is—it may happen. Lots of people are helping me… us … to prove I did nothing wrong… but it could still happen. Mary and I have talked about it, and if it should, she would want you to continue to live with her."

Mike remained silent.

"Mary loves you *almost* as much as I do. Were you worried what would happen to you if I went to prison?"

"No... I just don't want to be *away* from you..."

"Mikhail, we can still pray—ask God to show the right people I didn't do anything bad. But we can't know how God will work things out. You could talk to Brother Earl about it, you know. I think Brother Earl knows God pretty well. Okay?"

"Okay. I'll try not to cry anymore."

"It's all *right* to cry. Some people say it takes a real man to cry and show his feelings. It's not at all the same as being a cry-baby."

They lay quietly for a while. When it was time to return to Mary and Earl's, they locked up and walked out to the truck.

"Hey, Papa, did you really kiss Miss Mary… more than once?"

Alex grinned and answered, "More than once. And you are not allowed to ask any more questions on this particular subject." They both laughed, Alex realizing this was probably *not* the end of this conversation.

~ 35 ~

June was near an end.

Alex spent his days making crafts, selling them as fast as they were completed. He'd finally bought new wood to continue, and was making a good profit.

The phone rang at seven o'clock Monday morning. Earl answered, and Dan Lawson asked to speak with Alex.

Concerned, Earl went quietly to get Alex, who had just gotten up.

"It's Dan… for you. He didn't say what he wanted."

"Hello… Dan?"

"Good morning, Alex. I need you to be in my office at one this afternoon… per Chief Autry. Alex, he called me at *home* this morning. At. My. Home. *Never done.* But he told me to set up the meeting."

"What's it about?"

"I don't know. If it's good, he gave me no clue. Worst case scenario is… to be perfectly honest… if it's *not* good news, they may revoke your bail. I hope to God that will not be the case, but I'm bound to warn you—if it's bad, you might go straight back to jail from my office."

Alex's heart sank.

He thought he'd agreed to be there, but only vaguely remembered hanging up the phone.

Thankfully, Mike was still in bed. He needed a little time to swallow this, to absorb what might be.

Earl stood. Waiting. He'd heard only one end of the conversation, but could figure out it wasn't necessarily good news.

Alex repeated the conversation as best he could. Earl took charge.

"Okay, this is what we'll do. I'll call Anna and tell her to invite Mike to do something today. I know, I know, you promised Mike you would tell him everything. So you'll tell him you have to go to the lawyer's office and you don't know what they want. You can't scare him to death when you don't know what it is. Then Mary and I will go with you. It's likely Ilene will beat us there. Agreed?"

Alex nodded. Then he prayed.

Earl would pray as well, but as he dialed Anna's number, his concern for his friend's life was overwhelming. He'd thought they might soon see the proverbial "light at the end of the tunnel." Now, though he didn't want to admit it, his fear was that the light might prove to be the notorious train coming straight at them.

❄ ❄

Dan Lawson was in his office by nine. He had a calendar full of morning appointments, but the meeting at one o'clock called by Chief Autry crept into the forefront of his thinking all morning.

Against all the rules, even his own, he had grown close to everyone involved in the Nordin case.

It began with his friend of many years, Ilene Carpenter, then Aleksander Nordin himself. He had felt drawn in to this man's agony in proclaiming his innocence. Finally, his personal attachments to this case grew to include those he thought of as Alex's extended family.

In my years as a lawyer, I've seen many criminal types. Some can pull the wool over the eyes of even those who should know better. The evidence against Nordin solidly points to his guilt... even to finding a painting in his place. It makes little sense to believe in his innocence, but I'm convinced he's not capable of theft and smuggling, or even lying.

There's always a chance of completely misjudging a client, so maybe I'm only ninety-five percent sure. But I'm rooting for this man. Not the case, the man. It's become personal.

Dan's secretary, Carol, announced Chief Autry's arrival at twelve forty-five. Dan had him come in immediately, expecting some preliminary information.

After offering coffee or any variety of soft drinks, Dan leaned back in his chair, attempting a casual air. "Well, what do you have for us this afternoon, Chief?"

His expression revealing nothing, the chief answered, "All in good time, Lawson. I'll wait until Nordin arrives... with his entourage, I expect."

A few minutes before one, Alex arrived, with Mary holding his arm. Earl followed with Ilene.

Chief Autry caught Dan's attention and winked.

Dan cringed. *The man actually seems to be enjoying this. Can he be so cruel?*

❋ ❋

Dan had each of them seated as they came into the office. Obviously, Chief Autry was to have the floor, so he motioned him to his own large chair behind the desk, and walked around to sit among the others.

Autry remained standing behind the desk, his expression unreadable.

At one o'clock, the Chief began. "Everyone is here, so I'd like to bring you up to date. I believe you knew the cousin, Arta Nordin, had been located in Nashville. She was in custody, but only for questioning. Her story, however, had many holes from the beginning. As we expected, the longer she was confined, the more nervous she became. We told her we had located her boyfriend, known as Tank Johnson, but we told her nothing more.

"At the time, we couldn't arrest Tank. We warned him not to leave town, and informed him an agent would be posted to watch him twenty-four hours a day. We're pretty sure he was trying to figure a way to get out of the country, hoping to do so before Arta fell apart.

"We believe Tank somehow managed the theft of the paintings while employed by an American construction company in Russia. We think he met Arta completely coincidentally.

"When he learned she was planning to travel to the United States, he saw it as an opportunity—perfect timing to take advantage of a rather gullible young woman."

Chief Autry watched each face as they began to comprehend—he was unraveling facts having nothing to do with any involvement of Alex.

"Tank Johnson gave Arta the remainder of money she needed for her trip. We don't know whether he yet had a plan for sending the paintings with her. But when Mikhail Nordin's name came up, Tank encouraged her to take the boy with her.

"What, after all, could be more foolproof than traveling with a small boy who carried his own case? We believe he revealed a complex story of lies about the paintings and why he needed to hide them—only at the very last minute before Arta's departure. It may have even been that very morning, giving her little time to think it through."

As Autry spoke, going through everything he was allowed to tell them, he tried not to rush. He truly wanted them to see the big picture.

Only then did he begin to hint of Arta's confession, clearing Alex of all charges.

He'd watched them all as they glanced at each other, hoping, but afraid to be overly optimistic. He saw Mary Marshall's grip on Alex's hand, and the tension in the muscles in Alex's arm around her shoulder.

Tears were welling up in Ilene Carpenter's eyes, and unabashed anxiety in Earl Marshall's.

Even Dan Lawson, who had practiced law more than thirty years, seemed to be taking this case personally. He was well aware Dan had resented his not sharing the information prior to the meeting.

He'd paused for what seemed an eternity to his captive audience. Finally, he walked around the desk to Alex.

"Mr. Nordin, I have never been happier to be wrong about someone. Tank Johnson is now in jail, charged with theft, international smuggling and a few additional charges. Arta is being charged as an accessory. You, sir, have been completely exonerated of any wrongdoing—of having any knowledge whatsoever about the theft or the subsequent smuggling."

They all seemed to be holding their breath. He observed every face. Then he turned his full attention back to Alex.

"You are free of what I know has been a nightmare. I am aware this predicament has deeply affected all of you, as well as a little boy who will be happy to have his Daddy back.

"Congratulations, Mr. Nordin, you are free of this, *free* to live your life. And I will add my apologies for the difficult time you've had."

He put his hand out to Alex.

By now, Chief Austin was actually smiling as Alex stood to shake his hand. It seemed as if the others needed a minute to absorb what had happened. Then they began to talk, and to hug Alex and each other. Autry stepped back to enjoy watching the celebration.

Alex himself wished for better control of his emotions. But when relief washed over him, so did the tears. He embraced Mary as if he would never let go. When he composed himself a bit, he stepped back and looked at his friends.

"How can I tell you how grateful I am for what you've all done?" He began to choke up again.

Earl took the few steps to him, embracing him. "I think we have a little boy to see, don't you?"

They prepared to leave the office in much different spirits than those of earlier in the day.

They were happily sharing their gratitude with one another—especially to the man whose first name they didn't even know, and never thought to call friend, Chief Autry.

Earl phoned Anna from Dan's office. "Bring Mike home right away.

"Yes, yes, absolutely—it is *great* news!"

As he completed the call, Carol, who had listened at the door unashamed, said to Earl, "Congratulations. I'm so happy for everyone."

He whispered something to her, and kissed her on the cheek before leaving. She had never witnessed so much happiness in one room.

❋ ❋

After sharing the good news with Mike and Anna, they went out for a celebratory meal, Dan included.

Returning to Mary's, they sat together, finally able to relax completely. They recounted again and again the facts and gaps filled in for them by Chief Autry.

Noticing Mike nodding off after ten o'clock, Alex carried him to the bedroom, and the group began to disperse. Dan was the first to leave, then Ilene and Anna, all giving Alex one more hug.

Earl sat in the big overstuffed chair grinning at Mary and Alex. He gave a long exaggerated stretch, yawning. "It's been a long day… but I can stay up all night celebrating this wonderful day. How about I make another pot of coffee?"

He got up and took a few steps before looking back. He began laughing. "*Kidding*, I'm kidding, you two—I'm going to bed. I *know* you two hate to see me go, but I'm out of here."

Mary muttered, "You rat… about *time* you got out of our hair."

Alex stood to give him a brief hug before Earl left the room, laughing heartily.

"Have to say I'm glad to have you alone for a while," Alex admitted to Mary.

They sat back down on the sofa, close, happy to shut the world out for a while.

He took her in his arms, hungry for her touch, her warmth, her love. He whispered, "Mary, my dearest, I want to love you for a lifetime."

"Oh, yes, darling Alex, a lifetime…"

~36 ~

Morning newspaper's headline (grudgingly reported by Harry Bledsoe)…

NORDIN GUILTY, NORDIN INNOCENT? TAKE YOUR PICK

Few details have been released by the FBI. However, it has been revealed that evidence strongly suggests the theft of valuable miniature paintings from Russia was accomplished by Leroy Lloyd Johnson, also known as "Tank" Johnson, of Nashville. Accomplice, Arta Nordin, apparently smuggled the paintings into the United States.

Aleksander Nordin, formerly of Russia and currently a resident of Mt. Seasons, apparently had no knowledge of the theft or smuggling, and all charges have been dropped. All ten paintings have been recovered. No other details are available.

(Editor's footnote: The citizens of Mt. Seasons look forward to the reopening of Carpenter's Carpentry on a full-time basis. Nordin's work has been highly recommended by local citizens.)"

❄ ❄

The newspaper or its headlines were the last thing on the minds of those in the house on Oak Grove Street.

Everyone except Mary slept late. She dressed quickly, but had given some thought as to what she'd wear today. She pulled on casual black pants and slipped into a light-weight red sweater, pulling her auburn hair back in a large gold hair clasp. Going into the kitchen, she tied on a red apron and began cooking.

Alex came into the kitchen, and put his arms around her waist, nuzzling her neck. She turned to kiss him lightly. "Good morning," she murmured. "I'd like to serve you a breakfast that hasn't burned."

He grinned, gazing at her with wonder… she loved *him*.

"Okay… for now." He ran his hand softly over her back before pouring a cup of coffee and sitting at the table.

She turned back to the stove, trembling at his nearness, reminding herself again that the nightmare had ended.

She was cracking eggs when Mike came into the kitchen. He hugged her around the waist. "What we having, Miss Mary?"

"Well, honey, I'm cooking bacon, sausage and eggs, and making toast. Sorry, I don't do biscuits, but I could manage pancakes if you'd prefer, since it's a special occasion."

"I like bacon and eggs. Can I make my own hot chocolate?"

"Sure," she answered, as Earl came in and poured a mug of coffee.

Alex announced, "I called Anna and asked her to come over for breakfast… or a little later if she just wanted coffee."

Earl gave him a puzzled look. He knew Alex and Anna had resolved their feelings and were friends, but didn't quite get this, especially since she was here last night.

"The gang's all here!" Anna shouted as she came through the front door, and quickly to the kitchen. She hugged Mike, saying, "Good morning sunshine! And everyone else."

Mary had filled large platters with breakfast foods, and everyone was seated. She winked at Alex; he rose to walk to her. He placed his arm around her shoulder and gave it a squeeze. They were both grinning.

Earl suspected he knew now what was to happen.

"We could not wait for a formal occasion, so decided to have a breakfast celebration." Alex blurted. "Last night I asked Mary to marry me. Thankfully, she said yes!"

Earl and Anna exclaimed happily and began to push their chairs back, but Alex held up a hand.

"We called Mr. and Mrs. Marshall early this morning. Mary assured me they were very early risers. They gave us their blessing. But there is one more thing we need.

"Mikhail, you know what permission means… so we are asking *your* permission. What do you say?"

Surprising everyone, Mike did not answer immediately, but appeared to be seriously considering the question. He looked intently at Mary. Alex began to squirm a bit, wondering if he'd made a mistake by doing it this way.

Finally, Mike said shyly, "Miss Mary?"

"Yes, honey?"

"When you get married... can I call you Mama?"

"My sweet boy," Mary replied, with tears streaming, "I'd be *honored* to have you call me Mama."

He grinned widely and climbed up onto the kitchen chair. Standing to raise his arms, he announced, "You have permission!"

Everyone's big question was, "When?"

"We haven't set a date," they explained.

Alex added, "I'd like to get my business better established, now that my reputation has been cleared."

"Time to strike with all you got, Alex," Ilene had encouraged. "You've been the topic of conversation for just about every living soul in the county. They know who you are and what you do and how good you are at it... so let 'em know you're lining up business right and left. Make 'em worry they'll miss out if they don't sign a contract right away."

Alex was amused and thankful for this woman who never seemed to tire of encouraging him.

Mary interjected, "And I plan to more seriously explore the possibilities of opening a dress shop. I'd enjoy bringing new ideas to this area from Chicago—not only clothing, perhaps accessories as well."

She and Alex had agreed they needed time to date and spend time together without the pressures they'd experienced since they met.

She added, "I'd say we've already experienced what it means to stick together *for better or worse,* though."

Mike made no pretense of being happy about the delay.

"Probably in the spring, Mike."

"Okay." He turned back to his comic book momentarily. His expression suddenly appeared troubled.

"Mike, what's wrong?"

"Papa, you know our book, *The Clock*?"

"What about it?"

"The story about the wicked stepmother. When you marry Miss Mary, I want her to be like my *real* mother... I know I had a real mother when I was born, and Mary will be my second mother... but I don't want her to be a *step*mother ... just my *mother.*"

"Mike, Mary wants to be as close to being your *real* mother as she can. We planned to talk to you about this later, but she wants to adopt you when it's possible. That means she will be your legal-*forever* mother."

Thrilled, he wrapped his arms around Alex, "Thanks!"

Miss Parker's wedding was the next week.

Alex bought a new suit and one for Mike as well. They would need them for his wedding in the not-too-distant future.

With Mary, they happily attended and enjoyed Miss Parker's wedding, and dreamed of their own.

~ 37 ~

One thing continued to bear on Alex's mind. He'd pushed it aside, but it persisted.

Arta.

It proved difficult to learn where she was being held, but Dan Lawson was able to locate her a few hours away. He agreed to keep his inquiries confidential, but made arrangements for Alex to visit.

Alex phoned Ilene. "Could Mike spend the day with you tomorrow? I have out-of-town business.

"You're sure it's not inconvenient? Thank you. Put him to work. I'm sure there are things he could help with."

Alex dropped Mike off before seven-thirty. He began the drive to visit the cousin who had attempted, and almost succeeded, to destroy his life.

He had seen Arta only twice, and most likely wouldn't see her again after today. The authorities had obtained affidavits from him. They didn't believe his appearance would be necessary at her trial, or the one of Leroy Johnson, better known as Tank.

The three-hour drive seemed longer. He could think only of what she had attempted do to him. To Mike.

Entering the big-city jail brought back memories of the feeling of incarceration, causing him to shiver. After emptying his pockets, answering questions, completing paperwork, *and* being searched, he was finally escorted to a visitor's room.

He was seated at a table with a large glass barrier between visitor and prisoner.

Arta entered, walking toward him without realizing his identity.

As she began to sit, she recognized him. She gasped slightly and turned pale as she slowly settled into the chair. She looked down, but said nothing.

"Arta, ты знаешь кто я? (Arta, do you know who I am?)

She nodded. "Английский, пожалуйста." (English, please.)

Though surprised at her request, he continued in English. "Please look at me—you owe me that."

She raised her head. He realized he hadn't had a clear memory of her face.

There are no distinctive qualities. Her face isn't memorable in any way. So plain... sad. Her entire demeanor is sadness... beaten. What was my impression when I entrusted Mikhail to her? Reliable... sturdy... dependable. I don't remember seeing her smile, even then. Neither do I remember seeing joy, even in anticipation of a journey to a new country and new life. I didn't spent much time with her—I wish I had.

A realization struck him... one he didn't like.

Like Tank… I used her.

Her look of dejection isn't entirely new. I believe she had it before. I don't know what I expected to see or feel. But, I'm sorry for her.

"Arta, I needed to see you in person—in order to put this behind me."

She didn't move. No reaction, no emotion.

"I came *hoping* to be able to forgive you."

She seemed to simply stare ahead, but he could see tears in her eyes.

Is she hearing my words?

She finally spoke, haltingly. "Aleksander. I am sorry. For what I did. I am sure no one will ever understand. Sometimes even I don't. I was taught to do right. I believe in God. But I had no one… ever… who truly made me feel loved. I felt alone."

She stopped.

Is that all? What did I expect?

She watched his reaction.

"Arta, I know what you did, but I'd hoped to hear from you why you attempted to blame *me*. For what your fiancé did and your part in it. Can you explain?"

Her look changed slightly, as if she finally saw him and was completely aware. Clearing her throat, she began to speak in a strange mix of Russian and English.

She had been attempting to speak only English to the Americans.

Timidly, she began. "When I meet… met… Tank, I believed he was the one I'd waited for… he loved me, and I was special. I believed it… for a long time.

"I knew nothing of the paintings until early the morning of the very day we left for America. Tank brought them, with the little case, to my home. He told me a long story about how he has them... I do not remember all of it. I know... knew... something sounded wrong. But he tells me more of America and how he loves me.

"So I helped him take the lining loose from the case he'd purchased. We put the little paintings inside the lining and I sewed it back. Soon Mikhail and I... we were waving good-bye. Already I know I did wrong... I was lying to America, and making a lie out of a little boy.

"I let Tank take away who I was, what I believed in. The devil convinced me I deserve to be loved. This was what I had to do to prove how much I deserved love from Tank.

"He tell me I will take the little paintings out before I take Mikhail to Blancha. Then, I think, *I will leave one... if something goes wrong...*"

Nearly choking on stifled sobs, she continued, "I guess that was the worst of all. I thought if something happened, we'd blame it on you.

"When I see Tank to give him the others, he says I am a stupid girl. I tell him I did for him, I love him, nine paintings are enough. He was angry. But then he say yes, he love me and for me to stay in the hotel while he gets money for paintings. Then he will return, or call, and we will be married.

"But I *knew*...

"When he gave me the little kiss before he left... there was no love. But I hoped, anyway.

359

"I wait, and he does not come or call. I have not much money. I have to leave.

"It is big city, Nashville, how would he find me? Then I think… maybe he is caught… maybe *police* cannot find me… but they do. He's in jail somewhere. I don't know where, but I hope not to see him again."

Her tears were falling freely, but without a sound. "I'll pay for the rest of my life for the terrible things… I've been praying—but I don't deserve to be loved, or anything. I caused much hurt. I know you hate me. I hate myself—and I hate Tank for uncovering the evil inside me."

Suddenly, she stood.

She seemed to pull herself together, gathering courage and anger together. More forcefully, she said, "I hope now it is all cleared up for you."

"Arta, please sit," Alex answered quietly.

She looked unsure. But she did as requested.

"Arta. I'll not minimize what you did. I came to see you because I *had* to—I had to do it… for *me*. I don't know another way to explain it.

"I don't understand your actions, but I understand desperation.

"You are *wrong* about some things, though. I don't hate you. And you *do* deserve love. *God* continues to loves you, Arta."

Surprised, she stared at him.

"I wanted to thank you, too, for getting Mikhail here safely. It was a lot to ask of you, adding such a burden. I know it was never your plan to hurt him… or me. But you agreed to it.

"What is important for *me,* today, is that you know I've forgiven you. Without reservation.

"And that *God* will forgive you, if you ask. He loves you more than anyone.

"I wish you well. I've prayed about this, and about you. I'll continue to pray for you to receive a lighter sentence. Though I don't know whether it will help, I'll write a letter to request it."

She whispered, "Thank you. I never expected anyone to care about me again… in any way."

She continued, in a more normal tone. "I will be sent back to Russia. Wherever the trial is, I expect to be in a Russian prison. If I ever get out, I will at least be home, and that is my wish.

"Thank you for seeing me, Aleksander."

He put his hand flat against the glass, and she put hers against it from the other side.

They spoke not another word.

Driving home, Alex whispered a prayer.

"Thank you, Lord, for guidance. I felt burdened, with no understanding of why.

"You showed me forgiveness was needed— for me to *give* it, as *you* forgive me.

"Thank you for grace, and for lifting my burden."

~ 38 ~

The remaining months of summer seemed to go quickly with its days of sunshine, friends, laughter, and love… the fragile strands that make life good. Freedom. Alex relished and was keenly aware of it in every aspect of life.

Mike burst through the door, returning from a visit to Ilene. His bicycling to visit had become a weekly habit.

"Hey, Papa… you're whistling again… like the seven dwarfs in *Snow White*… they say whistle while you work… but maybe you could whistle something I know..."

Alex stopped working, ran to grab him, tickling him unmercifully.

"So… you want me to learn new music, do you?" They were both laughing as Alex put him into a chair.

"Well, I do got an idea about it."

"*Do got* an idea? I believe it's past time for school to resume."

"I *have* an idea. *Snow White* is on at the picture show in Coalton, but just this week … kind of a special showing... I know it's far… but I never got to see it since it came out before I was born… I like the music in it… sometimes the music teacher at school played the record."

Actually pausing to catch his breath, Mike continued, "Could we maybe go?"

"I'll check on it. That's a maybe."

Mary was delighted with the invitation to go down the mountain to Coalton, for supper and *Snow White*.

Alex drove Mary's car. The evening was perfect. *Snow White* was a hit, Alex promising Mike he would try incorporating some of the songs he'd heard into his whistling. Mary simply laughed at the whole scenario. The weather was pleasant, and Mike settled comfortably into the back seat for the drive home.

Alex was content as the soft music played on the radio and he thought of this new family-to-be. They rode in a comfortable silence, Mary snuggling closer to him, occasionally glancing up dreamily.

Oh, Lord, life can be so good.

Mike was asleep in the back seat when they returned to Mary's house. Alex lifted him out and transferred him into his truck. Mary stood with him for a few minutes in the moonlight as they came together in a warm embrace. Releasing each other and looking down at a peacefully sleeping Mike, it was a perfect moment. Alex kissed her again lightly, climbing into the truck and driving home.

Mike didn't wake even when Alex lifted him out of the truck and carried him in through the shop to his bed.

Kneeling by the bed, Alex thanked God for this child and for protecting them in the transitions of these last years. "Thank you, Lord, for protecting Mike *all* his life."

He'd finally accepted the death of his dear Vera, and was thankful for the new life he'd been given.

"Lord, please continue to bless us with peace, and forgiveness for my multitude of mistakes in judgement, anger, impatience, and lack of faith. Again I thank you for Earl, who has helped me come to this point in faith. Help me to be a good husband and a blessing in Mary's life."

I've always been in your hands, Lord. I just didn't see you.

❋ ❋

September.

School began as usual, the day after the Labor Day holiday.

Mike was excitedly beginning the second grade, his new teacher being Mr. Morton. "I'm glad, 'cause I know what to call him… men are always just *Mister*."

The carpentry business was flourishing. By Thanksgiving, Alex was flooded with Christmas orders.

In the second week of December, he was completing a custom-order rocking horse. He imagined the child, Nancy Patterson, seeing it on Christmas morning. She was four years old.

Nancy's father had told him they'd had a period of time when they feared losing her to polio. She'd been diagnosed when she was two, and spent a year in treatments.

Mr. Patterson explained, "One of the most difficult things was the necessity of her spending most of a year in a special-care facility in Coalton. So little is known about polio. Our fear was the horrible disease taking over and her spending the remainder of her shortened life in an *iron lung,* it breathing for her.

"Thankfully though, she was declared *cured* six months ago," he beamed. "She has a slight limp, but a small thing compared to our fears. This Christmas will be an extra-special celebration."

❄ ❄

The crunching of tires on rocks, patches of ice, and tree limbs, interrupted his thoughts. Alex turned to look out the window, seeing a tall, slender man getting out of an expensive car.

He was dressed in a suit. He wore dress shoes that were polished and buffed so bits of sun seemed to bounce off them. And he carried a briefcase.

Alex felt sick, memories of the year flowing through him.

I don't think I can do this again. What else could there be?

Going to the door, he prayed, "Lord, please continue to hold my hand, give me peace and wisdom to face whatever is coming."

He opened the door as the man approached. The man appeared to be barely thirty, smiling confidently, and walking with a long, relaxed stride.

"Good morning. I'm Junior Batson, with the law firm of Smith, Smith and Batson."

He extended his hand. "Are you Aleksander Nordin?"

Alex shook his hand, hoping Mr. Batson didn't feel the trembling coursing through his body. "Yes. May I help you?"

"I think you can. I'd appreciate it if you would invite me in."

"I'm more inclined to ask if I should have my lawyer present, Mr. Batson."

"If you will allow me in for a few minutes to explain, you may certainly call your lawyer if you feel the need. Please?"

Alex warily stepped back, holding the door open to motion the man inside. He hoped this would not prove to be a mistake. He guided him to the kitchen table.

"Before we begin, Mr. Nordin, I'd like to see some identification, preferably your passport, or a driver's license. I believe I am in the right place but you can understand my not wanting to share information with the wrong person."

"Mr. Batson, I'd like to see your identification first. I've learned a few things this year."

Identifications were exchanged quietly, though Mr. Batson pointed out, "If you will notice, my company card shows we specialize in estate law."

At the stove, Alex poured two cups of coffee, not attempting hospitality—he needed the warmth of the cup in his hands, hoping it would steady him.

"Thank you, Mr. Nordin. Please, may I call you Alex? I'd be more comfortable if you'd call me Junior."

Alex simply stared at his coffee.

Junior felt for him and realized he needed to get his business stated without further delay.

There was apparently to be no idle conversation with Alex.

"I'm aware of what you've dealt with this year. This is *not* bad news."

Junior had hoped to see a sign of relief in Alex, but it would obviously take more than his reassurances. He pulled a thick file from his briefcase.

"I'd intended to ask a few questions first, Alex, simply to pique your interest about your sister, Blancha. I know she left Russia before you were born, but I hoped you'd go back in your memory, as far back as your parents discussing her marriage. She married an American named David Aldredge.

"I'd hoped you might have some vague memories of hearing why they settled in the small town of Mt. Seasons."

Junior raised his eyebrows questionly. Alex didn't respond.

"There was a *reason* they settled here, Alex. I'd hoped she might have even mentioned it after you arrived. It was a fact rather well hidden, or pushed out of sight by the few who knew about it. With Abe Snider's incarceration, people began to talk about him.

Facts and long-forgotten memories were revived, *retrieved* from memories, I guess."

"Mr.... well, Junior... I've put Snider's actions behind me. I've even forgiven it as best I can, thankful truth won out.

"He will be punished and I want nothing more. My name has been cleared. I don't want a lawsuit, if *that's* what you have in mind. I will not agree to one. Can't people just let the situation alone?"

Becoming more agitated, Alex wanted to put an end to whatever was being plotted. "Look, I *know* Blancha had no money. She loved her husband. When he died, she had no choice but to work. She was a kind soul and gave more love and caring than anyone I know. She was the saving of my son, Mike.

"If not for Blancha, we would have had no chance to come to America. Her soul is at rest, Junior. I can think of no reason to begin dredging the past again. Not for her, me, Snider, or *anyone*."

"All right, Alex. Please calm down. I'm going to attempt to condense this. Just listen."

Junior Batson talked for more than an hour.

Alex quietly shook his hand as he left.

Returning to the table to sit, he mulled over what he'd learned. Junior had been honest in the beginning. It wasn't bad news... but perplexing.

What direction should I take with this? I need to talk with a lawyer... Dan. But not yet, I have to have time to work it out in my mind.

❊ ❊

Alex sat on the floor to paint the small initials, *a.n.*, on one hoof of the completed rocking horse for the Patterson's.

He leaned back to assess the effect, remembering his conversation with Mary, who had encouraged this addition. "Honey, you are a true artist, and artists sign their work."

"On a set of fine cabinets, it would be called desecration," he'd answered.

She'd insisted the smaller customized items were different, and his customers would appreciate it.

He drove to the Patterson home and turned into the drive, seeing Mrs. Patterson wave from the window and point toward the garage. In a few minutes the garage door opened.

"Oh, Mr. Nordin, I've been so anxious to see it," exclaimed Mrs. Patterson. He set it down inside the garage, removing the blankets. She touched it carefully, moving her hand over the sleek saddle, and leaning to examine the lower part and rockers.

"You've put your artist mark here— wonderful. It's perfect, Nancy will be so thrilled."

To do what I love, and be paid for it and appreciated. Unbelievable.

It had been a satisfying day. As Alex drove home, an idea began to take shape.

I believe I may have the perfect plan to close the chapter Junior Batson presented.

୨୨୨

"Thanks be to God
for his indescribable gift."
II Cor. 9:15

୨୨୨

~ 39 ~

Christmas

Mike was out of school and full of excitement. Christmas was only five days away. He rode his bike to Ilene's every other day. If Alex hadn't been so sure of Ilene's delight in the boy, he would have worried about him driving her '*round the bend*, an expression he'd learned from her.

Alex was excited as well, but memories of Christmas only the year before came to mind.

He, Mike, and Blancha had been happy just to be together. They'd had so little, but the love they'd shared would never be forgotten.

So many changes in only a year. He'd been devastated at Blancha's death after such a short time with her. He'd wondered how he would go on, how he and Mike would live, and where the blessings had gone.

But look where your life is now.

Yes, he had a business again—work to do to provide for his family. More importantly, a healthy, happy, son, and a family-to-be… Mary.

Where did these good things come from?

"Thank you, Lord. All good things come from you."

How he would've loved sharing this with Blancha, but he hoped, somehow, she knew.

"My precious sister, you helped make this possible."

❋ ❋

Christmas Eve night.

The Christmas Eve service at church brought a multitude of bittersweet memories.

For Alex, thankfulness overshadowed everything.

Afterwards, Alex and Mike drove to Mary's for the night. Earl had a late date with Carol.

Mary turned on the record player to play Christmas albums by Perry Como and Bing Crosby.

"The music is our background music for elegant dining," she explained to her rather mystified and delighted guests.

She had prepared late evening snacks to enjoy by candlelight. This being a first for Mike, the effect quietened him down considerably. Later, he hung his stocking by the fireplace, giving no arguments about it being bedtime.

As Alex returned from settling Mike in bed, he sat close to Mary on the sofa in front of the glowing fireplace.

"We need to remember to have more candlelight dinners," he whispered, "not only was it very romantic, it left Mike nearly speechless. But *now* is for us." He put his arms around her and she pulled closer to him.

"Oh, Alex, I cannot wait to be your wife... to share *every* evening with you... and night..."

She looked up at this wonderful man, soon to be her husband.

I love everything about him.

I love the way he looks at me with such intensity, the slight curling of his hair above his collar, his strong arms, the warmth as he holds me... and his sincerity. He can seem so vulnerable—I love his decency, and honesty. He is the answer to my prayers.

She lifted her chin as their lips met and parted, so filled with love for each other.

Finally sighing and pulling back slightly, Alex asked in an emotional, slightly husky voice, "Could I give you my Christmas gift tonight, while we're alone?

"Yes... if you want."

"Good."

Within minutes, he'd left the room and Mary heard doors closing from the direction of Earl's room. He reappeared, carrying a rather large piece of furniture.

"Alex, what..."

In one move, he set his load to the floor, and stepped to take her hand.

"Come see."

"Ohhhhh, Alex... it's the most beautiful thing I've ever seen."

"I think you call it a *hope chest*. It's solid mahogany, lined inside with cedar—I'd hidden it in Earl's closet a few days ago."

"Oh, darling, the design, so detailed... you must have worked on this for weeks—I adore it!

"You're right. They're often referred to as hope chests—a special place for a young girl to save things for use in her wedding or first home, in hopes of finding the right man. I, on the other hand, *found* my perfect man."

Excited, she took the few steps to retrieve a small wrapped package from beneath the Christmas tree. "My gift for you is perfect for *this* very moment."

No thought of what it could be, he removed the paper.

Mary had ordered petite brass plates.

Custom-Built by
Aleksander Nordin,
Carpenter's Carpentry

"One is to be added inside one door of each set of custom-made cabinets. *Not* desecration, darling. Simply your version of the slogan of a new greeting card company, *Hallmark*™— *Because you care enough to give the very best.*

"Your name on your custom cabinets authenticates the same sentiment."

Deliriously happy, she hugged him tightly. "The *first* will go inside my beautiful cedar chest."

Christmas morning, Mike naturally woke up first. Reaching over to pat Alex, he whispered, "Hey, it's here… it's Christmas morning."

"It's five thirty, Mike."

"I know! It's been morning a *long* time."

It was only slightly earlier than Alex had expected.

"All right. Go *quietly* knock on Mary's door, then Earl's."

After all, they might be *waiting* to hear from him.

The four of them walked into the living room together.

Standing in the center of the room was a gleaming red bicycle, complete with an over-sized green bow, Mike's gift from Alex and Mary.

They watched his face, delighted.

"Whewwww!"

Mike seemed rooted to the floor, eyes large, sucking his breath in. "A *new* bike. Wow! A basket, horn... everything... tassels on the handlebars... *sooo* shiny!"

Laughing, Alex ruffled Mike's hair, saying, "Well, do you plan to look at it from the doorway, or do you think you might want to ride it?"

Running to it, he shouted, "Wow, I'm gonna' ride it all day! Thank you!"

"Earl, with tears of gratitude, uttered, "I believe this is the best Christmas morning I have ever experienced."

The Christmas feast was at Pam and Bill Marshall's at noon.

It was an incredibly wonderful Christmas for the Marshall and Nordin families.

~ 40 ~

New Year's Eve

Mary was ecstatic. She would be seeing this New Year in with the man she loved. They planned to attend a small party with friends at a nearby restaurant, and she and Alex had agreed to leave around eleven. They very much wanted to celebrate alone at midnight.

She looked forward to being Mike's mother. She already loved him so much. He was to spend the night at Ilene's, with the promise of board games and snacks while they listened to the radio until midnight.

"I don't know which of them is more excited," Alex reported.

She stood in front of the mirror. She wore a new cobalt blue dress, the long sleeves with buttons from the wrist to the elbow, and a scooped neck.

The strand of pearls Mother gave me for Christmas will be perfect with this dress. Mother knew I would recognize them as having been Grandmother's.

I could barely speak when I opened the package, tears spilling over. I told her I never expected to receive them before... and my words stuck in my mouth as I stammered... but Mom laughed as she interrupted.

"Mary, I know you expected to get them only when I died. Well, I want to see you enjoy

them. I hope you will wear them on your wedding day, but they are not to be saved for special occasions."

I'll wear them on my wedding day, but tonight as well.

My wedding day! I can barely contain my happiness thinking of being Alex Nordin's wife, and sharing everything with him.

She put the finishing touches on her hair before slipping into her dress shoes. Looking at the clock, she walked to the living room to wait for her Prince Charming.

Tonight will be so lovely. Then New Year's Day—I'm not sure to which I most look forward. Tomorrow we will share a great deal of news with the family

Just after eleven, Mary and Alex drove from the party to return to her house. She sat close, feeling his warmth, almost wishing the drive were longer. She'd left a bottle of wine chilling for their toast to the New Year. They were content driving in silence.

Alex's thoughts were almost identical to hers as they neared her house. *I savor simply being near her. She is so beautiful, and tonight wearing the pearls with the beautiful dress of blue, so perfect with her auburn hair. All combined with the sweet scent of her perfume— she took my breath away yet again. Soon to be my wife. Incredible.*

I love the way she moves, her voice, her generosity, her loyalty… the feel of her lips… the softness of her skin. I adore the way her eyes narrow slightly when she's impatient.

And the twinkle in her eyes when she's had an idea. I love everything *about this woman.*

Entering the house, Alex helped remove her coat. After hanging it in the closet, she walked back to him and they shared a tender embrace.

Mary walked to the record player to turn on an album of mellow love songs—Perry Como, her favorite.

"Sit on the sofa... I'll be right back."

He'd worn brown slacks and a tan pullover sweater, which she'd declared to be her favorite color for him. As she left the room, he removed his top coat and reluctantly walked to the sofa.

When she returned with the wine and glasses on a tray, she'd added special cheeses and crusty bakery bread. They'd enjoyed a full meal earlier, but this would be just right to end the evening. She sat beside him, removed her shoes, and leaned closer.

"God has been so good to us, Alex. The coming year will be the happiest of my life. But, you know, it may sound strange, but this past year has been pretty wonderful. In spite of everything, we found each other. The fear of losing you only intensified my appreciation for what we have."

"Sounds like a toast," he laughed.

He continued more seriously, "I do feel the same. Happy New Year, Mary. May we have many more together."

They touched their glasses together and leaned back.

"I feel lighter than since I was a boy, Mary

"I feel there are no burdens in my life… meaning I'm bringing nothing into our marriage to weigh you down. I can come to you clean, so to speak, ready to fill our lives with good things."

"I'm glad. You finally feel free of the difficulties and nightmares of this year, and everything before. But I'm ready to share *whatever* comes."

As the clock struck twelve, they came close, sharing the moment, and dreaming of the next New Year's Eve.

Alex finally rose, looking at the woman he loved so deeply. "I hate to say good night, darling, but tomorrow is *here*, and I'm looking forward to our time with family. I know they will be surprised—and *happy* with our announcements."

Though it was cold, with a dusting of snow on the ground, Mary followed Alex onto the porch in her stocking feet. They were sharing a last kiss as Earl drove up. With a tap on his horn before exiting his car, he was across the yard as Alex headed toward his truck.

"Good thing I showed up when I did," laughed Earl. Alex waved as he pulled away.

"You've got a good man, there, Sis."

As they hurried into the warm house, he gave her a playful swat and quickly moved out of her reach before adding, "Sure hope you don't corrupt him."

~ 41 ~

A New Year
1948

Alex drove to the Marshall's home for lunch.

Mary would ride with Earl.

Ilene, and her son, Joey, would bring Mike.

Mary opened the front door as Alex got out of his truck. "I was watching for you. Happy New Year... again."

He put his arms around her and whispered, "I've missed you since last night."

In the living room, Mike ran to Alex, who grabbed him to pitch him into the air, Mike squealing and laughing. Anna had invited Jimmy Greenwood, who was close by her side. Ilene and Joey were involved in conversation with a woman Alex didn't recognize.

"Hey, Mom," Earl called out as he came through the back door, "I checked the gate lock—the dog won't get out."

He gave Alex a quick slap on the back. "Come over here, I want to properly introduce you to Carol."

Mary smiled, more aware than anyone how often Earl and Carol had been seeing each other. Alex was intrigued, and wanted to know more about the woman.

Earl proudly introduced Carol. Alex realized his friend was actually glowing with happiness.

Did men glow?

Perhaps he beamed.

As the others began talking, Alex had a few minutes to observe Carol. *She does indeed have beautiful brown eyes and lovely hair, as Earl described, and a happy laugh. She's only about an inch shorter than Earl, and not slim, but a nice build—wonder if I should be noticing that? Carol's brightly-colored blouse compliments her coloring.*

More importantly—she's having great difficulty taking those brown eyes off Earl. She's not in the least ill at ease, relaxed, and obviously very much in love with my best friend.

"Very nice to meet you, Carol, officially anyway. I know I met you in Dan's office, possibly twice, but I seemed to be in a mental fog."

Earl laughed. "I've invited her to your wedding, as my guest. I want her to get better acquainted with everyone."

A few minutes later, Dan Lawson arrived. He was the last guest, and Pam came from the kitchen to announce, "Dinner is served."

She had prepared the traditional ham, glazed with brown sugar, spices, and sliced pineapple, as well as turnip greens, hog jowl, black-eyed peas, corn on the cob, sweet potatoes, and cornbread.

At the table, Bill spoke. "Let's join hands to thank God for this meal, as well as all other blessings. And thanks to Pam for cooking all our favorite foods.

"You know, of *course,* this family is not superstitious.

"But," he added with a wink, "she included the greens and black-eyed peas for good health and wealth... just to be sure."

They all laughed, and bowed to thank God for an especially good beginning to their year.

After the sumptuous meal, Mary and Anna began clearing away dishes from the two tables. Carol began gathering the empty glasses. "Oh no you don't, Carol," Anna protested, "you are a guest, and are to make yourself comfortable."

Carol laughed happily. "I'm *comfortable* helping you girls—I much prefer this to feeling like a guest."

Mary and Anna exchanged glances, each thinking Carol just might not be far from *being* family rather than guest. Mary knew Earl was negotiating for a house of his own a few blocks from hers—perhaps he wasn't thinking of living there alone.

❀ ❀

New Year's *Revelations*

After the sumptuous meal, most everyone stretched out in the living room. A few went for a walk. Mike, who didn't consider it cold until the large snow shovels came out, headed out to play with the neighborhood children.

A new snow had fallen during the night, making their world appear pure once again, gleaming white, and without blemish.

Later, Pam began brewing fresh coffee and readying the dessert table.

Everyone together again, Earl stood. He waited until he had everyone's attention.

"Today is a special day, the first day of nineteen-forty-eight, and as Dad said earlier, we each have much for which to be thankful.

Today is also the day a few of us decided to be perfect to share news of *more* good to come. I've cleared it with Mom—dessert will follow our news."

They exchanged questioning glances and settled back to listen.

"Alex asked me to be the spokesperson today, but, it's *his* story. With the exception of Mary and Dan, very few others know about it yet.

But you are the people closest to Alex, though some of you are extended family. But he wanted you to hear everything factually as soon as possible. It's complicated. I won't attempt to cover every detail, but we want you to have some understanding of the whole picture. I will preface with this—there *is* a happy ending."

"Well," Bill interjected, "you certainly have our undivided attention, son. Let's hear it."

"All right. This information came to Alex only recently through a lawyer, Junior Batson.

"The story begins with The Snider Real Estate Company, established many years ago by George Snider.

"George was Abe Snider's *grandfather*. George grew up in a poor family with good moral values, which served him well in business. He valued family above everything.

"He had only one sibling, a much younger sister. Because of the age difference and his beginning to work long before finishing high school, they were not close.

"When George began to make a success in business, he regularly sent money to his parents, and after their deaths, to his sister. He tried to keep in touch, but eventually, due to her many moves, they lost contact.

"George had only one child, a son named Lincoln. His son joined him in the real estate business after completing his education.

"Lincoln, too, was a good, honest man, and their business thrived. Over the years they added the investment company.

"Out of the blue, George's sister contacted him. He was delighted. She was seriously ill and hoped to see her brother before she died. He made the trip out of state to visit.

"You may think she wanted money. But she wanted only to see him and have him meet her son, David, who was about to go into military service.

"George was deeply touched and asked David to keep in contact. He visited his sister once more before her death, but did not see David again.

"Years passed—about five. Finally, David came to visit his uncle. He brought with him his new bride, Blancha. This, of course, was Alex's sister.

"She married David Aldredge, making her Abe Snider's second cousin by marriage."

Earl watched everyone's face as these facts registered.

"George Snider's nephew, David, seemed to have inherited his uncle's feeling for family. He liked what he saw of Mt. Seasons. Because it would also bring family ties, he and Blancha decided to make their home here. He found a small house for rent, not realizing it was owned by the Snider Company.

"After a while George Snider was convinced his nephew was a sincere, honest, hard-working young man. So he had a codicil added to his will.

The codicil stated that when he died, the house would be signed over to David and Blancha, free and clear.

"George was about sixty by then. His son, Lincoln, mid-forties. Lincoln *also* had only one child, a son named Abraham. This is where the story gets complicated, nearly unbelievable.

"In a period of less than a month, several things happened. George died of a massive heart attack. The next *week*, even before the reading of the will, Lincoln *and* the Snider Corporation's lawyer were killed in the same car accident.

"This left Abraham Snider—Abe—the sole heir. He was also the executor, which gave him access to his father and grandfather's papers. As far as anyone can ascertain, Abe was the only person into whose hands came a copy of the codicil to his grandfather's will.

"In any case, he took no action regarding the codicil and, at some point, destroyed what he thought were the only copies.

"David Aldredge, Blancha's husband, died the next year.

"Abe could have then, though late, made things right, and relieved much of Blancha's burden. But he simply, angrily, collected rent from the dear woman until she died.

"However... and this is the best part... a long-time secretary of George Snider's had kept copies of some of his personal papers, apparently with his knowledge. She moved away shortly before his death and died years ago. Her granddaughter recently found the box containing copies of George Snider's papers, including his will and the codicil.

"The granddaughter lives in Kentucky but had fond memories of visiting Mt. Seasons, so had continued to have the county newspaper mailed to her. So, she knew about Abe Snider being convicted of arson and insurance fraud. When she found the will and codicil, she said she honestly didn't know whether she should do anything, but finally decided to contact local officials. God *bless* her.

"Bottom line... Blancha Aldredge was the rightful owner of the property and the house Abe Snider burned. This makes Alex her heir, the rightful owner of the property."

Silence in the room reigned, but soft gasps could be heard from time to time. Now the gasps were becoming louder, and Earl recognized low questioning voices.

Raising his voice to quieten them, he continued.

"*Now*, the part you will find most interesting. Alex will be paid the value of the house and furnishings and anything destroyed by the fire.

"He will be paid the value *as listed and valued* by Abe himself when he filed the insurance claim. This amount will be paid from Snider's estate, plus all the rent Blancha Aldredge paid during her lifetime... plus interest... *plus* a lump sum the judge added as a settlement.

"Abe Snider has agreed to this, in writing, in order to avoid further prosecution. Numerous additional charges could have been brought against him because of his actions, and. non-actions.

"As it stands, Abe will have a chance of eventual release from prison, where he will *definitely* spend time for the arson and insurance fraud charges. He realized if other charges were added, there would have been no question—he would spend the remainder of his life in prison.

"When he *is* released, he will have very little, financially."

Earl looked at each person in the room, enjoying the moment.

Mike had risen from his chair to return to Alex's lap.

Alex finally spoke. "I discussed all this with Mary, then with Dan, as my lawyer. Only then did I speak with Earl, as he is to be involved in, as Paul Harvey says on his radio program, *The Rest of the Story*.

"Good has come from tragedies. Earl will explain what we will do with the money… Blancha's money."

"To summarize," Earl explained, "Alex signed documents to put the money into a trust. I will head a foundation, with a board of directors, and have a specially-equipped home built on the property that should have come to Blancha. It will be used to house patients with temporary special needs"

The idea had come to Alex as a result of two people. First, the Patterson's daughter, who had to be away from her hometown to receive care. Second, Freddie Anderson, the young boy Earl had mentioned months before with a different problem, but who had needed care not locally available.

Earl explained further, "There are many details yet to work out, but the financial advisors we've consulted have agreed the money is sufficient, if handled carefully.

"Alex? The clincher is yours."

Standing, as Mike moved to another chair, Alex said in a choked voice, "It will be called *Blancha's House*."

The Marshalls' home was full of discussions and happy tears. All were thrilled about the lovely gift Alex was making to Mt. Seasons, on behalf of his sister.

Still standing, Alex held a hand out to Mary, who came to stand beside him.

Coughing theatrically to regain everyone's attention, Alex announced, "We have one more item. *Mike*... listen carefully. This announcement is brief.

"When the lawyer first approached me about the matter of the Snider property and everything you've heard today, I feared more bad news. A feeling of dread came over me. Images of the things I'd gone through last year came to mind.

"Again, I realized how quickly life can change. There may be only a breeze moving gently through, pleasantly bringing blessings— but a breeze can turn into a raging storm, blowing in to destroy everything you love in life.

"I realized I didn't want another minute of *my* life to pass... or *Mary's*, without our being together, sharing clear *or* stormy days."

He squeezed Mary's shoulder.

Elated, she announced, "Alex and I, with *Mike*, will be married in ten days. Saturday, January tenth!

"Consider this your invitation."

Stepping to Mike's chair, he leaned down to pick him up. "Mike? How do you like *this* idea, buddy?"

"Yay!" he shouted, as everyone began to applaud and congratulate them.

"*Now*, dessert is served," Pam announced.

"It appears this family is beginning a *very* good new year!"

~ 42 ~

Preparations

With only a week and a half, no printed invitations could be ordered. An announcement would be made at church, Mary's immediate family lived in town, and Pam Marshall would phone a few out-of-town relatives.

"The rest of Mt. Seasons will be taken care of, don't you worry," Pam laughed. "Between the telephone party-lines and Sister Hamby, bless her heart, everyone will get the word."

After the announcement, and departure of a few of the guests New Year's Day, Mary became unusually quiet. She and Alex were sitting near the corner of the room. She looked at him and reached to take his hand.

"What's wrong?" he asked.

"No one from *your* family will be here. I'm so sorry, darling."

Alex was touched at her love and caring.

"No, and I would have loved for my family to know you."

Her hand was warm in his. He looked at the engagement ring on her finger, soon to be complete with the addition of the wedding band.

"Mike will be there, and you will soon make us a family of three," he answered.

"You know how much I love your family. I've long thought of Earl as my brother. I no longer have any emptiness, Mary. You complete me."

"Oh, Alex, I love you so."

"I've thought of one thing," he responded. "I'd like to ask Ilene if she would honor me by… I suppose I mean, sitting in as my mother at the wedding.

"She's done so much for me and I have come to think of her as a mother. She could be escorted in just after your parents, and sit on the front row. What do you think?"

"It's a wonderful idea. She will be thrilled."

❀ ❀

"Knock, knock, knock. ding-dong, ding-dong!"

Alex happily knocked on Ilene's door and rang the doorbell at the same time.

"Come *in*," she said, quickly opening the door. "Glad you called—you're just *full* of it, aren't you? And grinning like a Cheshire cat! What in the world is up?"

Ilene always got right to the point.

"Well, I need another favor," he said enthusiastically."

"All right, what do you need?"

More seriously, he began, "Well, you know I have no family here other than Mike. So… at the wedding … I'd like for you to be escorted in… and sit on the front row, as Mary's parents will be. I'm asking… would you represent my mother?"

Her eyes filled with tears as she put her arms around him without a word. He returned the embrace, hugging her tightly.

When she drew back, he grinned mischievously. "Seems I discovered a way to make you speechless. May I take that as a yes?"

"Alex Nordin, you are a rascal. But *nothing* would please me more than to be considered your second mother—on your wedding day or any other. I love you as a second son."

"Where in the world would I be without you? I love *you,* dear lady."

Mary and Alex had agreed on a simple service from the beginning. That had been a good decision; trying to pull everything together in less than two weeks wasn't easy.

Mary had been overjoyed to find a large archway made only of grapevines, with narrow white ribbon intertwined. She'd spotted it soon after entering the local florist shop. It was the only thing she wanted in the sanctuary other than white pillar candles on pedestals at each side.

Miss Emily Watson, the owner of the shop, was an elderly woman who had never married, but delighted in helping make brides' dreams come true.

She didn't understand Mary choosing this archway when there were several in gold and silver.

"I want you to be pleased when you come into the sanctuary, Mary. Honestly, this one has been used only for small outdoor weddings. The rental fee is very small."

As if second-guessing herself, she added, "Oh, I hope I didn't offend. If your budget is tight, I completely understand. We can work something out for *any*thing you choose."

Mary assured her this was the one she liked. Then she chose a large spring arrangement for the reception.

"I know it's a winter wedding, Miss Emily, but we had originally planned to have it in the spring. And my heart *feels* like spring."

She hugged the elderly lady and whispered, "And, Miss Emily… there is no urgent reason for this wedding other than pure love."

Everything came together. The wedding was to be at two o'clock the next day.

Alex had planned to be up early. Before the alarm sounded, Mike jumped into his bed.

"Just one more day. We're getting married *tomorrow*, Papa… we got a lot to do today, don't we? Are we gonna go to Miss Mary's before rehearsal tonight? Can I wear my new suit tonight, *and* tomorrow? You gonna cook breakfast now or do I hafta have cereal… it's okay though if you don't wanna cook, I like cereal… but maybe Miss Mary will cook breakfast lotsa days after we get married…"

Alex sat up to throw a pillow at him.

~ 43 ~

Wedding **D**ay

🔔

Ilene Carpenter was proudly escorted to her seat on the front row. She was stylishly dressed in a beige suit of silk chambray, a soft pink blouse with ruffles at the neck, and a hat perfectly matching the suit. The pearl earrings, dyed-to-match shoes, and white gloves completed her elegant look.

Across the aisle, Pam Marshall wore a lightweight wool suit in pale pink, also with dyed-to-match shoes, a white blouse, and a gold broach and earrings. And, of course, white gloves.

Bill Marshall, in a new black suit, would be seated beside his wife after escorting Mary down the aisle. They were both thrilled to see their daughter marry this good man.

The organ music began as Alex and Mike came into the sanctuary to stand in front of the archway, each wearing their dark blue suits, with white shirts and blue ties. Mike was the only support Alex needed, in essence making him the *best man.*

Earl, also in a black suit, albeit rather well worn, stood to one side waiting to perform the ceremony.

Everyone turned to look as Anna, her sister's maid of honor and only attendant, appeared at the double doors at the back of the sanctuary.

She began her walk down the aisle, seeming to glide. Glowing with happiness for her sister, she wore a pale peach-colored, ankle-length dress, and ballet slippers.

Her hair hung in one thick braid intertwined with white baby's breath. Alex caught her eye and winked, thinking briefly she was missing her signature color of pink.

As Anna came to the front and turned to face the audience, the volume of the organ began to rise as *Mendelssohn's Wedding March* began. Everyone stood for the entrance of the bride.

Mary stood for a moment in the wide doorway before beginning her slow walk down the aisle. Radiant with joy, she was exquisite in the simple elegance of the ankle-length white gown with a princess neckline. She wore pearl earrings and the strand of pearls her mother had given her. Her auburn hair pulled back only slightly, she wore a circle of white roses on her head over a short veil.

She held her father's arm, seeming to float down the aisle. Bill Marshall was beaming as he placed her hand in the hand of Alex, and walked to sit beside Pam.

Earl performed the ceremony with the most joy he'd ever experienced performing this ministerial duty.

The vows were traditional, but brief, as requested. As he neared the end of the ceremony, he observed them intently.

"God has blessed you in so many ways. May your marriage and home always be filled with love.

"Now, as we stand before God and all these witnesses, I pronounce you, Mary Beth Marshall, and you, Aleksander Makar Nordin, to be husband and wife. What God has joined, let no one separate.

"Alex, you may now kiss... *my* sister... *your* bride."

Alex leaned in to lift Mary's veil. Their eyes only for each other, he embraced her. They delighted in their first marital kiss, as their hearts soared. After an interval, to the amusement of all, Earl seemed to be attempting to let Alex know the allotted time for the kiss had passed.

Earl then motioned everyone to be seated again. Alex looked at Mike, who came to stand between the couple. The three of them turned to face the audience, and joined hands.

Earl came around to stand in front of the three. "Mikhail Oleg Nordin, known to most of us as Mike, do you promise to honor this marriage and accept Mary Marshall Nordin into your family, acknowledging her as the lawfully-wedded wife of your father, from this day forward?"

"Yes, sir," Mike answered enthusiastically.

"Finally, Mike. Do you also happily promise to love her, and acknowledge her as your mother?"

"Yes, sir, I sure do!"

As expected, sounds of joy and laughter rippled through the audience. Earl then raised his voice to conclude…

"Ladies and gentlemen, on this day, the eleventh of January, in the year of our Lord, nineteen hundred and forty-eight, I am pleased to present to you, Mr. and Mrs. Aleksander Nordin and Master Mikhail Nordin. "

Not a dry eye anywhere, the second round of applause was thundering, continuing as the new Nordin family dashed up the aisle.

~ 44 ~

The Reception

The reception would necessarily spill out from the parlor into the wide hall and entry way.

As the happy couple exited the sanctuary, the County Herald photographer was positioned. His camera flashed in rapid succession as he followed them into the parlor. After several additional flashes as the ladies instructed them of their positions behind the wedding cake, he waved cordially. "Thanks!"

The traditional receiving line formed quickly, as Ilene instructed them about the proper order in which they should meet their guests.

"How does she know these things?" Earl asked his mother. "I've performed a good many weddings, but I can't hold a candle to her, remembering all these details."

Bill and Pam Marshall were at the head of the line, the first to greet the guests and thank them for attending. Ilene was next, then Earl, as the minister, the bride, groom, and Mike, with Anna at the end. Soon the line was moving as guests were greeted, hugs, pats on the back exchanged, and good wishes flowing freely.

Also at Ilene's instructions, a gift table had been set up against a wall, in spite of Mary's protests.

"Mary, people are going to bring gifts whatever you say.

"So you might as well provide a place for them, else they'd have to stack them on the floor—now *that* would be tacky."

By the time the receiving line was organized, Mary noticed the table overflowed with gifts, some on the floor, after all.

Pam and Anna had made the beautiful three-tiered wedding cake. It was topped with the tiny bride and groom, which had been on Pam and Bill's much smaller cake over thirty years earlier.

Miss Emily Watson served the cake… *to assure it was done properly.* Several ladies brought in stacks of clear glass plates and punch cups, which they referred to as *crystal.*

Others had made the mixed-fruit punch and began serving as soon as the first guests exited the receiving line.

Bowls of mixed nuts and pastel colored mints were in several locations around the parlor

The Gosden family had surprised Alex and Mike with their attendance, having received a note from Mary.

"Well, Mike," joked Bob J, "where you going for the honeymoon?"

"Kids don't go on honeymoons, Mr. Gosden," Mike explained seriously. "Mrs. Ilene told me just the bride and groom can go. I'm gonna stay with her while they're gone, and I get to start calling her Granna Ilene.

"Papa and Mary are going to Nashville.

"It's a big city and they're going to stay in a fancy hotel three nights. Hey, *didja* know I got a Grandmother and Grandfather Marshall?"

"Sounds good, Mike. You know, I have a surprise for James, and I saved it for today."

"A surprise?"

"Yep, we're moving back to Mt. Seasons as soon as school is out in Memphis. We're moving here to *stay*. I have a job at the big hardware store and lumber yard in Jessups."

He looked at James, adding, "We'll be renting a *house*."

Mary and Alex glanced in boys' direction, before turning back to Miss Emily Watson.

Miss Emily had finished serving cake, and now deemed it an appropriate time to talk with the newly married couple.

"Mary, your selection of flowers was perfect, as *well* as the grapevine arch."

Miss Emily turned slightly toward Alex, but continued looking directly at Mary. With a twinkle in her eyes, she added, "And, my dear, I especially approve of your handsome groom."

Alex was beginning to fidget when Miss Emily turned to claim his full attention.

She sweetly placed her hand on his arm. "You, young man, made an *excellent* choice."

He smiled at her kindness, and bent down to kiss the cheek of this feisty little Southern lady.

"Thank you, Miss Emily. I agree."

Satisfied, she turned to walk away.

"She's something special, isn't she?" he whispered to Mary

"Yes. She's never seemed to have family, yet is always helping others."

His arm around her, he was still in awe of this delightful woman being his wife. He felt tears stinging his eyes. "Mary, my *wife*… I still can't believe you're mine… to begin our lives *together*. I love you so."

"Yes, darling." With a mischievous giggle, she whispered, "And *I* am ready to begin our honeymoon. You?"

They glanced around the room. Guests had quieted down and some of the ladies were beginning to collect plates and cups. Anna was coming across the room with Mary's bridal bouquet.

"Okay, you two. It's time to throw the bouquet. Then you can make your get-away. Not figuring you're ready to be alone or anything, but it *is* time."

Anna raised a hand. "Everyone. If you'll make room for the bride and groom to move to the front lawn, the bride will throw the bouquet."

Mike had crossed the room as they began heading outside. Alex leaned to pick him up. "Won't be able to pick you up much longer, buddy, but give me a big hug before we leave. I know you'll have a great time at Mrs. Ilene's."

"Yes, sir, I'll be good. We're gonna bake a new cookie recipe and have popcorn every night. But … I'll be glad when you and… Mary… *Mama* … get back … so we can start being a family."

"Son, we are a family *now*—it's official."

To no one's surprise, Mary's car was covered in streamers, *Just Married* signs, and a good assortment of empty cans tied to the back bumper.

The day was cold, but the sun shone brightly. Poised on the steps, Mary was prepared to throw the bouquet to the group of about a dozen laughing, excited, single women.

She turned her back to them, pitching it backwards over her head as hard as she could, turning quickly to see who'd caught it.

Out of the corner of her eye, she was sure Anna's hands were on it.

Then, as if it hadn't happened, Carol's hands held the bouquet high in the air, obviously thrilled, as everyone cheered.

Alex spotted Earl in the crowd and their eyes met briefly.

Oh yeah, he's blushing... I don't think it will be long before this family has another wedding.

Pam Marshall handed Alex a white wool cape, which he placed around Mary's shoulders as they began moving towards her car.

Brides customarily changed into a travel outfit before leaving with the groom, but Mary had preferred to remain in her wedding dress.

Alex took Mary's hand.

"*Now*—let's get to car!"

They ran through a heavy shower of rice being tossed by the crowd of cheering well-wishers, Mike in the lead.

After a brief struggle with the keys, Alex had Mary and yards of the white dress tucked into the car. He laughed as he ran to the other side, amid the new shower of rice.

Inside, they rolled their windows down and waved as the car noisily began moving towards the street, every can clanking on its own, and streamers blowing in the wind.

The cheers could still be heard as they drove out of sight, raising the windows to close out the chill.

~~~~~~

Mr. and **M**rs. Nordin began the drive through Mt. Seasons.

Mary sat close, holding Alex's hand.

"I love that you stayed in your dress. You look like a dream—and I don't want to wake up."

It *is* a dream, darling, a dream realized."

Leaving Mt. Seasons, they turned onto the highway towards this new chapter of their lives, happily anticipating their first as a family.

~ 45 ~

Finale

At the newspaper office, Harry Bledsoe authorized front page for the wedding photo of Mt. Seasons' best-known couple of the moment. It was news.

The headline, ***Happy Ending/Beginning.***

In the church parlor, Pam and Bill Marshall sat, thoroughly exhausted, and clearly elated at the blessings of the day.

Anna held the hand of Jimmy Greenwood, dreamily wondering if she might be taking this step with him… someday.

But she was in no rush, which was why she'd shifted the bouquet to Carol's hands when they both briefly touched it.

Earl had his arm comfortably around Carol, mentally rehearsing the question he would ask next week.

Mike and James were collecting left-over mints and nuts, planning their summer, though months away.

Ilene Carpenter beamed. "I am simply happier than a woman my age has a right to be."

At his mother's side, Joey Carpenter added, "I'm pleased to have witnessed a happy ending to the *Nordin Story.*"

Behind him, Dan Lawson exclaimed, "Amen!"

The sentiment could have been echoed by Junior Batson, the Gosden family, and many others, including Clyde Autry (formerly known only as Chief), who left as quietly as he had entered.

Other guests were atwitter, discussing the wedding and the events of the past year. It would be good conversation for the remainder of the year

As the group dispersed, a gentle breeze peacefully caressed the trees, as bits of snow glistened in the remaining light of day.

∼ THE END ∼

Made in the USA
Columbia, SC
22 October 2017